Wereworld

Books by Curtis Jobling

Read the whole Wereworld series!

Wereworld Book 1: Rise of the Wolf

Wereworld Book 2: Rage of Lions

Wereworld Book 3: Shadow of the Hawk

Wereworld Book 4: Nest of Serpents

Wereworld Book 5: Storm of Sharks

CURTIS JOBLING

VIKING
An Imprint of Penguin Group (USA) Inc.

VIKING
An Imprint of Penguin Young Readers Group
Published by the Penguin Group
Penguin Group (USA) Inc.
375 Hudson Street
New York, New York 10014, U.S.A.

USA / Canada / UK / Ireland / Australia / New Zealand / India / South Africa / China
Penguin Books Ltd, Registered Offices: 80 Strand, London WC2R 0RL, England

For more information about the Penguin Group visit www.penguin.com

First published in 2013 by Puffin UK, a division of Penguin Books Ltd.
This edition published in the United States of America by Viking,
an imprint of Penguin Young Readers Group, 2013

LIBRARY OF CONGRESS CATALOGING-IN-PUBLICATION DATA IS AVAILABLE
ISBN: 978-0-670-78558-2

Printed in U.S.A.

3 5 7 9 10 8 6 4

Set in Elysium Std Designed by Jim Hoover

For Matilda Rose Cullen

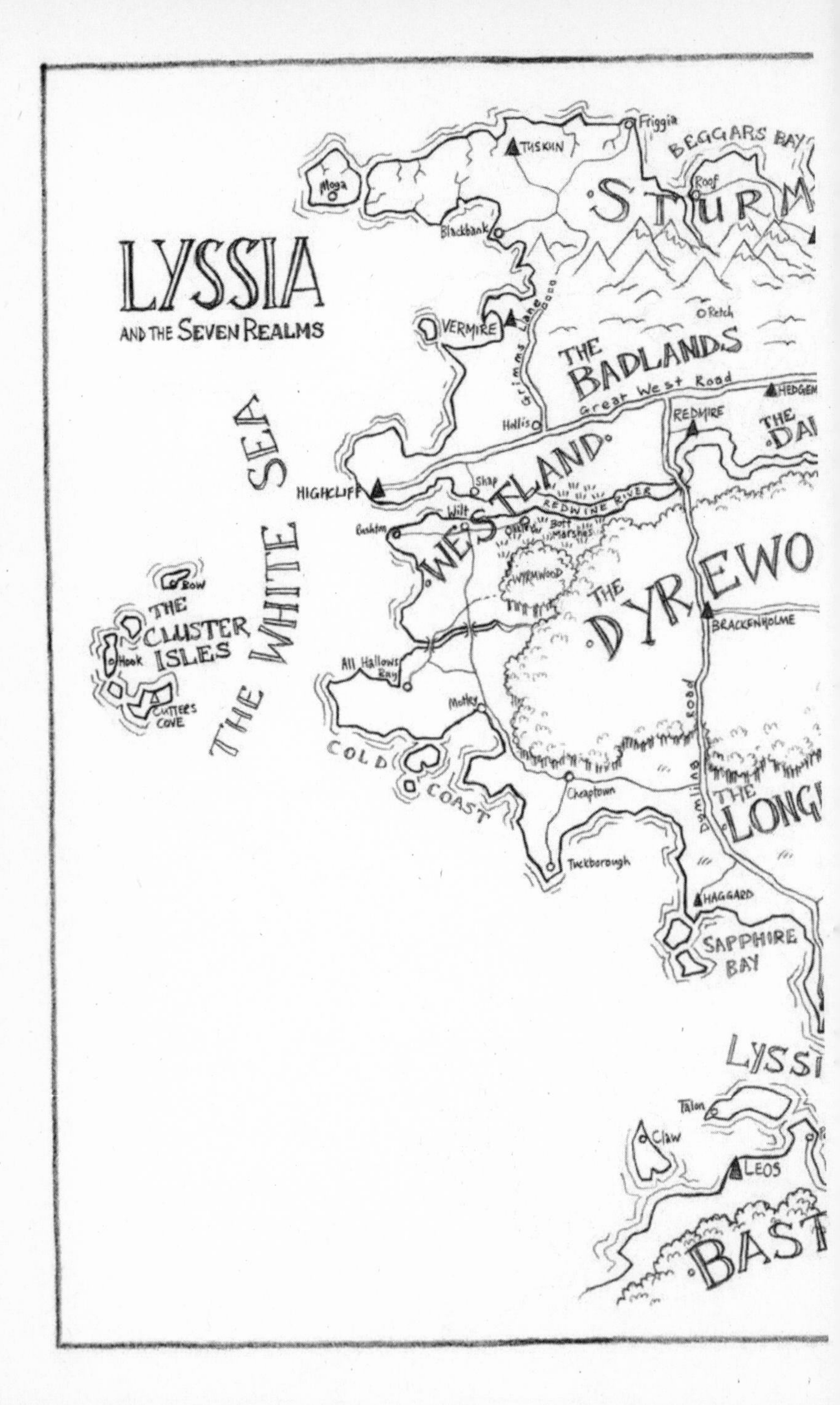

LYSSIA
AND THE SEVEN REALMS
THE WHITE SEA
Moga
TUSKIN
Friggia
BEGGARS BAY
Roof
STURM
Blackbank
VERMIRE
Grimms Lane
Retch
THE BADLANDS
Great West Road
HEDGEM
Hollis
REDMIRE
THE DA
HIGHCLIFF
Shap
WESTLAND
REDWINE RIVER
Wilt
Bashtin
Bott Marshes
WYRMWOOD
THE DYREWO
BRACKENHOLME
Bow
THE CLUSTER ISLES
Hook
CUTTERS COVE
All Hallows Bay
Motley
COLD COAST
Chaptown
Demilian Road
THE LONG
Tuckborough
HAGGARD
SAPPHIRE BAY
LYSSI
Talon
Claw
LEOS
BAST

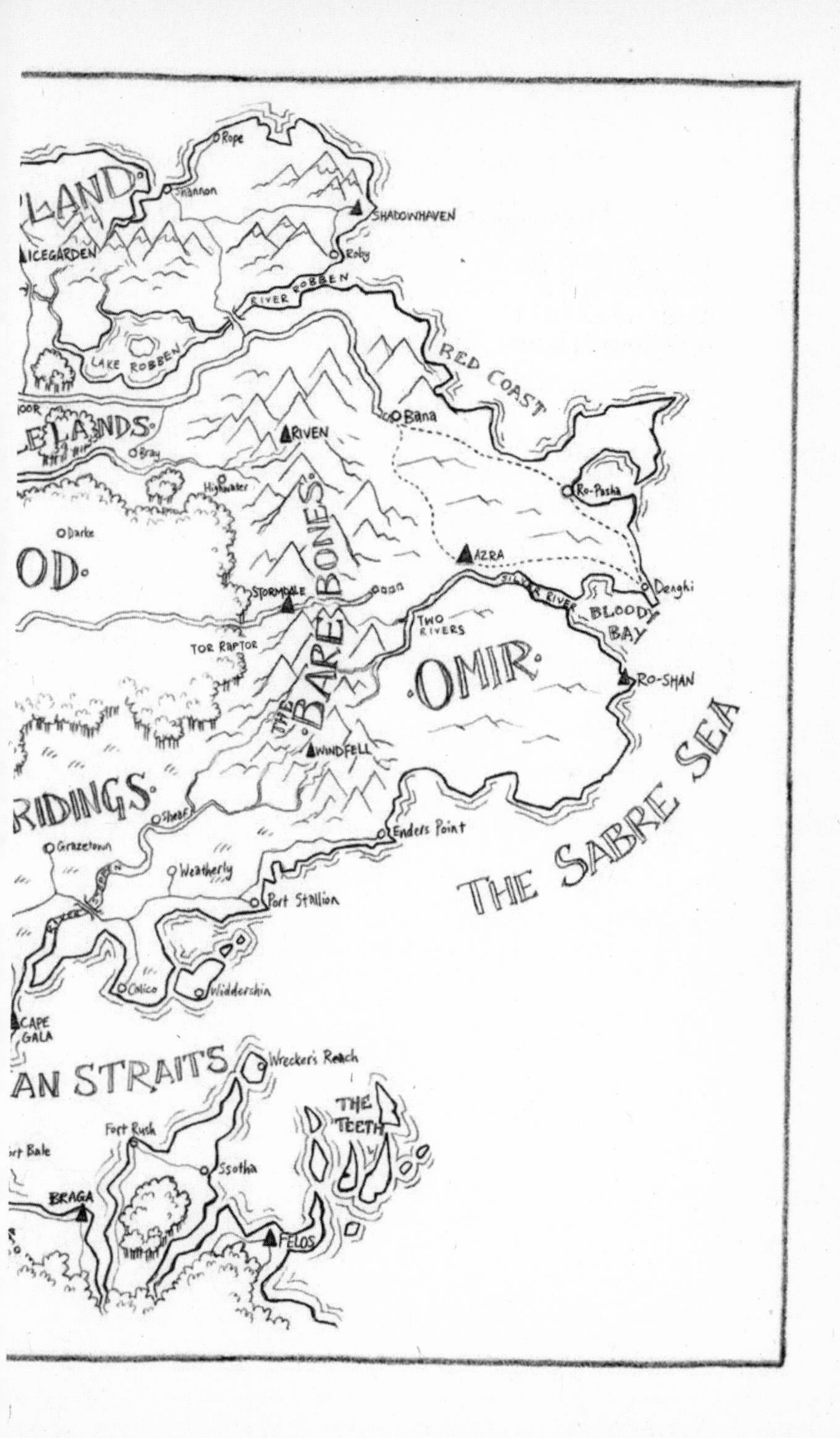
Rope
LAND
Shannon
SHADOWHAVEN
ICEGARDEN
Roby
RIVER ROBBEN
LAKE ROBBEN
RED COAST
Bana
LANDS
Bray
RIVEN
Highwater
Ro-Pasha
Darke
OD
THE BARE BONES
AZRA
STORMDALE
Denghi
SILVER RIVER
BLOODY BAY
TWO RIVERS
TOR RAPTOR
OMIR
RO-SHAN
WINDFELL
THE SABRE SEA
RIDINGS
Sheaf
Enders Point
Grazetown
Weatherly
Port Stallion
Calico
Widdershin
CAPE GALA
AN STRAITS
Wrecker's Reach
THE TEETH
Fort Rush
Ssotha
BRAGA
FELOS

CONTENTS

CAST OF CHARACTERS

THE WOLF AND HIS ALLIES

Drew Ferran, last of the Gray Wolves, rightful king of Westland.

On the High Seas

Count Vega, Prince of Cluster Isles, Sea Marshall for the Wolf, former captain of the *Maelstrom,* member of the Wolf's Council. Sharklord.

Baron Bosa, the Whale of Moga, captain of the *Beluga,* former pirate.

Captain Violca, captain of the *Lucky Shot.*

Mister Ramzi, first mate on the *Lucky Shot.*

Captain Eric Ransome, new captain of the *Maelstrom.*

Figgis, first mate of the *Maelstrom.*

Harriers of Hedgemoor

Lady Gretchen of Hedgemoor, former fiancée of Lucas, a leader of the Harriers. Werefox.

Trent Ferran, Drew's adoptive brother, former member of the Redcloaks, a leader of the Harriers.

Captain Lars Gerard, former captain of the Boarguard, current commander of the Harriers.

Hawklords

Baron Gryffin, former leader of the Hawklords of Windfell, now deceased, father of Shah.

Lady Shah, healer, daughter of Gryffin.

Bearlords and Family

Duke Bergan of Brackenholme, member of the Wolf's Council. Bearlord.

Duchess Rainier, wife of Bergan. Foxlady.

Lord Broghan, son of Bergan, Greencloak commander, now deceased. Bearlord.

Lady Whitley, daughter of Bergan, Greencloak scout. Bearlady.

Staglords

Magister Wilhelm, healer of Stormdale, Hector's uncle. Boarlord.

Duke Manfred of Stormdale, member of the Wolf's Council. Staglord.

Lord Reinhardt, son of Manfred, acting leader of Stormdale. Staglord.

Lord Milo, son of Manfred, younger brother of Reinhardt. Staglord.

In the Desert Realm

King Faisal of Azra, true king of Omir. Jackal-lord.

Krieg, gladiator, survivor of the Furnace. Rhinolord.

The Behemoth, gladiator, survivor of the Furnace. Mammothlord.

Other Werelords

Wergar the Wolf, former King of Westland, Drew's father, deposed and killed by King Leopold.

Queen Amelie, White Wolf, dowager Queen of Westland, widow of Wergar and Leopold, mother of Drew and Lucas.

Count Fripp, Lord of Bray. Badgerlord.

Lord Conrad, Horselord leader of the defense in Cape Gala.

Duke Brand, the Bull of Calico.

Other Human Allies

Baba Soba, a wise woman of the Romari.

Yuzhnik, Romari fire-eater and strongman.

Master Hogan, older scout, Whitley's mentor.

General Harker, commander of the Watch in Brackenholme.
Quist, senior Greencloak.
Machin, Greencloak.
Captain Reuben Fry, archer from Sturmland.
Bo Carver, Lord of thieves.
Pick, young girl thief.
Mack Ferran, Drew's adoptive father, father of Trent, killed by the Lionguard.
Tilly Ferran, Drew's adoptive mother, mother of Trent, killed by Vanmorten.

THE CATLORDS AND THEIR ALLIES

The Lions of Leos

High Lord Leon, Elder of Lions, father of Leopold, grandfather of Lucas.
Leopold the Lion, late deposed king of Westland, father of Lucas.
King Lucas, self-crowned King of Westland, Drew's half-brother, son of Leopold and Queen Amelie.

The Panthers of Braga

High Lord Oba, Elder of Panthers, father of Lord Onyx and Lady Opal.
Lord Onyx, the Beast of Bast.
Lady Opal, the Beauty of Bast, sister of Onyx.

The Tigers of Felos

High Lord Tigara, Elder of Tigers, grandfather of Taboo.
Taboo, granddaughter of Lord Tigara, gladiator in Scoria.

The Cheetahs of the Teeth

Lord Chollo.
Lord Chang, son of Lord Chollo.

Onyx's War Council

Count Costa, Vulturelord.
Duke Krueger, Rhinolord.
General Skean, Cranelord.
General Gorgo, Hippolord.

Sheriff Muller, Bandit-lord of the Badlands, the only human member of war council.

Doglords

Lord Canan of Omir, ruler of Pasha, rebel king engaged in civil war against King Faisal. Doglord.
Lady Hayfa the Hyena, ruler of Ro-Shann, enemy of King Faisal.

The Ratking

Vanmorten, Lord Chancellor of Westland, most powerful member of the Ratking family.
Vankaskan, dark magister, Hector's former master, killed by Drew.
War Marshall Vorjavik, twin of Vorhaas, killed by Lord Reinhardt.
Vorhaas, twin of Vorjavik, commander of the Lion's army in the Dalelands.
Vex, youngest Ratlord.

Wyldermen and Their Goddess

Vala, evil wereserpent goddess worshipped by the Wyldermen, killed by Drew.

Coldblood, shaman of the Wyrmwood, killed by Drew.
Darkheart, formally known as Rolff, son of Coldblood, versed in wild magicks.

Other Werelords

Magister Shuriko, court physician to the Panthers of Braga. Giraffelord.
Magister Shappura, Shuriko's deceased father. Giraffelord.

Other Human Allies
Major Krupha, Redcloak commander.
Sergeant Kramer, Redcloak guard.

SCORIA

Lord Ignus of Scoria, owner of the Furnace. Lizardlord.
Count Kesslar of Haggard, slaver. Goatlord.

Djogo, former captain of Count Kesslar's mercenaries and slaver, now Drew's ally.

THE KRAKEN, HIS ALLIES, AND HIS PRISONERS

Lord Ghul, the Kraken, Squidlord of the Cluster Isles and Sea Marshal of the Lion's fleet.

On the Hellhound
Captain Deadeye of the *Hellhound*. Sharklord.
Florimo, navigator, imprisoned by Ghul. Ternlord.

Finch, ship's cook.
Captain Hobard, imprisoned captain of the *Motley Madam*.

On Other Ships
Sea Marshal Scorpio, commander of the Bastian Fleet, captain of the *Bastian Empress*.

Captain Mesner of the *Beggar's Bride*.
Captain Zigler of the *Nemesis*.

Cutter's Cove
Hackett, Steward of Cutter's Cove. Crablord.

Colm, sergeant of Krakenguard.
Captain Flowers, member of Krakenguard.
Sergeant Callow, member of Krakenguard.
Casper, known as Skipper, ringleader of pirate children, former cabin boy of the *Maelstrom*.
Gregor, enslaved boy, brother of Kit and Pearl.
Pearl, enslaved girl.
Kit, enslaved boy.

THE BOARLORD, HIS ALLIES, AND HIS PRISONERS

Baron Hector, dark magister known as Blackhand, ruler of Redmire, former member of the Wolf's Council, ruler of Ugri. Boarlord.
Vincent-vile, the phantom of Hector's dead twin brother.

Crowlords
Lord Flint, son of the deceased Count Croke of Riven.

Prisoners
Duke Henrik, White Bear, Lord of Icegarden, cousin of Duke Bergan, under siege by Baron Hector.
Lady Greta, White Bear, magister, sister of Henrik, under siege by Baron Hector.
Duchess Freya, healer, mother of Duke Henrik and Lady Greta.

Human Allies
Ringlin, captain of the Boarguard.
Ibal, head jailor of Icegarden.
Two Axes, Ugri warrior.
The Creep, Ugri scout.

PART I

PERILOUS PASSAGE

I

Lackeys and Lickspittles

WITH WINTER FINALLY relinquishing her cruel hold over the Cold Coast, All Hallows Bay had gradually returned to life. The piers and jetties, home to only the hardiest vessels weeks earlier, were now crowded with boats of all sizes, weatherworn fishing skiffs bumping up against the barnacle-encrusted hulls of their huge, oceangoing cousins. The taverns and inns, so quiet during the harshest months, now thronged with life, sea captains and merchants haggling for bargains while less fortunate souls drowned their sorrows. The streets thrummed with activity, spring bringing hope to the people of the bustling port. All Hallows Bay was alive once more, but it came at a cost.

A Lion once more ruled Westland. The newly crowned

King Lucas had reclaimed his father's stolen throne from the young Werewolf Drew Ferran. The Catlords of Bast had sailed to Lucas's aid, strengthening his hold over the Seven Realms and helping to put the Werelords of the Wolf's Council to the sword. The Lion's ranks had swelled, warriors from across the vast continent of Bast heeding his rallying roar and landing on Lyssian soil. Shape-shifting Werelords of all color and size had marched to support Lucas, their enslaved homelands ensuring allegiance. Lucas ruled with an iron paw, squeezing every copper from his people's pockets and pressing them into his army of Redcloaks. He turned wives into widows as he sought to destroy the last of the Gray Wolves and all who supported Drew.

The Lionguard's presence had never been more apparent in All Hallows Bay. Many of the locals kept a wary distance, the violent reputation of the king's soldiers well-known to all. As with every land under Lucas's control, the Lionguard raised a force from the indigenous population. Though many people were reluctant to "take the red," some were happy to swear fealty to King Lucas. The Redcloaks of All Hallows Bay had a large proportion of the latter, made up of rogues and ruffians. The odd Bastian captain or Lyssian from more noble stock broke up their numbers, but for the most part the Lionguard were a cruel bunch. Rarely a day went by without brutality, ensuring the locals remained fearful of their so-called guardians.

Whitley sat in a booth at the back of the smoke-choked bar,

the hood of her traveling cloak raised around her face. Though she kept her head dipped, her eyes missed nothing, passing over the inn's clientele. There were few present whose homeland she could name. Olive-skinned sailors from the south rubbed shoulders with the pale-fleshed men of the north, granting the Drowning Man a cosmopolitan feel. One fellow strode past her booth, his face wrapped in an Omiri kash, the favored headdress of the Desert Realm. His eyes narrowed as they caught hers before he joined his companions in the recesses of the bar. Whitley stared into her half-empty mug, avoiding further eye contact. Here she was, one of the most wanted therianthropes in all of Lyssia, right under the Lionguard's noses but lost in a sea of strangers.

She and her companions had witnessed Redcloak justice as they'd made their way down the steep, cobbled streets toward the harbor. The grisly remains of King Lucas's enemies hung from gibbets beside the road as a warning for all. Whether they were guilty of genuine crimes or not, Whitley would never know, but none deserved such a fate. Her father, the Werebear Duke Bergan, had executed men in the past. Such ceremonies were not for public consumption: they were a means to an end, the punishment for crimes committed, and were carried out behind closed doors. The torment ended with the ax blow—that was the law back in Brackenholme. Whitley couldn't imagine the pain the families of the gibbeted criminals were now feeling, their loved ones swinging in the cages, crows and gulls pecking at their corpses. The king's justice was a cruel business, and judging by the number of gallows that lined the streets of All Hallows Bay, business had been good.

"A crowd gathers."

Whitley glanced up, the imposing figure of Yuzhnik materializing beside her table. The Romari strongman squinted through the dirty glass windowpanes to the street outside. Whitley followed his gaze, lifting her head to observe the commotion. Sure enough, a boisterous mob had assembled in the darkness, the blurred red cloaks of the Lionguard faintly visible by torchlight as they led a prisoner through the street.

"Another hanging? Another murder?"

"It's none of our business," replied Yuzhnik, coldly cutting the chat short before their anger could rise.

He was correct, of course, figured Whitley. They weren't in All Hallows Bay to attract attention. The fishing port was a stepping-stone that would take her out to the White Sea, where the true destination lay. Sighing, she pulled her attention away from the window and back to her giant companion.

"Did you find him?"

"I found *her*," said Yuzhnik, scratching his jaw ruefully. "I spoke to her first mate, Mister Ramzi. You'll find Captain Violca aboard her ship, the *Lucky Shot*."

A short, glowering man lurched away from the bar as if on cue. His drooping mustache glittered, the long black hairs twined through golden hoops. He nodded briefly to Yuzhnik as he passed by, making for the door.

"That's the fellow. A pirate if ever I saw one."

"When does she expect us?"

"Anytime you're ready. Violca will depart once the bells of Brenn's temple ring out ten times and the watch are settling bar brawls. The *Lucky Shot* has other . . . *consignments* to collect before she sails. And I'm sure Violca will be picking up business right up until she hauls anchor. Smugglers can't be choosers."

Whitley reached up, placing her hand in Yuzhnik's huge, weathered palm. The Romari flinched at her touch, looking down with surprise. She gave him a squeeze.

"You'll be heading back to the forest now?" she asked quietly.

"Indeed, my . . . friend." Yuzhnik smiled, stopping short of calling her a lady. It wouldn't do for them to get this far only for his good manners to reveal Whitley's true identity to those around them. "The forest" was the name they used for the Bearlady's homeland, the woodland city of Brackenholme, deep in the heart of the Dyrewood.

"My people escorted you here as promised. Worry not; Violca can be trusted. Baba Soba said the captain's always been a friend to the Romari. This makes her a friend to you and 'the shepherd.'"

Whitley smiled at the mention of "the shepherd," another fitting code name.

"Speaking of the shepherd, where is he?" added the Romari, his gaze wandering around the room over the assembled patrons' heads.

"He's out on the stoop. I think he wanted to avoid drawing any further attention our way. After all, half of Lyssia's looking for the one-handed man."

She polished off her mug of tea, squeezing out of her booth to stand beside the Romari.

"You'll look after my mother?" asked Whitley. The question was unnecessary: the Romari people had sworn fealty to the Wolf and his allies, and that meant the people of the Woodland Realm.

"We shall look after *all* of your people, little one, for as long as it takes. The roads in and out of the forest will remain ours: only death awaits those foolish enough to travel them. Just come back, and bring an army with you."

Whitley nodded, comforted by Yuzhnik's words. Picking up her pack, she set off through the door, the Romari behind. Stepping out onto the stoop, the young woman looked both ways, searching for her companion who awaited them in the darkness. There was no sign of him.

"You say you left him out here?" said Yuzhnik, frowning as he walked stiffly down the steps.

With night settling over All Hallows Bay, the harbor front had transformed since their arrival that afternoon. Market stalls had been cleared from the cobbles, replaced by stacks of lobster pots, traps, and nets, the town's fishermen unloading their catches by lantern light. The boatmen kept their heads down, steering clear of the cronies who assembled around a set of charred stocks. Whitley watched on with wonder as others disappeared indoors. Windows slammed shut and curtains were drawn as the harbor became the playground of the Lionguard and their followers.

The mob numbered a dozen, cheering three soldiers on as they dragged a young man forward, a wolf's head daubed on his bare chest in black pitch. One Redcloak held a flaming torch as another shoved the boy into the stocks. The beam snapped down, securing his head and wrists into the wooden frame as the crowd jeered. The onlookers disgusted Whitley: here were the sympathizers who embraced the occupying force, pandering to the enemy's whims and securing favor while their neighbors suffered. As their captain unfurled a whip, the crowd stepped back.

"I know you can all hear me!" he shouted, his voice booming through the emptying streets. "Don't be shy: open your shutters! Take a peek at what awaits if you side with the Wolf!"

The Redcloak paced away, letting the cord trail through the dirt in his wake. Another soldier readied his torch, holding it high for all to see. Whitley suddenly pieced together the youth's fate. The tar on his chest, the flame, the burned stocks:

the Lionguard intended to set *fire* to the boy! One old woman threw a rock at his head, the lad's knees buckling as blood streamed from his brow. Whoever the youth was, and whatever he'd done, he didn't deserve this.

"Lackeys and lickspittles," muttered Yuzhnik, spitting into the dirt contemptuously. "Where *is* the shepherd?"

Whitley stopped in her tracks, reaching out to grab hold of the Romari, her eyes trained straight ahead beyond the mob.

"Brenn help us. . . ."

The Redcloak captain shook a ripple along the whip's length as he extended his arm back, preparing to strike. A wicked snarl splintered his face as he unleashed the leather toward the captive youth, sending it licking through the air. But the whip's tongue never reached the boy, the attack suddenly caught fast behind the Lionguard. The soldier's arm snapped, a wail escaping his throat as his whip was savagely yanked back. The Redcloak whirled on the spot like a spinning top, his dislocated arm flapping in a grotesque fashion before he ended up in the dirt. The mob and remaining Lionguard turned as one, looking past their injured officer toward the approaching figure.

This hadn't been part of the plan. They were supposed to slip unnoticed through All Hallows Bay like ghosts, phantoms on the wind. Standing on the inn's stoop, Drew Ferran had felt that familiar, sinking feeling as the boy and mob appeared. He couldn't stand by and do nothing. He'd wandered around the crowd, disappearing into the shadows at their backs, readying himself to intervene. He focused his heart and mind, breathing quickening as the beast's blood raced through his shifting body. Dark hairs cut through his weather-beaten flesh as his muscles grew, groaning beneath his studded leather armor.

The fallen Lionguard tugged a knife from his belt with his free hand, raising it high as he staggered to his feet. He snarled and rushed his shadowy assailant, mangled arm trailing uselessly in his wake. At the last, terrible moment he realized what manner of beast he was facing, the Werewolf leaping up into the soldier's torso and launching him skyward toward the shrieking mob. The guard somersaulted through the air, limbs flailing before crashing back to earth on his head. Drew Ferran, the Gray Wolf of Westland, bounded forward.

The crowd—so brave moments earlier as the soldiers abused their prisoner—turned to run. While the soldier with the flaming torch remained beside the stocks, his companion lowered his pike. The Werewolf twisted as he rushed the man, the heavy blade catching him below the breastplate. Drew snarled, feeling the steel slice past his guts. He brought his left arm up, fast and hard, an uppercut heading straight for the Redcloak's chin. The steel-capped stump of his wrist caught the man's sweet spot, ligaments snapping as the jawbone crumpled. The pike tumbled to the ground as the Lionguard dropped, choking and fumbling at his shattered face.

The remaining Redcloak was already swinging his torch. Drew tried to step clear, but the Lionguard's fury saw the brand home, striking the Werewolf hard in the face. Burning flowers bloomed before his eyes, the torch's bright light blinding him. Sparks showered his head and smoke scorched his throat as his fur smoldered. Drew knew only too well the danger of fire, having witnessed firsthand the damage it could do to therianthropes, in spite of their magical healing abilities. He raised a thick forearm to his face, trying to wipe the heat from his eyes, but it was to no avail: the white glow filled his vision. The Werewolf recoiled as the Lionguard seized the initiative.

"Can it be true? The legendary Wolf my masters fear, here, in All Hallows Bay? And frightened of a little fire?"

The soldier jabbed the brand into the blinded Werewolf's wounded hip. The torch sizzled as it met torn flesh, the Redcloak giving it an awful twist as Drew howled in agony. The guard backed up, his fingers reaching inside the collar of his steel breastplate. All the while he swung the torch in great arcs, keeping the stunned Werewolf back.

"Think of what they'll say about me!" He laughed manically. "Sergeant Kramer, the man who caught the Wolf!"

With a triumphant sneer he tugged a signal whistle out on a cord of leather and placed it to his lips. With his other hand he swiftly plunged the torch back toward the pitch-soaked youth in the stocks.

The flames never reached the captive boy, the arm's

progress cut short by Yuzhnik's descending ax. Severed limb and burning brand clattered to the ground as the Redcloak wailed in horror. The flat of the blade silenced his scream, striking his temple with a sickening crunch.

Whitley dashed to Drew's side, holding his pained face in her hands as his features shifted. The dark, burned hairs receded, his muzzle shortening, drawing flush to his skull. Thick, powerful canines slid up into his gums, grinding back like an ivory portcullis. The yellow eyes dimmed, the fearsome Werewolf slowly returning to the boy from the Cold Coast. Drew blinked as he tried to focus on his friend.

"So much for us keeping a low profile," Whitley whispered, brushing Drew's singed hair from his eyes. The young Wolflord managed a smile, wincing at her touch.

"I thought you knew me by now," he replied. "I'm not the best spectator."

The Romari brought his ax down onto the stocks and splintered the bolts, aware that the fishermen stood in a huddle, watching. Yuzhnik lifted the terrified youth from the broken wooden blocks and put an arm around him.

"They say you're a Wolf's man, lad? Whether you were or weren't, reckon you might be now."

One of the fishermen rushed up, beckoning the group frantically. "Hurry! The Redcloaks' snitches will have spread word of what's just happened. There'll be more here, soon enough."

Whitley glanced around the marketplace, catching sight of inquisitive faces peering from windows. She heard the distant cry of the mob, calling for the watch's attention. She turned to Yuzhnik.

"What are the chances of Violca taking the *Lucky Shot* out early?"

"You'd better hope she's in a generous mood," said the Romari, turning back to the fisherman. "Lead on, friend."

Whitley set off after Yuzhnik as the Romari and the young prisoner followed the fisherman deeper into the docks. She stopped, realizing that Drew hadn't followed. The young Wolflord stood by the broken stocks, his hand drawn over his face. She dashed back to him, taking him by the arm.

"Hurry, Drew. Now isn't the time for dawdling."

"Believe me, I've no desire to linger," replied the youth, turning his tear-stained face to Whitley. His red-ringed eyes stared straight through her.

"I'm blind."

2
Deathwalker

HIS BARE FEET *slapped against the cold stone flags, each step bringing him closer to the tower's summit. Moonlight reflected off the dark walls of the winding staircase, the brickwork's definition growing sharper as he neared the roof. Weary legs lifted him ever higher, his limbs possessed with a life of their own, carrying him inexorably toward the star-dappled heavens. The spiraling rope banister ran through the palm of his blackened hand, skeletal fingers grasping and hauling him the remaining few steps, out onto the top of the Bone Tower.*

The wind tugged at him, threatening to send him staggering over the edge. The wizened lightning rod, scorched black by the elements, groaned in its housing where it was bolted to the parapet. He was aware he was dreaming, but the creaking metal and sensation of the air rushing around him were sickeningly real. He could smell the ice on the breeze from the snow-capped mountains, taste the blood and smoke of battle from far below, and feel the cruel, cold caress of the Sturmish elements as the north's ill winds bit into his flesh. He stepped closer toward the edge, the city of Icegarden suddenly sliding into view as he came to a halt beside the crumbling crenulations.

The fires burned to the south, the White Bear's fortifications tasting the flaming pitch of the Lion's army. The battlefield spread across the Whitepeaks' slopes, great swathes of icy meadows now turned to rivers of churned slush, spring's unavoidable appearance aiding the Bastian advance on Icegarden. Campfires twinkled out in the Badlands, home to Lucas's mighty force. Closer to Icegarden the beleaguered camp of the trapped Bearlords huddled, its fires far fewer, its number greatly reduced. His eyes didn't linger upon his enemies. They weren't the reason for his midnight stroll.

He lifted his right foot into the air, raising it until it landed on the white stone parapet. The brickwork was rough and uneven against his sole, the sensation chillingly realistic. Just a dream, he reminded himself. Even so, he fought his body's desire to lift the other foot, to follow its brother up onto the tumbledown stones. Another blast of wind buffeted him.

I'd like to wake up now, *he told himself, his subconscious mind sharp enough to banish the nightmare when he'd endured enough. Only the dark dream wouldn't relinquish its hold on him. His right leg straightened, drawing his left up into the air to land beside it on the parapet edge. He looked down, his toes curling over the top of the uneven stone block, the void beyond. The vertigo he'd endured as a child suddenly hit him hard, grasping his heart and squeezing tight. His knees trembled, one more gust hammering at the pale flesh of his torso, prodding, poking at him, pushing him forward.*

Then came the whisper:

I can kill you whenever I wish . . .

Hector felt the world turn, his stomach lurching as something hard hit him in the guts. He was flying through the air, stars spinning overhead before his back hit the cold hard flags of the Bone Tower's roof. Beside him lay the panting figure of Ringlin, chief among his Boarguard. The man's arm still rested across Hector's stomach, the tall soldier's quick thinking having caught the young magister. It had been Ringlin's grasp that had knocked the air from his lungs, yanking him back from a fatal fall to the palace rooftop hundreds of feet below.

"My lord," gasped Ringlin, withdrawing his arm, breathing hard as he crawled onto his knees. "The roof . . . what were you thinking?"

Hector lay where he was, staring up at the twinkling sky, fingers twitching spasmodically as breath steamed from his lips.

"I wasn't . . . *thinking.* I thought I was dreaming."

Ringlin unbuckled the brown cloak from around his shoulders, draping it over his master.

"You turning into a sleepwalker? Had a friend of mine back

in Highcliff who was one o' them: walked straight off the jetty and into the harbor. They found his body the next day, but not before the crabs had nibbled him to pieces."

He reached around Hector, helping the Boarlord sit up straight. Ringlin dabbed at the back of the magister's head, his fingers coming away bloody from where he'd struck the flagged roof.

"Sorry about that, my lord. Small price to pay, though, eh?"

"Indeed," agreed Hector, woozily, trying to regather his senses. "How did you know I was in danger?"

"You passed a chambermaid in your stupor: she came to alert me. I figured you didn't sound yourself so came looking. I just followed the trail of confused servants and it led me here."

"Thank you, my friend," said Hector, struggling to his feet, the Boarguard helping him rise. It felt odd that Hector should consider Ringlin a friend, especially in light of the circumstances that had forged that friendship initially. The death of his brother, Vincent, had brought Ringlin and another rogue, Ibal, into his service, the two men having worked for the slain Boarlord. His brother had been killed by Hector's own hand—an accident, though that fact counted for little in the eyes of his twin's ghostly vile that both haunted and served him. Hector had been trained as a magister, a healer, but had turned his back on the fairer arts of late, concentrating his knowledge on the realm of necromancy and communing with the dead. After his death, Vincent had returned in the form of a vengeful vile, a spirit that in turn tormented and comforted Hector. As for Ringlin and Ibal, what had started out as a distrustful business arrangement had grown into something more. Whether it was a genuine fondness, Hector was reluctant to say. His last true friendship hadn't ended well, he figured, thinking back to Drew.

"Reckon you had another of those bad dreams? You've been having plenty lately."

"This was no dream. I witnessed everything, Ringlin. I was locked away inside my body, seeing everything as clear as you before me now. It was as if I was . . . *possessed.* As if something had taken a hold of me . . ."

His words trailed away, his mind leading him back toward Vincent.

"Grim words, my lord. You fear it's your brother, don't you?"

Ringlin was no fool. The rangy rogue had frequently witnessed Hector's struggles with the Vincent-vile. At first, Hector's outbursts must have appeared to the Boarguard as deranged babblings, the magister arguing with the voices inside his head. In time a pattern had appeared, the outbursts intensifying whenever Hector channeled his dark magicks, often hissing his brother's name in anger. The young Werelord now stood at the height of his powers, seemingly in total control of the vile. Vincent's torment had all but ceased by day, the spirit dutifully obeying Hector's commands as and when it was called upon. The nights, however, were another matter.

"Perhaps," said Hector, his voice lacking conviction. He knew full well that the vile was behind his perilous sleepwalking. But how far would his brother take things? Why would the vile send him to the top of the Bone Tower, a footstep away from death?

"Is he listening to us now?" asked Ringlin, glancing across Hector's shoulder as if the vile might suddenly become visible to him for the first time.

"He's always here; he never leaves me," whispered Hector. "Although he remains suspiciously silent at present. Where are you, brother? Why so shy all of a sudden?"

Hector had gotten used to Vincent's presence since his death, haunting his every deed and bending his ear. That banter had dwindled in the last few months, since Hector had seized Icegarden from Duke Henrik, attacking the White Bear's city with his army of Ugri warriors.

"Do you finally know your place, Vincent? Is that it? You realize my power is absolute?"

Ringlin shifted awkwardly. "It may not be wise to antagonize your brother, my lord, especially with your night walks still unexplained."

Bless him, thought Hector, *he still doesn't realize that Vincent sees and hears* everything *I do. He may be silent at the moment, but there isn't a thought that passes through my head that he doesn't feed upon. Is that not so, brother?* The vile remained ominously silent. Hector shivered, despite Ringlin's brown cloak.

"We shall speak in greater detail regarding my brother later," said the Boarlord, clenching his black fist, the skin drawing tight over the knuckles. He stared out over the land beyond the city walls.

The beleaguered camp of the Bearlords lay below, temporary home to Dukes Henrik and Bergan, while farther away the fires of the Catlord forces burned. Hector had once been a friend of Bergan, the Lord of Brackenholme, but those days were long gone. Hector had sided with the Lion for a brief time, before news of the Catlords' treachery had reached his ears. Lord Onyx, the Pantherlord who commanded the king's armies, wanted the Boarlord dead, having sent the Werecrow Flint to carry out that very deed. Onyx had seen the power that Hector wielded, his mastery over the dead, and rightly feared the young Wereboar.

But Hector had chosen his own path now. Flint and his Werecrow brethren had become unexpected allies, the Lords of Riven fearing treachery of their own at the hands of the Catlords. The Crows had spent too long as the whipping boys in Lyssian courts. Alongside Hector, the greatest necromancer the Seven Realms had ever known, they would forge a mighty new future where Boar and Crows ruled over all humans and therians, mastering the mountains and the lands below.

Hector's eyes narrowed as he caught sight of something

moving across the sky in the distance, the moonlight catching its pale wings as it circled the Catlord camp. Ringlin spied it, too.

"Another of the Catlords' allies," said the Boarguard warily. "An avianthrope of Bast, no doubt. Perhaps a Cranelord? Their numbers grow daily, Onyx calling upon the aid of fellow Werelords from his homeland. I fear the force he's gathered down there, and exactly what it's made up of. What creatures do you suppose he's mustered to his side? And how soon before they finally strike out and crush the Bearlords?"

"Spring is here," replied Hector. "Perhaps Onyx still fears the advantage that Henrik and Bergan have of the higher ground. The Sturmlanders know the Whitepeaks better than any force, especially an invading army from the jungle continent. The weather may have become that bit more tolerable, but even with far greater numbers the Bastians would be fools to rush their attack. They play a waiting game: they intend to starve the Bearlords and the Sturmish out of the mountains."

"You do realize, my lord, that the Beast of Bast still wants you dead? You've betrayed your oath to Lucas, taking Icegarden for your own and siding with the Crows. You've as good as signed your own death warrant: once Onyx and his army have vanquished the Bearlords, surely we're next."

"Next to be vanquished?" Hector laughed. "And I thought you were a gambling man, Ringlin."

"I like a wager, but the odds look stacked against us. Just *look* at the size of that army!"

Hector nodded, appreciating the point his man made. "I don't disagree—that's a frightful force Onyx and Lucas have gathered—but you underestimate the hand we hold. Not only do we have the impregnable walls of Icegarden surrounding us, but we have my Ugri warriors from Tuskun bolstering our ranks alongside the recently arrived Blackcloaks of Riven. And all the while their Crowlord masters control the sky. It would be sheer folly to mount an attack on my city. We truly hold all the aces."

Even shivering and in shock from his awful sleepwalking, Hector couldn't help but feel good. After all the trials and terrors he'd faced, his fortunes seemed to be on the turn. He had an army of brutal warriors at his disposal and powerful allies in the Crows who seemed to both respect *and* fear him. And somewhere, deep within the Strakenberg mines, the ancient artifact known as the Wyrmstaff remained hidden. With such a staff in his grasp, who knew what magicks he could unlock? What host he might be able to command? Hector had prisoners within the cells beneath the palace, prisoners who *knew* where that staff was. It was only a matter of time before he held it. His enemies could call for his head all they wanted: he was safe in Icegarden.

"And what if the word from the Crowlord is true, my lord? Does that not impact upon your plans?"

Hector winced, Ringlin's words like a knife to his back. He knew full well what his Boarguard referred to. News had reached Icegarden on Flint's dark wings, information that Hector was struggling to comprehend: Drew Ferran, the last of the Gray Wolves of Westland and the first real friend he had truly known, was alive. A severed hand was all that had been recovered of the Wolf in the Horselord city of Cape Gala, the remainder of Drew's body never found. Most believed he'd been eaten alive by the undead horde who had swarmed the citadel, while a rumor had persisted that he'd escaped. That rumor had gained momentum in recent weeks, strengthened by numerous sightings.

"Whispers of the demented and desperate, nothing more," said Hector, trying to dismiss the comment with as much flippancy as he could muster.

"You can't believe that," replied Ringlin. "This came from men of Riven who faced the Werewolf in Stormdale, soldiers loyal to you. Lord Flint's own brother fought him on the battlements."

"They must have been mistaken."

"How easy is it to mistake a lycanthrope?" asked Ringlin, forgetting himself for a moment. "Remind me again how many Werewolves still live?"

Ordinarily, the rogue might have expected a withering look from his master, but on the matter of Drew's reappearance Hector couldn't hide his mixed emotions. When to his mind Drew had been dead, his decisions had been so much easier. With his friend gone and the Wolf's Council broken, it was quite clear what path he had to take through life. He was to forge his own, a new path that ultimately led to him taking power not just over the Dalelands but farther afield, right across Lyssia. If Drew did indeed still live, how would he react to the choices the young Boarlord had made? Hector avoided Ringlin's gaze, bare feet gingerly crossing the cold flags toward the stairwell.

"There are other lycanthropes who may yet live in this world, Ringlin. The White Wolves of Shadowhaven roamed the north not that long ago. Perhaps it was one of Queen Amelie's kin that the Crows and Rats faced in Stormdale."

Ringlin paused, considering his words. "As I understand it—my lord—Flint was quite specific when describing the creature that fought alongside the Staglords. If Drew *does* live—and that hasn't been confirmed, I know—then what would you do? How would your actions tally with your old friend?"

Hector finally turned back to his Boarguard, sneering. "For a reformed footpad, you certainly have a way with words. Where did you learn such insight and diplomacy?"

"On the streets, for the most part," he said, before adding, "and in your esteemed service, of course. You didn't answer the question, my lord. What if Drew lives? Do you fear he'd disapprove of the path you've taken?"

"Wherever my friend's been, that he should rise from the dead and return to the fray, I'm confident I can make him understand the reasons for my actions. Do you think I've anything to feel shame for, Ringlin? Speak freely."

The informal chats between them had increased since their arrival in Icegarden. Hector truly trusted the tall soldier's counsel, finding few others he could depend upon for frank and honest answers.

"You've killed folk, both human and therian. You did away with Vega, murdered Slotha to impress the Lion, and left a trail of bodies in your wake."

"I'd hardly call it a trail. A few dead Skirmishers from Onyx's lot, that's all."

"But you ordered your Ugri into battle against the Sturmlanders when you seized this city. You sent me and Ibal out into the cold to kill in your name. If a man dies at your command, then his blood's on your hands as much as the blade that did the deed."

When Hector thought about it that way, the number he'd slain grew dramatically. The capture of Icegarden from the Sturmish had been a swift and bloody affair.

"Regardless, Vega had to die. He betrayed Wergar years ago; it's only natural he'd betray his friends again. He couldn't be trusted."

"By you, perhaps, but wasn't he loyal to Drew and the Wolf's Council?"

"You're worse than my cursed brother's vile sometimes!" Hector snarled. "Why the persistent questions, Ringlin? Do you deliberately try to cast doubt in my mind?"

The rogue raised his hands passively. "You asked me what I thought. If you mean to convince the Wolflord that your actions were for the greater good, then there can be no doubts: you need to *believe* that yourself. Do you?"

"Of course I do," blustered Hector. "The Wolf's Council was a shambles once we lost Drew. Manfred turned his back on me, judging me before I'd even said my piece. Bergan's a spent force, a shadow of the Bearlord I once knew and respected, and if rumors are true his own city of Brackenholme was sacked by the Wyldermen." He pointed back beyond the city walls. "Where are the proud men of the Woodland Watch, coming to their liege's aid as he huddles on the slopes of the Whitepeaks? I see no army."

Ringlin nodded as Hector continued ranting.

"Should Drew return to me, he'll find I've procured an army, a force powerful enough to defeat our enemies from Bast and drive the Catlords once and for all from Lyssia. He couldn't do it with the bickering Bears, Sharks, and Stags. Between us, we can return the Seven Realms to their former greatness! This would be a source of great happiness for all."

"And if he disagrees with your methods?"

Hector faltered, words failing him momentarily. The wind whipped at the pair of them suddenly, howling as it raced past the tower top, causing them to seize hold of one another until it died away.

"It would not gladden me, Ringlin, for Drew to stand

against me. But if he did?" Hector cleared his throat, raising his voice. "Then . . . then the Wolf shall not figure in the brave new Lyssia that awaits us."

Ringlin smiled approvingly as Hector found he'd surprised even himself.

"There," said the rogue. "You've said it: a world without Drew Ferran, should it come to it. Don't you feel better, now the words are out there?"

The gurgling voice of the Vincent-vile briefly materialized in Hector's ear, gone again as quickly as a whisper on the wind. The magister managed a smile as he set off down the stairwell, the lanky Boarguard close behind. *If it were truly better to speak such a thing,* he thought, gripping the rope handrail as he stepped down through the darkness, *then why do I feel sick in the pit of my stomach?*

3

GRACED

IN EVER DECREASING circles, the avianthrope descended into the war camp, drawing closer to the command tent. Wings clapped at the air, alerting the elite Bastian guard below. The golden-skinned warriors looked up, raising spear and aiming bow at the approaching Werelord. As the flying shape-shifter neared the ground, fire and torchlight illuminated thick dark plumage, a great ruff of white feathers rattling around the visitor's disjointed neck. Powerful talons snatched at the earth as the avian landed, and the Bastian soldiers relaxed their weapons. The towering Werelord stepped between them, great strides carrying him into Lord Onyx's tent, his crooked throat twisting to allow his head to clear the door frame.

The Vulturelord crossed the rugged floor, sharp toes receding with each footfall, his body shifting as he stalked toward his equals. Stuffed animal heads and skulls dangled from the canvas ceiling, Onyx's trophies staring down at the avianthrope through glassy eyes and hollow sockets. A bell jar sat atop a squat wooden plinth, a gray clawed hand floating within, pickled and preserved for all time. This was the Werepanther's most favored prize: the hand of the Wolf.

Two enormous black jaguars slept before an open hearth in the center of the chamber. A circle of stones kept the burning logs in place as smoke curled up toward a chimney hole at the tent top. Eleven of the twelve seats around a great oval table were taken, their occupants staring at the array of maps that were pinned to its surface by an array of bones. Goblets sloshed as the gathered players muttered over their drinks. Now the war council turned as one, witnessing the last of the Vulture's features fade as the sickle beak transformed into a hooked nose.

Lord Onyx, the Beast of Bast, rose from his huge wooden chair at the head of the table, gesturing to the vacant seat opposite.

"So good of you to join us, Count Costa; I feared you'd been distracted by a carcass in the mountains. I was hoping it might be a dead bear . . ."

The bald-headed count bowed to the Pantherlord before taking his seat, reaching forward to pour himself a goblet of wine.

"If you want me scouting the Whitepeaks, my lord, then don't expect me to be the first at your table. My work's unorthodox by nature, stealth and subterfuge as important as keen senses. I could of course remain close to your side like so many of your other, oh-so-capable commanders," he said, smiling as he cast his beady eyes over the table.

Chests puffed out as all present blustered at Costa's comments, their voices rising quickly in defense. One officer spoke louder than the others, a barrel-chested brute with a great, wobbling jaw. He snorted as he jabbed a thick finger at the Vulture.

"Don't be casting aspersions about this council, Costa. We each have a role within King Lucas's army, duties that keep us tied to this camp and our men. Besides, if I had wings, do you not think I'd be fluttering around these miserable mountains spying on our enemy?"

Costa scoffed at the claim as he took a swig from his goblet. "A Hippo with wings? I'd pay gold to see that, General Gorgo!"

The Hippolord gnashed his teeth, his features trembling as his leathery flesh darkened. The great tusks began to appear at either side of his broad mouth, skin splitting as the ivory blades emerged from his jaw.

Onyx reached down, a mighty hand snatching Gorgo by a tusk. "Put those away," he growled, shaking the general before releasing him.

Gorgo's hands went to his face as the tusks began to

recede, horrified at being manhandled by the Pantherlord. His fellow commanders of the Lion's army looked away, sensing the general's embarrassment.

"As I was saying," said Costa, "the night's the only time that's safe for me to scout. General Skean, a fellow avianthrope, will vouch for the danger of the skies in daylight."

An elegant, elderly Werelord nodded sagely, his long fingers reaching out to brush over the map, lingering over Icegarden.

"Costa's correct," said the Cranelord. "The Crows own the sky while the sun is up—my kin and I are far outnumbered by Flint and his black-feathered brothers. The night is another matter, though, when the Crows return to Icegarden to roost, with only a couple remaining on the wing. If you want a good look at our enemies—both the Bearlords and the Boarlord's rabble—then the night is the best time for Costa—"

"What did you discover?" interrupted Onyx, locking his eyes upon the Vulturelord.

"The Bears remain utterly surrounded. There are maybe a couple thousand of them, strung out behind their barricades along the snowline. We block their way down from the mountains through the foothills, while many of Hector's Ugri warriors patrol the land beyond Icegarden's walls, picking off any Sturmlanders foolish enough to try and return home. If any soul somehow found his way into the city, he'd find the soldiers of Riven have swelled the Boarlord's force."

"What condition are Henrik's men in?" asked Gorgo. "They must be at death's door by now. What are they living off? Their fallen comrades?"

"They're wasting away, General, but far from cannibalizing their dead. The Sturmlanders are resilient: they know these mountains and if anyone can survive out here, cut off from their own supply lines, it's them."

"What of Duke Bergan?" asked Sheriff Muller, the only human member of Onyx's war council. "Any sign of the Bear of Brackenholme?"

Costa glowered at the man disdainfully. "You think I had time to wander through their camp and check every tent, Muller? I've no idea about Bergan's condition or whereabouts, but we can be confident he hasn't found a way out of that camp. There is none; he's trapped."

"The weather's been Henrik's greatest ally over the last couple of months," said Gorgo, the Hippolord's broad lips flapping as he turned to Onyx. "With the Lyssian winter behind us and warmer weather on its way, their end is nigh. The sun warms the blood of our brave men of Bast: a renewed army waits to take to the field. General Skean and I have the troops in position. We're ready for action, by your command, my lord."

"Which brings us to Baron Hector," said Onyx. "The Crows of Riven have flocked to Blackhand's side, clearly fearful of their future in the Seven Realms. As they should rightly be: the infighting that ruined the assault on Stormdale was thanks in no small part to their petty bickering and jealousies. The Rat war marshal Vorjavik died that day, and I don't doubt that Crowlord talons left their marks upon his corpse."

"It seems an oath means nothing to the Boar." Gorgo snorted. "That's the Wolf *and* the Lion he's turned his back upon now, not to mention his brief alliance with the Walrus Queen. Blackhand's in good company with those filthy birds from the Barebones."

"Both the Boar and the Crows have outlived their usefulness," said Onyx. "It was always clear to me that our Lord Magister was a dangerous individual. The perverted magicks he can harness—communing with and controlling the dead—have no place within our society. Flint was supposed to dispose of the Boarlord, but it seems I underestimated the Crow's capacity for treachery."

"It's just a shame they were able to take Icegarden for their own before handing us the keys to the city gates," said Costa, polishing off his drink.

"No matter," grumbled Gorgo, the Hippo curling a hand into a clublike fist. "We crush the Sturmlanders. Then we crush the traitors." He punched the table in an unnecessary show of conviction, prompting a weary head shake from Costa.

"You make it sound so simple," said the Vulture. "The weather may be turning to our favor, but the stalemate remains. Our warriors find these mountains a fearful place, having seen so many of their brethren fall upon the white slopes. I doubt many will be in a hurry to race toward the Strakenberg, even with half of Bast at their backs."

A trumpet sounded close by in the camp, a rousing voluntary that caused the twelve members of the war council to look up.

"Is the camp under attack?" asked Gorgo, rising from his chair. "What fool would blow a horn at this time of night?"

One after another, the officers stood, following Onyx toward the tent's entrance.

"That's no alarm call," growled the Pantherlord as he disappeared through the door.

A procession of Redcloaks marched down the churned-up avenue that cut through the heart of the encampment, heading straight toward the command tent. Bastian Goldhelms and Lyssians alike came out of their billets to see who had arrived, lining the muddy lane as the column strode past. At the head rode a dozen scarlet-caped cavalrymen, their chargers stepping gracefully through the mud. Behind them came four files of the Lionguard, fifty deep, rank upon rank of crimson-caped soldier, striding stiffly, shoulder to shoulder. The lines parted as they assembled before Lord Onyx, falling into regimental position on either side of the command tent.

With the rest of the war council gathering at his back, Onyx glowered at the Lionguard that had arrived unannounced, each of the Redcloaks avoiding his glare.

"Well, then?" roared the Beast of Bast. "Where's your commanding officer? Who would think to arrive in *my* camp at such an hour, without a word of warning being sent my way? Is he really so keen to meet the maker?"

More horses trotted down the dirty road, the campfires throwing light over them as they came into view. Eight more cavalrymen rode in formation, a pair of riders between them traveling side by side on two magnificent steeds. A robed, hooded figure sat on a tall black stallion, a heavy cowl obscuring his face from view, but Onyx knew the rider well enough: Vanmorten, Lord Chancellor of Westland, Wererat of Vermire, and the most powerful member of the famed Rat King family. Beside him, sitting proud atop a great gray warhorse, rode a most unexpected guest.

The soldiers all bowed low as the warhorse trotted forward. Even the assembled members of the war council bent at the knee, all except for Onyx, who stood with his hands on his hips, a look of genuine surprise rising across his hard features as Lucas approached. The young Lion looked down at the Werepanther, reining his horse to a halt a few feet from Onyx.

"An unanticipated pleasure that you should grace us with your company, Your Highness," said Onyx, managing to smile but making no attempt to hide his annoyance.

If the Panther's manner was intended to unsettle the Lion, Lucas showed no sign of upset.

"Since when, dear Uncle, did the arrival of Westland's king

not warrant a show of manners from *all* in his presence?"

Onyx's eyes widened, his lips curling contemptuously as he looked to Vanmorten. The Wererat's hooded head turned away, avoiding the gaze of the Beast of Bast. The Panther looked to those nobles who were members of his war council, each still low to the ground, knee in the mud.

"He has to be joking," the Panther whispered to Costa at his side, but the Vulturelord remained crouched, his head dipped.

Lucas nudged his warhorse's flanks with his heels, and the massive mount stepped closer to Onyx, dipping its head aggressively until only an inch separated the two. The Pantherlord growled as the horse snorted and stamped the ground between them. *Who is this child that he should come before me, the Beast of Bast, and show such disrespect? I have* made *this boy, provided him with an army and a backbone where his own father was unable! Is* this *how he repays me?*

A tremor ran through the ranks of assembled Lionguard, the tension heightening with each passing moment as Onyx refused to bow. It might have been his hearing deceiving him, but the Werepanther was convinced he could hear swords loosening in their scabbards.

Lucas leaned forward in his saddle and spoke in a low, conspiratorial voice. "Believe me, Uncle, I understand your discomfort. This is terribly awkward. I know you've been out here in the back of beyond for some time, away from court life, but there are certain rules of etiquette we have to adhere to. It's a show, if you will, for the men; reaffirms who's in command, whom they're fighting for."

Gradually Onyx bowed his head, his chin coming to rest upon his chest while his brow gave the warhorse a firm butt across the nose.

"Your Highness," said the Beast of Bast, slowly bringing his head back up. The other Werelords and soldiers now rose, following the Pantherlord's lead as the atmosphere shifted to one of relief. Lucas adjusted the simple iron crown that encircled his head, brushing a few blond locks from his brow in the process.

"It's *Your Majesty* now, remember, Uncle? I grew tired of waiting for a gang of lesser lordlings to gather and say yea or nay to my claim." Lucas sighed, swinging his legs around in his saddle. Several of the Lionguard rushed forward to support him as he slid from the horse, throwing their red cloaks over the mud before him to protect his path on his walk to the command tent. Onyx walked by his side, his commanders in turn following them. The boy had enjoyed a growth spurt, the Panther noticed; his chest had filled out, an attempt at a mustache had appeared over his lip, and his head was now up to the Panther's shoulder. *Still a sprat, of course,* Onyx mused, himself a staggering seven feet in height.

"Why wait for the approval of the Horses, Stags, and Bears?" Lucas announced, striding into the tent. "It's merely a matter of time before their opposition's crushed once and for all. Who can stand in my way? No, the coronation was carried out some weeks ago in Highcliff before the priests of Brenn's temple. My Lord Chancellor was chief witness to the deed."

Onyx glanced back, spying that Vanmorten hadn't joined them, instead hovering by the door. He distrusted the Rat—though, in fairness, Onyx distrusted most everyone.

"You would not join us in my tent, Lord Chancellor?" asked Onyx menacingly. "You've nothing to fear here—you're among friends. This isn't like you to be so shy."

Lucas suddenly nodded to the Wererat, gesturing for him to leave. "Bring them, Vanmorten, and be quick about it."

The tent flaps fell back into place as Onyx turned and followed the young Werelion. Lucas stood before the pedestal that bore the glass jar. He peered at the Werewolf's hand within, tapping the glass with a gloved finger.

"The Rat is quiet, *Your Majesty,*" said Onyx. "I'm surprised my sister didn't bear witness to your coronation. Surely a Cat of Bast, one of your own kind, would have been a better choice of witness before the eyes of your Lyssian god."

"Opal had already left," said Lucas, straightening from inspecting the grisly trophy. "She's taken to the seas to snuff out the piracy that's dogging our navy. She's a very capable woman, my aunt. It does rather make me wonder whether she might have been a better choice to lead my army in this conflict."

The collective gasp of the gathered Werelords threatened

to blow out the candles that burned around the chamber. Gorgo stared at the Panther, mortified, while the rest of the therians turned their gazes to their feet.

"You would question my command? Need I remind you who I am, cub?"

Lucas turned on the Werepanther and snarled, the downy yellow hair below his nose thickening into wiry golden whiskers as his lips filled out, canines bared, growing by the second. The sleeping black jaguars woke, adding their own chorus to the Werelion's throaty growls.

"You forget yourself, Uncle. The last time I checked, it was the Lion that ruled over the Seven Realms. I'm the King of Westland, lord of all Lyssia, and you should know your place. I won't be so easily . . . *manipulated* as my father was before me."

Onyx smiled with an easy charm as if Lucas were a newborn in his lap. "You think you can do better with my army, *Your Majesty*, then you're most welcome to—"

It was a glib, throwaway comment that Onyx regretted instantly.

"Fine, I'll take full responsibility over the army, henceforth," said Lucas, calming as he spoke, his fangs slowly shrinking. "Thank you for all you've done, Uncle, and do not think me churlish—I'm still in need of your assistance. Annoying though it is that you've thus far been unable to break the White Bear's resistance, I'm sure with our combined cunning we'll crush them beneath our paws."

Onyx glared at the Werelion as the young king assessed the war council, continuing his grand speech.

"It warms my heart to see so many of our subjects from Bast here, close to my side in this trying time." The assembled therian lords all bowed to the king respectfully, their eyes flitting Onyx's way, watching and waiting to see what the Panther might do next. "One day, once this dreadful rebellion is put to rest, I should dearly love to travel to Bast and pay my respects to the Forum of Elders. And I shall be sure to visit each of your homelands. My uncle has only words of pride when he mentions your provinces that have sworn fealty to the Catlords. It means more than words that you would come to my aid, my lords, in my hour of need."

"Lord Onyx and the Forum of Elders called us, Your Majesty," said Count Costa, the Vulturelord picking his words very carefully, "and we came. Our word is our bond."

Good fellow, Costa, thought Onyx, managing an almost imperceptible nod in the avianthrope's direction, but the count caught it. *You know who your true masters are; let's hope the others don't forget, either.*

Lucas nodded sagely as if Costa's words in some way reflected deep loyalty to him. "I have a bold vision as to how we may defeat our enemies, both in Sturmland and beyond."

"Something we foolishly haven't yet considered, perhaps?" asked Onyx, his deep voice tinged with anger. A movement by the door caused all but Lucas to turn.

The Ratlord, Vanmorten, reentered the tent, a trio of savage-looking men close to heel. Though they were unarmed, there was no doubting how dangerous they were. One was completely naked, blue woad bands encircling his filthy limbs like bolts of azure lightning. Another bore a crude mask of white paint over his face in the style of a skull. The last—the one Onyx had to assume was their leader—wore no markings, no tribal insignia to differentiate him from his companions. His matted hair hung down his back, his broad bare shoulders rippling with muscles. The warrior's glare settled upon Onyx, a meeting of champions as they measured one another warily.

Sheriff Muller stepped forward, aghast, reaching for the sword on his hip. "Your Majesty, these are Wyldermen!"

"Stay your hand, Muller," snapped Vanmorten. "What a knack you have for stating the blindingly obvious! The king knows full well who they are."

Though Onyx had heard of the Wyldermen, this was his first encounter with the wild men of the Dyrewood. He was struck by their intensity, the rage that seemed to simmer below the surface as they eyed the assembled Werelords suspiciously.

"These are your secret weapon?" snarled Onyx. "A gang of bush-dwelling denizens of the haunted forest?"

"Their leader is Darkheart," said Lucas, his attention

returning to the hand in the jar. “He is the son of Coldblood, shaman of the Wyrmwood, a man murdered by our mutual enemy, the Wolf. He is well versed in Wyrm Magicks just as his father was before him.”

Onyx growled. “Wyrm Magicks? The backward beliefs of these savages are going to help us defeat our enemies? I hadn’t taken you for a superstitious child, Your Majesty.”

Lucas turned back to Onyx, his amber eyes shining bright. “Wyrm Magicks and something else, dear uncle.”

“What else?”

The king hooked a thumb and raised it into the air, tapping the glass jar beside him. Ripples ran through the liquid, causing the Werewolf’s hand to slowly rotate.

“My half brother, Drew Ferran,” replied Lucas. “He’s going to lend a helping hand.”

4
The Captain's Table

DREW SLAMMED THE fork down into the tabletop, metal thrumming as it quivered, buried in the wood.

"If it's all right with you, my ladies, I may just use my fingers." Drew sighed. Dining was difficult enough one-handed; being blind was adding a fresh element of danger and unpredictability to the Wolflord's dining experiences. He'd chased his meat and vegetables around the tin plate long enough. Now he snatched up the food and began to make short work of it.

"I did offer to cut it up and feed you," said Whitley from across the table.

"Thanks, but I'm not a child who needs spoon-feeding," Drew replied, trying to hide his frustration with a gravy-spattered smile.

"Don't feel enslaved to etiquette when you dine at my table, Your Highness," said Captain Violca from where she sat at the table's head, her voice light and musical.

Drew hadn't seen the woman's face, but she'd made a striking impression upon his mind's eye. The scent of her perfume had preceded that first handshake when he and Whitley had been bundled aboard the *Lucky Shot* in All Hallows Bay, and her grip had been like steel. There was a strength in that handshake that reminded Drew of his mentor, Duke Bergan. Violca was clearly a woman to be respected.

"You're too kind," he said, splintering a rib and worrying the marrow from the bone. "And Drew's just fine."

Violca had given the two full use of her cabin aboard the *Lucky Shot,* bunking in with her crew while she had such esteemed guests aboard. Yuzhnik had left them in the port, taking the unfortunate youth who had been tortured by the Lionguard under his wing as he sought a way back to the Dyrewood. He would deliver the message back to Brackenholme that Drew and Whitley had safely met up with Violca.

"Your eyes," said the captain. "How do they fare?"

"Badly," replied Drew, pausing to raise his fingers to his brow to readjust the bandage. Whitley had cleaned and dressed his wounds, putting an herb-soaked cloth across his scorched eyes and binding it behind his head. The ointments had begun working already, soothing and taking the heat from his skin, but when he'd awoken that morning Drew had been disappointed to find his vision was no better. Then it came to him: *fire*. Alongside silver, flames were certain to harm him, his therianthropic healing ineffective against such injuries. Bright lights played before him, as if he'd stared into the noon sun. He fumbled with the bandage, sensing it loosening the more he tried to straighten it.

"Here, let me," said Violca. "You're not the first young man I've bandaged aboard the *Lucky Shot*."

Drew heard her chair scrape along the floorboards as she rose and walked down the table toward him. He felt her fingers brush his face, untying the bandage before gently tightening it once more. She deftly secured it in place with a knot that wasn't going anywhere. Drew felt the color in his cheeks.

"How long before I can see again?"

"Keep thinking that way, and with optimism like that you could recover from death!" Violca observed.

"This blindness could be permanent?"

"I've no idea—I'm sure Lady Whitley would agree you need a magister to appraise your wounds, work some healing cantrips upon you. This is beyond what little knowledge I have of medicine, especially as you're a therianthrope."

What I wouldn't give to have Hector by my side right now, thought Drew.

"Then, what happens next is entirely in Brenn's hands," he said.

Violca laughed teasingly, placing her hands on his shoulders. "Your god of forest, fell, and fen won't help you upon the White Sea. You're in my world now: it's Sosha you need to start praying to, Drew Ferran."

Whitley cleared her throat, causing Drew to start and Violca to withdraw her hands. When she spoke, Drew sensed an air of annoyance in her voice.

"Gods to one side for a moment, Captain, do you know the whereabouts of Bosa's ships?"

"No, but they've caused mayhem among the Lion's fleet," Violca said, returning to her seat. "Initially the Whalelord attacked the navy in Moga, leaving it in flames before striking at ports throughout the Cluster Isles and along the coast. Hook, Blackbank, Vermire itself: almost nothing's been spared Bosa's blades."

"This is the army we need," said Drew, pushing his plate away, the last remnants of his meal polished off. "Bosa sounds like my kind of fellow."

Violca laughed. "You've never met the baron, have you? Let's just say he's a colorful chap. I'm not sure you could ever truly rely upon his aid. He lives by the barter—if you want his allegiance there has to be something in it for him. Something of value."

"They said similar things about Vega, yet he proved his worthiness. Perhaps we can offer Bosa a position in the Wolf's Council, a place at the high table, so to speak."

"Bosa's an enigmatic old Whale, at one time possibly the

wealthiest Werelord of the Sea. He's frivolous and fanciful. I really couldn't guess what kind of deal might whet his appetite. Be on your game when you meet him, though. He's a shrewd customer."

"Just get me to him, Captain, and I'll do the rest."

"Easier said than done," said Violca, sucking her teeth. "The tide seems to have turned of late, and Bosa's pirate fleet has suffered at the Squidlord's hands. For a while it seemed that the Whale had the measure of the Kraken, Ghul, but I've heard from various sources that some captains who were aligned with Bosa have turned against him. Perhaps all is not well within the Whale's merry band. I'm used to smuggling contraband past the navy, not seeking out a renegade Werelord, the most wanted pirate in the White Sea. This may take time."

"Time's a luxury we can ill afford, Captain," replied Drew sadly.

"What other news have you heard from the wider world?" asked Whitley. "We've been starved of information, first recovering from Vala's attack on Brackenholme and then finding the quietest path to All Hallows Bay. With the whole Seven Realms at war there were few people on the road to pass the time of day with. We caught scraps of information in the Drowning Man, but how much of that's hearsay is hard to tell."

"I wouldn't put too much faith in tavern rumors, my lady," trilled Violca. "Buy a man a drink, and he'll likely tell you whatever you want to hear. Deathbeds and battles are the best place for unearthing the truth, and the White Sea's seen its fair share of both lately."

"I don't understand," said Drew, his head turning as he followed their conversation blindly.

"A man thinks he's dying, he'll want to make his peace with his god and speak the truth. We've found many a broken or wounded vessel in recent months, bodies bobbing alongside the flotsam and jetsam of sea battles. The few breathing souls we fished out had tales to tell."

Violca went quiet suddenly, and neither woman spoke.

"What is it?" asked Drew. "What's the matter?"

"I'm wondering just what Lady Whitley heard in All Hallows Bay," the captain playfully replied.

"What might I have heard?" asked Whitley keenly. Drew sensed an anxiety creeping into his friend's voice.

"About your father, Duke Bergan," said Violca to Whitley. "And how he lives."

"Truly? Bergan, alive?" gasped Drew, his heart soaring with the news. "How do you know this is no rumor?"

Drew heard Violca's voice change tone, softening almost to a whisper as she addressed Whitley.

"They say your father has been sighted among the forces of Duke Henrik, my lady, on the slopes of the Whitepeaks. He lives. A dying Redcloak confirmed as much, as he bled out on the deck of the *Lucky Shot* after one of Bosa's battles."

Drew rose from his seat and reached over the table, his

open hand reaching for Whitley. He found her trembling fingers and closed his own about them.

"I thought he'd been killed," she choked out, tears and laughter mingling. "First I lost my brother, Broghan, and then I feared Father had been taken from us. Praise Brenn," she added, gripping Drew's hand tightly.

"Brenn would not have been so cruel as to steal them both from you, Whitley," said Drew.

"Brenn had nothing to do with my brother's murder," said the Bearlady, her joy momentarily stifled. "It was Lucas who killed Broghan, as commanded by that monster Werepanther, Opal. If there is any justice in the world, I'll have my vengeance."

Drew had heard all about the events in Cape Gala, where Opal, Lord Onyx's sister, and her Bastian army had descended upon the home of the Horselords. Many had been butchered, but the execution of Lord Broghan had sent the greatest shockwaves through the hearts of Drew's loved ones. He tugged her hand, commanding her attention.

"We will see justice done, Whitley," he vowed.

Drew turned his head back up the table.

"Find me Bosa, Violca. His fleet, no matter how ragged, is the first step toward building us an army that can win this war. As Calico withstands the attacks of the Bastian navy in the south, so Icegarden shall break the back of any siege Onyx mounts upon it."

"You think Icegarden can withstand a siege, Drew Ferran?"

said the sea captain sadly. "Duke Henrik's forces are camped on the slopes of the Whitepeaks, not by choice: they've already been turned *out* of their city. Icegarden's fallen."

"Fallen to Onyx?" gasped Whitley. "Then the war in the north's already lost."

"No, my lady," said Violca. "It is another enemy who has taken Icegarden, a foe to both the Lion and the Wolf. The Crowlords have seized the Sturmish capital, under the command of the magister Blackhand."

"Blackhand?" said Drew. "Where has this magister sprung from?"

"He's a Boarlord," replied the captain. "Baron Hector of Redmire."

"There must be some mistake," Drew said. "Hector's a friend of ours, a good man. He wouldn't be involved with the Crows. I've seen their kind—I fought them in Stormdale—and Hector would die before siding with those villains."

"I know what I heard—"

"Then you heard *wrong*!" Drew snapped angrily.

The room was silent for a moment, the only sound that of the lanterns swinging from their brackets and the crew working abovedecks. Violca's chair slid back once again as she rose.

"If you'll excuse me, my lord and lady, it's about time I spoke with my men."

"Please," said Drew, raising his hand. "Forgive me, Captain

Violca; I meant no disrespect. But it's impossible for me to believe what you tell us is true. It must be hearsay, a rumor of the worst kind."

"I understand your concern. I'll leave you with the remainder of your meal. Cook will clear up when you're done."

He heard her booted footsteps head toward the door that exited her cabin.

"Captain," said Drew, "I'm sorry if I caused offense, especially as you've been so gracious to us. Smuggler you may be, but there'll be rewards awaiting you in Highcliff once this dreadful conflict's over."

"The only reward I seek is peace returned to Lyssia, Drew Ferran. Try and make that happen, please?"

"I'll try," replied Drew, managing a smile, "if you try not to believe too many rumors."

Violca opened the door and paused in the threshold.

"That's the funny thing about rumors," she replied. "You can't really pick and choose them."

"How do you mean?" asked Whitley.

"The source of my information about Blackhand," said Violca, "was the same dying Redcloak who informed me of Bergan being alive. I've never been one to call a dying man a liar. Good night, my lord and lady."

5
Outlaws

WHILE THE LIONGUARD infantrymen traipsed through the drizzle along the Low Dale Road, their commanding officer, Major Krupha, could have been a million miles away. The only soul in a troop of thirty to be on horseback, the veteran campaigner towered over those below, their muddy boots slipping through the mud as they steered clear of the horse's hooves. Sparse woodland dotted the land on either side of the road, the first green of spring marking their branches. Krupha was already thinking about the meal that awaited him back in Hedgemoor, the city of the Foxlords that he was charged with policing. *City? Hardly.* It was a peasant village compared to the cities of his homeland, Bast. It did have a few redeeming features. The claret that came down the Redwine River was very fine, invariably finding its way to his table. The hunting was good, when he could be bothered to find his way into his saddle. And the offerings from the kitchens were almost as fine as those back home in Braga. Almost, but not quite.

The weather in Lyssia was something he'd never get used to. Krupha had never before seen snow, and if he never saw it again it would be too soon. With the winter behind them, snow had turned to sleet and then rain. The near constant downpours were wearing away at the spirits of his men, and he yearned for heat. That the Dalelands were known as the Garden of Lyssia came as no surprise to the major, considering the copious rainfall. Still, Hedgemoor Hall was a splendid place to shelter from the elements; the Foxlords had spent their boundless wealth wonderfully, building a palace of great beauty in the heart of the Dales. Krupha toyed with the idea of bringing his wife and many children over, once the war was won. He would of course have to clean up the hall beforehand—wives had a habit of disliking the impaled heads that symbolized the bloody work he carried out in the name of his masters, the Catlords. Krupha shook his head. Women and war: the two would never mix.

He had spent the last two days in the company of General Vorhaas in Redmire. The Wererat, brother to the Lord Chancellor, Vanmorten, was the commanding officer of the Lion's army in the Dalelands and overlord of the entire realm. Krupha was concerned by the upturn in bandit activity throughout the Dalelands. Several small groups of the Lionguard had been murdered in remote outposts of the Dales, especially around Hedgemoor. But to Vorhaas's mind, the major was worrying over nothing. From what he'd seen of these troops, he was unimpressed. Quite possibly they got what they deserved.

The Lionguard of the Dales were thugs, lacking the nerve and know-how of better-trained warriors. The Wererat longed for a handful of his Vermirian Guard to knock them into shape, but this was wishful thinking. Unfortunately for Vorhaas and Krupha, they were stuck with the Lionguard, since the elite fighting forces were all in Sturmland under Onyx's command. The soldiers Krupha had to work with never ceased to amaze him, breaking limbs and cracking skulls where strong words would have done the trick. As for the Foxguard in Hedgemoor, they were disbanded, thrown out of their barracks and put to work as a labor force. Those who objected joined the scowling rows of their decapitated comrades on the walls.

Krupha glowered at his Lionguard. The line was staggered, having abandoned the orderly formation they'd departed Redmire in. No Bastian force would break rank while they marched like this. He didn't have the energy to berate them, though. They were all weary, the journey along the muddy Low Dale Road a most miserable affair.

Two of the soldiers slowed directly before the major, causing his horse to suddenly halt, stirring him from his reverie.

"Why have you stopped, you imbeciles?" shouted Krupha. "Keep moving!"

One of the men directly before the commander's horse pointed ahead. "A wagon stuck in the road, sir."

Krupha looked past his men and the quagmire of ruts and puddles. Sure enough, a farmer's wagon stood skewed across the road, blocking the troop's passage. The vehicle had swung off its path, its back end sliding down into the ditch at the roadside. A peasant girl stood tugging at the reins of a shire horse, trying to urge it up the incline, drawing the covered wagon away from the muddy gutter. Five of the Lionguard had already run forward to see if they could assist. The girl stubbornly shook her head, rust-colored hair spraying water as she tried to control the beast.

The major snarled, tapping the flanks of his mount and urging it through his men. The Redcloaks reluctantly shifted to either side, allowing Krupha through. Ahead, he could see the Lionguard trying to help the girl draw the horse up the embankment. Initially his intention was to simply tell them to shove the wagon and horse entirely out of the way—the child was a fool to have lost control of her charge in such conditions. But as he drew closer, the veteran warrior felt a familiar feeling begin to nag at him. Krupha was a professional soldier who had fought across Bast and now Lyssia. One didn't become a major without a gift for sensing danger.

Krupha's eyes glanced to the trees at either side of the road.

The girl was slight, struggling with the belligerent animal. One of the Lionguard took the reins, allowing her to step clear as he wrestled with it. She stood to one side, the ringlets of her dirty red hair hiding her face.

"Get back!" shouted the major. "Away from the wagon! It's a trap!"

But it was too late. The cover of the wagon was already tumbling away as the undergrowth on either side of the Low Dale Road burst into life. The girl bounded into the midst of the Redcloaks, spinning through the air, soldiers screaming as her clawed hands tore at their flesh.

The canvas tarpaulin fluttered free from the wagon frame as the men within immediately unloaded their weapons. Arrows and crossbow bolts whistled into the Lionguard, joined by a host of missiles that flew from the trees beside the road. Spears, rocks, and slingshot stones rained down onto the startled Redcloaks. Already, ten of the Lion's men lay across the road, wounded and dying. The ambushers wore no uniform to speak of; their ragged clothes suggested they were more farming folk than warrior stock. Gradually the Lionguard tried to regroup, stepping over their fallen comrades, readying their longswords, and raising their shields. Four of them now clustered around the ferocious red-haired girl, seeking to bring her down before more of their number fell.

Gretchen glanced back to the wagon, catching sight of her companions struggling to clamber free. Their bows discharged, they'd whipped their weapons up from the floor of the cart as the Redcloaks had rushed them, trapping them inside the timber frame. She'd hoped they would be by her side by now; instead, she faced the enemy alone. The Lionguard commander's panicked horse reared up nearby, its feet kicking at the air as its master struggled to control it.

Gretchen surrendered herself to the beast. The claws were joined by daggerlike teeth, the muzzle of the Werefox extending through her face. This wasn't the first time she'd channeled her therian side—in recent months as she'd struggled to stay alive, becoming the fox had saved her skin. She and her growing band of companions had encountered savage Wyldermen in the Dyrewood, bandits in the Dalelands, and the mercenaries and murderers who worked for Prince Lucas. Her ability to change into the Werefox had meant the difference between life and death, not just for Gretchen, but for those she now called friends.

Russet hairs bristled across her body, her back arching, spine and rib cage cracking within her torso as she shifted. Gretchen screamed, a brittle roar that she spat out into the men's faces. Three of the Redcloaks recoiled in horror, the sight of a shifting therianthrope still the stuff of nightmares for many humans. Only one kept his nerve, lunging forward with his sword while his friends faltered.

Gretchen saw the blade coming, twisting her body so it narrowly missed her belly. Her jaws came down, snapping over the man's sword hand, grinding bone and tendon. With a squeal of agony the soldier released his weapon, tumbling to the mud to nurse his limb. His comrades stirred into action, unleashing a volley of blows at the Werefox. While two sliced thin air, the third found its mark, glancing off Gretchen's thigh. The enraged Fox cried out, snatching past the Redcloak's reach and thrusting her hands into the top of his armor. Clawed fingers found their way around and through his breastplate, burying themselves into the flesh of his collarbone on either side of his chest. She clenched her fists and snarled, yanking the man off his feet and throwing him into one of his companions.

All about her, men struggled for dominion over one another, the road now slick with mud and blood. The last man on Gretchen slammed his shield into the therianthrope, sending her tumbling onto her backside. His silver-blessed longsword slashed down, but the transformed Werefox rolled clear as the lethal blade cleaved the mud. Her foot came up to kick him but his shield was there, deflecting the blow. Now the Lionshead sword stabbed down, coming straight for Gretchen's red-furred throat, ready to kill the werecreature with its outlawed silver edge. She moved at the last moment, the blade missing her neck but cutting through her cloak as it sank into the road, pinning her in place.

The Lionguard ripped a dagger from his belt, immediately

seizing the advantage to slash into her stomach. The blade left a trail of white-hot pain in its wake as Gretchen feared her belly might split at any moment. One clawed hand went to her guts as she drew her legs up, her other hand raised, swiping at the Lionguard in vain. His dagger went high, about to strike the killing blow against the trapped Werefox.

Suddenly the man was bowled out of the way as one of Gretchen's comrades caught him in the midriff and tackled him to the ground. With mud covering every combatant it was hard to tell friend from foe until they acted. Gretchen tried to move, but she was still secured to the earth by the longsword and afraid her stomach might open. She looked across at the two men as they fought beside her, yards away. The Redcloak was on top, her savior below as the soldier's hands throttled him. The dagger lay nearby in a filthy puddle.

Her comrade's arm snaked out from beneath the Lionguard, a three-fingered hand scrabbling in the mud for the knife. Trent Ferran, the adoptive brother of the Wolflord Drew, caught hold of the blade, dragging it into his palm as he lunged up. The Redcloak's eyes went wide as the dagger vanished into him, his grip on Trent's throat slackening instantly. The young man beneath rolled the dying soldier away before scrambling across to Gretchen.

The Lionguard commander turned on his horse, retreating back down the road. A handful of his soldiers disengaged with their enemies, running after him as he galloped in the direction of Redmire. Trent's eyes settled on the wound in her guts, but Gretchen looked past him toward the fleeing Redcloaks.

"Come back!" called Gretchen as some of her men gave chase. "It's over. For now . . ."

She winced as her body began the painful process of shifting back to human form, her bones bending and muscles burning with discomfort. "Today we've put a marker down. Lucas can send his troops into the Dalelands as much as he likes, but if he's expecting a warm welcome he'll be disappointed."

"That was Major Krupha, my lady," said a bald man who wore a leather smock, his full ginger beard fanning out across his broad chest. "I'd recognize that tall streak o' yellow anywhere. He's the one what did my apprentice in when they took my smithy in Hedgemoor. I'll see him dead if it's the last thing I do."

"Him and the rest of the Redcloak swines, Arlo," said another man, to a chorus of cheers.

"Save your backslapping until we get back to the camp," said Trent, standing over Gretchen. Though young, he had a confidence about him, as if he'd been born into a life in the military. His voice was strong and assured as he addressed the twenty men who had gathered.

"Take what you can from the fallen Lionguard—weapons, armor, provisions, whatever you can find. Do it quickly; who knows if there are more of Krupha's men back down the road? Either way, he'll be with General Vorhaas before dawn and there'll be a manhunt for us. We'll need to be long gone by then."

The fighters immediately set to work stripping what they needed from the dead. Gretchen watched, a sense of pride washing over her after the first real victory of their small band of outlaws. The Harriers of Hedgemoor they called themselves. They'd attacked small guard posts before now in recent weeks, striking quick and fast, killing the odd Redcloak and spreading fear among their ranks. But this had been a mission for them, a true test of their mettle and what they were capable of. The group might have been made up of blacksmiths, farmers, ratters, and woodsmen, but they were slowly becoming soldiers.

"Is it bad?" Trent asked, returning his attention to Gretchen and glowering at the knife wound in her stomach.

"I daren't look," she replied as her friend took hold of the sword that kept her stuck fast in the mud. He tugged it free, throwing it to one side as he knelt beside her. He winced as the two of them inspected the injury. Gretchen's hand was slick with dark blood, bubbling between her fingers.

"I'll bind it, but I'm no magister," said Trent. "The healer can look at it when we get back to camp. You just thank Brenn it wasn't a Lionshead blade."

Trent reached down and lifted her into his arms. He had been a member of the Lionguard in a previous life, when he'd thought his brother had been responsible for their mother's murder. He'd been wrong, of course, horribly wrong. Drew wasn't the enemy at all. He may have been a therian lord, a Werewolf, and the rightful king of Westland, but he was still his brother. Gretchen hoped the two might yet be reunited, should they ever find one another. They'd heard the rumor that the Wolf was alive and had returned to Lyssia.

"I can walk, Trent," said Gretchen. "Really. You can put me down."

Reluctantly, he lowered her to her feet as she gingerly stepped onto the road, holding her stomach. It was typical of Trent to be concerned. The two had grown close the past few months as they had been thrown together escaping the horrors of the Wyldermen's attack on Brackenholme. Despite knowing her temperament well, Trent hadn't wanted Gretchen to take part in the ambush, but there'd been no dissuading the Lady of Hedgemoor.

One of their companions approached, carrying a sword in his hands. He was only a few years younger than Gretchen and Trent, a boy really, with an unruly mop of blond curls that were clotted with blood.

"You got a head full of blood, Tom," said Trent.

"It ain't mine, sir," said the lad, a former stable boy from Hedgemoor, turning the weapon and holding its handle toward Trent. "Your sword."

"You dropped your Wolfshead blade?" asked Gretchen.

"Left it in a Redcloak," said Trent, taking the weapon from Tom and nodding his thanks. It was his father's old sword. "Good of him not to run off with it." He dipped his head, catching Gretchen's gaze from beneath his tousled blond fringe. "Before we go anywhere, you need that bandaged," he said, nodding toward her wound. His face was stern and serious, the look he gave her like that of a parent scolding a child. "You're sure I can't carry you?"

"Walk on, Ferran," she replied, determined not to appear weak in front of the Harriers as the fox's blood still coursed through her veins. It was typical of him to worry about her, and it rankled. She wasn't a girl anymore, and she wasn't weak. She was a strong young woman—and a therianthrope at that—and she was as capable as any man present when it came to fighting.

"Move out!" she called, taking command of the group.

Reluctantly, Trent set off after Tom, throwing an arm around the boy as he went.

"Up front, young'un," said Trent, managing to smile as they rejoined the men. He looked back at Gretchen just once, his blue eyes unblinking as he glared at her.

You're not finished, Trent; is that it? thought Gretchen as he disappeared through the crowd. *Good. Neither am I.*

6
CONSPIRATORS

"IT GOES AGAINST all that's holy, and I won't be a part of it."

Sheriff Muller stared out of the ruined farmhouse, his brow knitted with concern. Directly behind him, General Gorgo paced back and forth, snorting and shaking his head as the three-quarter moon cast a blue light over the Badlands and Whitepeaks below.

"I'm with the sheriff," said the Hippo. "Whatever Lucas has planned with these Wyldermen, I don't like it. I was warned about these wild men when I first stepped foot on Lyssian soil. They're not to be trusted, heathen cannibals. No good can come from such an alliance."

"My greatest concern," said Count Costa, "is the fact that we're forced to meet in this pile of rubble." He sat astride the ruined wall, looking back at the camp. "Since when could a young Lion kick the Beast of Bast out of his tent?"

The Vulturelord looked to where Onyx stood, the giant Werepanther filling the frame of the broken doorway. He wore breeches and an intricately jeweled leather waistcoat, his only concession to the harsh northern weather. His muscles rippled, flesh shining purple in the moonlight. His command tent had been claimed by King Lucas and his entourage, leaving Onyx to find fresh quarters. He'd taken another tent, close to the Lion's, but the affront was plain for all to see. The commander of the Catlord army had been deposed by the boy: there would be consequences.

"The young Lion is king of this land," said Gorgo. "You'd do well to remember that. It's for him we're here in the first place, fighting his war."

"Really?" said the Vulture. "I don't recall ever swearing fealty to some Lion of Lyssia. My bond is to the high lords in the Forum of Elders. My people serve Bast."

"You're not *in* Bast, my lord," said Muller. "I'd mind what I say if I were you. That army out there serves King Lucas; your words are treason to their ears."

"I'm being wasted here," replied the count, addressing his comment in Onyx's direction. "I was never one for playing the game of government, and I'd never imagined that was your domain, either, my lord. We are *warriors*, Onyx: send me to Omir where I can be put to good use. Join me if you like. While Field Marshal Tiaz battles the Jackals in the sand, my Vulture brothers fight the Hawklords in the sky. That's a war we can win, as opposed to the stalemate we suffer here. Let's push home our advantage in the Desert Realm, and leave the Lion to play war here with the Sturmish."

"We cannot abandon our troops," interjected Gorgo. "A quarter of this army is made up of Bastians. I wouldn't leave my men under the command of . . . a *boy*."

"So this is it?" said Costa, casting a hand over his companions from his lofty perch before tapping his own chest. "Are we four the only ones concerned by the turn of events? That Lucas should arrive here unannounced, in league with Wyldermen, doesn't bother the other members of the war council?"

"It may bother them, but they're afraid to speak up," said Gorgo. "Half of them don't have the imagination to realize the danger of consorting with these wild men. They simply follow orders. As for General Skean, the Cranelord may well disagree, but he's a guarded one. He'll be watching from afar, keeping his distance—he'll show his colors later in the game, mark my words, when he's nothing to lose and everything to gain."

"And the rest of your Bastian werebrothers?" asked Muller.

"They'll be concerned, I'm sure, but they look to Onyx for guidance. After all," said Gorgo, turning to the Werepanther, "it was His Grace who called us to this land in the name of the Catlords. We are all sworn subjects to the felinthropes, weapons for his kin to direct. The fact that a Lionlord rules the Seven Realms must cast a cloud of confusion over their loyalty. Whose orders trump whose?"

"A very fine question." Costa smiled. "Time will tell, I expect—"

"There's only one question that's up for debate," said Onyx at last, startling the other three. "What business does he have with this Wylderman, Darkheart? How can this shaman aid our war effort?"

"How many of the wild men were in his party?" asked Gorgo. "Twenty?"

"Aye," replied Muller. "Hardly an army, is it?"

"He plans something with the Werewolf's hand," said Onyx. Drew Ferran's limb was a trophy from the battle for Cape Gala, lost as he escaped the Horselord city, biting through his own flesh and bone in order to free himself from bondage. The severed hand had remained in the Pantherlord's keeping ever since, a constant reminder of his enemy's remarkable strength, desire to survive, and sheer bloody-mindedness.

"But what could he do with the hand?" asked the sheriff.

"If I knew that, do you think I'd have sought your counsel at this late hour?" growled the Panther. "Wyrm Magicks, Lucas mentioned."

"Perhaps this shaman has some way of using the Wolf's limb to discover his whereabouts," said Gorgo, suddenly animated. "That *would* be helpful; something we could use to hunt him down."

"If Wyrm Magicks are anything like Blackhand's sorcery, who knows what Darkheart might be able to conjure?" replied Onyx.

"He could just be deluded, of course," said Costa idly. "I mean, a wild man from the woods? Is he really someone we should put our faith in? Perhaps it's the king we should be most worried about, to have been seduced by a shaman."

"Whatever his plan," said Muller, "I can tell you now, my men won't stand for it, and neither will the Lionguard. These are men of Westland and the Badlands. They know all about the Wyldermen and their ways, worshipping ancient dark gods and feeding on human flesh. There's been centuries of bad blood between the wild men and the free people of Lyssia. If the king thinks we'll fight alongside them, he's mistaken."

"Muller's right," said Gorgo. "Having Wyldermen in camp can only breed discord among our troops. What is the king *thinking*?"

"You should ask him if you're so concerned."

At the sound of the stranger's voice, Muller and Gorgo both spun, the sheriff's sword swiftly out of its scabbard while the Hippo stamped the ground. Costa was suddenly poised and ready to leap down or take to the air. Only Onyx remained motionless, his back turned to the interloper who had appeared from the shadows to the rear of the ruin.

"Who goes there?" asked Muller, taking a few steps through the rubble, the moonlight throwing great shadows over the dilapidated farmhouse.

"Come out of the shadows, Lord Chancellor," said Onyx without turning. "Don't be shy. We're all friends together, are we not?"

Vanmorten materialized from the darkness, his black robes disengaging from the ruin's gloom. Muller recoiled at the sight of the Ratlord, while Gorgo sneered. Costa remained where he was, his hand resting upon the scimitar at his hip, eyes never leaving the Wererat.

"How long have you been there?" asked Muller suspiciously.

"Long enough, isn't that right, Vanmorten?" said Onyx.

The Ratlord's scarred hand emerged from his robes and waved about airily. "I heard . . . things," he said breezily. "I heard King Lucas's advisers expressing *concerns* over his tactics. I heard talk of those lords sworn to protect and serve the Lion refusing to carry out the king's commands. I heard human and therian voice alike expressing concern over the king's arrival in this camp—the camp of the king's *own* army."

Vanmorten came to a stop a dozen feet from Onyx and his companions. "Now tell me, my lords," he said, raising a burn-scarred finger toward the conspirators. "Did I hear correctly?"

Onyx finally turned to confront Vanmorten. "Show me your face, Ratlord."

"What?"

"I've never trusted folk who hide themselves away," said the Panther, holding his arms out wide. "Take a good look at me, Lord Chancellor. I carry no weapons; I've nothing to hide. If we're to speak frankly, lower your cowl."

Muller took a step back from the Ratlord, all too aware of the infamous injuries Vamorten had twice received at the hands of Drew Ferran.

"I shall do no such thing," replied Vanmorten, his cocksure attitude swiftly evaporating.

"Ashamed, are you?" said Onyx, nodding. He took a casual step in the Ratlord's direction, his arms still out wide, huge hands open. "Understandable. Since you're hideously deformed by the actions of the Wolf cub, with a face so disfigured your own mother wouldn't kiss you."

"Bite your tongue!" snarled the Rat, taking a step back. With the Werepanther demanding his attention he hadn't noticed that Costa had disappeared from the wall. Onyx continued.

"Always sneaking around, Rat, you and your brothers. The eyes and ears of the Lions of Westland, in every court across the land—that's your way, isn't it? Sneaky and insidious, the lot of you. A suitable family motto, perhaps?"

"I am Lord Chancellor! How dare you speak to me this way!" Despite his protests Vanmorten kept stumbling backward. He hissed as his body shifted beneath his robes, the thick, dark material rippling as he began to change.

Costa's foot kicked the Wererat in the small of the back,

propelling him forward toward Onyx, who was already changing. The Werepanther's clawed hand shot into the folds of the cowl, catching Vanmorten about the throat as he shifted. Onyx lifted the Ratlord off the ground, rising all the while as his muscles, legs, and bones expanded to accommodate the Panther.

Muller and Gorgo watched on, absorbed by the encounter, each horrified by where it might end. Vanmorten struggled, raking at the felinthrope's dark skin, but it was like cured leather, toughened by battle. Onyx reached forward with his free hand and tugged the black cowl away.

The sight caught even the Panther by surprise, so hideous was the Rat's visage. The flesh across the right-hand side of his face was completely missing, discolored skull on show around the jaw, Vanmorten's big pink eye bobbing lidlessly inside the socket. The other side was simply livid, burn-scarred flesh, where no healing balms had ever succeeded in their work. As Onyx squeezed the Ratlord's throat a black tongue snaked out of its gasping jaws, bringing with it the stench of rot and ruin.

Onyx sneered, shaking the writhing Rat in his fist.

"I'm not some little lord of Lyssia, Rat. I'm Onyx, the superior of any Werelord in your Seven pathetic Realms. You face the mightiest of all the Catlords and you *dare* to bandy threats?"

Vanmorten spluttered while the others watched. The Ratlord squealed, the life ebbing from its limbs.

"I give you a gift this night, Vanmorten. I give you life."

Onyx tossed the Wererat to the ground before his mighty feet, where the crumpled Lord Chancellor lay wheezing as he nursed his throat. The Rat quickly receded before the Panther as Vanmorten shrank into the shadows on the floor.

"You're *mine* now, Rat. Mine to command, should I wish anything of you. My will's all that need concern you henceforth. Run your errands for the king, but nothing he says in confidence to you must remain so—you'll report back to me. The Wyldermen, the Lion's enemies, his plans: you're *my* eyes and ears beside the king now. Or I'll take my gift back and give you what you deserve. Understand?"

Vanmorten nodded feverishly, his breath rattling in his throat.

"Now," said Onyx, wiping the Wererat's spittle onto the crumbling brickwork, "let's finish this quickly. Your master, the king: what's his business with the Wyldermen? Speak."

"The one . . . called Darkheart . . ." said Vanmorten, rubbing at his throat, "the shaman wants the Wolf's hand . . . for his ceremony."

"What ceremony?" asked Costa, poking the Rat with his foot.

"The full moon approaches . . ." rasped the Lord Chancellor.

"Why does Darkheart need the moon?" asked Onyx.

"He says it must be done under its light," said the Wererat, struggling to his knees, replacing the hood of his robes. "He needs the blood of the Wolf to make it happen."

"Speak straight, Rat, not in riddles," said Gorgo.

"He's sworn he'll stop at nothing until he and his fellow wild men kill the Wolflord. A bargain's been struck. The king will give the shaman what he needs—the blood—and in return for this the Wyldermen have promised to lay waste to the Bear's forces in the Whitepeaks. Once this is done, they'll hunt down and kill Drew Ferran and his friends. The plan can't possibly fail for us—we win either way."

"How can you put so much faith into a bunch of Wyldermen?" asked Onyx, the puzzle not quite fitting together. "What's to say the wild men won't get butchered the minute they attack Henrik's army?"

Vanmorten smiled as he massaged his throat, the white of his teeth catching the moonlight within his cowl.

"Oh, it won't be humans who attack the Sturmish."

"A therian force?" asked Costa suspiciously.

"Not therian, either." Vanmorten laughed, rising to his feet and straightening his robes.

"What then?" asked Onyx.

"Demons, Your Grace," said the Lord Chancellor. "Demons."

PART II

BOUND AND BEATEN

I

THE KRAKEN'S REACH

THE WORLD SHOOK suddenly, jarring Drew from his sleep before depositing him from the chaise longue onto the cabin floor. The sound of timbers grating screeched throughout the *Lucky Shot*, a wailing roar that threatened to split the hull in two. Disoriented, Drew gripped the boards with his hand and bare feet, nails sharpening into claws as he held his position. Bottles smashed and valuables clattered as the shelves of the captain's cabin emptied themselves across the chamber.

"Whitley!" Drew yelled, as the ship juddered and lurched.

"I'm here," she cried, out of her bunk now and quickly beside him. He felt her arm across his bare shoulder, her face next to his. Her panicked breathing could be heard over the cacophony, hot and frantic in Drew's ear. The shouts of crew members now surfaced above the din.

"Stay here," she said.

Drew snatched at her arm. "Where are you going?"

"Up top, to see what's going on!"

"I'm coming with you," he said, standing unsteadily as the ship was buffeted again.

"You are *not,* Drew—you're blind, for Brenn's sake! Stay here; I'll be back down." She placed a hand on his chest, gentle but firm. He felt her lips brush his cheek below the bandage that covered his eyes. Then she was gone, calling back as she went, "Do *not* leave the cabin, Drew. It's not safe."

Drew heard the door slam shut, and he was alone in the chamber while the world turned about him. The crew's cries had become screams, the clashing of steel joining the maelstrom of noise.

"I was never good at taking orders," Drew muttered, staggering across the chamber with his hand reaching out until he felt the chaise longue.

Drew made his way along the couch's length until he found his weapon belt at its head. He stepped into the loop of leather, hiking it up around his waist before pulling it tight. The buckle locked into place, the scabbard swinging at his hip. He staggered forward, banging into the wall and feeling along its length until he came to the door. Snatching the handle he yanked it open, stepping out into the corridor.

He'd been able to make some sense of the ship's layout since they'd come aboard in All Hallows Bay, but that had been when the *Lucky Shot* was traveling unhindered across the sea. She was now under attack, and as the vessel pitched once more and Drew landed on the staircase, he realized he was anything but sure of his surroundings. The sound of combat was louder now, racing down the steps from the decks above. If he were to enter the fray in this condition, he'd be cut down in moments, but he couldn't hide below while Violca's crew were butchered.

Scrambling up the staircase, Drew found the hatch was closed. He put his shoulder into it, only to find it held fast. Beyond, he could hear the screams of the crew joined by the wild laughter of others: the Lion's fleet? Had the Kraken found them? Drew crouched on the steps, reaching up to tear the bandage from his face. White light flooded his field of vision. He blinked, willing his eyes to focus, to make sense of his predicament, but the blinding glow remained. Drew's eyes were lost to him, but there were other senses he could call upon. He let out a snarl, his mind racing back to those earliest memories of the beast. Running wild through the Dyrewood, the sounds and smells of the forest all around him, his senses on fire. The snarl became a growl, then a roar.

Whitley ran along the deck through the pitch-dark night, hurdling tumbling barrels and ducking swinging rigging, three pirates hot on her heels. Each wore the Red in his own particular style, a nod of homage to Lucas and the closest any would get to a uniform. One wore a scarlet bandanna around his head, another a neckerchief, and the last a red jacket squeezed over his fat belly. As she ran, she looked across at the giant black ship that dwarfed the *Lucky Shot*, ropes and grapples securing them together along her port side. Twice the length of Captain Violca's ship, with an additional towering deck, it was a brute beside a child. The crew of the smuggling ship were putting up a valiant fight, but the battle would be over soon enough. If Drew weren't incapacitated, perhaps they might have had hope. As things stood, their last chance for victory lay in the hands of the girl from Brackenholme.

With each desperate stride, the trio of cutthroats closing in, Whitley let the bear into her heart. She leapt toward the starboard rail, catching hold of a trailing rope from the rigging as she took to the air, her nightdress torn free by a pelt of rippling fur. The hemp went taut as it held her weight, Whitley swinging out and around in a great arc. As she flew back toward the ship, the three men skidded to a halt, and the Bearlady launched into their midst. Whitley's feet slammed into the chest of one, his lungs crunching as the air was smashed out of them. Her trailing claws raked another, sending him screaming toward the rail.

The last was the fat pirate in the red jacket. With his companions taking Whitley's attacks he'd found his opening when her back was turned. His cutlass tore down, slicing into her back. Whitley twisted and lunged for the man, catching him in the belly with her jaws. The pirate screamed, striking her face repeatedly with his weapon's basket handle. Each blow reverberated through her skull, combined with the agony of the wound to her back, but she didn't relinquish her grip. The weapon might not have been silver, but the injury was critical. If she continued to fight, she'd lose more blood; if she rested, her therianthropic powers could take over and begin the magical healing process. Instead she held on with weakening jaws.

A bestial roar shook the ship, accompanied by the sound of splintering timber. The pirate struck Whitley's nose once more, causing the Werebear to finally release her grip. She fell back onto the deck, a wave of dizziness sweeping over her. The man struggled to stand, grinning, but the smirk didn't last long. The needle tip of a rapier emerged through his chest, clean through his heart, before the blade was whipped out of his back as he slumped onto his companions. Violca stood in his place, flicking the blood from her blade, the first mate, Ramzi, at her side.

"Quickly, my lady," said Violca, helping Whitley rise. "We must get you and the shepherd off the ship. Mister Ramzi's prepared a boat for you at the stern. He'll see you to safety."

The Werelady looked down the ship toward the prow. The

fighting was thickest there, at the point where the enemy had piled aboard. With no lantern light and the moon and stars hidden by cloud, only the occasional dim flash of a blade could be seen as smugglers and pirates warred with one another.

"I left the shepherd below. I thought he'd be safe there."

"Well, he's no longer below, and he's far from safe," replied Violca, catching sight of something large and dark bounding across the foredecks, into the heart of the melee. "Go now! I'll bring him to you!"

Ramzi placed his arm under Whitley's to support the injured Bearlady. He led her swiftly down the ship's starboard side, the girl glancing back all the while as the captain raced off to where the fighting was worst. She was soon lost in the darkness and the screams of the dying.

2

The Mother of Icegarden

HECTOR GRIMACED, PINCHING the bridge of his nose. The pain persisted, a constant strain behind the eyes that lanced through his head like a hot poker. He pushed his right palm into his eye socket, trying to massage the headache away. Opening his red-ringed eyes he focused on the woman who sat chained to the chair before him.

"Why do we have to play these silly games?" he asked miserably.

Duchess Freya glared back, with a look of withering, unrivaled hatred that made Hector feel terribly small. Chained though she was by Sturmish steel manacles, the magick rolled off her in waves. He could scarcely believe that the most powerful of the Daughters of Icegarden, magisters of the

Strakenberg—and mother to Duke Henrik and Lady Greta—was a prisoner before him. The Boarlord spied the bruises that marked the White Bear's face and neck and shivered. His henchman, Ibal, stood by the door, jailer to many of Hector's prisoners and witness to all their interrogations. But his usual nervous giggles had all but vanished in the presence of the duchess, the Boarguard sensing her aura of power.

"A game would suggest entertainment," she replied. "I can assure you, Blackhand, your visits don't amuse me."

"Yet still you make me ask the same question, day after day, offering me no answer. Do you think I enjoy this pantomime?"

"Honestly?" replied the duchess. "Yes. I think you do."

Hector snapped his fingers and pointed at her, spittle dribbling from his snarling lips. "You're trying my patience, my lady. Are you so foolish that you'd hasten the pain?"

"Ask your question, you sick little boy," said the elderly therian, turning her face from him in defiance. She fixed her eyes upon Ibal, who looked away. "Bring me your pain; see what it gets you."

Hector's left fist rose slowly, his dark robe falling away to reveal gnarled, black flesh. He flicked it open as if releasing a trapped butterfly from his hand, sending his brother's vile racing on its way toward the duchess. He watched as the smoky phantom, visible only to Hector, swirled around her, circling like a shark around its prey, awaiting his command. He flung his hand forward, the Vincent-vile raking the Bearlady's face as it rushed past. As Hector's arm came back the other way, it struck Freya once more, the chair she sat on rocked forward onto its front legs, threatening to bring her crashing face-first to the ground. Ibal took a step forward, making to grab the seat just as it clattered back to the stone-flagged floor.

Hector breathed hard, noticing that the pain in his head had lifted while his brother's vile was at work. The vile wasn't content unless it was put to use. Torture and murder were its pleasure, and it could never get enough of either. It sickened Hector that the spirit had such a hold. While the Boarlord was ultimately in command of the vile, it seemed to be growing in confidence of late. The sleepwalking, the silences, the headaches; they were all connected to Vincent, and Hector feared what might come next.

He looked up, Freya's cries bringing him out of his daze. Her head snapped back and forth, the spectral killer continuing to attack, a tornado of hatred that whipped and whirled about her, lashing out indiscriminately and tearing at her flesh. Hector snapped his black fingers, calling the vile back to heel. It ignored him.

"Vincent!" he shouted, tearing his black hand through the air. Reluctantly, the vile ceased its barrage of blows, snaking back to Hector and coiling around his shoulders. Hector shivered as he heard the phantom snicker.

"Your Grace," he said. "The Wyrmstaff: where is it?"

"I knew your father, Blackhand," said Freya, her voice a

whisper. Her long white hair had fallen across her face but he could still see her eyes. They were wet with tears, her disgust replaced by sadness. What happened to you, child?"

Hector was taken aback. He'd expected the same tirade of abuse she'd flung his way every other day for the last few months. Instead he got sorrow and sympathy, and it didn't sit easy with him. His lips trembled as he tried, and failed, to maintain his composure.

She pities you, brother, hissed the Vincent-vile at last, its voice now hot down Hector's neck and dripping with malice. *This wrinkled old Bear thinks she can appeal to some good within you. Show her there is none. Kill the old witch now, and take whatever answers you need from her still-warm corpse!*

"No!" shouted Hector, causing Ibal to jump and the duchess to flinch. "I won't do that!"

"You're talking to your phantom again, aren't you?" said Freya, her eyes narrow as she searched the room's shadows for Vincent. "I may not see the vile, but I know when necromancy's at work."

Hector took a step back, horrified by the White Bear's grasp of his power.

She's bluffing, brother. Kill her! Silence her poisonous words!

But Hector didn't stop the duchess. He let her continue.

"You think you could torture me for weeks on end without my understanding your magicks? The vile is the servant of the dark magister, Blackhand. I see how the power has polluted, corrupted you." Her eyes settled upon his skeletal limb, which he hurriedly withdrew.

"You're ashamed, aren't you, boy?" she said quietly.

Hector shivered, afraid to answer.

"It's not too late. You can make this right."

Hector stepped closer, crouching as he brought his face close to Freya's. The nighttime horrors, the rage that possessed him, his distrust of those he once loved and held dear—he knew in his heart of hearts that this was all wrong. He was the boy from Redmire again, blocking out the malevolent words of his dead brother as he searched the White Bear's eyes for answers.

"How can I make it stop?" he whispered.

Freya smiled and spoke slowly, her voice a husky growl. "Unfasten my manacles, Blackhand. I may be a tired old Bear, but I still have teeth and claws. Let me put an end to your pain, before you take another life."

The magister recoiled as her words sank in. The shred of reason that had been present a moment earlier began to fade as a dark cloud gathered in his mind. His face contorted from one of wide-eyed need to abject fury.

What did I tell you, Hector? hissed the vile. *Kill her! Do it, now!*

The Boarlord snorted, a low grunt rising in his throat as he felt his mouth throb. He shook his head, trying to worry the pain away, but could feel his jawbone aching. His teeth began to grow, slowly jutting from his gums, as a hitherto unknown strength began to emerge. His heart, so often weak, was suddenly robust, pumping blood around his frail body. His eyes leveled with Freya's as he brought the flat of his hand back, ready to strike her.

The cell door suddenly flew open, clanging on its hinges as the occupants of the room turned in surprise. Ringlin stood there, panting hard.

The black mood that had taken hold of Hector was blown away, replaced by a bout of dizziness. His men jumped forward, catching the baron before he collapsed. He looked up at Ringlin, his voice weak as he refocused on the man, the Boar fading from his face.

"What's the matter?"

"You must come at once, my lord. It's the Crows."

3
Dead Eyes

THE PRISONERS KNELT on the deck of the *Lucky Shot*, hands tied behind their backs, most with their chins on their chests. Violca kept her head up, staring down any of the pirates who dared look at her. She was struggling to see through one eye, a deep brow wound sending a steady stream of blood trickling into her other. She ran a tongue against her teeth, feeling a number loosened. She counted how many of her men were still alive: a dozen, perhaps? Barely more. So long as she kept her enemies' eyes fixed on her face, it was drawing them away from her hands, which were working feverishly upon the ropes that bound them.

"Huge great dog, wasn't it?" said one of the pirates, scratching his head. "Ain't never seen anything like that before."

They're talking about the Wolflord! Violca realized.

"I thought it were a big cat, like one o' them giant beasts Onyx has."

"Bit Ribchester's head clean off, it did!" said another, laughing nervously. "His head were still screamin' as it rolled down the deck!"

"Took some killing, whatever it was," said the first.

"Wasn't dead when we pushed it over the side."

"Whatever it was, it's fish food now."

The heavy footsteps of the enemy ship's commander sounded as he stomped down the gangplank onto the *Lucky Shot*. Violca recognized him immediately as Captain Deadeye, his misshapen face known by all. Well over six feet tall, he had a downturned mouth, a jutting underbite pointing skyward. His eyes were spaced a touch too far apart, no doubt on account of his therian side. He was one of the ugliest men she'd ever clapped eyes upon.

"An unexpected surprise to run into the *Hellhound*, Deadeye," said Violca, "especially at such an antisocial hour. If you'd wished to pay me a visit, there were easier ways of attracting my attention. A meal next time I'm in Cutter's Cove would have done the trick, a bit of small talk and business over a cup of wine?"

"Your smart mouth isn't as pretty as I recall, Violca," Deadeye said with a sneer as he came to a halt in front of her, hands on his hips.

Her eyes landed on the pair of cleavers that were strapped to his thighs, her fingers still twitching as she tried to work them free of the rope.

"I'd have painted them with lipstick instead of blood if only you'd sent word that you were coming. This is such an ugly way for us to start a conversation."

"Conversation? This is an interrogation, witch," said Deadeye. "Where are your passengers?"

"I'm carrying no passengers. Does the *Lucky Shot* look like a ferry to you?"

Deadeye crouched before Violca so that his drooping face was close to hers. "You had therians on board. Two of them."

How does he know about the Wolf and the Bear?

He slapped her hard, freeing two of the teeth that had clung to her gums. She lifted her head up slowly and grinned, revealing a gap in her bloody smile.

"The Werelords," said Deadeye. "Where are they?"

Violca spat at him. "Long gone, you ugly thug!"

Deadeye's monstrous face contorted as he brought his hand back, ready to strike her again. Then he stopped, staring behind her. Slowly, his downturned lips shifted into a hideous smile.

"Not quite," said Deadeye, his black bug eyes refocused on Violca.

Violca glanced back and her heart sank. Two pirates carried Whitley's limp, unconscious body between them, while Ramzi walked in front of another pair, his hands behind his back.

"I'm sorry, skipper," said the first mate as he was led toward Deadeye.

"It's all right, old friend," she replied. "You did all I asked. Looks like we didn't win this one."

Deadeye laughed. "I only see one loser here!"

Violca watched as Ramzi walked up to the captain of the *Hellhound*, reaching an arm out to shake the giant Werelord by the hand.

"Good work, *Captain* Ramzi," said Deadeye. "Your compliance is appreciated. Lord Ghul will be pleased by your deeds. Consider the *Lucky Shot* your own, as agreed. Just remember who your masters are."

Violca lurched forward, the ropes falling free, grabbing a cleaver from the holster on Deadeye's thigh. She pulled it loose and hacked at the Werelord, who in turn swung the traitorous Ramzi into her path. The cleaver hit the sailor square in the chest and buried deep into his breastbone. His eyes went wide as Violca tried in vain to rip it free.

Deadeye pulled Violca away from the dying Ramzi and lifted her into the air, holding her tightly by the biceps. She struggled and lashed out at him, kicking wildly as he hefted her aloft like a father might do a toddler. She stared down in horror as he began to shift, his shoulders broadening, pink flesh fading to a cold, lifeless gray. His head transformed, chest and chin merging into one great curving jaw as his skull expanded sideways. The bulbous eyes blinked on the sides of the creature's head, solid balls of the most soulless, cruel black.

"Dead eyes," she whispered.

However hideous Violca had thought him before now paled into insignificance. As Werelords of the Sea went, he was as monstrous as they came: a beast of the ocean and slayer of men. She looked about frantically, pleading to the pirates, but they turned away. Violca screamed as Captain Deadeye, Hammerhead of the *Hellhound,* brought her kicking and thrashing into his monstrous, hungry jaws.

4
THE EMISSARY

"LEAVE HIM, FLINT!" shouted Hector as he strode into the giant throne room, Ringlin and Ibal on either side of him. His feet skipped along the marble floor, magister's robes hitched up, as he raced to the crowd who had gathered before the dais. His Ugri Boarguard and the Crows turned as he approached, the Werelords laughing at the Baron of Redmire as he pushed his way through them. At their center, Lord Flint, their leader, towered over a crouching soldier. The avianthrope was part transformed, black beak open as he screeched at the helpless human, scimitar raised high. His wings were just emerging when Hector shoved him away and to the floor.

The Crows turned to Hector as one, drawing rank around their sibling and cawing angrily in unison. Ringlin and Ibal stepped forward, grabbing the beaten man and dragging him behind their master. The remaining Ugri in the hall moved as one, rushing to their liege and flanking Hector.

"You dare lay a finger on our brother?" shouted a lord of Riven.

"I'd do it again, and worse, I promise you!" Hector yelled back, raising his black fist at the Crows. They each glared at the hand, understanding the implied threat.

Flint pushed his well-meaning siblings aside, barging his way to the front of the group. The strongest of the Werecrows, if he feared Hector as his brothers did, he wasn't showing it.

"Why do you defend this human? This emissary from the Bearlords? There's only one message we should send back to Henrik and Bergan, and that's this fool's severed head thrown from the walls!"

"There'll be no killing," said Hector. "This man comes under the flag of parley. We grant him that. We're not monsters."

Flint's dark, glassy avian eyes blinked suspiciously as Hector turned to the unarmed soldier. The right-hand side of the man's face was swollen where Flint had struck him. The Boarlord managed to smile and offer his regular hand. The soldier didn't take it, instead straightening his filthy gray cloak and bowing briefly.

"Captain Reuben Fry," said Hector, disappointed that the man wouldn't take his hand. He'd always been fond of the archer. "It's good to see you, though the circumstances of our meeting saddens me greatly."

"It's General now, my lord," said Fry stiffly.

"Congratulations, General Fry! You always were a fine soldier; you deserve the recognition."

"I come to you with words from Duke Bergan, my lord," replied the Sturmlander, ignoring Hector's small talk.

"What words would those be?" interrupted Flint. "*'We surrender'*?"

His brothers laughed as Hector raised a hand to silence him, his eyes still fixed on the Wolfguard general.

"Speak, Fry."

The man cleared his throat before continuing. "The Dukes of Icegarden and Brackenholme ask for clemency, and safe passage out of the valley. North of the Strakenberg is their preferred path, taking the Whitepeaks Way, preferably under cover of night."

"Why not head south out of the mountains?" one of the Crows called out mockingly, to a chorus of guffaws and squawks.

"Our men are weak, my lord," replied Fry, ignoring the Lords of Riven. "If they remain down there much longer—even with knowledge of the land—they'll die. They're exhausted, starved; some are diseased. Grant us a route out of there and we'll go quietly."

"What's to stop you launching an attack on Icegarden once you're close enough?" asked Hector. "The Whitepeaks Way would take you directly past the walls of the city."

"We no longer pose any threat to you," said Fry, pointing south angrily. "Our army's half dead. If you refuse us access to the Sturmish mountain road, you're as good as killing us all."

"I'm not refusing you passage, Fry. But I ask one thing of the dukes: submission. They need to kneel before me, swear fealty and obedience. They need to acknowledge my position as Lord of Icegarden. Only then will I grant them a way out of the valley."

Fry sighed. "That'll never happen, as well you know. Let us by, my lord, I beseech you. We're a broken, spent force."

"The Bears are wounded beasts now, but in time they'll heal, and then what? They never return? You leave me as custodian of Sturmland, ruling over their people?" Hector shook his head. "No. This needs doing now to avoid unpleasantness later. They come to me, unarmed, unaccompanied, and they both kneel: Henrik and Bergan. Those are my conditions. My *only* terms."

Fry stared at him. "Nothing could make you change your mind?"

Hector smiled sadly.

"Beyond those walls there's a war raging," said Fry, his voice strained. "While you sit inside this palace, there are men and women fighting and dying out there for a free Lyssia. The

Catlords won't stop when they've defeated us. You'll be next. These walls have stood for centuries—I was born within them—but you can't keep out Lucas forever. And what life will you have until then, locked away inside this city? You'll be a prisoner, Hector," he said pitifully.

"I'm doing this for a bright new future, Fry," he replied, wagging a black finger at the Sturmlander. "One where the Boarlords are no longer at the bottom of the heap and the Crowlords rise up the pecking order. *That* will be the new order to Lyssia. Don't underestimate our strength, nor what other assistance I can call upon."

Fry's gaze fell upon Hector's mummified limb, nausea washing over him. "You were once an honorable young man. Can you not be that again?"

"I'm still a—a good man . . ." stuttered Hector. Ringlin stared hard at him, nodding calmly.

"You killed Bo Carver, or at least your men did," said Fry, glancing at the Boarguard. "You'd even have killed poor Pick if you'd had your way—a child."

"She lived?" exclaimed Hector with surprise. "That gladdens me. I . . . regretted what happened there."

"She lives despite the attention of your thugs. We were lucky to find the girl in the snow, frozen half to death. She told us what had happened. I wouldn't have believed it if we hadn't seen it with our own eyes. Having your Ugri attack us when we returned to the city? What's *possessed* you?"

A fine choice of words. The Vincent-vile chuckled. *Enough listening to this idiot, brother. Let the Crows work their magic on him. His head should be careening over the walls by now. You show too much compassion.*

"It's clear to me that the Seven Realms need Werelords of action," said Hector, still trying to explain himself. "The Wolf's Council stagnated, lost its way once Drew disappeared."

"The Wolf's Council was a gathering of good, passionate men!" Fry exclaimed defensively.

"The Wolf's Council's redundant," said the Boarlord, trying to change the subject.

"But you've heard the rumors, haven't you, my lord?" said the Sturmlander. "Drew has returned. Those Lionguard and Skirmishers we've dragged wounded from the battlefield told us as much. Your friend lives, Baron."

Hector smiled as calmly as he could.

"Ringlin and Ibal, I'd like you to personally escort the general from the city. See that his weapons are returned and no harm comes to him." Hector saluted the Graycloak. "Good to see you, Reuben Fry. Be sure the next time we meet that you bring the Bearlords to the throne room of Icegarden, bowed and begging for my blessing."

The two rogues took Fry by the arms and led him roughly from the hall. The Crows snarled at him as he was led away, all except for Flint, who glowered at Hector.

"You're weak. Compassion like that will come back to haunt you."

"It was hardly compassion. He came begging for my assistance, and I gave him none."

You can lie to the Crow, but you can't lie to me, hissed the vile in Hector's ear. *You* do *care for your old friends. Listen to the bird, brother. He speaks sense.*

The magister stalked away from the dais and the crowd, heading for the Bone Tower. He needed to clear his thoughts, take some air, get away from the Crows and their bullying words.

Bullying their words may be, Hector, but they're true. The Bear and his people should mean nothing to you anymore.

"Kindness can kill you quicker than silver. Whatever feelings you still have for these people, you need to bury them, Blackhand!" Flint called after the departing baron as he sheathed his scimitar. "Before they bury you."

5
Courtship

BY THE PENDULOUS light of a swinging lantern, Whitley stared into the mirror, horrified by what she saw. Her dress resembled something she might have clothed a doll in as an infant. It was a gaudy affair, full of ruffles, pleats, and ribbons. She might not have been a lady of the court like Gretchen or the other Wereladies of Lyssia, but she was aware of what passed for fashion in Highcliff. This frock was an antique from a long-forgotten time, its musty stench catching in the back of her throat. It had been laid out on the bed, waiting for her when she awoke.

The wound on her back had been cleaned and dressed, and her therianthropic healing had accelerated the repair. Who had taken care of her, she had no idea. She had awoken with a splitting headache, the decanter and empty glass on the dressing table providing a clue as to why. She picked up the bottle and sniffed the sweet medicinal aroma. How long she'd been drugged for, she had no idea. It might have been weeks, but the aching wound in her back told her it was more likely a day or two at most. Whitley shook the enormous frilled sleeves. She looked ridiculous, but it was the least of her concerns. Drew's whereabouts were at the forefront of her mind.

A knock at the door made her jump.

"May I come in?"

"What if I say no?" replied the girl from Brackenholme.

A key turned in the lock and the door opened, and a large, shadowy figure filled the frame. He ducked to enter the cabin, heavy booted feet stomping clumsily as he crossed the floor. In one hand he carried a wooden tray, on which a steaming bowl was balanced alongside a hunk of buttered bread. Whitley's stomach rumbled as the man carefully placed it on the dressing table beside the tumbler. Hungry though she was, she feigned disinterest.

"Who are you? Why did you attack the *Lucky Shot*?"

"Who else were you traveling with, my lady?" asked the man as he stepped away from the dresser, looming into the lantern light. He was as big as her father, no mean feat considering how imposing Duke Bergan was. But while the Bearlord had a full, wild head of hair, the giant before her was bald, and spectacularly odd looking. His face was long and drawn while his beady eyes were slightly too far apart. His downturned mouth ensured his expression was fixed somewhere between sad and disappointed.

Good, thought Whitley. *If he's asking who else I was traveling with, perhaps that means he and his men didn't find Drew. Perhaps he's safe.*

"I was traveling alone," replied Whitley, before adding, "not that it's any of your business. Why did you attack Captain Violca's ship?"

The big man wagged a long finger and tutted. "No. You don't get to ask the questions, little lady. You answer mine. Understand?"

His black eyes watched her, unblinking. Whitley couldn't help but stare back at them, finding them both alluring and alarming at once. There was a distant quality to his gaze, something disconcerting that nagged at the Bearlady's nerves. Motionless as he was, the room was charged with the threat of violence. Whitley nodded silently.

"You traveled with someone aboard the *Lucky Shot,*" said the tall man. "I was never one for tricks. They annoy me, and when I get annoyed, I break things. Who was with you?"

"Honestly, I was—"

"Don't tell me you were alone, my lady, please. For your sake. Just the truth will do."

He took a step closer, causing Whitley to back up and bump

into the mirror. The man cocked his head, watching her. He reached out and gently brushed his fingers against the ringlets of brown hair that fell around her face. She shivered, recoiling at his touch, the temptation to call upon the bear appealing but for the fact that she'd still be trapped. She might kill the brute, but she'd still be stuck aboard his ship with however many other villains to contend with. Whitley looked away as the man slowly removed his hand.

"Does my manner offend you, my lady? Do you find me uncouth? I apologize if so. I've been told I'm a humorless wretch before. Only the once, mind: folk never say it twice."

She brought her eyes back to him. "You really don't need to call me 'my lady.' It's quite unnecessary."

"This would be another of those silly games that I don't like, my lady," said the man, his drooping lips quivering as he showed his teeth.

Whitley flinched at the sight of them, crooked, hooked, and yellow. The smell that escaped his mouth reminded her of rotting fish. She gagged as he smiled.

"You see, I know who you are, Lady Whitley."

Her eyes widened at mention of her name. She couldn't help it: even if she'd wanted to deny it her reaction had betrayed her. She glanced toward the open door and the corridor beyond. If she was going to try to escape—Brenn knew where to—then she was going to have to act quickly. The tall man clearly knew far too much. *Did he know that her companion was Drew?*

"I know you had another with you, a gentleman . . . The late Mister Ramzi told me you boarded his ship in All Hallows Bay, two of you. Now, I would ask dear Captain Violca who this other fellow was—Ramzi said the crew called him 'the shepherd'—but she is sadly no longer with us. Who was he, my lady?"

Whitley fought to keep her composure—the man was missing Drew's identity. "One of my father's men, from Brackenholme, sent to protect me," she replied.

"Now, I might have believed that, but he didn't do a particularly good job, did he?"

"What do you mean, you might have believed that?" she exclaimed, the starched ruffles around her wrists shaking. "I'm telling you the truth."

"You think you can outsmart—"

The crystal decanter smashed into the man's face, sending a bloody ravine racing across his temple. The bottle had remained hidden in the voluminous right-arm sleeve of the hideous dress, Whitley releasing and catching it by the neck before swinging it at her captor. The brute staggered to one side, crashing into the bedpost as Whitley made to dash by.

Stunned though he was, the man still managed to throw his hand out as she ran past. His forearm was around Whitley's throat now, quick as a flash, holding her tight from behind. The other hand reached down, snatching the heavy bottle from her before she could strike him again. He tossed the decanter onto the bed, lifting his hand to her neck. She felt his rough fingers firm against her throat as he brought his face over her shoulder alongside hers.

"You're telling lies again, little lady, and lies make Captain Deadeye very cross," he whispered into her ear. "My men from the *Hellhound* who boarded that boat came upon an unexpected assailant. One said it was a wild dog, another a big cat like one might find in Bast. Some said it was a bear, my lady." He laughed. "Imagine that: a bear aboard a boat! Present company excepted, of course."

His laughter died away, the only noise that of the timbers creaking and the sea beyond the portholes. He turned her in his arms, holding her out before him by the throat. His torn face wept dark blood, but his voice remained calm and controlled.

"Now tell me, what beast was that, tearing around the *Lucky Shot*, taking chunks out of my crew?"

"Perhaps Violca had a dog aboard. I never saw all of the ship, I stayed in the cabin—"

"A dog that wore a sword and scabbard on its hip? That's a very sophisticated dog you're speaking of, my lady."

"I can't help you," said Whitley, growling. She was tiring of this Deadeye's badgering and bullying. His black eyes bulged as she snapped at him, and he held her throat that little bit tighter.

"This creature with the sword was last seen being run through by a number of my men with spear, cutlass, and harpoon. He was thrown overboard eventually, much to my annoyance. I'd have liked to inspect that body as it reverted back to human form. Still, therian or not, the White Sea will have claimed him by now. Come, my lady, stop this silliness. Put your teeth away and tell me who that poor soul was."

Whitley cried out as her jaws cracked, the skull of the bear taking form. She thought of her father, her brother, and all those who'd wronged her family. A rage was growing inside as she imagined Deadeye's men slashing and hacking Drew before throwing him into the freezing sea. They'd killed him.

"Perhaps your stay aboard the *Hellhound* as my . . . *guest* will jog your memory, Lady Whitley. Think on, my dear. See if you can recall seeing anything. Little details like that can save a man's—or a woman's—life."

"Take your hand off my throat, you ogre," she snarled. Her hands came up to swipe at him, but he stepped back swiftly, his reach strong and long enough to keep her at arm's length. Instead her shifting claws raked at the skin of his forearm, trying to puncture the flesh. She kicked out, but he lifted her, banging her against the mirror. She felt the glass crunch where her back impacted with it, her feet coming up and lashing out in vain.

"I could be a friend to you. You're a long way from your home in the forest. Terrible things can happen at sea. If you stay by my side, you'll be safe. No harm shall come to you, not so long as I protect you."

"In return for what?" Whitley growled, the bear still rushing to her aid.

"A partnership," he replied. "Marriage," he clarified, before darting forward with his other hand. Both of them were around her throat in an instant, and for a moment Whitley was convinced he meant to throttle her. Instead she felt something cold against her skin; then she heard a sharp snap and a crunching sound as a metal collar was fastened around her neck.

She couldn't breathe, her airway shut off even as he let go and she collapsed to the deck. She scrabbled across the cabin, clawed fingers raking at the floorboards as she gasped for air. It wasn't just the collar that strangled her. *Marriage? To this gruesome beast?* Her skin crawled with horror, and ripples of fur raced across her body.

"Relax, my lady," said Deadeye. "Relax and you may yet live. Control the beast." The captain watched as she writhed across the cabin floor in agony.

"Come, little princess, you should be able to control this creature by now," he said, his crooked smile revealing those terrible teeth. "How silly to run away from the safety of Brackenholme without first mastering control of your therianthropy. Prove your worth, not just to me, but to yourself, Lady Whitley. Only the strong survive the White Sea."

Whitley bucked and squirmed, her eyes bulging as she fought to control the Werebear. She tried to imagine her home, her room in Brackenholme Hall, curling up beside her mother, head in her lap. She imagined Duchess Rainier's gentle hands caressing her face, brushing her hair. Gradually she felt the beast recede, the coat of dark fur replaced by her pale, sweat-slicked skin.

"There," said Deadeye. "I'm impressed. You'll make a worthy addition to the *Hellhound.* I sense we'll achieve great things together, Werelords of both land and sea brought together."

The captain set off toward the door, his heavy feet making the floorboards rattle beneath Whitley's face.

The door slammed shut. The Werelady struggled to her knees, crawling across the cabin floor until she came to the base of the dresser. She gripped the table's edge, her claws having vanished, and hauled herself to her feet. A disheveled face stared back from the mirror. Whitley pulled her straggled hair to one side, examining her neck.

A silver chain encircled her throat, the skin scored and scratched by her struggle. She leaned in closer toward the fractured, polished glass, running a finger along the collar's thick, solid links. She turned it around her throat, drawing and dragging it where it sat flush against her skin. A padlock held it together, the ugly choke chain fastened tight. She stifled a sob. Drew was gone, murdered by the crew of the *Hellhound,* his body tossed to the deep. She shivered at the touch of the silver against her fingertips. She belonged to Deadeye now.

6

Foul-Hooked

DREW LET OUT a cry. His body screamed with the memory of the battle aboard the *Lucky Shot,* each and every wound on fire, awakening him from his troubled sleep. Initially he imagined he was still dreaming, trapped in an awful nightmare. As he bucked and writhed, he felt the attacks anew: two sword blows to the chest, a crushed right shoulder blade, and a searing pain through the guts where a harpoon had skewered him. His eyes flew open, but his vision remained flooded by the blinding, bright light. He flung his arm out, reaching for something, anything that might tell him where he was. The world was no longer rocking: he was on dry land, *but where*? He heard something move close by, his fingers snatching in the sound's direction. Warm flesh—a wrist?

He grabbed it as the owner tried to pull free from his feeble hold.

"He's awake!"

It was a child's voice, raised high in alarm. Something hard—a boot, perhaps—caught Drew in the face, sending his head to one side, his nose bursting with the impact.

"Gerroff 'im, you rotten sod!" snarled a deeper youthful voice. A stick struck Drew across the temple, his head bouncing the other way as he relinquished his hold. He was nauseous from the unexpected blows, each having caught him utterly defenseless.

"Hit 'im again!" shouted the first voice. "He nearly tore me leg off!"

"Leave him be!" A feminine voice spoke now, equally young, followed by a scuffle of some kind. Drew growled as he shook his head, trying to clear away the disorientation and bring forth the wolf. The stick whacked him hard in the breastbone, sending him collapsing back. He landed on some kind of rough pallet, obviously what had passed for a bed while he'd slept.

"Growl one more time, pal, and we'll wale on you like you've never known," said the second voice, clearly itching to deal out more pain.

"Skipper said don't hurt him," said the girl's voice, "so keep your stick to yourself, Gregor."

"He might call himself Skipper, but that don't make him the boss o' me!"

"Keep your voice down," the girl hissed. "Hackett will hear you!"

"Please," gasped Drew, raising his hand in submission, "I'm not looking for a fight; I just want answers!"

"Hush," said the girl, her hand going over Drew's mouth. "The last thing we need is Hackett's men coming knocking."

"Take your hand off his mouth, Pearl," said Gregor. "You don't know where he's been."

"We know exactly where 'e's been," said the boy Drew had originally grabbed. "Rottin' on this mattress for the last two days. How 'is wounds ain't killed him, Sosha only knows!"

"Wait," said Drew. "I've been here for two days?"

"Near enough," said Pearl. "Thought you were gonna bleed out, number of wounds you had."

"You looked like shark bait." Gregor laughed. "I've seen chum with more life when we pulled you out the sea."

"Skipper said we should bring you back here, keep you safe," added Pearl.

"Who's Skipper?" asked Drew.

"Jumped-up little squirt," said Gregor. "Thinks he can boss us all around."

"He ain't bossing nobody," snapped Pearl. "He's trying to keep us alive, stop Hackett and the Krakenguard from tossing any more of us into the tide."

Drew waved his hand, trying to attract their attention. They went silent.

"Would it be all right if I sit up? Can I expect any of you to kick, stamp, or *wale* on me?"

"Get up, mister," said Pearl, clearly the most levelheaded of the three.

"But no funny business," added the first boy, with about as much menace as a puppy.

"Off your high horse, Kit," said Pearl, admonishing him.

Drew laughed.

"What's so funny?"

"Kit," replied Drew, sitting up and rubbing his jaw. "I had him down as a Pup."

"Wouldn't laugh too loud if I were you, pal," said Gregor. "If Hackett's men don't find and kill you, we might just leave you to Kit. He's pretty handy with a knife."

Drew winced as the boy suddenly poked him in the back with his stick.

"He could finish whatever job those wounds started on you."

"Stop playing stupid games, Gregor," said Pearl quietly, her voice drawing close to the Wolflord. "He ain't gonna cause us no harm. You're blind, ain't you?"

Drew nodded, staring ahead into a white world of nothingness. "I was burned some days ago, a brand to my eyes. I haven't seen since."

"You've really been in the wars, haven't you, mister?"

Drew managed a smile. "That's the second time you've called me 'mister.' How old do I appear to you?"

"Into your third decade?"

"I've seen sixteen summers," Drew replied.

"Sweet Sosha," said Gregor. "Your ma must've given you tough chores!"

"He ain't much older than us, then," said Kit.

"No fooling you, is there, Kit?" replied Gregor. Drew heard the sound of a playful smack from one boy to another. *Just what Trent and I might've done in happier times,* he mused with a sigh. Perhaps these boys, too, were brothers.

"You say you pulled me out of the sea. What happened?"

"Gregor found you," said Pearl. "It's him you need to thank for saving your life."

"Thank you," said Drew.

"Don't be so quick with your gratitude, pal. I don't much like you being here, right?"

"How did you come across me?"

"You were foul-hooked—found you tangled up in my nets."

"*Your* nets? *You* have your own fishing boat? But you're only a boy."

"You ain't much older," replied Gregor defensively. "Besides which, we do what we're told since Ghul rounded all the older folk up."

"So now I'm your prisoner?"

"Well, you certainly ain't going anywhere."

"Skipper says we're to watch over you until you get better," added Pearl.

"Ignore Skipper," said Gregor. "I say what's what, and I say you stay put. You go wandering off you'll get us all hung. I want you where I can keep an eye on you, y'hear?"

Drew sensed the boy would be more than happy to see harm come to him should the need arise. He winced as he tried to get comfortable.

"Fetch a bucket of seawater, Kit," said the girl as she maneuvered around the injured lycanthrope. "Reckon I need to change this bandage. Injuries ain't been cleaned since we first dressed 'em."

Drew heard the creak and rattle of a rickety door as Kit left, Pearl immediately setting to work.

"You said . . . you said the older folk had been taken away?" said Drew, trying to continue the conversation to take his mind off the pain of the bandage removal.

"Aye," replied Gregor. "Fathers and mothers, all gone. Ghul's had 'em rounded up. How else do you think he's winning this war?"

"I don't follow," said Drew, gritting his teeth as Pearl tugged the soiled cloth away from his flesh. "I thought Bosa had gotten the best of Ghul. That's what we heard on the mainland, anyway."

"Things change awful fast in the Cluster Isles," said Pearl.

"The Whale had the Kraken on the run, with every free pirate on the White Sea sailing to his side. But Ghul's no fool. The Squidlord knows how to break the backs of his enemies. . . ."

"How does taking your parents help him defeat Baron Bosa?"

"Just about every man who sails the White Sea has family or loved ones in Cutter's Cove," said Pearl. "Every pirate is somebody's son or daughter."

"Ghul got tired of being hounded by Bosa's fleet and took everyone connected to Bosa's renegades. That's pretty much every free man and woman in the Cluster Isles," Gregor explained.

"Where to?"

"Out to sea," the boy replied. "Dunno where, but whatever he's done it's had an effect on the Whale's ships. Whole crews have turned themselves over to Ghul, every soul aboard getting clapped in irons."

"What's he doing with those he's kidnapped?" asked Drew.

"No idea," said Gregor. "Little news gets to us here in Cutter's Cove. Ain't no ships coming into the harbor, only the military. They fly the Lion's red and gold, plus others—black flags from some distant land."

"Bast," whispered Drew.

"What?" asked the boy.

"You mean, where," Drew replied. "It's a jungle continent, south of Lyssia. That's where the Lion's reinforcements have come from, shiploads of soldiers from overseas."

He'd traveled to the White Sea with the hope of finding Bosa. To hear that the Whale's fleet was being whittled away, just as Violca had suggested, made Drew's heart sink. And what had become of Whitley, he dreaded to think.

"Was there any sign of the ship I'd been on when you fished me out of the sea?"

"No," said Gregor. "If it was Ghul's men that attacked you, then there's a few likely outcomes, none of them good. The crew will have taken the Red and sworn fealty to the Lion, or else they'll have been taken to the same place as our parents. Maybe they're all dead. Either way, that ship belongs to Ghul now."

"One of my friends was aboard," said Drew, sick with worry.

"Then you'd best pray the Kraken's in a merciful mood," said Pearl, tugging the last tattered cloth from Drew's back. He cried out as Pearl gasped.

"I don't believe it. The wounds have healed! They're—"

Pearl's words were cut short by shouting outside. A whip crack and a child's cry sent shivers racing down Drew's battered spine. More calls followed: it sounded like a chase was under way, the calls of the men slowly growing distant. The door suddenly creaked open as a panting Kit returned to the room. Drew was utterly lost, still unsure of whom he was with, let alone his surroundings.

"What's going on?" he whispered.

"Looks as though the Krakenguard collared Kit," said Pearl quietly. "Here, let me look at that."

"I'll be fine," said the young boy. Drew heard the anger in his voice as he tried to stifle his sobs.

"Collared him?" asked Drew. "Why would they beat him for fetching a pail of water?"

"There's a curfew at night," replied Gregor. "You take your chances if you're out after dark. Did he follow you, Kit?"

"I lost him on the front. This bucket had better be worth the skin it cost me."

"Good lad," said Pearl. "Seems our guest's wounds are healed, Sosha only knows how. May yet need that bucket for the whip welts on your own back, little brother."

"So where are we now?" asked Drew as he heard the bucket get handed over, the salt water strong to his nose. "And I mean precisely."

"You're in a hut in Cutter's Cove—one of many—and it happens to be our home," said Gregor. "You understand why I ain't keen on Hackett's men finding us harboring you now? They're killers. There's been four hangings already this last week. We all got homes in the town, but they turfed us out, stuck us in this work camp in sheds and lean-tos. And they work us like slaves, trawling the sea and tilling the land for them. We weren't born to serve others. We're the Pirate Isles—we plunder, we steal, we take what we want. Cutter's Cove was once home to the most feared captains of the White Sea. Ain't a soul on these islands who ain't connected to piracy in some way, shape, or form."

"Ain't a soul *left* on these islands, apart from us children," added Kit.

"They've taken *every* adult?" asked Drew incredulously.

"All the able-bodied."

"So there are *some* adults left in Cutter's Cove?"

"A few dusty old seadogs and retired tavern wenches. The town's manned by children now, forced into labor by Hackett and the Krakenguard."

"And who's Hackett?" asked Drew, struggling to piece the puzzle together.

"He's the Steward of Cutter's Cove," said Pearl, tearing a cloth from somewhere and dunking it into the bucket. Drew heard the water slosh as the girl soaked it in brine. "Hackett runs the place in Ghul's absence. He's one of them Werelords."

"You won't ever find a meaner piece of pond scum than the Crab," added Gregor. "Let me help you with that, sis."

Drew listened to the younger boy's sobs as his siblings saw to the wounds the whip had dealt him.

"You mentioned Skipper," said Drew. "Who's he?"

"He's the jumped-up little toad who thinks he can tell us what to do," said Gregor.

"And he works with Hackett?"

"Sosha, no!" exclaimed Pearl. "He's one of us, another kid, but he's got big ideas."

"Big ideas for a small fry," muttered Gregor. "Thinks he can turn up and just start telling us what to do."

"Gregor's bitter because Skipper's half his size."

"He thinks we should do as he says just because he's served time on a ship," said the boy moodily. "That don't make him better than us."

"So then where's Ghul?" asked Drew. "If Hackett runs Cutter's Cove in his absence, where's the Squidlord?"

"That's what Skipper's trying to find out," said Pearl. "He and a few other lads took a fishing boat out, to see what's happening out there. We're just praying they make it back here."

"I hope my friends make it back," said Gregor. Drew heard the boy spit. "As for Skipper, Sosha can take him, for all I care."

"You really don't like him, do you?" asked Drew.

"You've Skipper to thank for still being a free man, pal," said the boy, his breath warm on Drew's face. "Believe me, I'd have handed you over to Hackett when we dragged you ashore. He's the one who said we needed to hide you. The way I see it, the longer we do that, the longer we put ourselves in danger with the Crablord's men. If it weren't for your little guardian angel, and the song and dance he made over keeping you safe and alive, you might've been hanging from the gallows in Cutter's Cove by now."

Drew heard the boy rise. "Lights out, Pearl. Guards'll be round shortly."

"Wait," said Drew suddenly. "I had a sword on me when I was tossed overboard—at least I think I did. I don't suppose it was still in my weapon belt when you found me."

"Weapon belt? Sword? Are you having a laugh? You must have lost it, and I'd be grateful, too, if I were you. A piece of steel would've dragged you to the ocean bed for sure, dirtwalker."

"So you never saw it, then?" said Drew, irritated.

The stick was under his throat instantly, cutting off his air supply.

"I don't take kindly to accusations. Your sword's gone. If you ask me, Skipper's a fool to protect a dirtwalker like you. What makes you so special, exactly?"

"Leave him alone."

The voice was new to Drew, coming out of nowhere, causing Pearl and Kit to gasp.

"Never heard you come in," grunted Gregor to the new arrival. "Taken to creepin' round like a mouse, have you, Skipper?"

"If it keeps me alive, I'll creep like a roach," said the boy quietly, his voice strangely familiar to Drew. "Step away from our guest, Gregor."

"Or what? I'm getting tired of you flouncing round like you own the place, just because you once served some highfalutin Werelord. You're no better'n us, *Skipper*."

"Maybe not. But I'll put you in the dirt if you cross me, Gregor, I swear to Sosha. Now clear off."

Drew heard the bigger boy depart, Pearl and Kit following him to the other side of the hut, where they were soon engaged in muted conversation. Drew blinked, gray shapes shifting through the white mists that fogged his eyes. *Is my sight returning, or is my mind playing tricks on me?*

"My lord," whispered Skipper, his voice suddenly close to Drew. "I can't believe it's really you."

"Do I know you?" asked Drew hesitantly, afraid of what the answer might be.

"I should hope so," said the boy. There was a lightness to his voice, as if he were smiling.

"I can't see—I'm blind," said Drew.

The boy gently traced his finger around the Werelord's eyes. "It's me, Drew. It's Casper."

PART III

SCARLET SEAS

I

Below the Surface

STARING UP INTO the clear blue sky, the water of the Redwine lapping about her ankles, Gretchen couldn't help but be transported to her childhood. There was a pool, in a glade, deep in the heart of her father's woodland, far removed from the city. When she was a child her nurse would accompany her, leaving the young therian to play to her heart's content. Occasionally her friends might join her in the glade, girls from other courts across the Seven Realms, daughters of nobles her father entertained. They would laugh, and play, and sometimes just lie on the bank, staring at the clouds while their toes dangled in the pool. This was a place secret and special to the ladies of Hedgemoor. Her mother had told her about it, and Gretchen had hoped to tell her daughters about it. One day.

She sighed as the daydream jarred her back to reality: that day would never come.

Gretchen allowed herself a moment more of relaxation, closing her eyes while the Redwine massaged her feet, the sounds of spring surrounding her. She caught the distant voices of her men from their campsite, the odd peal of laughter carried on the wind to her secluded spot. She ground her teeth. If she could hear them, who else might?

Sitting upright, she reached a hand through the grass to snatch at her boots, her eyes trailing over the river. They skimmed over the moss-covered outcropping of a rock, its tip breaking the surface as the Redwine raced around it. At that instant, the "rock" shape blinked. She dropped her boots, her eyes flying back to the river, just in time to see it disappear.

Gretchen kept very still, her eyes fixed on the surface of the water. *Are my eyes playing tricks on me?* She was tired and weary, her Harriers constantly on the move, changing camp from day to day, never staying in one place for too long. Trent had the most military experience in the group, but he wouldn't lead. That task was a Werelord's; this was Gretchen's role. The command of the band had fallen upon her shoulders, and the responsibility weighed heavily. She squinted at the spot in the river where the head had surfaced, her eyes growing bleary as the water constantly moved. *No,* she thought. *I'm not going mad. There was a head there . . . wasn't there?*

"What's the matter?"

Gretchen jumped, startled by the voice that had crept up on her. It was Trent. She looked back to the water.

"I saw something."

"In the river?"

"Of *course* in the river," she said with irritation.

"I was only asking," he replied gruffly.

She turned and glared at him.

"We might be in the wilds, on the run from the Lion's army, but don't forget your place, Ferran."

Trent arched an eyebrow at her before glancing over the rushing water.

"It was probably a fish, Lady Gretchen. You'll find most rivers are full of them," he replied cheekily.

"I know a fish when I see one," she snapped, tugging her first boot on.

"It'll be that other thing, then: a duck." The tone of his voice was playful, but Gretchen was having none of it.

"Can't you control the men in my absence?"

"I beg your pardon, *my lady*?"

"I want them ready to march at a moment's notice. We're not so far from Redmire, Ferran—our ultimate target, remember? I'm surprised half of General Vorhaas's army hasn't descended by now, with the racket they're making."

"Can you really blame them for being in good spirits? They've much to be proud of, with victories over the Lionguard from the Low Dale Road to the edge of Badgerwood.

We've achieved a great deal in a short space of time."

Gretchen sighed. "We are but a fly that irritates the fat rump of Lucas's army. Do you think these 'victories' reach the Lion's ears, or those of Onyx? They won't have heard about our skirmishes. They probably take us as seriously as Muller's idiots in the Badlands, and we're a tiny fraction of the sheriff's number."

"Why the sudden pessimism?" asked Trent. "Do you forget what the Harriers consist of? We've cobblers, bakers, coopers, and builders. These aren't warriors or mercenaries. They're honest, normal men who fight for freedom. Sure, they may have forgotten themselves for a moment, but don't deny them a little pleasure."

Trent set off walking. "I'll go and speak to them, but don't expect me to berate them."

"Save your legs and your breath, Ferran," said Gretchen, tugging her last boot on and standing. "I'll speak to them myself."

The Lady of Hedgemoor made to walk past Trent, but he grabbed her by the forearm and pulled her back to him.

"Unhand me!" she exclaimed.

"Not until you give me some straight answers."

"You forget who you speak to, Redcloak."

"I don't forget a single thing, Gretchen. If you think you can sneer at me like something you've scraped off your boot after everything we've been through together, think again. Call me Redcloak all you like if it makes you feel superior, I don't give a Ratlord's behind, but I deserve an explanation. Why are your claws out?"

It was a figure of speech, but it was true. Gretchen stared at her hands, clawed as the fox flashed through her, ready to lash out. She tried to pull free but Trent's grip remained firm.

"You've been irritable with me for the last month, ever since we hooked up with the Dales men," he continued. "Are you afraid to be seen speaking to me in front of your subjects?"

Gretchen laughed. "Brenn help us, you think an awful lot of yourself, Ferran, don't you? It must be wonderful when the world revolves round you!"

"This from *you*, of *all people*?"

"It's not who you are or where you come from, it's how you act with me," she snapped. "You're always fussing around me, like I'm a child. I'm quite capable of looking after myself!"

"This is about the other day, isn't it? When we attacked Krupha and his men? You're picking a fight with me because I wanted to make sure your wound was seen to, is that it?"

"I wasn't the only one injured—there were others in our number who were wounded!"

"You'd taken a blow to the stomach!"

"It was a glancing blow, and you forget—I'm a therianthrope. I *heal* when others don't."

"So I'm guilty of caring for you, then? Is that any reason to continually pick fights?"

"You need to treat me as you would any man in the Harriers," Gretchen replied.

"But you're *not* a man, let alone just anybody. You're a Werelady, a figure of hope, a cause for the Dalelands to rally behind!"

Gretchen yanked her arm free and started walking, leaving Trent to gasp with exasperation before following.

"I thought you were different from your brother," Gretchen spat out over her shoulder, "but you're just as pigheaded and stubborn as he ever was. Is it just the Ferran boys who are soaked in chivalry or every man along the Cold Coast?"

"How are we supposed to act? You're a noblewoman. A lady who was betrothed to Lucas not so long ago. You can't be the pampered princess and the freedom fighter at the same time."

She spun around and leveled on him.

"Take a look around you, Ferran. Do you see me living any differently from the rest of you? I sleep under the same stars, in the same muddy ditches, soaked by the same stinking rain."

"Don't give me that," said Trent angrily. "You may think you're one of us, but believe me, the men in that camp treat you differently. You get the first of the rations, you get the pick of the spots to sleep, and some of them treat you with more respect than they would their own grandmothers. Face it, Gretchen: you're more important than any of us."

"I can't do anything about how *they* treat me! What do you want from me?"

"I don't expect you to do anything about it. You're a therian. You have your place, we have ours, whether you'll admit it or not. We can never be like you. You were born to rule, we were born to serve. There's no shame in it, for Brenn's sake—you can change into a beast, you're impervious to most things that could kill a man. You have to be better than us, or what chance do we have of surviving this war?"

Gretchen stood motionless. She knew she was unlike any of them. She'd been raised to consider herself better than humanity: that was the way of the Werelords. But now it sickened her that all of her comrades had been treating her differently.

Trent set off to walk past her. "Perhaps that's why you're so happy to play me like a fool."

Her hand flew out, instinct triggering the attack. But before she could strike his face, Trent had caught her by the wrist. Her other hand came across to hit him, but he snatched it, too, out of the air. The two stood face-to-face and hand in hand, the Werefox snarling at the boy from Westland.

"I thought we'd grown close in the Dyrewood," Trent said, his cool blue eyes focused on hers. "When it was just you and me, it felt like there were no barriers. We were just two friends, depending upon one another. Yet now, it's like you're ashamed of me."

Gretchen growled. "Let go of me, Trent."

"Why the shame?" he continued, ignoring her protestation.

"Is it because you can't bear to admit there might actually be something between us?"

She lashed out with her leg, her foot cracking Trent across the shin and sending him falling to the grass-covered riverbank. As she tumbled to the ground he pinned her down. She snarled, her fox teeth sharpening ever so slightly. Trent stared back, jaw set and firm in the face of the therian girl, hands still clasping hers tightly.

"You abhor the fact that a human could mean so much to you, don't you?"

"Pah!" she spat out, trying to tear free again. "You've an inflated opinion of yourself, Ferran," she gasped, writhing beneath him, trying to work her knees free to launch a crippling kick.

"No," he said, smiling without feeling. "It's not me at all, is it? It's him."

Gretchen didn't need to ask who "him" was. She wanted to tell Trent that it had nothing to do with his brother, that Drew had no impact on their relationship, but she'd be lying. She was torn by her feelings for each of the Ferran boys: the memory of Drew and how he'd made her feel, and the way she'd come to look upon Trent as more than just a friend through the terrible dangers they'd faced together.

She opened her mouth to speak, to deny that her aggression had anything to do with the heir to the throne of Westland, the Werelord at the heart of the war of the Seven Realms. Her green eyes frantically searched Trent's as he stared down at her. The words caught in her throat, her feelings betraying her. *Say something,* she thought. *Prove him wrong, even if he's right!*

At the moment she was about to speak, Trent kissed her. She struggled halfheartedly, her sharp teeth catching his lips, but Gretchen's facade of resistance was crumbling beneath her desire for the kiss. She should have bitten him, torn a strip from him for his impertinence, but the anger she'd felt for him moments ago was gone, and with it the beast receded.

Trent broke the embrace and pulled away. A drop of blood bloomed on his lower lip where her teeth had snagged him. Again, Gretchen wanted to speak, but this time to tell Trent what she truly thought of him, how he made her feel: safe, secure, special. But the young man spoke first.

"I won't be second best to him," he whispered, releasing her and jumping to his feet.

Trent stalked away toward the Badgerwood. Gretchen watched him go, none of her usual quick-fire ripostes coming to mind. She turned back to the Redwine, the apparition she'd seen earlier in the river forgotten. Calm though it appeared, the Werelady knew better. Currents raged beneath the surface, as turbulent as the thoughts that clouded her mind.

2

Skipper

DREW'S EYES WATERED, the faint outlines of his fingers fluttering as he waggled them back and forth. The strain induced a blinding headache, but he pushed it to one side, willing his vision to focus. The field of white was now gray, broken by the shifting shadows as he brought his ghostly digits closer to his face. *This is progress,* he thought, fighting the urge to holler with delight.

"Be careful," said Casper. "If the wind changes, your face might stick."

Drew jumped at the voice. He'd been concentrating so hard that he wasn't even aware that Casper had entered the hut. The siblings had left him alone all day, the others hard at work outdoors for the Krakenguard. They'd hidden him beneath blankets when the foreman had collected them, and he'd stayed in the hut since then.

"You really do sneak around a lot. How long have you been there?" asked Drew.

"Long enough to see your eyes nearly burst from their sockets."

"I might be blind, but I can hear that grin from here. Why aren't you out there working with the rest of them?"

"Like you, I ain't supposed to be round here," said Casper. Drew heard the boy sit down. "Being cabin boy aboard the *Maelstrom* hardly won me any friends, especially among your enemies. I, too, need to stay hidden. I've been hiding out in the harbor, beneath the jetties. Ain't nobody lookin' for wanted men—or kids—there. Gregor, Pearl, Kit, and the rest of the children have been press-ganged into labor by Hackett's men. They count 'em in and count 'em out—if any are missing, they come looking and dish out some hurt. If I turned up at roll call, I'd be as good as stickin' my neck through the noose."

It was good to hear the boy's voice again. Drew had only spent a brief time in Casper's company, back when his ordeals had begun. Count Vega the Sharklord had captured Drew and stowed him aboard Vega's ship the *Maelstrom*, delivering his prisoner to King Leopold. But when Drew and his allies—including Vega—defeated the Lion, Drew had given the pirate Vega a place on the Wolf's Council. After shaking off his distrust of the Sharklord, Drew had come to depend upon the pirate prince in matters both political and personal.

Throughout it all, Casper had been close to his captain's side, the nearest thing Vega had to a page boy.

Since Casper—or "Skipper," as the children of Cutter's Cove called him—had appeared the previous night, Drew hadn't gotten a chance to properly speak with him. It was clear that the boy had assumed a position of power among the enslaved youngsters. He knew that Bosa's fleet had been scattered across the ocean by the Kraken. But Vega's whereabouts still eluded him.

"How are your eyes, then?" asked the boy.

"On the mend. It's gradual, but I can make out shapes again. Who knows, I might be the new lookout aboard the *Maelstrom* by this time tomorrow!"

"Over my dead body," the boy said with a snort. "That's my job. You stick with ruling Westland, my lord."

Drew dropped his joking tone. "We never got to speak properly the other night, Casper. You only half said hello before you were off again."

"Sorry about that. I had to speak to some of the other lads first. They've put a lot of faith in me. Was amazed to find you still here when I got back, to be honest. Hated to think what Gregor might've done."

"You don't like him?"

"I don't mind him. He's only looking after his own. He doesn't trust me."

The boy's relationship with the others sounded complicated, but there was only one thing Drew wanted to know right now.

"Where's Vega, Casper?"

"Taken alive by Ghul, along with many other pirates from the Cluster Isles who opposed him."

"What happened to the *Maelstrom* and her crew?"

"Got took from the captain, didn't she? We were heading north, around the cape of Tuskun toward Sturmland. The captain and Duke Manfred were set for visiting Icegarden. Only someone had different ideas—tried to do away with my master and threw him overboard. I followed him over the side. Neither of us saw the *Maelstrom* again. I'd die for that man," added the lad, with utter sincerity.

"Who tried to kill Vega?"

"Your pal, the Boarlord. Shivved him with his fancy dagger while his men threw a sack of cannon shot around the captain's neck and tossed him into the sea."

Drew shook his head, unwilling to believe it. "Hector wouldn't do that. I know him. He's a good man: he's no killer."

"Saw it with my own eyes," said Casper quietly. "With respect, don't question what I witnessed, my lord. Not after what Blackhand did to my captain. If Count Vega were still here with us, he'd tell you as much himself."

Drew grimaced, the bile rising in his throat. There was

that name again: *Blackhand.* The wicked magister who now ruled Icegarden.

"This ain't news to your ears, is it?" asked the perceptive boy. "You've heard other bad things about your Baron Hector, ain't you?"

"Things I wish I hadn't," replied Drew, forcing back his misery. He couldn't believe that Hector had actively sought to take Vega's life. There had to be another explanation for this and the events in Icegarden.

He took a lungful of air, trying to clear his head of his friend's betrayal.

"Just when you think you know someone—" started Casper.

Drew broke in. "So how did you and Vega escape a watery grave?"

"I dove in, tore the sack from about the captain's throat, and kicked up to the surface. Found myself adrift with him, didn't I? Well, I've always been a strong swimmer—reckoned I got that off my old man, so the captain said. So I put my back into it, keeping him afloat until he came round. We're lucky he's a Sharklord and that the knife wasn't silver—the captain woke up enough to swim a bit, too, if you can call it that, but between us we had a good idea which direction land was. Got picked up by a fur trader's wee ship off the Tuskun coast. From there we eventually made it back to Moga."

"That's quite the tale of survival. Vega owes you his life. So what happened then?"

"Captain and I went to war beside Baron Bosa," Casper said proudly. "Took the battle straight to the enemy. Lion, Squid, and all ships that flew the Black Flag of Bast—they were scared witless by the Whale's attacks. For a good time we had 'em on the run. That was before they started with the kidnappings: taking folk from their homes, loved ones and the like. Didn't take long for sailors to start turning themselves over to Ghul, whole shiploads of pirates switching sides for fear of what the Kraken might do to their families."

"So your fleet shrank?"

"Family's a powerful thing."

"You're not wrong. How did you end up here?"

"We were working aboard the *Beggar's Bride,* Captain Mesner's ship, with the count serving as first mate. Mesner had a reputation on the White Sea before this war even kicked off. Big man, full of bluster and bravado. He and Bosa went way back."

"A good man, then?"

"Once, perhaps. Last thing the count said to me was that Mesner was behind the ambush. We were way west of Hook Island, moored up, keeping watch over the Clusters for Bosa. There should've been nothing at our backs but open water. Instead two of Ghul's ships took us by surprise. Mesner must have tipped the Kraken off. He had no family; reckon it was gold that turned him. In any case, I managed to escape in a rowboat during the melee. That was three weeks ago. I've been here ever since."

"What have you been doing in that time?"

"Trying to get this lot to fight back, for starters. We may be smaller than Hackett and his men, but we outnumber them ten to one. We could defeat them if we pulled together."

"And where's Vega now?"

"Me and a couple of other lads took a fishing skiff the other day, followed the rumors out to sea. Found what we feared the other night."

The boy was quiet for a moment as he composed himself. "Lord Ghul's built a sea fortress, right at the heart of the Cluster Isles' crescent. That's where he's taken my captain, and no doubt the others, too."

"A sea fortress? But what island could he build it on, in the middle of the bay?"

"That's just it. There ain't no land out there. It's a tower in the sea."

Drew was confused by the boy's description. "I don't understand how he could've built a tower without land, Casper."

"Nor do I, but I saw it well enough myself."

"Are you sure? You said yourself it was at night."

"Ain't nobody on the White Sea got eyes as keen as mine, Lord Drew. I wasn't lookout for no reason. That's why the captain kept me close: Count Vega always said I was his best investment."

"How close did you get to the fortress?"

"Not very; sea was full of ships around it. If we'd have tried to get nearer they'd have sent us to the bottom—"

"Did anyone see you come here?" Drew asked, interrupting him.

"If I don't want to be seen, I don't get seen. The camp was empty, anyway. Children were all to work, at the docks, on the boats, and in the fields. There weren't even any guards when I came through."

"Well, there are now," said Drew. "Someone's out there."

They could both hear the footsteps now, attempts at stealth betrayed by the squelching of mud. Drew dropped his head, allowing the wolf in enough to heighten his senses. There were multiple figures approaching from different directions, all closing on the hut. He could smell sweat and metal, alcohol and tobacco.

"Stay put," whispered Casper.

Drew heard the boy stand and snatched out at him, catching his ankle.

"Are you crazy?" he growled, the beast barely restrained. "Where are you going?"

"I'll draw them away. They *can't* find you, my lord," he said, ripping his leg free from Drew's grip.

Then he was gone, the door slamming shut as he made a break from the hut. Bursts of obscenities were followed by the shouts of the guards as they gave chase. Then came a sound that made Drew's heart stutter in his chest: the wail of a boy. The guards had caught Casper.

Casper ripped a chunk of flesh from the forearm that held him tight and spat it into the mud. His hand burst free from the panicked guard's grasp, and he raked his fingers down the man's face, ripping red furrows into his cheek. Another soldier jumped forward as his comrade struggled with the enraged boy, blood pumping from his maimed arm.

"You little—"

The flat of the guard's hand struck Casper's face hard, sending his head ricocheting into the wounded officer's jaw. The soldier released his grip as the two collapsed into the mire. Casper rolled onto his back, blinking and seeing stars as the men stood over him.

"I thought you said he wouldn't put up a fight, boy," said a third guard, calling to a figure behind him. Casper tried to refocus as a boy emerged from the huts at their backs.

"He's supposed to be blind," replied Kit nervously. Casper's heart sank at the boy's betrayal.

"Then what do you call this?" squealed the soldier, clutching his torn limb with trembling fingers. "He's an animal, blind or not!"

"He's wild is what he is," snarled the third man as Kit walked closer. "We should kill him here. No point dragging him back to Hackett only for him to cause more trouble. Who knows what else he might do, given half the chance."

"Hang on," said Kit warily. "That ain't him."

"Aye," said the officer who had struck Casper. "You said the stranger had one hand. This one's got two!"

"Then who's this?" asked the wounded soldier, giving the boy a kick. Casper whimpered as the boot hit his ribs, causing him to double up in the mud.

"That's Skipper," said the nervous boy, peering around the guards, unable to look Casper in the eye.

"You've betrayed us all, Kit!" gasped Casper.

"By giving the stranger over to 'em? This buys me and mine favor with Lord Hackett!"

"You've put yourself and your family in danger," cried Casper. "You can't trust them! Run, Kit!"

"There'll be no running," said the sergeant.

"More importantly," said the third guard, "where's the lad with one hand?"

There was a blur of movement as a dark shape shot from the shadows between the nearby huts, catching the sergeant as it leapt by. The man was gone, dragged off between the ramshackle buildings before his companions had time to react.

"Sweet Sosha!" squealed the wounded guard. "What was that?"

"Sarge!" called the other man, nervously weighing his sword in his hand. "You there, Sarge?"

"This ain't right," said the first guard, stepping over the concussed Casper, cradling his arm against his belly. "Sarge said we were to just grab the lad in that hut and take him to Hackett. You set us up!" he said, rounding on Kit with an enraged snarl. His good arm came up and down in a sharp, savage motion, and the boy fell to the mud. "You promised us there was someone sheltering here, someone the Crab would want. It was a trap all along!"

The wounded guard kicked out at Kit, but the boy didn't respond, lying unmoving on the ground. "Well? Answer me!"

"Leave him be, Colm," said the other man, his eyes flitting between the filthy huts, searching for their enemy. "So there's two of 'em. They're just kids."

Of the sergeant, there was no sight, no noise. The guard reached down and grabbed Casper by the hair, dragging him to his knees before him. He raised his sword and placed the tip against Casper's spine, poised to thrust down.

"You see this?" he shouted. "I don't know who you are, boy, but we can make this easy. You give us the sarge, we give you your little mate back. And we walk away, right?" As he turned back to the shadows, there was a resounding *clang* as a blood-smeared helmet flew through the air, striking his own armored head. The impact was enough to send him staggering back, the sword point wavering from where it hovered over Casper's neck.

The Werewolf bounded forward, leaping over the kneeling boy and hitting the guard in the chest. The two went down, the sword tumbling to the mud as the man tried to defend himself. The lycanthrope's head loomed over his, lips peeled back to reveal teeth as thick as spearshafts. The beast turned its head in Casper's direction as the man screamed, fumbling for his weapon belt.

"Defend yourself," Drew growled as the boy struggled to his feet, the wounded man reaching for him.

A stabbing pain rocketed through Drew's abdomen, cold steel scoring his stomach.

The guard looked down the lengths of their bodies to where his hand clutched the bloody dagger. He brought his face back to the Werewolf's, the beast's pale yellow eyes staring through him. The man's cry of horror was cut short as the Wolflord's jaws snapped at his face.

Casper felt the first guard catch him by the shoulders, yanking him from his feet. The man swung the boy high like a rag doll before sending him crashing into the ground. The soldier reached down to pick up the sword that lay in the mud, but Casper was one step ahead, lashing out with a kick and catching the man's torn forearm. The guard bellowed, instantly retracting his wounded arm as Casper grabbed the weapon.

Stumbling clear, the guard's eyes flew to the Werewolf that now crawled off the body of his dead companion. Then he turned from the growling beast to the crouching boy with the blade in his hands. He backed up against one of the huts, nowhere to run, his arm weeping profusely. Dropping to his knees in the filth, he stared warily at his enemies. The boy rose, lifting the heavy blade in both hands, the tip wavering at the sole surviving guard.

Casper glanced at the Werewolf as it paced between the buildings, twisting its head and sniffing at the air. Blind though Drew was, there were other ways for him to find and strike his enemies. The lycanthrope snorted as he found the guard's scent, suddenly crouching, poised to pounce at any moment. Casper looked down to where Kit lay motionless in the mud. The boy's eyes were closed, his pale face turned to one side, half submerged in a puddle. Even from a distance Casper could see he was dead.

"What . . . what is that?" gasped the injured guard, staring at Drew. "Is that the *Wolf*?" he asked, never taking his eyes from the beast.

Casper stepped forward, the weapon heavy in his hands, but he held firm. The guard's throat bobbed, his eyes wide, torn between the boy and the Wolf.

"You killed Kit. You're a murderer."

"I'm a soldier, boy," gasped the man. "Put the sword down before you do something stupid. Perhaps Hackett might spare you—"

"He was a child, and you killed him."

"What *is* that monster?" the guard cried, ignoring the boy's accusation.

"I only see one monster here," replied Casper coldly. He could feel sweat pooling against his palms as he gripped the sword's handle. "I ain't never killed a man before."

The guard gulped. "You don't wanna start now," he whispered.

A clawed hand touched Casper's shoulder, gentle but firm. A squeeze was all it took to draw him away from the villain and the dark act that might follow. Casper stumbled back, light-headed and unsteady on his feet, as the beast turned its bloody muzzle back to the Krakenguard. Slowly, the Werewolf's lips peeled back, teeth bared, jaws opening.

"Please," whispered the soldier, his eyes wide with terror. "Sosha, no!"

The wounded soldier made to scream, but the sound never escaped his lips, the Werewolf's fist striking him clean across the temple and plunging him into a deep and troubled sleep.

3

The Shark, the Shackles, and the Shanty

"SING ME ANOTHER shanty, old-timer. Something involving a handsome sea captain this time, and the colorful death of a spineless squid."

While his fellow prisoner struck up a tune a few feet away, Count Vega, buccaneer pirate prince and former captain of the *Maelstrom*, leaned forward and allowed the chains to take his weight. He glanced at the outlawed silver manacles fastened tight about his wrists, the links of steel securing him to the wall at his back. Vega looked down at the waves raging in the darkness far below. The occasional spume of white froth materialized, caught in starlight before vanishing from sight. The constant rocking motion was familiar to his sea legs, but the sheer distance from the ocean remained alarming. He'd climbed what he'd thought were tall crow's nests before, where the pitch could fling a man to his death, but nothing compared to this.

"When the black-hearted *Maelstrom* hauls out of the
dock,
Sail for the Shark and to death in the dark!
To see these poor fellows, how on board they flock,
Hey ho, to death in the dark!"

Vega smiled at the shanty, a variation on an old favorite from the Cluster Isles. The elderly chap singing was a navigator by the name of Florimo, imprisoned for the composing and singing of a defamatory ditty about Lord Ghul's parentage. Judging by the harmless chap's apparent dementia it struck Vega as cruel beyond words for the Squidlord to be holding him prisoner, but few of the Kraken's actions surprised him. Florimo had been kind enough to recount the offending song to the count, and the two had quickly become friends.

Vega strained his neck farther, inspecting the tower's curving walls. Other figures were manacled to the structure's exterior, above and below. *Captive captains like me?* he wondered, the occasional wail sounding over the ocean's roar. Walkways, ladders, and bamboo gantries crisscrossed the wall in all directions, allowing the jailers access to their prisoners.

"O'er whiplash and squall hear the Squid's sorry wail.
Sail for the Shark and to death in the dark!
Such is the price for the Kraken's betrayal,
Hey ho, to death in the dark!"

"Shut that racket up!" came a shout from above. Vega looked up, spying a couple of figures jumping down the walkways, drawing close to where he and Florimo were chained.

"Racket?" the senile old sailor piped up in shock. "You wouldn't know a fine tune if it bit you on your—"

"Silence!" yelled the heavyset man as he swung down from the platform overhead, landing with an almighty rattle on the runged floor. He rose quickly, a head shorter than the Sharklord but twice as wide. Lord Ghul had paid Vega a visit each day since his capture, the sea marshal of the Lion's fleet dishing out torture at every opportunity.

"Do my words offend your delicate ears, my lord?" crooned the toothless Florimo. "Oh, but your poor, sweet lugholes! Free my treacherous hands from these chains and I would cut my tongue out if it should please you!"

Vega's grin was short-lived as the Squidlord grabbed Florimo by the throat.

"If I wanted your tongue, you tatty old bird, I'd tear it from your scrawny throat myself." The Kraken sneered, his broad hand rippling beneath the prisoner's jaw. "You're only alive because your miserable plight amuses me, you wretched excuse for a sailor. Too infirm to sail ship, to haul rope, to mop decks—I wouldn't trust you with the slop bucket—you'd probably drown in it!"

"Strictly speaking, my lord," spluttered Florimo, "I'm a navigator, and such duties are beneath—"

Vega watched in horror as the flesh of the Kraken's hand tore apart between thumb and forefinger. The gash ran up the sea marshal's arm like a fault line, severing the limb in two as the twin appendages thickened. All the while, the remainder of the Squidlord remained unchanged. Ghul had complete mastery over his therianthropy, able to control individual portions of his form as only the greatest Werelords could. The digits disappeared, fused into the transforming skin of the Weresquid, the pair of tentacles beginning to burst forth circular suckers that shone with sharp teeth. One writhing limb caressed Florimo's face as the man cried out fearfully, the razor rings catching his skin.

"I could flay the flesh from your body," whispered Ghul, his voice gurgling as if partly submerged in water.

"Leave the old man alone, you wobbling sack of guts," called Vega. "It's me you're here to torment, isn't it?"

The Kraken glared at him, drawn away from the assault on Florimo. His lips peeled back, revealing the shifting insides of his mouth. Vega's stomach lurched at the sight of the Squidlord's beak, grating and snapping where teeth should have been. The other tentacle snaked through the air toward the count, rising up like a cobra, ready to strike.

"Leave them be!" a woman cried as she swung down from the gantry overhead, landing on the lurching deck with easy grace.

Ghul reluctantly released his hold on the old sailor's face, the tentacle slipping away to reveal circular cuts scarring the man's cheek.

"My lady," said Ghul submissively, even managing an awkward bow.

"You can drop the courtesy," said the woman. "Such a title has never sat well with me, and we both know I'm certainly no lady."

"You've sat on my throne for years, Ghul, yet you still bow like a hunchbacked cretin," Vega taunted the Squidlord.

The woman's black skin shimmered by the starlight, her shaved head cocked to one side as she turned to look the Sharklord up and down. "I'd be careful what you say if I were you, Count Vega," she purred, the accent in her velvet-smooth voice revealing her homeland as Bast. "The only reason you're here now is that my dear friend Lord Ghul has very strict orders to keep you alive. You have him to thank for the very fact you draw breath. Consider that the next time you mock the Lord of the Cluster Isles."

"Thank you . . . er . . . my lady," said Ghul, struggling to fulfill her request.

"Call the Kraken what you like," said Vega, "but there's only ever been one Lord of the Cluster Isles. I made that title my own, remember, Ghul? You'll be calling yourself a pirate prince next, I wager. Dress yourself in a bonnet and crown yourself Queen of the Sirens for all I care—it won't change what you are."

"And what's that, little fish?" asked the Squidlord, stepping up to the woman's side.

"A backstabbing, lying, thieving bag o' blubber," Vega stated plainly.

Ghul laughed. "I'll only take offense at that last bit. Those other three things? Well, we're pirates—that's what we do, isn't it?"

"Some, perhaps, but there's a code that many abide by. You broke that code long ago, many times over."

"I make the law, just as you did before me!"

"I abided by the law, even when I ruled in Cutter's Cove, just as I did aboard the *Maelstrom*. All men are equal in my eyes."

"Some are more equal than others." Ghul laughed, his tentacles recoiling as he slowly shifted back to human form.

The woman raised a hand between the two men, signaling an end to their confrontation. "I didn't travel from Highcliff, Lord Ghul, to witness your spat with the Sharklord."

"Forgive my impertinence, but why *have* you traveled here, Opal?" asked Vega. "An interest in my predicament? Don't get me wrong, I'm terribly flattered that one as important as yourself has taken my well-being to heart."

"So you know who I am, Count Vega?" asked Opal, looking down the length of the fortress wall.

"Your reputation precedes you," replied the Sharklord. He'd heard tales of how striking Opal was and now that she stood before him, he could see they weren't mere rumors. "As your brother's might is spoken of throughout the known lands, so is your elegance. If Onyx is the Beast of Bast, then you are indeed the Beauty."

Opal faced him again. "I wasn't expecting such eloquence from a man who has been chained to a wall, facing the elements, for the last three weeks. You flatter me," she said with a smile, while the sneering Ghul watched on.

Vega's teeth sparkled as he threw her his best roguish grin. Wars were fought on many fronts. This wasn't the first time Vega had been held captive by the opposite sex, and it was a game in which he was well versed. Even ravaged and exhausted, manacled to a rocking tower by silver and steel, he wasn't entirely unarmed. He still had his charm.

"No flattery, though admittedly not all accounts have been so kind. You do, after all, represent an invading force in Lyssia. I've met the odd soul who described you as a monster, but I see now that such stories are ludicrous propaganda."

The count wasn't a fool. He knew Opal was almost as deadly as her brother. He'd heard of what she'd done in the Horselord palace of High Stable, publicly murdering Duke Lorimer before ordering Lucas to slay the captured Bearlord, Broghan. He needed to win her over, and from there perhaps escape, but he needed to be careful. He was playing a dangerous game with a deadly foe.

"Don't listen to him," said Ghul. "He deceives you!"

"Quiet, Ghul," said Opal, her eyes fixed on the Sharklord with unblinking fascination. "You don't think me a monster, then?"

"I've yet to see anything that would give me that impression."

"You don't know me, Vega."

"Nor you me. I understand if you consider me your enemy. But look at us—we're being civil, are we not? Our differences don't have to end in bloodshed."

"They don't *have* to," she said, as the fortress rocked suddenly once again. The Catlady almost lost her footing, and Ghul reached out and grabbed her by the forearm.

"Be careful, Opal," said Vega, his voice thick with concern. Ghul's jaw fell open, annoyed that the Shark had stolen his thunder. "You risk much already by climbing down these walls to speak with me. Why not move me inside the tower so we can continue our discussion? Keep me manacled, by all means—I am, after all, your prisoner—but perhaps we could conduct this conversation in more hospitable surroundings?"

"Don't worry about my safety, Count Vega," Opal said as she disengaged the Kraken's hand from her arm. "I'm a Panther of Bast. I'm sure-footed anywhere, even on your White Sea."

"Of course, how silly of me," he said with a smile.

Opal stepped right up to Vega until they were nose to nose. Her perfume assailed him, sweet and intoxicating, while her flawless skin glistened with sea mist. He might have been laying on the compliments, but he wasn't lying. She was truly one of the most attractive women he'd ever encountered.

"I find you fascinating, Vega," she whispered.

"The feeling's mutual," he replied.

"In more peaceful times, perhaps something beautiful might've blossomed between us."

"Something may yet."

"If it did, would you give me your loyalty?"

"Yes."

"Would you give me your heart?" she asked breathlessly, moving her face past his, her lips brushing his cheek.

"I fear I would."

"Would you give me your ship?"

Vega sucked air through his teeth. "That's a devil's question to ask a pirate prince!"

"You've caused us a great deal of trouble in recent months, Count Vega," the Catlady said huskily, sniffing at his sweat- and salt-soaked shoulder. He felt her fingertips tracing a circle over his heart. "You must understand, that makes the high lords of Bast and the Lion of Westland most unhappy. We're grateful to Lord Ghul for capturing you. You were proving quite the thorn in our side."

Vega laughed as the Kraken smiled proudly. "Take off my manacles and let me hug my old friend, show him how thankful I am," the pirate prince deadpanned.

Opal continued, ignoring Vega's jest. "You and your friend from the north, Baron Bosa, have systematically dismantled the king's navy from Moga to the Cold Coast, leaving King Lucas's fleet in disarray."

"That's some of my best work," he replied cheekily. She opened her hand, her fingernails now brushing the skin of his chest.

"I've been sent here to bring you to account, to escort you back to Highcliff where you'll stand trial for crimes committed against the Lion of Westland."

Vega winced as he felt a nail snag his skin. "A trial, you say? A fair hearing before Lucas?"

"I didn't say it'd be fair," Opal replied as her nails caught his flesh once more, deliberately this time. He'd misjudged Opal, badly. "King Lucas has a terrible temper. One should avoid crossing him at all costs."

"The fool's crowned himself?" snarled Vega. "It means nothing. The only true king is the Wolf!"

He gnashed his jaws, fighting to keep his own inner beast back for fear of having his hands severed by the manacles.

"I see you do have some fight in you after all," observed Opal. "Perhaps we'll become better acquainted, and I'll get to see more of the shark as we sail back to Highcliff. But if you'll bear with me, I have work to do first. As you can see, Lord Ghul's been busy rounding up the remnants of your dwindling fleet. There are plenty of sea captains—once loyal to you—who need questioning. They're fighting with one another to tell me Bosa's whereabouts. It's amazing how persuasive one can be when one imprisons the families of every pirate in the White Sea."

"Chaining folk to a sea fortress tends to focus their minds," agreed the Kraken. "It helps one see what's at stake when loved ones are strung from the walls."

"While also making your fortress unassailable," added Opal. "After all, who'd launch an attack on this structure without fear of harming their family?"

"You've been taking innocents hostage?" shouted Vega as he felt Opal's forefinger jab into his chest, the clawed tip cutting a bloody trench into his skin.

"None are innocent—they all sided with the Wolf," she replied as she concentrated on her handiwork.

"They're all guilty by association." Ghul laughed.

Vega cried out as the Pantherlady's claw completed its ragged circuit across his torso. His head hung limp as he looked down at the crude heart shape Opal had scored into his skin, directly over the one that beat within.

"As for you, sweet Vega, I'll hold you to your word," she said, smiling all the while. "I've been away from my children for far too long. While I fight a war in the name of my nephew, they remain in Bast, apart from their mother's bosom. This pains me. You might understand if you had children of your own: it's a love like no other. So, I'll take you up on that offer. Once I deliver you to Lucas and he removes your head from your shoulders, I'll take your heart from your chest. Call it a memento of my Lyssian adventure. It'll be a nice gift to take back to my homeland of Braga, a delicacy my dear children may feed upon."

Opal stepped along the walkway, taking hold of a ladder rung.

"He's all yours, Ghul," she said. "Just don't kill him. That honor shall be the king's."

With that, she scaled the fortress wall, back into the belly of the tower.

As the Kraken stepped up to the shattered Sharklord, he shook his arms out in both directions, the limbs splitting and rippling into four monstrous tentacles. Florimo turned away, unable to watch what would follow.

"Now," said the Weresquid as a serpentine length of flesh caught Vega beneath his chin, lifting his head. "Had something smart to say to me, did you?"

Vega spat at the monster.

"Good," said Ghul, wiping the spittle from his face with his shoulder. The tentacle gripped the count's jaw, holding his head in place while another squirming limb recoiled, preparing to strike the Sharklord.

"That was just the answer I was looking for."

4
STRANGE COUNSEL

"THAT'S A LOT of keys," said Ringlin.

"There are a lot of cells," replied Hector.

Ibal unhitched the brass ring from his belt and stepped up to the door. His chubby fingers rifled through the jangling keys, his master watching patiently. While Ringlin had assumed the rank of captain of the Boarguard, empowered to command the Ugri in Hector's name, Ibal had been given the position of head jailer in Icegarden, managing the cells below the palace. They had sat empty before the magister and his allies took the city, but no longer: the jail was now occupied by former members of the city watch, terrified courtiers, and any others who opposed the Boar and the Crows. The cells of Icegarden had never been so full.

"I'm not sure why you keep coming back here, my lord."

"Did I ask you your opinion, Ringlin?"

"It's just . . . I'm not sure what good speaking to him does."

I can't say I blame him, hissed the Vincent-vile. *Why do you seek the counsel of this pathetic creature when you have me to call upon? Who knows you better than your dear, sweet brother?*

"I don't expect you to understand, Ringlin," replied Hector, ignoring the vile. "I just need you to obey."

"As I always have done, my lord, and shall continue to."

"That you dislike this prisoner comes as no surprise. You and he have history, do you not? You may wait here if you find his company so unpalatable."

"No," said the former thief, a look passing between him and Ibal as his shorter friend finally found the key he searched for. "I'll stay with you, if that's all right. I'd prefer to hear what he has to say, sift the lies from the truths."

Hector turned to Ringlin while Ibal turned the key in the lock.

"You don't get it, do you? I trust him as much as I trust you, albeit for very different reasons. You've proved yourself to me, time and again, delivering all that I ask of you. You've earned my trust. He, however," said the magister, hooking a black-gloved thumb and gesturing toward the cell door, "will never leave this cell and accepts his fate. He has no reason to lie. He can speak plainly in my company—and does, I might add. He's a dead man, for all intents and purposes. I've found death can be quite . . . liberating for a soul."

Hector closed his hand into a fist to emphasize this point. It wasn't lost on Ringlin, the captain shuddering at the thought of the dark magicks his master commanded and the vile that did his bidding. Ibal pushed the door open and stood to one side as his friend and his liege entered the cell.

A torch guttered in a bracket beside the door, an unusual concession for a prisoner but one Hector had been happy to permit. The chains that kept the man captive ensured he couldn't reach the flaming brand. The metal links were secured firmly to the wall, the finest Sturmish steel keeping him restricted to the corner of the cell. A bucket was positioned as far away from the rear wall as possible, a mattress running the brickwork's length providing the only true comfort for the prisoner. The man sat on the rough bed, a blanket draped over his shoulders, the end of the chain manacled about his left ankle. He looked up and smiled as Hector and Ringlin stepped into the chamber, the sea serpent tattoo that rode the right-hand side of his face rippling into life.

"You come to empty the slop bucket, Ringlin?" asked Bo Carver. "Be a good chap, try not to spill it."

"You're lucky you're not wearing it, Carver," said the former thief with a sneer as he took his position by the door. The torch crackled beside his face, casting shadows across his glowering visage. "This was still a jail cell, last time I looked. You want to mind your lip, Thief Lord."

"You've made quite the success story out of your sordid little life, haven't you, Captain Ringlin? Both you and the waddling simpleton out there."

Right on cue, Ibal peered around the open doorway, a sickly giggle escaping his wobbling lips. Carver smiled as Hector looked on in silence.

I do like it when they fight, whispered the Vincent-vile giddily, the specter making invisible circuits around the magister.

"Seems any footpad can rise up the ranks in the Boarguard," said Carver, "if he's prepared to leave his principles behind."

"You're one to talk. You've been a prisoner for Brenn knows how many years, first in Highcliff and now here in Icegarden. Lord of Thieves? Lord of Jails, more like."

"I sleep with a clear conscience, though, Ringlin. It may be a filthy mattress in a dingy cell, but I know I've never betrayed a fellow thief. I fear you can't say the same."

Ringlin stepped forward, towering over the chained prisoner.

"I sleep in a luxurious bed, in a warm room, the hot food in my belly lulling me to a land of pleasant dreams. You think about that, Carver, as you're lying here in the dark, the torch dead on the wall and only your 'morals' for company."

Hector clapped his hands.

"I think that's enough posturing from you pair of peacocks," said the Boarlord, sitting down on the cold floor in the cell's center. "Ringlin, be a good man: go see if Dame Freya requires anything from us. I feel badly that we parted on such . . . cross words earlier. Fetch her any food she or her fellow Daughters require. I'm in a generous mood," he added, before turning his back on the rogue.

Ringlin scowled at the smiling Carver for a moment longer. "As you wish, my lord," he replied before turning and heading through the door. "But the sewage bucket can stay here."

"That's no way to talk about dear Ibal," called the Thief Lord after him. The jailer giggled beyond the threshold in the dark corridor, as Carver settled back onto his mattress.

Hector adjusted the metal brooch that held his cloak together, a charging boar fashioned upon it, before straightening his cloak.

"A trinket of tin from the Dalelands?" asked Carver. "Bit sentimental for Lord Blackhand, the Monstrous Magister of Icegarden, isn't it?"

"Prince or pauper, I feel it's important to remember where one comes from," he replied with a smile. "I'm still the Baron of Redmire, and it's brass, not tin."

"So," said Carver, knitting his hands together and resting them on his raised knees, "back for another inspiring talk?"

"Don't flatter yourself, Carver. I don't come to you seeking advice, though I do find you to be a tremendous vessel to pour my thoughts into. Who would have imagined you'd be someone I can tell my innermost secrets to?"

"The feeling's not mutual, I'm afraid," said the Thief Lord, giving the steel links a brief shake. "Keeping a man chained has a way of breaking down his trust for you."

Hector smiled. "I don't come here to torment you. You and I have an understanding. You know you'll never leave this cell. You simply can't: you know too much about my business, about what's gone on here, my intentions—"

"And about your little demon," interrupted Carver, waving his hand through the air.

The Vincent-vile hissed like a cornered alley cat, itching to be released. *He thinks he* knows *me. Let me acquaint myself with him, brother; give me a moment alone with Master Carver . . .*

"It's no secret that I have command over certain forces. It's called communing, Carver."

"'Necromancy' would be a better word, no?"

Hector cocked his head. "You know more about magistry than I expected, though your choice of words is questionable. 'Necromancy' has such chilling connotations."

Carver laughed. "Whereas what you practice is utterly benign, dear baron? What harm could possibly come from speaking with the dead?"

"It doesn't *have* to be sinister," said the Boarlord irritably.

"Whatever innocent reasons you might have once had to dabble with the dark arts have long since vanished. It's consumed you, hasn't it?"

"Consumed? It's enlightened me. The scales have fallen from my eyes."

"So much so that you abandon reason and good judgment. You surround yourself with murderers and cutthroats, Hector. The Crowlords as brothers in arms? They're despised by their own mothers, let alone their neighbors!"

"A means to an end, Carver. Allegiances shift all the time."

"You've changed *your* allegiances more often than Ibal changes that bucket," he said, gesturing to the slop pot in the corner of the room. "Nobody will trust you before long, Hector. You've betrayed everyone you've ever sided with. You think the Crowlords trust you? They're killers. I'd be dead if they had their way; it's only your sick interest in my welfare that's kept me alive. No doubt Flint's already plotting how they can extricate you from their future regime."

"I don't trust them, either."

"But what way is that to live?" replied Carver. "Waiting for the knife to strike your back?"

"They need me as much as I need them. I need their eyes over the Whitepeaks, the soldiers of Riven who've marched into Icegarden. And the Crows would be lost without my Ugri and their knowledge of these frigid lands. They also appreciate the power I wield," Hector said, clicking the gloved fingers of his left hand.

Carver shivered. "*Presently* they may need you as much as you need them, but things can change quickly, Boarlord."

"Indeed, and with luck on my side I intend to see good

fortune swing my way before Flint and his brothers get a whiff of favor."

"So you're still torturing an old woman, just to find some relic that might not even exist?"

"The Wyrmstaff exists, and Freya knows its whereabouts. I just need to prize that information from her."

Carver laughed. "You make it sound like you're extracting a tooth! Why stop at tormenting her with your little demon? Why not work with the tried and tested methods of torture: broken bones and torn-out teeth?"

See, hissed the vile, boiling through the air in front of Hector, its black smoky body shimmering with sadistic excitement. *The bald thug's no fool. He appreciates my methods!*

"No!" shouted Hector, to his brother's spirit as much as the Thief Lord. He tore his hand through Vincent's ethereal form, the dark cloud that only he could see parting as his fingers ripped through it. "I won't harm her any further!"

Then you'll never find the Wyrmstaff, gloated the fading vile.

"Was that outburst for the benefit of me or your invisible friend?" asked Carver, shaking his head. "Why the obsession with some old staff from a time long gone? You've got what you wanted, haven't you? Wasn't it Icegarden you desired? Didn't you want the other Werelords to take you seriously? Not just the Lions and Catlords but your brethren from Lyssia: Bergan, Manfred, and Vega? I'm sure they've got the message by now."

"They'll all be accounted for. Your old acquaintance Vega's already dead, his body swallowed by the sea. My Ugri warriors will find Manfred and Queen Amelie and they'll join you in these cells soon enough. And getting Bergan to bend his knee before me is only a small part of what I desire. It's knowledge I seek."

"Knowledge of what? How it feels to be friendless? A betrayer of trust?"

"Arcane knowledge, Carver. An understanding of the building blocks of magick, power over life and death."

"Stop now, Hector, while a shred of sanity remains," replied the Thief Lord.

The magister smiled. "Don't worry about me, Carver. I haven't lost my mind: everything I do is based upon reason and deduction."

"You're deluded. I know my folklore, Boarlord: can't think of many tales of necromancers that have happy endings."

"Then it's time to write a new chapter into your storybook, Thief Lord," said Hector. "You know your letters, don't you? You can chronicle my exploits in your free time."

"This will end badly, Hector."

"Try not to fret, my friend," said Hector, standing. "It's my head that's on the block, not your tattooed work of art."

"If your Crowlord friends find your back with their knives, my head will roll, serpent and all."

"Then you'd better start praying fate's pendulum swings

my way, Carver." Hector walked to the door, pausing to turn back. "By the way, your protégée, the girl—Pick—lives. She didn't die that night when she escaped Icegarden."

"A morsel of good news," said Carver, nodding. "How do you know?"

Hector smiled. "I can't say, but I thought you'd want to know. I'm your guardian angel, Thief Lord—the only thing standing between you and those black-winged devils out there. Consider that next time you try to convince me of the error of my ways."

5

Banquet for a Bride

DEEP IN THE belly of the *Hellhound*, Whitley stared across the dining table at the vacant seat opposite. A plethora of plates and trays lay before her, laden with food, dishes and bowls loaded with roasted vegetables of every color, their smell intoxicating. An enormous portion of rare beef sat glistening on a giant platter. Abovedecks, running feet thundered, the occasional cloud of dust dislodged from the ceiling boards to drift down over the banquet. Behind her, the ship's elderly cook, Finch, busied himself in the shadows. Having shuttered all the portholes, he now wrestled with a bottle of wine, which finally released its hold on the cork with a satisfying *pop.* Finch reappeared at her side, reaching across the table to pour claret into the captain's goblet.

"Where's Deadeye?" asked Whitley, watching the wine glug into the cup. Her eyes caught sight of the golden key that hung from the cord around Finch's neck, her only means of escape from the cabin. Finch wasn't just her cook; he was her jailer, the Sharklord's eyes and ears when he was up top.

"The captain'll be with you shortly, m'lady," replied the cook, finishing his duties with the bottle.

"I asked where he was, Mister Finch. Why the runaround above? What's going on?"

"Sounds like we're under attack, m'lady," said the old man as he crept back into the shadows.

"Under attack?" she exclaimed, spinning to face him. "By whom?"

"Couldn't tell you, m'lady," said Finch. "I wouldn't worry, though. It's nighttime and the captain's a cunning soul. The enemy could sail within ten yards of the *Hellhound* and miss her. Black sails, black timbers, as black as hell itself. There's a reason she's painted the way she is."

"The windows—that's why you've shuttered them?"

"Blackout, m'lady," he replied, tapping his nose with a sly wink. "Best way of ensuring we ain't seen. Like I say, your husband's a smart old fish."

"He *isn't* my husband," Whitley snapped.

"Not yet, mistress, but that's surely just a matter of time, ain't it? You should be grateful for his lordship's attention. Once he delivers his shipment of silver weapons to King Lucas, you'll be all his; rumor has it his second port of call will be Sosha's temple for the wedding. A bride in spring—is there anything more lovely?"

Whitley glared at Finch, who grinned back. The prisoner wore another gaudy old hand-me-down dress from yesteryear, its musty stench disguised by a rich perfume. Apparently, it had belonged to Deadeye's mother in an age long gone. The fact that the Sharklord made Whitley wear the dresses added an extra level of creepiness to their encounters and further confirmed his disturbed state of mind to the girl. The chain around the Bearlady's throat was as good as a wedding ring, tying the young girl to the deranged pirate captain. She was at his mercy.

As the noise continued overhead, Whitley looked at the covered portholes, slats locking each in place. The old cook stood by the cabin door, watching her. Choked though she was by the loop of metal, she could still fight, and there were plenty of items close to hand that could be turned into weapons. But before she could act, there was a rap at the door. Finch stepped across and took the key from around his neck. Placing it into the lock, he gave it a twist and the door opened. Captain Deadeye appeared from the dark corridor beyond, stooping as he entered his staterooms.

"That'll be all, Mister Finch," said the captain. The cook bowed and disappeared through the opening, swinging the door shut behind him. Deadeye gave the key a turn and withdrew it from the mechanism before striding to the table.

Whitley watched as the towering sea captain moved to the chair opposite. He ducked as he sat, avoiding the wrought-iron lamp that swung from the roof, his huge misshapen head swooping beneath the lantern's passage. Tossing the key onto the table, he picked up a napkin and flapped it open. He gently placed it on his lap, smoothing it out before picking up his cutlery. Above, the bedlam continued, the creaking of decks and slamming of timbers threatening to dislodge the lamp or bring down the ceiling at any moment. Disregarding the din, Deadeye leaned forward, stabbing the beef with his fork and proceeding to carve a juicy red slice from it.

"You look beautiful this evening, my love," said the captain to Whitley.

She smiled demurely, staring at the empty feasting dish in front of her, as big as a shield. Everything about the captain's table was extreme. Even the cutlery was oversize and ungainly, the knife and forks closer to gardening tools than dining implements.

"My sweet, are you not eating?" asked Deadeye, carving himself a second and third slice of meat and slapping them onto his giant porcelain plate.

Whitley shivered, his endearing words like acid on her flesh. "I'm not hungry . . . my lord."

She had learned to at least feign respect for the captain during her stay aboard the *Hellhound.* That initial encounter when he'd collared her, challenging her to control the beast within, was just the start of her education at Deadeye's hands. He required total submission, utter obedience from the girl who was to be his wife. Whitley's bruised cheek was evidence enough of his brutal demeanor. The fight had soon gone from Whitley—at least outwardly—as she allowed the Sharklord to dominate her in all matters while she plotted her escape. From conversations over the dining table to the clothes she wore, Deadeye had final say on all things, and it pleased him greatly.

"Mister Finch went to a great deal of trouble to prepare this banquet for us. These are the spoils of the Garden of Lyssia, the finest produce from across the Dalelands. I would have assumed something here would whet your appetite," he said, cutting one of the steaks in two.

"Don't let me stop you; please help yourself, my lord," she replied meekly.

"To these vegetables?" he said scoffingly. His laughter was forced and guttural. Deadeye didn't strike Whitley as a man who laughed often. "Not really to my tastes, my love."

He jabbed a huge piece of beef with his fork and tossed it between his downturned lips. Whitley watched as the captain chomped away at it, jaws open all the while. She cleared her throat and smiled at him as he stabbed at the next piece of meat.

"I couldn't help but notice the commotion above," she said. "What's happened?"

Deadeye raised a thick forearm and smeared a bloody dribble of grease from his jaw. "Bosa's ships, three of them. If I had another boat, I'd take the fight straight to them, but we need to be cautious. Let them pass. I'll send a bird back to the sea fortress, call for reinforcements from Lord Ghul."

Whitley had heard mention of this fortress on numerous occasions since being captured. It was where the *Lucky Shot* was taken to, while the *Hellhound* kept her route for Highcliff. Those men in Violca's crew who had remained loyal to their mistress were clapped in irons in the belly of their own ship. Whitley had no idea of what awaited them at this fortress, clearly Ghul's base in the White Sea, but she suspected their fate would be unpleasant.

The events aboard the *Lucky Shot*, and what had followed, had put a purpose in Whitley's heart. The crew of the *Hellhound* had killed Drew, tossing his butchered body overboard. The rightful king of Westland—*her Drew*—had been cast into the ocean to be eaten by the fish. Deadeye had seen to the death of Violca himself. She'd heard as much in grotesque detail from Finch. Whitley was set on a course for revenge, against Deadeye, Lucas, Opal, all of them. Her heart was full of rage for those who had taken her loved ones from her. She'd make them pay for their murders.

"I thought the *Hellhound* was one of the mightiest ships of the White Sea, my lord," said Whitley, without a hint of sarcasm. "Is she not powerful enough to ambush them now? To strike out of cover of night and split their ranks?"

Deadeye stopped chewing for a moment, his black eyes leveled on the girl.

"The *Hellhound*'s a match for any ship, but three against one are odds I dislike. And we don't want to split them. No. We wait for them to pass; we call for assistance. We take all three of the Whale's ships rather than just one."

"Of course, my lord. I didn't mean to question your judgment. I'm sure you know best."

Deadeye grunted as he picked up another slice of meat, tearing it from his fork.

"We shall remain at a distance," he said, spitting food as he spoke. "I don't care to dine alone, my love. Please, eat."

Whitley rose from the table and straightened her skirts. Pushing the chair back, she picked up her plate, balanced it on one hand, and began to progress around the banquet. Deadeye reached forward again, sawing at the beef, the blood now driving him into a feeding frenzy, all decorum lost. He snarled as the meat separated, spilling its juices across the table. Whitley maneuvered closer to the captain, reaching tentatively toward the bowls and dishes with her clunky fork. She speared a trio of roast potatoes in quick succession before daintily depositing them onto her plate.

"How can you be sure those ships are Bosa's, my lord?

There are many who sail the White Sea. You could be mistaken, couldn't you?"

"Even from this distance and by starlight alone I recognize one of them," said Deadeye, smacking his greasy lips as he feverishly devoured the beef. She'd seen him feed this way before, the Sharklord getting gradually more distracted as he gorged on the barely cooked flesh.

"How did you recognize it?" Whitley asked, stabbing a floret of butter-drenched broccoli from its trough.

"It's the *Maelstrom*."

Whitley's knees buckled ever so slightly at mention of Vega's ship. Thankfully Deadeye was lost in his feeding, pupils rolling in their sockets as he made increasingly ecstatic noises with each mouthful.

"Count Vega's ship? Does this mean one of your most bitter enemies is nearby?"

She was well aware of what the Sharklords thought of one another, having heard firsthand just what Vega thought of Deadeye and the Werelords who served the Kraken. He felt nothing but hatred toward the Weresquid's allies, each of them having played their part in dethroning him, turning him out of Cutter's Cove as they sought favor from the old king Leopold.

Deadeye managed a spluttering laugh, almost choking on the meat as his downturned mouth threatened to turn up for a moment, revealing rows of lengthening teeth. "I know exactly where that sprat is, and he's not aboard the *Maelstrom*. No, Vega provides danger to nobody. Lord Ghul has my cousin in hand."

"Then who pilots the *Maelstrom*?" asked Whitley, placing the huge plate onto the table's edge beside the captain while she leaned across him. She grabbed a ladle and scooped peas and corn onto her dish. Unseen by Deadeye, she caught a stool from under the table with her foot, dragging it beneath the huge skirts before raising her heel onto it. Replacing the serving spoon, she picked up her fork again in one hand, the heavy plate in the other.

"Sosha only knows," said the Sharklord, his voice low and gurgling as he abandoned his cutlery to reach forward and rip great strips from the beef. "It's been missing for months. For it to turn up now suggests Vega still has friends out there. Friends of Vega's are friends of Bosa's. That makes them all enemies to me."

As the Sharklord's hands turned gray and clawed and dragged a huge piece of meat onto his plate, Whitley struck. She drove the fork down with all the strength she could muster, sinking it through Deadeye's right hand. The tines slipped between the bones and sliced out the other side. They proceeded to cut cleanly through the beef beneath before hitting the porcelain of his blood-spattered plate. The dish shattered into a dozen shards as the fork finally buried itself into the battered oak tabletop.

Deadeye's scream took a moment to come, a split second

as the pain raced to his brain and sent the alarm bells ringing, jarring him from his feeding frenzy. When the wail came Whitley had already jumped onto the table, launching herself up off the stool to land with a thud among the banquet. Her dish was in her white-knuckled hands, catching the Sharklord flat in the face. The plate exploded, leaving shrapnel studding the captain's head, jagged pieces of pottery pockmarking his flesh.

As Deadeye's head recoiled, the force of the blow sent therian and chair toppling backward, his features shifting fast. The only thing that stopped him from crashing onto the cabin floor was the giant fork pinning his hand to the table.

Whitley wasted no time, jumping up toward the lantern that swung from the ceiling, fully aware that the screaming master of the *Hellhound* was already lurching forward again, his furious face juddering as the shark surged to the fore. His jaw cracked, the mouth shifting into a gnashing maw of monstrous teeth. The bones of Deadeye's face shuddered as he morphed, forcing the darkening skin to go taut as it stretched over the Hammerhead's skull. The sharp nuggets of porcelain came flying from his flesh where they'd been embedded, exploding from the wounds like bolts from a crossbow. The Wereshark's ghastly eyes blinked on either side of his anvil-shaped head, leveling upon the girl who stood over him on the table.

The girl from Brackenholme was ready, screaming as she brought the heavy iron lamp down onto Deadeye's head. The glass shattered, crowning the Sharklord in a shower of flaming oil that raced over his skin from head to toe. Whitley snatched up the key from the tabletop before leaping clear of the burning Hammerhead. She landed in a tumble, skirts tripping her as she crashed toward the door, the room burning behind her. Forcing the key into the lock, she gave it a hard turn, the mechanism rattling as it cranked open. She glanced back as she swung the door open, seeing Deadeye rising from his chair, wreathed in orange fire. The enormous skirts caught in the door frame as the terrible Sharklord upturned the table and began to stride toward her, ignoring the flames that devoured his flesh. Whitley tore herself out of the dress, leaving the hideous outfit hanging from the threshold as she stumbled into the corridor in her slip, blind with terror.

6

Cry Wolf

"RIDICULOUS! SOLDIERS DON'T just *vanish*!" yelled Lord Hackett, rising from the throne and striking his captain with the back of his hand. The Crablord's heavy hand hit him like a shovel.

"How hard is it to fetch a one-handed boy from the work camp? How many men have you sent?"

The captain rubbed his jaw as he answered his master. "That's the third group we've sent in two days, with none to return. I'm not making this up, my lord. The work camp's no longer a safe place for the Krakenguard."

Hackett stamped toward the captain, causing the man to retreat down the steps of the dais, cowering from the Werelord. The throne room of Cutter's Keep, empty but for a handful of steel-helmed soldiers of the Squid, echoed with Hackett's footsteps. The Crablord's balding head glistened with sweat, the few remaining lengths of straggly red hair unfurling from where they were plastered against his scalp.

"Just listen to yourself, whimpering like a soiled bairn!" Hackett laughed. "That camp's full of *children*, Captain Flowers, weary ones at that. Nippers we've worked to the bone and beyond. Their parents are gone—mothers in chains, fathers in gallows. They're terrified of us. How in Sosha's name does that make 'em dangerous?"

"I can only tell you what I know, my lord," said Flowers, nervously standing his ground in the face of the furious Crablord. "Since Sergeant Callow went in there the day before last with that boy, we've sent two more groups in to find out what's happening, first four and then six men. None have returned. It's not about the one-handed boy anymore; this is about our men vanishing. That's thirteen of the Krakenguard gone, sir."

His men made the sign of Sosha behind him, a ritual that wasn't lost on Hackett.

"Cut the superstitious rubbish out right now. I'll give you all thirteen lashes if I see one more prayer!" He glared at Flowers. "Any sign of the boy who lured them in?"

"The one called Kit who said they were harboring the fugitive? None. The children drew rank yesterday and today, utterly uncooperative."

"Did you not whip 'em? Put 'em in the stocks and gibbets?"

"Some remain there presently, but none have anything to say. They know what's going on, but they all choose beatings over confession."

"Hang a few of 'em," said the Crab, turning his back and stomping back to his seat as he ran a hand over his threadbare scalp. "Do it where their siblings can see 'em, nice and high. That'll loosen their tongues."

"Furthermore," added Flowers, "the children didn't turn up for their work detail this evening."

Hackett stopped in his tracks. This was unheard-of. He'd been running Cutter's Cove since his liege, Lord Ghul, had taken to the White Sea. His regime had been brutal, his laws draconian, punishing the slightest misdemeanors with the whip, dismemberment, or death. This was the only language the children of pirates understood, and it had worked. Until now.

"What do you mean, they *didn't turn up*?" he asked incredulously.

"The foreman and the Krakenguard waited for them at the docks at dusk until the moon rose. None appeared."

"Then why did they not *fetch* them?" spat out Hackett, his face red with rage.

"The men, my lord," said the captain nervously. "They're . . . anxious. They fear something bad approaches. The omens are—"

Hackett's hand flew out, shifting as it slipped around Flowers's throat. By the time it closed, the broad pincers of the

Werecrab were ready to snip the captain's head from his body.

"Tell me one more old wives' tale, Captain, and so help me I'll—"

"My lord!" shouted a guard, flinging open the throne room doors and sending them slamming back on their hinges.

The man rushed along the dirty indigo carpet that ran the length of the chamber up to the granite dais. Hackett watched as the man approached, his battered helm under his arm and a stream of blood flowing from his head. He dropped to one knee and bowed, spilling claret onto the bottom step of the stone platform.

"Speak, man," said the Crablord irritably, removing his clawed hand from Flowers's throat and slapping him away.

"Cutter's Cove's under attack, my lord!"

Hackett could hear the noise now, beyond the tall arched windows that looked out over the cove. He strode over, Captain Flowers and the wounded soldier close behind.

"By whom?" said the Crablord as he looked down over the port. Torches raced through the street, the screams and cries of combatants steadily closing on the keep.

"The children, my lord," said the bloodied soldier. "The children attack!"

In happier times, the twisting streets of Cutter's Cove rang with laughter and music, the folk who called the city their home reveling in good fortune as they enjoyed the spoils of victory. The reach of the pirates was long, to Sturmland in the north and the Longridings in the south, few seafarers avoiding their attacks. No times had been more prosperous than when Count Vega, Pirate Prince of the Cluster Isles, sat on the throne, leading his men to sea on his dread ship, the *Maelstrom.* Here was a Werelord who led from the front, who inspired faith and courage in his men, tales of his escapades spreading throughout the world's oceans.

But times changed, as did those who sat on thrones. Now, with the shadow of the Squid cast over Cutter's Cove for long enough, the streets ran with blood, dark rivers winding between sea-slick cobbles. The sounds of merrymaking had been replaced by the screams and cries of the daring and dying as the young men and women who called this port home fought back against their oppressors. The children of Cutter's Cove were done with taking orders. They were battling back, and they would live free or die trying.

Boys and girls of all ages rushed up the myriad lanes and alleyways, running in packs, carrying makeshift weapons in their small fists—torches, staves, nets, and knives, items salvaged from their farm stores and fishing boats, tools that their enemies had trustingly placed in their hands. Now they turned them against the panicked soldiers of the Krakenguard, overpowering the Squidlord's lazy warriors with their sheer numbers.

Leading the charge up the main street were the hardiest youths. Of the older boys ready to follow their fathers into a life of piracy, none were louder or more ferocious than Gregor, enraged by his young brother Kit's death. He swung a club around his head, his fellow fighters keeping their distance for fear of being clobbered. When the squid-helmed soldiers of the Krakenguard appeared in the street he made a beeline for them, driven by rage and revenge. Following close behind came his friends, keeping the soldiers back with pitchfork and staff while their companions overpowered them.

Two other figures picked the fastest route through the city as they made straight for Cutter's Keep. The boy known as Skipper was spry, but even he struggled to keep up with Drew Ferran. The young Wolflord sought out every foe he could find, doing his utmost to attract his enemies' attention and draw their blows. The last thing he'd wanted was for the brave boys and girls to be butchered. He held the beast at bay as he shouted and screamed, calling for the Krakenguard and luring them in. He had to—if they saw a Werewolf bounding up the lane toward them, they'd flee from the fight, picking their battles with the little ones instead. This was the only way.

The Squid's men came readily, confident their armor and shields would be enough. But the half-blind, one-handed boy was proving far more able than any imagined. Calling upon all that his adoptive father Mack Ferran and the Staglord Duke Manfred had taught him, Drew fought for his life and those of the youngsters around him. He listened to his enemies' footsteps as their boots hit the ground. He dodged blows, rolled beneath swipes, swerved around lunges, kicking and lashing out with bare feet and hand. This was his only concession to the wolf: at his finger- and toe-tips, thick dark claws had emerged, tearing through armor and finding the flesh of his enemies by the light of the stars overhead.

"Turn your bows on those two!"

The captain on the gatehouse grabbed two archers and almost shoved them over the parapets as he pointed out Drew and Casper. The boys leapt over a freshly felled soldier, the sixth man to fall to Drew already that night. That put the figure to a round dozen Krakenguard he'd dispatched in the last couple of days. Gregor and the other more vicious, vengeful youths had taken care of the rest who'd visited the camp, looking for their comrades and the poor, misguided Kit. It saddened Drew that it had taken the child's death to galvanize the work camp and confirm Gregor as his ally.

"Stay back, Casper," shouted Drew as he snatched up the fallen guard's sword and tossed him the man's shield. Casper caught the shield just as the bows sang. Two projectiles whistled through the air, one hitting the shield dead center as Casper brought it up before him. The second flew straight for Drew, but the lycanthrope was ready. Close as he was to the keep now, he allowed the wolf to the fore. He'd drawn the mass of attacks in the streets. He was where he wanted to be, knocking at Hackett's gate, the doors closed, the portcullis lowered.

The stolen sword flashed, the flat of the blade catching the arrow in midflight and deflecting it.

"Sweet Sosha!" gasped Casper, amazed at his friend's dexterity, and more besides. "You saw the arrow? Your eyesight's returned?"

Drew didn't answer, growling where he crouched, dark hairs racing across his bulging flesh. The youth from the Cold Coast was growing, his back arching as his physique changed. His sight was returning incrementally, but the wolf's other senses, heightened above and beyond those of a human, helped to compensate for his poor vision.

"Wait for the gates," snarled the Werewolf as he leapt into action, leaving Casper behind in the street.

Drew took to the air in a giant bound, landing upon the creaking awning of a ramshackle inn. His next leap took him onto the shingles of the neighboring building. The third leap propelled him through the air, across the road toward the gatehouse, sword scything down. The gate captain took the blade down his torso, almost cleft in two, while the two bowmen turned and screamed in horror at the Werewolf. Drew's jaws snapped and his feet lashed out, biting and kicking at the archers as bows, fingers, and hands clattered onto the rooftop.

Craning over the crenulations, Drew looked down into the courtyard. The odd soldier ran by, shouting fearfully. Jumping down into the courtyard, Drew landed on powerful lupine legs. The guard who worked the gate mechanism stood with his back to him, looking out through the gate via a slatted window. He turned as he heard the Werewolf land, his cry cut short as the lycanthrope skewered him to the wooden door by the sword and left him hanging. Drew took hold of the wheel, pulling hard, the chains above rattling as the portcullis rose and the gates swung open.

"Wolf!"

Drew looked up from the wheel, back toward the keep. A group had emerged, seven in all, six squid-helmed soldiers of the Krakenguard flanking a balding man in a garish rose-gold breastplate. The man pointed as he marched imperiously down the steps, a confident swagger to his gait. The elaborate crab sigil on his broad, shining chest told Drew all he needed to know.

"Who'd have thought it?" Lord Hackett laughed as he gesticulated to his men to fan out. "While half the known world is out looking for your rotten corpse, you walk right into my city, son of Wergar, allowing me the pleasure of taking your sorry life."

The Krakenguard moved quickly, encircling Drew, swords and shields raised.

"You'd be the bottom-feeder I've heard about, then?" growled the Werewolf.

Hackett chortled. "Good things, I hope?"

Hackett flexed his arms and Drew watched in grim wonder as the man began to change. The golden armor groaned under the strain of the Crablord's shifting body, his torso ballooning as hard, rigid plates of red shell filled the gaps between the sheets of steel. Hackett wobbled as he rose, his legs extending, almost skeletal and spiderlike as they lifted him higher from the ground. His flesh turned the same rouge tone, warty lesions appearing across his toughening, bony exterior. Hackett threw his head back to emit a gurgling cry, his mouth tearing open like some terrible bug, revealing twisting, hinged jaws that worked with an unnatural life of their own. The arms cracked and creaked, growing to awful proportions, forearms disappearing to be replaced by a pair of enormous, lethal pincers. Each was the size of a full shield, the long, serrated edges clicking together menacingly as the Werecrab scuttled toward the Werewolf.

Drew crouched low as the Crablord surged up to him, an open claw arcing over his head and snapping at thin air. The Wolf's leg flew out, striking the shin of one of its spindly legs, but the blow bounced off, the gnarled skin impenetrable. As another pincer came down, Drew swept his other foot about, taking the Crab's armored leg out from under it. Hackett went down on one knee as the Wolf jumped forward, between the Crab's arms, inside the monster's reach. Drew searched for a weak spot, a soft place where the armored hide didn't protect the creature. The Crablord's bald head twisted, extending from within its shell-covered shoulders, scrawny neck supporting the misshapen mass. Drew's teeth snapped at its face, the hideous mouth biting back, a mess of hinged teeth that moved independently of one another. A clawed hand caught the back of Drew's neck, squeezing hard and causing him to cry out. Keeping hold, Hackett raised the Wolf in the air and smashed him onto the floor of the courtyard. Holding the lycanthrope in place in its clawed grip, the Crablord raised its other limb, pincers twitching menacingly as it let out a gurgling roar of triumph.

As Hackett was about to strike, a roar rose from the city. A horde of children spilled through the mighty doors like a tidal wave, weapons held high and voices soaring. Some wore the scale mail they'd stolen from the Krakenguard, while others carried shields scavenged from the soldiers. Many had switched pitchfork for shortsword, staff for ax, as they flooded the courtyard. The six men who had stayed by Hackett's side turned and ran, dashing back toward the keep. While half of the mob went after them, the rest rushed to the Werewolf's aid, throwing pebbles, rocks, sticks, and stones at the Werecrab.

Hackett wavered as the missiles bombarded him. Drew seized the moment, snatching the elbow of the Crablord and gripping with all his might. Finally the skin relented, his claws disappearing into the flesh and sending pink froth bubbling from the joint. Hackett released his hold on the lycanthrope with a bellow before raising both pincers to rain hammer blows down. Drew kicked out, trying to roll one way and the other, but found himself trapped by the Crab's skeletal legs. Each impact sent tremors ringing through him, his therian bones resisting the initial onslaught as his flesh was pummeled, but he had little fight left in his body. Another blow might crush him at any moment.

Before the claws could come down in one more fatal flurry, two figures flashed past Drew. Casper raced alongside the monster, a shortsword in his hands, the blade clattering off the beast's spindly leg. Gregor leapt through the air, a Krakenguard's helm on his head, his club coming down to clang against Crablord's golden breast. It was enough to distract Hackett from his assault on Drew as he briefly lashed out at both boys. Casper was backhanded into the crowd, while the pincers caught hold of Gregor's shoulder. The boy was raised and shaken, his helm tumbling loose as he cried out. Hackett brought his other arm around, opening the awful bladed limb as it neared the boy.

"Drew!"

Risking her life between the Crab's stamping feet stood Pearl. She thrust something out to the stunned lycanthrope. It was the handle of a weapon with a white orb for a pommel. He recognized it immediately and reached out a battered hand.

The moon might not have been full, but the light was

enough to pour power into the ancient enchanted blade. Moonbrand shone white as Drew swung the longsword up, the weapon illuminating the Crablord as it sheared through its free arm. The taloned limb crashed to the floor, the stump of its elbow pumping blood and foaming froth. Gregor was instantly released, landing with a thump as the Werecrab snapped and slashed at the Werewolf, its scream high-pitched and chilling. Its coordination was gone, the shock of the amputated claw sending it into a blind fury. The children peeled back as Drew rolled clear, hugging the ground, waiting for another opportunity.

Moonbrand flew out again, this time cutting one of Hackett's legs out from under him, sending him onto his back. The Crablord rocked and rolled on his broad, round body, trying to right himself but finding no purchase with the ground. Its black eyes looked up, grotesque jaws yammering obscenities at the children who had gathered around it. Gregor stood over its head, holding something high and bringing it down with all his might. The severed claw of Lord Hackett, Crablord of the Cluster Isles and Steward of Cutter's Cove, fell down around his exposed neck, the pincers that had been his own weapon decapitating him like a guillotine.

Drew jabbed Moonbrand's tip into the earth for support, pushing himself up off his knees until he stood on tired legs. The children stared at their slain overseer while the terrified cries of his minions broke the night around them.

"This is no time to stand around," shouted Casper. "There's still work to be done!"

"To our brothers' and sisters' aid!" added Gregor as the crowd headed for the keep and the walls to see off the remaining Krakenguard.

A handful of children remained, the youngest who had survived the ordeal, gathered around Pearl. Drew lifted Moonbrand and flicked the Crablord's blood from the white blade. He smiled wearily at the girl through clouded eyes.

"Your brother said my sword was lost." He turned to the keep, ready to see the battle to its grim end.

"What can I say, my lord," said the girl as she hugged the small children around her. "We're pirates. Thieving's in our blood."

7
Locking Horns

HOLDING ON TO the rope with white knuckles, Whitley braced for impact. Over the roar of cannon fire and the cries of sailors, another noise joined the din. A wail as terrible as a banshee's sounded as the sleek gray ship that had flanked the *Hellhound* finally collided with Captain Deadeye's burning hulk. Whitley glanced down from the rigging. She watched as the jostling ships crashed against one another, the hulls screaming as they scraped and splintered. Pirates tumbled from each ship as the giants locked horns, shockwaves shuddering throughout both vessels. Ropes and grapples flew across from the attacking crew, finding purchase in the masts and decks of the *Hellhound* as the second and third ship drew ever closer.

Whitley's heart soared as the men of the *Maelstrom* prepared to swing across.

Whitley edged along the rigging of the mainmast, climbing ever higher, away from the clamor below. The fires that raged in the belly of the ship, quickly racing through the vessel, were her handiwork. The crew of the *Hellhound* ripped open a crate in the middle of the deck, revealing stacks of silver swords bound for Highcliff. The men whipped out the weapons, readying themselves for whoever boarded the privateer. Vega might have been under lock and key at the Kraken's sea fortress, but there were other deadly Werelords who'd sailed with him.

The Bearlady clambered onto the topmast, snatching hold of the wooden rungs that would carry her away from the unfolding battle below. If she could reach the topsail's yard, she might find somewhere where she could sit the fight out, safe from harm. With Deadeye's silver chain still around her throat, she had no chance to transform, no opportunity to call upon the bear. She'd dashed up from belowdecks, hugging the shadows en route to the mainmast. As the flames had licked the ship's aft from the captain's cabin, the *Maelstrom* and her sister ships had swiftly given chase. By the time Whitley had begun her ascent, Vega's ship had already engaged the *Hellhound*, each craft unloading its cannons into the other, payloads of blasting powder exploding in both their bellies. Whitley would pick her moment—leap into the sea if need be—to try to reach the

Maelstrom. But she wouldn't die aboard the Hammerhead's ship, and she wouldn't become his bride.

As if on cue, the hatch door burst open on the aft deck, a black cloud billowing around the emerging Sharklord. Whitley paused, eyes fixed on the monstrous Deadeye as he shook his head, gray skin blistered open, white flesh sizzling from the flames. His entire body was wreathed in oily smoke, shadowing his every movement. His beady black eyes scoured the deck, ignoring the battle that was now under way. Pirates from the *Maelstrom* had boarded the *Hellhound*, cutlasses clashing as they met with defenders. Another deafening roar split the air as the ships crunched into one another, skittling sailors as the *Hellhound* pitched hard to port, almost flinging Whitley from the topmast to the deck below. A shriek flew from her lips. The Bearlady clung to a rung with one hand, the other trailing helplessly at her side as the *Hellhound* lurched upright once again, her hull crumpling as the *Maelstrom* bullied and bashed her. Looking down, Whitley spied the Sharklord's eye fixed on her as she flailed overhead.

As Whitley kicked her legs out, wrapping one around the topmast, Deadeye stomped across the deck of his blazing ship. Any sailor from either ship who got in his way caught the brunt of his fury, his jaws biting and clawed hands raking as he ripped a bloody path through the battle. He reached the mast's base as the girl climbed higher, her heart pounding. Whitley's muscles burned as she ascended, her body weak after having spent what felt like forever imprisoned in the cabin.

Reaching over the main topsail, Whitley threw a leg over the yardarm and hauled herself onto the beam. She faced down the topmast toward the deck, her stomach heaving when she saw the Hammerhead racing up the mainmast toward her. He was fast and sure-footed, used to moving aboard a pitching ship. Whitley didn't trust the mast and its rungs; the rigging felt more familiar, like the swinging walkways that filled the Great Oak back in Brackenholme. Snatching hold of a rope, she dragged herself upright and reached onto the rigging. She edged along the topsail yardarm, her bleeding fingers gripping the netted rope hard. As she stepped onto the web, she saw a gray, clawed hand emerge on the topmast.

"Stay where you are!"

Whitley looked around frantically, unsure of where the voice had come from. It wasn't Deadeye, of that much she was certain.

"We're coming to you!"

She looked starboard toward the *Maelstrom*, where a pair of men had worked their way along their own mizzenmast, drawing closer to the *Hellhound* as their yards and sails collided. One of the men was old, with a sharp gray goatee beard and twirling mustache. The other by his side was younger, a scarf bound around his head, cutlass in mouth. The youth leapt from his ship's mizzenmast, flying through the air and snatching hold of a trailing rope from the *Hellhound*'s mainmast. By the time he'd landed, Deadeye was on the topsail yard, standing between girl and young pirate.

The smoldering Hammerhead's black pupils blinked as it regarded its foes, its sagging downturned mouth threatening to form a grin.

"In a hurry to meet Sosha, boy?"

The lad took the cutlass from his mouth and edged along the yardarm.

"Worry about yourself, Deadeye," he replied, his voice thick with fear.

"Please," cried Whitley. "Stay back! He's a monster!"

The young man advanced, ignoring her plea.

"Wait for me, Hob!" cried the old man from the *Maelstrom* as he swung across, snatching hold of the rigging, but the youth continued.

"Well, well, well," called Deadeye as the fight continued beneath them. "Captain Eric Ransome, as I live and breathe. They made you captain of the *Maelstrom*, then? You going to send this ship to the ocean bed, too? Got quite a reward on that dusty old head of yours since you turned on the Kraken. Pity I won't be able to present it to Ghul when I've swallowed it!"

"Take your best bite, Hammerhead," cried the old sailor as his feet landed on the yardarm. "I guarantee you'll choke on it!"

Ransome's footing was unsteady, the old pirate losing balance and slipping from the end of the beam. He caught hold of the long length of timber, hanging high over the churning waters between the two ships. Hob edged forward, his free hand snatching at trailing ropes for support as he traversed the yard like a tightrope. In his other hand he held his cutlass out, leveled at the enormous Wereshark.

"Please don't!" shouted Whitley, one last hopeful cry to the brave young sailor.

"Quit screeching, my love," said Deadeye without looking back. "I'll get to you in good time."

With the ship lurching, Hob seized his moment. He jumped forward, slashing vertically down at the Hammerhead, but Deadeye stepped back, effortlessly evading the youth. Another blow whipped back the other way, the Sharklord sucking his gut in as the blade ripped a line through his flesh. The monster laughed.

"You board the *Hellhound* and haven't the sense to bring *silver weapons*?"

The youth hung back for a moment, not responding. The Wereshark's laughter suddenly ceased as a clawed hand went to the wound on his stomach.

Hob spat into the wind, clearing his throat. "Tastes bad enough to a human, but Sosha knows how it feels in your guts."

"What was on that blade?" bellowed the Hammerhead as he tore and scratched at his stinging torso.

"It ain't silver," shouted Hob as he readied his cutlass. "But the captain reckons it's the next best thing. That's *wolfsbane*,

Deadeye, with just a hint o' rum! Let me guess which part you don't like!"

Whitley had to admire the inventiveness of Ransome's men. The herb, harmless to humans, was potentially deadly to a therianthrope: steel blessed with wolfsbane was the next best thing to silver. Unfortunately for Hob, his gloating was premature. He was laughing as the enraged Hammerhead leapt forward, his giant gray arms crossed before him. The cutlass came up but too slowly, the seaman lost in his moment of victory. As the claws flew back in either direction, one hand connected with Hob's shoulders, the other with his hips. Deadeye grabbed and ripped, tearing the brave youth into two bloody pieces, sending both tumbling into the melee below.

"No!" screamed Whitley as she clung to the ropes, the sails painted red.

"Silence, *my love*!" roared Deadeye as he briefly turned his haggard head her way.

Whitley could see his black eyes were swollen, bulging from his melted face, blood pouring from the sockets and the corners of his mouth. The wolfsbane was coursing through his body—Brenn knew how much damage it was doing, but clearly not enough: he was still standing, stamping along the yardarm toward the struggling Captain Ransome.

"You belong on the seabed with the other old wrecks, Captain," the Hammerhead said, wheezing, as he halted above the dangling veteran. "You should've gone down with the *Leviathan* when Vega scuttled you off Vermire!"

"Vega showed me there's more to a man's life than following orders, Deadeye," shouted Ransome as he clutched the yardarm in one hand. Below, the fight was reaching its terrible climax as the fires raged out of control.

Deadeye grabbed hold of the rigging and leaned down over the end of the beam, smacking his smoking lips as he revealed his terrible teeth. Ransome's free hand shot up, a dagger flying straight for the Hammerhead's throat. The Sharklord was too quick, snatching the old captain by the forearm as the blade's progress juddered to a halt a hair's breadth from his spoiled skin. Deadeye shook the man's wrist, the dagger falling into the night. He yanked Ransome into the air, rising as the *Hellhound* pitched forward into the sea, a great wave washing over the burning decks below and knocking all from their feet. The salt water sluiced through the vessel, rushing through the sundered hatches to flood the hold. Crates and cargo, lashed above and below, ripped free from where they were housed, crashing into the battling pirates.

A rope lashed Whitley, striking like a whip as it tore free from the topgallant mast. She looked up, spying the hemp's end where it was secured to the crow's nest. As the *Hellhound* rolled back, her foredecks rising high over the pounding waves, Whitley reached out and caught hold of it. She wound the rope around her wrists and braced herself as the ship tipped back, hard to aft, then she leapt from the beam.

"Give my regards to Sosha!" snarled Deadeye as he clutched the rigging in one hand, bringing Ransome toward his jaws.

The Hammerhead looked back at the last moment, instincts suddenly alerting it to the danger it was in, but it was too slow. Whitley emerged through the smoke, feet first, as the rope carried her through the sky above the *Hellhound*. Keeping her legs locked, she aimed her heels at the Sharklord's head. Both connected with an almighty crunch, splintering cartilage as Deadeye was catapulted from the topsail yardarm. Ransome spun in the air, tumbling past the topsail rigging. As the ship crashed back down into the sea, the Hammerhead fell, limbs snatching at thin air as he plummeted to the deck. Awaiting his descent was the open crate of silvered weapons, their glistening blades pointing to the stars. The monstrous captain of the *Hellhound* landed in a thunderous explosion of blood and metal.

The rope hit the mast, bouncing Whitley loose, the hemp ripped from her grasp. She tumbled, the world turning, darkness and fire around her as she followed Deadeye toward the deck. Her hands were snared suddenly, jarring her in midfall, her arms nearly tearing from their sockets as two firm hands held her by the wrists. She looked up, the weathered, drawn face of Captain Ransome looking down at her as he hung upside down from the topsail rigging.

"Hold on, girl," said the pirate, teeth gritted beneath gray whiskers. "I've got you."

8

The King's Justice

"I WOULD ASK you to reconsider, my lord. This seems an unnecessary risk."

General Vorhaas stood in the heart of Redmire Hall's entrance chamber, arms outstretched as his squire attached his ailettes. The Ratlord looked resplendent in his armor, the breastplate dark as night. His smile was confident, his mood relaxed, as Major Krupha paced anxiously by the great doors. Beyond the threshold, the sound of the assembled townsfolk was a constant rumble as the Lionguard marshaled the crowd. The entire population of the Boarlord capital was present, along with those from the surrounding farms and hamlets. Vorhaas was determined that none would miss the spectacle he had planned.

"You worry too much, Krupha," replied the Wererat, clenching his fist as the squire snapped the buckles on his second jet-black arm guard.

"The rebel attacks were on the rise for weeks," said the major. "For them to suddenly cease a few days ago? I don't like it. This signals something, an attack perhaps."

"It signals that their morale is broken," said Vorhaas, lowering his arms as his squire checked the straps around his suit. Like all the armor worn by the Werelords, the outfit was fashioned to grow with the metamorphosis, to shift as the therianthrope changed.

"You really think that?" asked Krupha. "What victorious act of ours broke their backs, exactly? For the life of me I couldn't tell you!"

"A few minor triumphs on some barely manned outposts hardly signals a change in the tide of war, Krupha," replied Vorhaas scoffingly.

"They attacked my retinue on the Low Dale Road, in broad daylight!"

The Ratlord turned and smiled sympathetically.

"I understand you must carry a sense of . . . shame for what transpired that day, Krupha, but you weren't at fault."

The major's skin prickled at the Ratlord's well-placed comment. The two had an understanding, born from fighting alongside one another in the name of the Lion king. Vorhaas knew how heavily the guilt weighed on Krupha's shoulders since the major had ridden hard back to Redmire on that fateful day, the sole survivor of his troop.

"There were thirty soldiers in my company, my lord. None were recovered, all presumed dead. The ambush was well coordinated; we're not talking about a gang of peasants throwing stones. These so-called Harriers were well drilled and disciplined. Of course I blame myself."

"Blame your hapless Lionguard for not scouting the road in a proper fashion, Krupha. You and I both know they're rabble, unfit to serve in a military force. Once we get today's ceremony out of the way, send word north to Onyx. Inform him I want some brave men of Vermire or Goldhelms from Bast sent down here, to bolster this army with some real military might. I'm sure my brother War Marshal Vorjavik didn't settle for second-rate soldiers."

Vorhaas jutted his jaw out as the squire finished adjusting the armor.

"Try not to let your misplaced concerns spoil a splendid day, Krupha. If any of these Harriers are still active in the Dalelands, today's execution should be a timely reminder of who rules this realm."

Vorhaas marched across to Krupha and extended his hand. The major took it, always impressed by the sheer might of the Ratlord's grip.

"Don't be getting cold feet now, Major. They're on the run. You should be able to enjoy a day such as this. Try not to fret."

Krupha bowed but remained silent as the general stepped in front of the doors, his right hand held out. The squire staggered up, carrying a long, half-moon ax before him in both arms. The Ratlord snatched it one-handed, shifting it lightly in his grip as if it were a toy. The major didn't share his commander's sentiments, but Vorhaas was in good spirits, and he wouldn't want anything to dampen them. The general's weekly ritual on the scaffold had become something of a tradition in Redmire, as the most heinous criminals were dragged up to the block to taste the Wererat's justice.

Vorhaas raised the ax and banged its heavy head against the entrance three times. The doors opened, the bright light of a fine spring day flooding the hall and illuminating the Werelord in all his finery. Vorhaas marched onto the wooden steps that rose from the street to the Boarlord mansion. Two Redcloaks held the doors open as the acting lord of the Dalelands marched down to the dusty street. A dozen crimson-caped soldiers flanked his route as he strode toward the scaffold that had made its home in the town square. Beyond the Lionguard stood the assembled people of Redmire, crowded into the street with more Redcloaks at their back.

Major Krupha had yet to return to Hedgemoor since the attack on the Low Dale Road, extending his stay in Redmire while he recovered. He just needed to get this day out of the way with, before acquiring a handful of the general's better outriders to accompany him back to Hedgemoor. Krupha had witnessed the ruthless efficiency with which the Harriers had ambushed his men. He wouldn't underestimate them again.

As the general stamped up the wooden steps of the scaffold, the brisk rap of a drummer's batons accompanied the Ratlord's progress. Krupha remained on the mansion's porch, his eyes fixed upon the crowd. A sea of bowed heads spread out before him, the eyes of Redmire fixed firmly on the ground. He estimated there were well over a thousand present, filling the square and the streets that led into it. This was far more than Krupha had wanted, but it was what Vorhaas had demanded. Every man, woman, and child was forced to attend. Previous executions had barely entertained an audience, only a handful of those sympathetic to their new masters. But the Ratlord wanted all the people to see firsthand what any attempts at revolution would bring them.

Krupha looked up at the sun, sitting high over the rolling hills that loomed north of the town. Noon: now was the time. His gaze passed over the busy rooftops that surrounded the square, terra-cotta tiles, timbers, and thatches jammed together higgledy-piggledy. The major scratched his frequently broken nose nervously, eyes narrow as he inspected the skyline. He turned back to the pair of Redcloaks who stood to attention beside the double doors.

"You two have a fine vantage point here. Keep your eyes fixed on the crowd at all times. Any sudden movements, let me know."

The Lionguard grunted their acknowledgment as the major looked back to the scaffold. He shook his head as he watched the townsfolk, wishing once again he was back in Hedgemoor. *Things must be bad,* he thought, *if I'm pining for the Fox city and not Braga. Stupid peasants. If only they knew just how powerful they were: they outnumber us fifty to one. If they had a backbone we'd be in trouble.*

"Come on, Vorhaas," Krupha muttered out loud, in earshot of the Redcloaks. "Let's get this charade done with."

A box wagon rolled out of the garrison building beside the mansion house, led by a pair of shire horses. A single driver rode the bench up front, the wooden cell bouncing at his back, its contents safely under lock and key. Six Redcloaks pushed the crowd apart as the wagon drove forward toward the scaffold, their pikes prompting the townsfolk to break before them like waves on a ship's prow.

Krupha shook his head as cries came from the mob, the people crushed against one another, the Lionguard and prison wagon forcing their way through their midst. *This could have been done behind closed doors. His head on a spike would've served the same purpose.*

"People of Redmire," shouted Vorhaas, turning slowly on the scaffold as he addressed the audience. "Lift your faces so I may be graced by your full attention!"

Right on cue the soldiers at the front of the crowd began to poke and jab the civilians. Within moments the panicked assembly were all looking Vorhaas's way, their anxiety rising.

"You're all aware of the punishments I've meted out over the past few months," continued the Ratlord. "Those who break the king's law face the king's justice." He raised the ax in the air to drive home the point before allowing it to fall with a *thunk* into the executioner's block.

"It gives me no pleasure to carry out these acts," Vorhaas lied. "This is a necessity, the only way we show the miscreants and rabble-rousers who would sow unrest in the Dalelands that their acts of terrorism and lawlessness will not be tolerated. These 'Harriers of Hedgemoor' seem to have garnered a foolish following in some quarters of this realm. Well, let me tell you: should news of anyone's sympathy with these villains reach my ears, the same fate will befall you as that which awaits today's prisoner."

He turned to the wagon as it rolled to a halt at the foot of the scaffold.

"Bring him out!"

The driver jumped around to the back of his vehicle, unlocking the box wagon's door. He stood to one side as a Lionguard emerged from within, leading a manacled man out after him, a bag bound around his head. Krupha allowed himself a smile. It had been quite the coup capturing the man, a rare victory for the Lionguard in the Dalelands. Much loved by the people of Redmire, he'd been the man the Harriers had rallied around when they'd first formed, a symbol of happier times when a Boarlord sat on the throne. Krupha and Vorhaas only hoped the man's execution would sound the death knell of the band of brigands.

The prisoner was led up the steps and onto the platform as the crowd's nervous murmurs began to build in pitch. Some in the crowd no doubt knew who the man was—Krupha could almost hear the man's whispered name flitting from lips to ear throughout the throng—but most were unaware of who was about to be executed. The Lionguard had caught him a week previously, the fortuitous words of a snitch directing the Redcloaks to the man's next attack.

General Vorhaas stepped up and whipped the hood from the prisoner's head.

"I give you Captain Lars Gerard, leader of the rogues known as the Harriers of Hedgemoor and enemy of the free people of Lyssia."

The gasp went up around the square. Curses and cries were thrown at the scaffold as the Lionguard momentarily had a fight on their hands. Some of the townsfolk surged forward, horrified by the sight of one of their own, a man so highly regarded, manacled and about to kneel before the block. This was too easy for the Redcloaks, the soldiers jabbing with pike, spear, and sword as the peasants fell onto their blades. The panic didn't die down, instead reaching new heights as the crowd now tumbled back, clambering over one another to avoid the sadistic Lionguard.

Krupha shook his head wearily. For all Vorhaas's love of pomp and ceremony, he was failing to see the bigger picture. Gerard, the former captain of Baron Huth's house guard, was a symbol of hope for these people so long as he was alive. Snuffing out that life would break the back of their resistance. But dangling him here before them, alive, invited chaos to erupt at any moment. The major placed his hand on his sword hilt, rattling it in his scabbard.

"Be alert," he said to the guards behind him. "This could turn ugly."

As if in response to his words, Vorhaas released a full-throated bellow, a screeching roar that echoed around the square and commanded everyone's attention.

The dark armor groaned as the therianthrope's torso expanded and elongated, his legs and arms thickening as he shook his ax in the air. His head seemed to buckle and fold in on itself, the top of his skull broadening and flattening. His flesh rippled as oily black hairs split the skin, erupting from every inch of his body. His jaws visibly dislocated as he threw his head back, his tongue lolling out swollen and fat as his neck ballooned and trembled. A snarling snout ripped forth, jagged teeth interlocking over one another as the Wererat's jaws clapped with monstrous delight.

Vorhaas now stood nine feet tall, squat legs apart supporting his lengthy frame. The onlookers screamed, even the Lionguard in awe of the transformed Ratlord. The mighty ax was now far more deadly, the strength of a transformed Wererat more than triple that of a man. Krupha had seen Vorhaas's act before; it held no mystique for him. His eyes were on the rooftops, where he briefly caught sight of a Redcloak moving from one building to another, bow in hand. He turned to the soldiers behind.

"Tell me, do we have any men on the rooftops?"

"No, sir, not that I'm aware of. They're all at street level."

Krupha looked back, searching for the figure again. He didn't see the same one, but he did spy another Redcloak on a roof a hundred yards farther around the square, sheltering in the shade of a chimney stack. This one also had a longbow raised, by the look of it. Old as the major was, his eyesight was still good, as was his knowledge of what the Lionguard were equipped with. Crossbows were the standard issue of the Redcloaks—longbows were unheard-of.

It came to Krupha just as the attack commenced. The thirty Lionguard he'd lost on the Low Dale Road, not a body to be found: their armor, their shields, their swords—their *red cloaks*—all gone. How could they have been such fools? How could the pathetic soldiers, this poor excuse of an army he'd been forced to work with, been so lax? They'd gifted the Harriers with disguises, and the outlaws had leapt upon the opportunity.

A flurry of missiles whistled down from the roofs into carefully picked Redcloaks, triggered by two of the Lionguard leaping for the scaffold toward the changing General Vorhaas, his back presently turned to them. One was ahead of the other, the cloak fluttering free to reveal a girl who was now all too familiar to Krupha, her long red hair trailing as she bounded toward the Wererat. With each step she changed, her skin shifting to a shimmering russet coat as the Werefox emerged. She leapt high as Vorhaas turned, alerted to the drama unfolding at his back by the startled faces in the crowd.

She landed on his head, limbs enveloping his jaws and pinning them shut. Gretchen wrapped herself around the Wererat's long skull, squeezing tight as Vorhaas threw his head this way and that, trying in vain to shake her loose. Gerard leapt clear into the crowd, quickly enveloped by the mob. The frantic Vorhaas brought the ax back and made to scythe at her, only for the second faux Redcloak to get in his way, deflecting the blow with a deft parry of a shining longsword. *Silver,* realized Krupha with dread as the crowd boiled over into an outright uprising.

Before the Ratlord could launch another desperate attack, the young, blond Harrier with the sword lunged in, the Werefox still clinging to the general's head. The blade disappeared into a gap in the Wererat's elaborate armor beneath the armpit. General Vorhaas, acting lord of the Dalelands, crashed to the scaffold like a felled tree as the Werefox girl sprung gracefully from his body, the longsword still stuck through his chest. Lady Gretchen of Hedgemoor turned her attention to Redmire

Hall as her companion bent to retrieve the Wolfshead blade from the slain Wererat. The two stared at Krupha over the sea of cheering townsfolk as the guards behind him disappeared into the mansion.

Not for the first time, Krupha ran.

PART IV

BATTLING BACK

I

The Sea Fortress of the Kraken

LIKE A TWISTED wooden spear erupting from the ocean, Ghul's sea fortress reached high into the gloomy heavens, defying the wind and waves of the White Sea. Around its base, a multitude of craft gathered, lashed to one another and the tower itself. Piers and pontoons branched out from the structure, the twisted spokes on a broken wagon wheel, covering the surface of the sea. Dusk cast her dark shawl over the ramshackle taverns that crowded the jetties, Ghul's men making merry within.

The drink-fueled din wasn't the only noise that filled the air. The cries of Ghul's prisoners floated down from the walls high overhead. More than fifty men remained lashed to the fortress or suspended from gibbets, many of them captains who had served Baron Bosa. Some were simply the outspoken loved ones of pirates who were still at large, sympathizers with the Wolf. Many more were imprisoned within, hostages that kept the Squidlord safe. One by one, the Kraken's enemies had turned themselves in, switching sides or surrendering their ships as they discovered their families were in danger. Bosa's fleet had dwindled in the last month, only a handful of vessels remaining loyal to the Whale. Soon none would remain.

A fishing skiff manned by a handful of youths bobbed closer to the sea fortress, carrying provisions from Cutter's Cove. They had already passed the Kraken's ships as they approached the tower, the pirates casting cursory glances over them before letting them by. The shipments were regular, bringing food from the city port to Ghul's war fortress. The parents of the enslaved children were no doubt chained up inside the tower or hard at work in the bellies of the many ships that hunted in the Lion's name.

The boat's single sail was lowered as the lads sculled closer, catching the attention of the soldiers who manned the floating harbor. Two squid-helmed guards stood beside a burning brazier on the jetty's end, warming their hands over the drum. The Krakenguard waved them through, the skiff squeezing between larger craft, its long deck draped in tarpaulin to protect its goods from the elements. One particular docked vessel loomed larger than any other, a Bastian man-of-war. The *Nemesis* was Opal's ship.

The Krakenguard lit pipes and traded jokes as the crew

of the long boat set about mooring it. The soldiers remained blissfully unaware as the gang of armed teenagers crept out from under the skiff's tarpaulin and onto the jetty. The oldest and toughest youths of Cutter's Cove struck swift and sure, thankful for the pirate shanties that drowned the soldiers' cries.

Drew threw the first guard over his shoulder, following the lads as they dragged the second beneath the tarpaulin. He was grateful for the descending darkness, although he feared for the safety of the youths who'd accompanied him. To attack the sea fortress was folly at any time of day. Should the time come when battle broke out, they would be fighting in darkness on the rocking and rolling decks of the sea fortress. He hoped their sea legs were better than his. Better still, he prayed it wouldn't come to that. The children of Cutter's Cove had suffered enough.

"Merle, Bonny," Drew said to the two tallest boys as he climbed under the cover with the others. "You two need to be near to that brazier, but not so near that anyone can make out your faces."

"Aye," said one of the rangy youths, adjusting his squid-helm. Most of the lads had procured armor and weapons from their enemies in Cutter's Cove. They already had the look of the Squidlord's warriors, only in piecemeal, ill-fitting uniforms.

Drew turned to Gregor. "It's been an honor fighting by your side," he said, shaking Gregor's hand. "I hope you all get home in one piece."

"Don't worry about us, Wolflord. We ain't goin' anywhere until you and Skipper do the job you came for. Them's our parents the Kraken's got locked up in that tower, remember?"

Gregor had proved his worth in the last few days, putting aside the distrust he'd harbored and working alongside Drew as they planned and put into action their attack on Hackett in Cutter's Cove. Alongside Casper, Gregor had unified the enslaved youngsters, galvanizing them into something that resembled a fighting force.

"You remember my signal?" asked Drew.

"It'll be hard to miss," replied Gregor.

"I hope we don't need it."

"Try not to worry and just get our families free," said Gregor. "If you need a distraction, we'll provide one."

"Good luck," said Drew, "and may Sosha watch over all of you."

With that, he hopped off the boat. Casper waited for him, crouched behind a stack of barrels near the head of the jetty, where it joined a broader main pier that ran to the fortress. This was one of the wheel spokes, a pontoon that was linked to the tower, set upon dozens of rafts and boats. The entire complex was a dizzying, chaotic collection of timber and rope, ships and walkways, somehow managing to stay afloat. The tower itself rose from a giant platform that sat high above the waves. Even in the fading twilight, Drew could make out the cages and walls that housed Ghul's prisoners, high above the tallest ships' masts. Gulls circled the fortress, cawing and screeching, landing on the gibbets to pick at those captives who had succumbed.

"What have you seen?" whispered Drew.

"It's exactly as Captain Flowers said," replied the cabin boy calmly.

Casper wasn't like the others. Years in Vega's service aboard the *Maelstrom* had hardened him. But for all his confidence, he was no killer, and the same couldn't be said for the boys at their back. Many had taken the lives of their tormentors in the last few days, and Captain Flowers was one of the few members of the Krakenguard who'd been spared their blades. As one of the few survivors of Hackett's force, he'd provided many answers to Drew's questions about the sea fortress.

Casper pointed toward the structure, where a tall arched opening broke the tower's twisting timber surface. Four of the Krakenguard stood there, maybe a hundred yards from their cover on the jetty. Beyond the portal, torchlight revealed a spiraling staircase.

"The front door," whispered Drew as Casper nodded.

"Be silly to go in that way when we know about the back entrance, eh?"

Casper grinned, but the expression was forced. He was no

fool, painfully aware of how close they were to death. Drew was in just as much danger as the boy from the *Maelstrom*: there were sure to be a few Krakenguard and pirates aboard the sea fortress who were equipped with silvered weapons.

"You first," said the cabin boy, gesturing to the jetty's edge.

Drew slipped over the side and lowered himself into the chill water. The cold instantly hit his extremities, but he pushed the pain to one side. With the enchanted Moonbrand weightless within its scabbard, his weapon belt floated beside him as he kicked himself along, ducking as he went under the next jetty. The boarded walkway passed by overhead as he swam toward the fortress, parallel to the main pier. Casper followed silently behind.

As the two emerged from under the jetty they kicked across a brief stretch of open water, one of the few areas around the construct that wasn't choked by boats or rafts. Another jetty barred their path; this time the young Wolf and his companion had to hold their breath as they kicked on, swimming under the obstruction. With only one hand to help pull himself through the water, the act was far from easy for Drew. Fortunately he had the very able Casper behind, pushing him on until he got clear of the timber. Surfacing on the other side, they found one more obstacle remained.

Of the dozen tall ships secured in the floating harbor, the *Motley Madam* was the smallest. With just two masts, and dwarfed by the *Nemesis*, she didn't command fear like her sister ships. At a glance she looked like a pleasure vessel to Drew, something a visiting noble might have sailed into Highcliff aboard. The fact that she was moored to the sea fortress told its own tale, though, confirming her to be a pirate ship. From where they bobbed, Drew and Casper could even make out the wooden windows concealed within her hull, cannons no doubt hidden in her belly.

On deck, they heard the laughter of men at play. The rattle of dice was unmistakable, the crew enjoying a relaxing moment aboard their ship. One sailor stood directly above the rear of the ship, clutching the rigging beside the aft rail, relieving himself into the sea. Casper turned up his nose and looked away, while Drew kicked back, away from where the sailor might see them. With a belch the man was gone, stomping back to his companions.

Casper pointed forward. "After you, my lord," he whispered, his mouth barely above the waves.

Drew swam on, hugging the pier's edge and the shadows that surrounded it, his eyes on the *Motley Madam*. To hear the men on board, so close by, made his stomach lurch. Reaching the steep sides of the central tower platform, Drew took another deep breath before diving down beneath the main pier. He passed between the rowboats and logs that had been lashed together, snatching at pockets of air before emerging on the other side. He glanced along the edge of the platform, squinting through the gloom, searching for the telltale sign of their route into the fortress.

Casper surfaced beside him, hardly causing a ripple, his eyes immediately leveling on the guards at the tower's entrance. They were barely twenty yards away and, while the pirates aboard the *Motley Madam* might have been relaxing, the Krakenguard at the fortress gate stood to attention, facing the bustling harbor before them. The walls at their backs were clad with great sheets of polished steel, making scaling them impossible. The waves constantly lifted Drew and Casper, threatening to wash them onto the platform. The pair gripped the floating walkways below the waterline, holding their breath when the sea rolled over them.

Drew finally spied what he was looking for, swimming on as he crossed the harbor to his target. The gulls gathered on the edge of the dock, dropping in and out of the brackish water, their activity intensified around a particular area. Drew gagged as he approached, spying all manner of detritus bobbing in the foam. This was the sewage port for the sea fortress, where the refuse found its way out of the tower. Fish heads and potato skins bobbed in the brown scum, the birds squabbling with one another for the pickings.

Drew paused for a moment, treading water at the entrance to the narrow channel that was cut through the platform. The trench was curved and dark, around a couple of feet wide, with a metal grille over the top that prevented folk from falling into it. It was angled to such a degree that gravity helped to carry its contents out to sea.

The Wolflord propelled himself forward, arms straight ahead. The water carried him a short distance up the effluence-filled chute, before he found he was above the tidemark. He was left to crawl the remaining distance, knees and feet struggling for purchase, one hand straining and grabbing. He felt the rotten timber catch in his fingernails, crumbling in his grip, the stench overpowering. A wave of claustrophobia assailed him and he fought the urge to cry out. What if he were to get trapped now? Was this how the last of the Gray Wolves would die? Could there be a more humiliating fate?

Drew pushed the panic away, forcing the fear from his mind. He snatched at the grille above, using the metal slats as anchors as he wormed his body on. Gradually, he saw the wall loom high overhead, the distance of the platform now covered, as he disappeared into the sea fortress sewers, consumed by darkness.

The third punch buckled the sluice grille, sending it splintering away from its housing. Drew's fist emerged from the ground, his elbow next, followed swiftly by his head and shoulders. Slowly he crawled from the sewage pipe, flopping onto his belly like a dying fish as he gagged and spluttered, vomit dripping from his slack jaw. He turned and reached his hand down the hole to snatch hold of Casper. The boy came up and out, collapsing onto the floor of the latrines beside the young Wolflord, the two retching and heaving as they gasped for air.

"We need to move," Drew rasped. "You know where you're going?"

"Aye, my lord. If Flowers was telling the truth, then the cell block's where I'll find the rebel pirates."

"Good," said Drew as he staggered to his feet.

"You got your bearings?" asked the cabin boy as he stood beside the lycanthrope.

"I'm heading up," said Drew. He might have been covered in sewage, but his heart was racing, his spirit soaring: *they were in!* His white smile broke through his filth-covered face, the teeth elongating and sharpening to deadly points.

"It's time for me to fetch you your captain, Casper."

2
Wolf Blood

LEANING AGAINST THE towering stone, Lord Onyx watched the unfolding ritual with keen interest. He didn't share his comrades' superstitions. While his fellow Bastian lords stood a healthy distance away, fearful of whatever Wyrm Magicks the shaman was conjuring, the Pantherlord remained within the ring of standing stones, intruding upon the holy site. Although the forests were now the sole domain of Lyssia's Wyldermen, there had been a time when their tribes had been scattered across the Seven Realms. The humpbacked hill in the Badlands that the crowd now gathered on was once one such site, the stone circle at the heart of the wild men's worship.

While the one called Darkheart danced and hollered before a roaring fire, his brethren formed a circle around him. Their arms were interlinked, bodies swaying from side to side, an ebbing tide of chalk and woad markings, bones and feathers. Their chant remained constant, beating out a rhythm beneath Darkheart's keening. The shaman wore a ram's skull over his own, crowned by rattling capercaillie feathers, his body daubed black with clay. He leapt and spun, pirouetting and prancing, his movements balletic as he circuited a crude stone table. His eyes were rolled back in their sockets, the glistening white orbs mirroring the full moon above.

A fully armored King Lucas stood behind the ring of Wyldermen, within the stone circle but apart from the ritual. His youthful face was illuminated by the bonfire, smiling as he watched Darkheart's dance. His lips worked as he tried to mouth the incantation, a foreigner unversed in the tongue. His eyes followed the shaman's every movement, the young Lion captivated by the ceremony. He held something round and white against his shining golden breastplate, partly obscured by the draping sleeves of his regal red robes. To his side, Vanmorten stood, black cowl around his face. The hood turned as the Ratlord glanced toward Onyx. *That's right, Lord Chancellor,* his eyes seemed to say, *I'm watching you.*

"You should put a stop to this," muttered General Gorgo at Onyx's shoulder. The Hippolord remained hidden in the shadows of the monolith.

"Why?" replied the Beast of Bast. "The king's happy. Let the child play."

"We waste time. The moon is full—we should be making the most of her light. I say we leave this sorry spectacle behind and march on the Sturmish now, as discussed."

"You know the king's orders as well as I," said Onyx. "We march on the Sturmish tonight, but *after* this ritual."

"I don't like it. Vanmorten said the Wyldermen would summon demons to fight for the Lion. Demons! They're dancing with darkness, as bad as anything that wretched Blackhand is involved in!"

Onyx stifled a laugh.

"I witnessed firsthand what Baron Hector was capable of. I can assure you, whatever 'demons' this Wylderman and his brothers conjure will pale in comparison. Despite his frail form and feeble bloodline, the Boarlord's an enemy we must all respect."

"You fear Blackhand?"

"You misheard me," said Onyx, returning his gaze to the wild men as they sang and swayed before the flames. "Respect and fear are very different things. I fear nothing—living *or* dead—but I recognize a worthy foe when I see one."

Four Wyldermen appeared from the darkness at the far side of the hilltop. They wrestled with something, gripping poles and ropes that were lashed around a large shape between them. The staves were held at arm's length, their noosed ends looped around the great, dark beast that fought to break free. Its snarls caused a ripple of excitement to pass through the onlookers, the assembled members of the war council muttering in raised voices at the creature's appearance.

"What are they going to do with that?" spluttered Gorgo.

"Perhaps if you stop asking questions and just watch, we may learn, General," growled Onyx.

As they neared the fire, the flames threw light over the captive wolf. It was a big male, no doubt a pack leader, caught by the Wyldermen a few days earlier. As well as the bonds around its neck, the warriors had bound its jaws with ivy, locking its deadly teeth away. White slather frothed from its peeling lips as the men dragged and pushed it toward the stone table.

"Good grief," said Count Costa, as he walked up the hill to join the two Werelords. "This is all a little over the top, isn't it? We're wasting moonlight here, watching this nonsense when we could be attacking the White Bear."

The Vulture came to a stop beside Gorgo, turning up his lip as he watched the Wyldermen hoist the wolf onto the slab.

"How are the other council members?" asked Onyx. He kept his voice low, their conversation restricted to hushed tones.

Costa glanced back at the rest of the war council. The remaining members stood in a huddle, Sheriff Muller among their number, aghast at the Wylderman ceremony. At their back, a mist had gathered in the valley, obscuring the Lion army's vast camp from view.

"They want to be away," continued Costa, "launching a midnight attack on the Sturmish. I think it's fair to say they're concerned by the king's choice of counsel—after all, nobody likes a cannibal—but they remain loyal to him."

"Blind loyalty," grunted Gorgo.

"It's what empires are built on," said Costa. "It's always worked for the Catlords, hasn't it?"

"If we had General Vorhaas here, we might be able to mount some kind of . . . intervention with the king, a means of stopping his consorting with these savages," said Gorgo. "Alongside his brother Vanmorten, perhaps the two Rats could influence the Lion."

"Perhaps we should call for him to return from the Dalelands," said Costa. "I could fly there myself and have him on his way."

"Sounds to me like you want a holiday in Redmire, Costa," Gorgo said, snorting.

"Nobody goes anywhere," growled Onyx. "We don't need to drag Vorhaas here to fight in our corner. The king's made his bed; now he must lie in it. Whatever comes is of his own doing."

The Pantherlord's eyes were fixed upon the young king as Lucas's head bobbed, following the song and dance of the wild men. The warriors were binding the snarling beast to the table, the dark green cords of ivy pulled tight around the wolf's body. The chant's tempo had increased, the shaman now working himself into a frenzy, his movements jerky and unnatural as if possessed by spirits.

The chanting ceased suddenly, as did the thrashing,

scything dance of the Wyldermen. The only noise from the stone circle came from the wolf as it growled and struggled against its bonds. The shaman turned about and stepped up to the circle of wild men. Each represented a different tribe from the ancient Dyrewood, each a survivor from the Wylderman bloodlines that had otherwise perished or been defeated in the Battle of Brackenholme. The once-diffuse tribes of wild men shared one thing in common: they had all worshipped the Wyrm Goddess, the Wereserpent Vala. But now that the Werewolf had killed Vala, Darkheart and his brothers had all joined forces with Lucas. The shared desire for revenge on Drew had driven them together.

The Wyldermen parted momentarily as the shaman beckoned the king to join him at the ceremony's heart. Lucas stepped forward quickly, eager to be immersed in the ritual, oblivious to all else around him.

"See how swiftly he rushes to the wild man's side?" hissed Costa. "I do hope General Skean and the others are paying attention."

Onyx squinted, standing upright as he tried to discern the finer details of the spectacle. Lucas handed the round white object to Darkheart, who received it with a bow. The king raised his hands to his mouth, stifling a cry of excitement. He was like a child on the night before his birthday. Onyx could see what the object was now: an upturned skull, a thick, dark liquid swilling about within.

"A human skull?" asked Costa.

"A bowl of blood," said Gorgo. "But whose?"

Onyx's eyes widened. *That's why they'd wanted Ferran's hand.*

"Wolf blood," he whispered in grim fascination.

The severed limb was irrevocably tied to the lycanthrope, its dead flesh holding that cold, enchanted therian blood like a sponge. Somehow, the shaman had extracted the blood and poured it into the skull. *But what can they possibly do with it? Summon a* demon?

Placing the skull bowl onto the head of the table, the shaman raised the flint knife in one hand and stared up at the moon. He moved the blade back and forth, speaking ancient words to the sky. He placed his other hand on the wolf, running his fingers through its wiry gray fur, the beast responding to his touch as it ceased its snarling. The hairs on the back of Onyx's neck prickled as if a crackle of energy passed through the air. Trees father down the hill began to creak suddenly, the wind rushing through their branches and causing them to shake like rattlesnake tails. The bonfire began to splutter, sending showers of sparks into the night.

"This is a grotesque pantomime," whispered Gorgo nervously, as Darkheart held the flint dagger high. "This isn't magick. I've seen more magick in—"

The dagger fell, punching through the wolf's torso to its heart. Instantly, the fire was quenched, plunging the hill briefly into darkness before it burst into life once more. But now the flames that danced were sickly green, casting a ghostly glow over the stone circle. Some of the war council cried out. Gorgo staggered back, seizing hold of Costa by the forearm. All around the hilltop, unnatural winds raced, invisible phantoms that swept between the standing stones, parting the Werelords or forcing them toward each other. Only Onyx remained unmoved, his eyes never leaving Darkheart. Growls, hisses, snorts, and snarls seemed to echo in the darkness, as if a horde of foul beasts were crawling and slithering up the hill toward the Bastian nobles.

"The green fire," said Gorgo frantically, the Hippo's tusks suddenly jutting from his wobbling jaw as he allowed his body to shift. "What's causing it? Some kind of blasting powder?"

"And the animal sounds?" asked Costa, his crooked beak already breaking from his face. He turned toward the shadows as if something might pounce upon him at any moment, his wings erupting from his back in an unconfident show of strength.

Onyx watched as Darkheart left the flint blade quivering in the wolf's corpse. He lifted the skull to his mouth and tipped its contents in. He poured it down his throat, some of the blood spilling over his mud-daubed skin and down his chest. His hands trembled as he removed the bowl from his lips and stretched his arms out wide. The skull dropped to the floor as Darkheart's head tipped farther back, his gaze fixed on the moon. The green flames blazed at his back, lighting the thick clouds from below as they billowed from the hellish bonfire.

The shaman fell suddenly to the ground, dropping to his knees as he bucked and writhed. Gorgo and Costa backed away from the stones, many of the war council now muttering that they should leave, that this was a mistake. Onyx spied Vanmorten retreating from the stone circle, putting distance between himself and the ritual's terrible finale. Even a few of Darkheart's fellow Wyldermen hesitantly stepped back from their juddering leader. Lucas remained motionless as Darkheart frothed and spat beside the unearthly green fire. The shaman shook and buckled, his movements blurring as if he might tear apart at any moment.

Then he was still.

The assembled onlookers held their breath, the only sound now that of the crackling fire, its emerald limbs stabbing skyward like a monstrous mantis. Darkheart rose, his movements slow and measured. The death tremors had been replaced by the calm, languid motions of the newly awakened. He lifted his chin and opened his eyes. They flashed yellow. *The eyes of a wolf.*

Darkheart beckoned the first of the Wyldermen forward, the warrior marked in blue woad stripes that banded his entire body, a stone-headed ax in his hand. The shaman took the ax from the wild man's hand and tossed it onto the grass. He whispered something, the fellow nodding as he turned his head to the side, offering his neck. Darkheart bit the man's throat hard, his sharpened teeth worrying the flesh. As the warrior fell to the ground, the next Wylderman stepped forward. The shaman slowly worked his way through them, biting the necks, shoulders, and chests of his brethren, leaving his mark on each.

The Werelords below were backing up as one, still watching the night and whatever phantoms were out there. They were soon swallowed by the rolling mist as they descended the hilltop. Gorgo and Costa rushed to keep up with them, even Vanmorten racing to join the Bastians, leaving Onyx to watch the wild men in horror.

"Fear," whispered the Beast of Bast. "So this is how it feels?"

The emotion was entirely new to him, and he didn't like it. He began to back away, a wave of revulsion riding over him as he slowly made sense of the macabre ceremony—the blood, the wolf, the Wyrm Magicks, the bites. Ancient human folklore told that therianthropy could be passed over through the bite of a Werelord. It wasn't true, though, just a myth used to scare children. The blood of the therianthropes—what Lyssians called a Brenn-given blessing and Bastians saw as a gift from their forefathers—was what separated Werelords from mere mortals. Onyx had just witnessed that most sacred blood passed across into humans. This was unheard-of on either continent. Who knew what the consequences might be?

As Onyx retreated from the stone circle, he caught sight of

Lucas watching him. The young Lionlord's red robe had been cast aside, golden armor shimmering emerald by the glow of the fire, his father's greatsword in his hands. He had his back turned to the Wyldermen as they fell to the floor, wailing by the light of the moon and the ghastly green flames. *This is the army the king promised, the warriors to help us defeat the Sturmish?* Slowly the wails of the wild men became howls. The boy was still smiling, Onyx noticed.

The boy had his demons.

3
Breaking Bonds

"I THOUGHT YOU said this fortress was impregnable, Ghul."

Opal stood on the balcony of the Kraken's war room, staring down the tower's length to the wharfs below. The pontoons, piers, and shackled ships all thrummed with activity, as liberated pirates battled Krakenguard and sailors. The fighting was fierce, the recently freed prisoners leaping upon their captors bare-handed, throttling Ghul's soldiers as they were stabbed in return. Only the Panther's flagship, the *Nemesis*, remained free of combat, her Bastian myrmidons having withdrawn the walkways that led to the floating harbor. Fires raged, the flames leaping from boat to jetty as burning men tumbled into the docks.

"It is," blustered Ghul. "Fear not: no harm will come to you!"

Opal snarled at the Squidlord, who recoiled from the balcony's edge. "I'm not some wetling Lyssian princess, Kraken," she growled. "You're speaking to a Werepanther. I fear nothing."

"It's just . . . the howl, my . . . my lady," stammered the Kraken. "If one were to fear *anything,* then—"

Tall though Lord Ghul was, Opal was still able to clap her hand over his mouth, her clawed fingertips squeezing the skin of his ruddy cheeks. Within the war room, Captain Skerrett watched impassively, the master of the *Nemesis* all too used to Opal's volatile temper. Ghul's senior officers and Krakenguard watched on from a distance, wary of the fierce Catlady and what she might do next. None stepped to their liege's aide; they knew who was truly in command.

"I. Fear. Nothing."

Opal released her grip, allowing Ghul to catch his breath.

"Understood," he said, nodding. "It's just that the howl seemed to signal the start of this attack. All hell broke loose at its sounding!"

"He's right," said Captain Skerrett, his fingers flexing over the pommel of his silver saber. "The Wolf's here, and he has help. He's behind this prison break. I'd urge caution. He might be within the walls as we speak."

Ghul shook his head. "Those scum may have escaped the

cell block, but the remainder of the fortress is locked down. We're quite safe up here."

"Considering the cells are within the fortress, I find that hard to believe," Opal said. She pointed at one of the Squidlord's captains. "You. Go below; take some Krakenguard with you. Inform my men on the *Nemesis* to prepare to sail."

The officer was off immediately, taking a couple of soldiers with him as he disappeared into the spiraling staircase. Opal turned to Skerrett as Ghul marched past her toward the stairwell, bellowing for his men to follow.

"Captain," she said with a smile, "fetch me my prisoner. We've delayed long enough."

Hopping off a walkway and onto another ladder, Captain Skerrett descended the tower wall followed by two crewmen from the *Nemesis*. The pair were more than enough to help him transport the prisoner to the Bastian flagship. If what Ghul had said was true, the Sharklord's spirit was beaten, his body broken. He landed on the bamboo-runged walkway at Vega's level, its bars fanning out from the wall, running beneath two weather-beaten prisoners who hung suspended.

One was a craggy old fellow who smiled at the captain's arrival, throwing him a wink. The other didn't move. Skerrett withdrew his shining silver saber. Vega's reputation preceded him, and the captain wasn't about to take any chances. The Sharklord hung motionless by taut chains and manacles, head bowed, arms twisted. The once-flamboyant, glamorous Lord of the Cluster Isles cut a very sorry figure, his body scored and scarred. Skerrett's men arrived at his back, standing unsteadily beside one another on the rickety walkway, glancing warily over its edge.

"Sailor, eh? Not so different, you and I," said the older prisoner.

"Of course we're not," replied Skerrett, his tone pleasant. "Perhaps if I was pinned to the wall covered in my own excrement, we could be twins!"

The old chap giggled as the captain turned to the count, sword at the ready.

"Don't tell me you can sleep through that racket," said Skerrett, peering briefly down into the bedlam below. Black clouds bloomed from one of the ships as a sudden *boom* sent its decks flying into the air. The blasting powder, so precious to the pirates of the White Sea, was a dangerous weapon. While it could inflict terrible damage upon one's enemy, a careless flame could scuttle one's own hopes—and vessel—in an instant.

He poked his saber at the count's exposed ribs. "Heads up, Sharklord." Skerrett sneered. "There'll be time to sleep when Lucas takes your head."

Still Vega didn't move, while the old prisoner tried to stifle his laughter. Skerrett switched his attention to the raggedy fool, whose eyes were fixed upon the runged walkway.

"Pray tell what amuses you, old chap. Share the joke?"

The mad wretch didn't answer, his eyes wide as he looked at the slatted floor. The captain glanced down, his booted feet splayed as he balanced on the bamboo struts. He gradually focused on the dark spaces between the bars, discovering a pair of glowing yellow eyes staring back.

Skerrett staggered back as the Werewolf's head exploded through the walkway, the bamboo splintering as Drew launched himself through it from where he'd clung underneath. The platform was tearing loose from the wall as the lycanthrope lunged for the sea captain, his two companions from the *Nemesis* screaming and tumbling into space in a shower of broken bars. Skerrett found a handhold and lashed out with his saber, puncturing Drew's flesh as the Werewolf tumbled, scrambling for a handhold. Each pipe and pole he snatched at came away, his clawed feet digging into the wall for extra purchase. When Skerrett's saber slashed at the hemp that held the remaining walkway in place, Drew feared his number was up.

Unfortunately for the Bastian captain, his steps had led him back toward Vega, who suddenly stirred into life. His legs encircled the man's waist, hauling him backward. Still trapped in human form by the silver manacles, Vega instantly put the chains to good use. The count pulled hard on the right manacle, the long length of chain rattling through its bracket as it hauled the left hand up with a clang. Ignoring Skerrett's butting head and slashing blade, the Sharklord looped the chain over the man's neck before allowing his body and left hand to fall again. Momentum did the rest.

The chain rattled to a cranking halt as Skerrett's throat crumpled with a resounding *snap* against the bracket. The saber tumbled from his lifeless hand, only for the Werewolf to fling a leg out, catching it with his clawed foot.

"A nice trick, Your Highness," said Vega from beneath his filthy fringe of black hair. "Now if you'd be so kind, young friend, can you help me down?"

"What's keeping Captain Skerrett?" snarled Opal.

Ghul's men who remained in the Kraken's war room said nothing, remaining a healthy distance from the Pantherlady. From the balcony she could see a number of ships had disengaged from their moorings, drifting clear from the burning harbor while fights continued aboard each. Ghul's own ship, the *Soultaker,* was ablaze, careering out of control as she collided with the *Nemesis.* Even from this height Opal could see her men of Bast had their weapons drawn, hacking and slashing at the Squidlord's pirates, stopping the panicked sailors from boarding their vessel.

"And your master?" she hissed at Ghul's men, pacing back

into the chamber and between them. "Where is he?"

"Defending his tower," said one of the Krakenguard at last, his voice laced with fear as the Pantherlady came face-to-face with him, teeth bared.

Right on cue a monstrous wail sounded in the depths of the stairwell, a gurgling scream that bore little resemblance to a human voice. The men all looked toward the darkened doorway before turning back to Opal.

"Lord Ghul?" she asked as the men solemnly nodded.

She leapt back to the balcony's edge, one clawed hand buried in the floorboards as she peered over the side. All order was lost below. If she didn't get to the *Nemesis* now, chances were she never would.

Glancing over her shoulder, she now noticed that the Krakenguard who remained continued to nervously stare at her, their silvered weapons drawn. *For me?* she wondered. They must have been aware of the fighting aboard the *Nemesis,* as her Bastians repelled their panicked comrades. Whatever bond the Catlords had with the Squidlord was in danger of tearing apart, if it hadn't already. Her role as adviser to King Lucas counted for naught now, with the world going up in flames around them.

Opal instantly thought of her two young children, back home in Braga. *What am I doing here?* They'd been apart for so long now, the Pantherlady sailing with her brother's fleet, keen to impress her father. High Lord Oba had his favorite in Onyx;

little that Opal did seemed to win affection. She wouldn't die in this floating fire, not for Oba, not today. Again, she turned to the sea. A number of ships were moving into view out of the darkness, illuminated by the flames of the burning harbor. The flags weren't of Bast or Westland or even the Kraken of the Cluster Isles. The five craft were recognizable to Opal instantly, and not just because of the silver wolf heads fluttering upon their black flags. These were the ships they'd hunted for months, fast approaching the sea fortress, coming straight for them like a shoal of sharks. Leading the pack was the *Maelstrom*, and at her side the white ship known as the *Beluga*, her bronze ram carving the water before her.

"Bosa," whispered the boldest of the Krakenguard, having drawn closer to look down from the balcony. "Here to reclaim his prodigy."

"Count Vega?" asked Opal, as a noise from the staircase made the pair turn. Lord Ghul had appeared, his broad frame filling the doorway, his neck disappearing as his eyes swelled in their sockets. His robes were spattered with gore, the Lord of the Cluster Isles having clearly been heavily engaged in the fighting below. The Kraken's beak snapped with delight as he dragged a boy into view, throwing him onto the floor of the war room before him.

"Who's this?" asked Opal, glowering at the child.

"Vega's precious cabin boy if I'm not mistaken," rasped the Kraken, body still transforming, robes cast aside.

The Werepanther watched on as Ghul kicked the stunned child forward and staggered into the chamber, at once impressed and disgusted by the monstrous spectacle. Bright flashes of pink and purple flashed over the Kraken's flesh, shimmering in waves across the mantle that his body had assumed. The Weresquid towered over the lad as another explosion caused the tower to shudder. With a wet rip, Ghul's arms and legs seemed to tear apart, at once vanishing to be replaced by eight ever expanding, terrible tentacles.

"We may yet leave here with a Shark in chains," said Ghul, his voice a wheezing burble. "And perhaps even a Wolf!"

4

Ballad of Butchery

TEN TORCH-CARRYING Bastian Goldhelms accompanied the Werepanther as he stalked across the frozen meadow, surrounded by the swirling fog. The ground was loose underfoot, spring's long reach extending high into the Whitepeaks, slowly turning snow into slush. The bodyguard was ceremonial, a feature for any Catlord who took to the field and a role held in high esteem by others in the army. Onyx had never actually needed a guard to accompany him—he was a living, breathing weapon, the most feared felinthrope ever to prowl the world. Indeed, ordinarily he looked upon the tradition with disdain. Yet on this night, he was happy for the company. There was only one in his party he was displeased to have present. Walking a few steps behind was King Lucas, resplendent in his suit of shining gold. On his hip he carried a hunting horn, his means of signaling the Wyldermen.

Fresh from their ordeal at the standing stones, Darkheart's warriors had been released into the fog by Lucas, while the commanders of the Bastian and Westland armies stood back and watched, aghast. The wild men who had been sent into the night toward the Sturmish lines bore little resemblance to those who had been guests within their camp. While still vaguely human, they were changing, metamorphosing. Their bodies seemed twisted, their muscles enlarged, and what hair was on their bodies had begun to spread. Where filthy nails had once tipped their fingers, claws had appeared. Beneath their dark, shaggy manes of black hair, their eyes shone bright and yellow while their razor-sharp teeth now looked that little bit longer.

The war council had been glad to see the backs of the wild men. The warriors from the Dyrewood had snarled at one another, lashing out with tooth and claw like dogs bred for fighting. To Onyx's eyes the Wyldermen, already savage and intimidating, had given up what humanity they had; they were feral now, truly more beast than man. The Wyrm Magicks that Darkheart had conjured, channeling into his brethren, had given them a taste of the therian gift. Such a thing was unheard-of, and how much of the wolf had crossed over was yet to be seen. But Onyx was confident of one thing: it could only end badly.

The Sturmish screams had soon sounded in the fog, signaling that the Wyldermen had found their prey. Onyx had heard the cries of men dying in battle before. Most souls who took to the battlefield were prepared for death when it finally came. They knew when the long sleep came it would be on the end of a spear, before an ax, or beneath a hail of arrows. But the wails that had sounded in the fog were new to the Pantherlord. They were the panicked, hysterical cries of horrified men, a frantic overture of terror. Just when Onyx thought the cries couldn't get any louder, they would lift up a notch. These were the screams of men who were facing a foe fresh from their nightmares, an end unlike anything they'd ever imagined.

Occasionally, the group passed a body lying in the slush, torn and opened up, the steam still rising from the Sturmlander's corpse. Thus far, they had encountered no survivors. As they passed between the giant wooden stakes that marked the outermost line of the Sturmish defenses, Onyx heard the king chuckle.

"They've made a terrible mess of these northerners, haven't they?" Lucas laughed. "I'd heard Sturmlanders were made of sterner stuff than this."

"Just like all of us," said Onyx as he stalked through the snow, eyes alert, searching for movement.

There were no more screams in the darkness, no more howls or savage cries. The battlefield was quiet for the time being, Darkheart's Wyldermen having disengaged as ordered when Lucas had called on the horn.

"Are you there, White Bear?" shouted Onyx as he came to a halt, his voice echoing across the field.

"Do you really expect him to come, dear uncle?" asked Lucas, but Onyx ignored him.

"Come out, Your Grace," he bellowed.

Onyx paused for a moment as he heard something move in the fog, off to his right. He trained his eyes on the mist as he continued his speech.

"Face me in combat, Henrik, therian to therian, and end this war. Fight me, and I'll allow the remainder of your army to leave the mountains. You have my word. Fail to show, and there'll be no mercy. No Sturmlander will leave the Whitepeaks alive. Think quickly. I give you a hundred breaths!"

Onyx stepped away from his companions toward his right, moving until the torchlight of his men was at his back. His eyes quickly adjusted to the gloom, picking out the details of a ghostly outpost, hastily abandoned. A pot sat upon a pile of glowing coals, the broth within bubbling, the dishes and plates of the Sturmish soldiers abandoned in the snow. The door to a bunkhouse creaked on its hinges, the lantern within still glowing where it hung from the wall. Boots, cloaks, and armor lay scattered on the floor, dropped by the men of Icegarden in their haste to escape the Wyldermen.

A snarl outside made Onyx step away from the door, peering around the side of the building. Through the fog he made out the dim shape of a body being dragged into the darkness behind the bunkhouse.

"He won't come."

Lucas had followed him. The Pantherlord turned away from whatever grisly scene was unfolding behind the building.

"He'll come. The lives of his people now depend upon it. He's seen what awaits them if he doesn't."

"He may send one of his champions again."

There was a mocking tone to Lucas's voice that Onyx disliked.

"They weren't my terms. I'd hoped we'd starve them out of the mountains, but that hasn't happened. This stalemate ends tonight."

"And you have my assistance to thank for our success thus far, Uncle," said Lucas smugly as the two walked back toward the Bastian torches.

"I intended to attack tonight regardless of whatever sorceries you cooked up with your Wyldermen, Your Majesty. The weather and the conditions are perfect. I would have backed myself and my fellow Bastian Werelords to end this siege tonight, with the moon at our backs. You cannot underestimate the power of my army, Nephew. That you have sent Darkheart and his brothers in instead adds an unpredictable element to the proceedings. Something I don't like."

"You cannot underestimate the potential for my Wyld Wolves, Uncle."

"Wyld Wolves?" Onyx retorted with a scoff. "They make a mockery of therianthropy. They no more resemble a wolf than they do a rabid dog. You play with fire, Your Majesty. I pray we all don't get burned."

The Bastian bodyguard suddenly jumped to attention, swords and torches raised before them, facing north toward the heart of the Sturmish camp. Onyx paced along the line in front of them, staring into the fog. He could hear them coming, armor clanking, horses whinnying, voices muttering.

"Onyx?"

"Duke Henrik," replied the Pantherlord as the crowd emerged through the mist like phantoms. "An honor to finally meet you."

"Spare me the niceties, Panther," said the Lord of Sturmland as he drew nearer upon his charger. "You've lost whatever honor you thought you had. You're a savage, Onyx. A monster. May you die a hundred deaths for what you've unleashed upon my people this night."

"Whatever damage has been dealt to your troops this night wasn't of my doing, Bearlord."

Henrik laughed bitterly as he reined his horse to a halt, the dozen riders who accompanied him doing likewise.

"You deny responsibility, Panther? You're the commander of this army, aren't you? They do as you say, don't they?"

"They do as *I* say," said Lucas, coming forward from the shadows behind Onyx. The Pantherlord raised his hand to quiet the king, but the boy wouldn't be silenced, a victorious swagger in his step.

"By siding with the pretender Drew Ferran, you've brought this upon your people. Whatever damage the Wyld Wolves have dealt you was of your own doing, Henrik. How fitting that my lycanthropes have wreaked bloody havoc with those who befriend the Wolf."

"They're not lycanthropes, boy," spat out Henrik, stamping forward through the slush and towering before the young Lion, Onyx trying to get between them. "They're aberrations, monstrosities. Even the Bastians are capable of compassion, but not those unholy beasts you set upon us this night, killing and feeding upon my brave, weary Sturmlanders."

The White Bear's face was twisted with rage and disgust. The duke was as tall as Onyx, though he lacked the Panther's broad build. His striking breastplate bore the image of a great raging bear.

"Kill him now, Uncle," Lucas demanded, baring his teeth, which shifted within his jaws.

"Lost control of your boy king, Onyx?"

"He never *had* control of me," snarled Lucas, trying to push past the Werepanther. Onyx raised a hand to the Lion's chest, holding him back.

"Enough!" bellowed Onyx, the king instantly mortified

by the Panther's command. "Let's get this done," he continued, turning back to Henrik. "Have you brought your second?"

"Indeed," said the White Bear as another figure approached from the assembly behind. Onyx's face lit up at the sight of his enemy's companion.

"We've never met, Duke Bergan, but I feel like we're old friends!"

The Bearlord of Brackenholme stepped up to Henrik's side, carrying his cousin's enchanted weapon, the White Fist of Icegarden, in his hands. He held the gauntlet of razor-sharp white steel claws out to the Lord of Sturmland.

"Don't fool yourself, Panther," said Bergan, his eyes fixed on Henrik as the White Bear prepared himself, slipping his left hand into the shining metal glove. "You'll find no friends in Lyssia. You can put a Cat on the throne, but we'll never call him king."

Lucas leapt suddenly with a roar, the Lion in him emerging, launching himself toward Bergan. The old duke unleashed a snarl, instantly shifting, his head beginning the change. Before the Werelion could attack the duke, Onyx snatched hold of Lucas by the shoulder, dragging him back and flinging him away. Lucas landed headfirst in the snow, shaking the white powder from his mane as he looked up with eyes full of rage.

"Stay back!"

Onyx's voice thundered as he faced down the Werelion. His body began to shift, muscles rippling as every inch of his huge frame expanded, swelling in size. He kept on growing until he hulked like a giant over the young felinthrope. The Werepanther's enormous dark head lit up suddenly as he snarled and revealed his teeth, bright white canines shining by the torchlight. An arm as thick as Lucas's torso extended toward the young king, a mighty clawed finger pointing at the boy.

"Stay where you are, Your Majesty. You may have trampled over my plans by sending your Wyld Wolves into the fray, but this is *my* fight. You might not understand the meaning of the word 'honor,' disgracing us in front of our noble brethren as you have, but I still do. This duel tonight is between myself and Duke Henrik. No others shall draw blood. The rules of engagement are quite clear: Duke Bergan and the Sturmish entourage must leave here unharmed."

As if to emphasize the point, Onyx extended a mighty foot, drawing a line in the sludge with a hooked toe.

"I would ask you—*kindly*—do not cross this line, Your Majesty."

Lucas didn't answer, instead snarling where he crouched. One of the Goldhelms stepped up to offer his arm, nearly getting it ripped off when the petulant Lion swung a clawed hand at it. Onyx turned back to Henrik, who had now also transformed. Finally, he had encountered a worthy opponent, the white Werebear as tall and imposing as the Werepanther. In human form, Onyx was clearly the more muscular of the two, but as therians he lost out to the sheer mass of the Bearlord. Henrik's shoulders, neck, and back shook with muscles, the beautiful white fur bristling in the breeze.

"They'll write ballads about this battle," said Onyx as he watched the ursanthrope with the utmost respect.

"There'll be no ballads for your death, Bastian," replied Henrik, flexing the White Fist of Icegarden. The Bearlord opened his palm, the enchanted gauntlet moving fluidly as claws of Sturmish steel emerged. Henrik turned the mighty paw one way and then the other, searching for the light of the moon.

"She's up there," said Onyx, "but you won't have her help with your trinket this evening, Henrik. I know all about your enchanted steel, and the effect of moonlight upon it. Seek no help from above—this fog is thick."

"The White Fist will still serve its purpose," said the Bearlord. "You have no second?"

"I don't need one," replied the Panther as he began to circle Henrik. "I've never backed down from a fight in my life, and am not about to now."

"And no armor or sword, either? So it's true what they say about you in battle?"

"That I need neither? That I'm fearless? That I *am* the weapon?"

"No," replied Henrik as he paced around the other. "That you're insane."

Onyx had to laugh. "Very good. So the prize at stake, are we agreed? For Sturmland?"

"For Lyssia," replied the White Bear as he lunged at the Panther.

Onyx met Henrik midcharge, the Werepanther's black clawed hands snatching the Werebear's paws. He squeezed with all his might, his purchase on the White Fist unsure, flesh against steel, while his other hand held Henrik's naked paw in a viselike grip. The two turned, digging heels into the snow, pushing against one another as their jaws gnashed in one another's faces. With each footstep the ground seemed to shake, the Sturmish party and the Bastian bodyguard all spreading out, forming a ring of onlookers about the combatants.

The Panther focused his attack on the Bear's right hand, driving all his strength into his grip and grinding Henrik's knuckles against one another. He felt the bones crack and pop inside the shaking paw, as the blade trembled, almost falling from his grasp. His other hand slipped free of the White Paw, the contest uneven, choosing to thump the steel fist and sending it recoiling. Onyx left the arm swinging, instead going for the Werebear's chest. His claws left furrows in the metal and sparks in their wake as his uppercut slashed up into Henrik's jaw. The claws connected deep in the white fur, as Onyx ripped it away. The fur turned dark around the Werebear's throat as the Panther drew first blood.

Now it was Henrik's turn to attack, the White Fist flying

back like a battering ram. The knuckled gauntlet hit Onyx like a hammer blow, crunching and splintering the ribs and folding him in two. The Panther's powerful legs lifted up off the floor as he relinquished his grip on the Bear's right paw. Henrik wasted no time, punching down with his maimed fist and catching the Panther's temple. The Bastian bodyguard gasped, already having witnessed their liege take more wounds in a moment than he'd ordinarily experience in a campaign.

The gauntlet followed, crashing down, only to strike at thin air as the Panther lashed a kick at the Bear. Henrik sidestepped, his neck a red bib, as he slashed down at the winded felinthrope with both paws. Onyx was too quick, leaping up into the Bear's arms before the claws could descend. His teeth snapped at Henrik's face as the ursanthrope chomped at his shoulder. All the while Lucas watched, pacing anxiously back and forth, willing the Panther on to victory.

Soon enough, the slush was black with mud and blood, the Werelords' bodies ravaged and exhausted from the relentless battle. Henrik's breastplate lay on the floor in pieces, the straps severed. Even now, in the face of possible death, Onyx found himself regretting the fog that surrounded them, with only a handful of witnesses to his monumental duel. Whosoever won the contest would be a worthy champion of any army. If the Bear lived or died, he'd earned the Panther's respect.

As the two fell to the floor in a wrestle, Onyx's claws raked down Henrik's left arm, catching at the point where the deadly White Fist, the cause of so much damage, sat snug to the Bear's limb. He gripped the steel and yanked hard, the gauntlet tearing loose and flying through the air to land at Bergan's feet. The Lord of Brackenholme snatched it up, looking for a way to pass it back to his cousin. Henrik drove his head in, smashing his broad skull against the Panther's and sending him stunned to his knees. Onyx lunged forward, jaws open, looking to launch a desperate attack on his foe, but the White Bear was leaping clear, swinging his now gauntletless left paw across Onyx's torso in the process.

Onyx crouched on all fours, quickly moving a clawed hand up to his stomach. He pushed himself upright, breathing hard, woozy and nauseous. His clawed hand held the flesh of his belly together, the cuts from the Bearlord's paw grievous. He smiled through bloody teeth as he looked up at Henrik. The White Bear stood wearily over him, his white fur painted red. He raised both paws into the air once more, enormous claws ready to strike.

"Well fought, Bearlord," whispered the Beast of Bast, finally accepting defeat. He relaxed and prepared for the killing blow.

It never came. The Sturmlanders cried out, even the Goldhelms joining them, as Lucas leapt forward. Onyx opened his mouth to scream, to shout no, to call the king back, but the greatsword of the Werelions was already connecting with the exhausted Werebear's neck. The first blow hacked the flesh, sending Henrik to his knees beside Onyx. The Bearlord's eyes were open, staring incredulously at the Panther until the second chop took his head off.

Before the Sturmish could even think about jumping to their lord's defense, the Wyld Wolves poured forth out of the night, swarming toward them out of the fog. The freakish lycanthropes bounded, springing, taking the knights from their whinnying horses. Some of the monsters leapt onto Henrik's corpse, tearing into the slain Werelord with ghoulish enthusiasm while the Werelion watched on.

"Betrayers!" roared a transformed Duke Bergan as two Sturmlanders tried to drag him away. "Brenn curse you all!" He retreated into the fog, surrounded by the terrible Wyld Wolves as they scattered his party.

"No!" shouted the Beast of Bast as he knelt in the snow, claws in his guts, his words lost on the transformed Wyldermen. "There's no honor in this, Lucas! Call off your Wolfmen!"

The Lion looked down at Onyx and snarled. "You forget yourself again, Uncle; it's *King* Lucas." He crouched beside the injured Werepanther as the butchery continued behind him. "And I'll do whatever I please."

5
Tentacles of Terror

AS THE FIRES raged in the harbor, choking the sky with black clouds, the tower of the Kraken was beginning to fall. Some said that magicks had gone into the citadel's construction, as powerful as those in Sturmish steel. True or not, though, no enchantment could help the sea tower now. A feat of engineering born from the Squidlord's ambitious mind, Ghul's floating fortress was on its last legs. Mighty cracks shot through its walls, fractures that raced from base to summit. Supporting beams that had been carefully considered and perfectly placed began to grind and groan, torquing and twisting beneath the strain of the palace's burning bulk.

Hooking the stump of his left arm over the rail, Drew launched himself onto the balcony, landing with a thump on the trembling decking. A quick glance into the chamber ahead revealed little, the air thick with smoke. Reaching back, he took hold of the weary Vega's hand, straining to haul the Sharklord up. Below the count, Florimo and other freed prisoners clung to one another, the walkways buckling beneath their feet. The exterior walls were alive with activity as pirates and sailors were released from shackles and gibbets, the fires spreading quickly over the structure's frame. Vega dropped to his knees as Drew bent over the banister to grab Florimo.

"Keep moving, Vega," gasped Drew. "There has to be a way down through the tower."

Vega stumbled on into the chamber, squinting into the gloom. The odd torch guttered in its bracket, failing to penetrate the darkness. The shrieks of combat echoed from the tower's depths, warning the count of what lay ahead. He shifted Skerrett's silver saber in his hand nervously, manacles and severed chains dangling from each bloody wrist. The captain of the *Maelstrom* did not feel himself. His ordeal on the walls of the sea fortress, starved and tormented by the Kraken, had left him a shell of the pirate prince he once was. His only desire was to be away from the terrible tower, as soon as was possible.

"Come now, old friend," came a voice from the darkness, causing the Sharklord to stutter to a halt. "You were going to leave without saying good-bye?"

Vega saw the shape appear now, materializing through the smoke. Many Werelords of Lyssia could change to allow aspects of the beast to the fore, to varying degrees; few could shape-shift entirely into the creature that Brenn's blessing had married them to. The old Serpent of the Wyrmwood, Vala, was one such therian who held complete control over the beast. Ghul, the Squidlord of the Cluster Isles, was another.

Covering the distance in quick time, three tentacles lashed out at the Sharklord. The first struck him hard, knocking him to the floor. The second swept him up, tossing him through the air, away from the balcony. The third caught him, pinning him to the war room wall with such force that the timbers splintered at his back. The silver saber quivered in the floorboards a few yards away.

"This is too easy," the Kraken's voice rumbled as its huge mantle bobbed into view, the wobbling flesh undulating with shades of indigo and violet. Any human features were gone, banished by the change. Head and torso had merged into the tall, bloated body of the Weresquid, eight monstrous limbs rippling out from beneath its swaying frame.

A tentacle drove Vega up the wall, grating the squirming count until his head hit the ceiling, the thick limb choking him.

"Put him down," snarled Drew as he stepped forward from the balcony. Moonbrand glowed in his gray furred hand, penetrating the pall of smoke that had filled the chamber from below.

"I don't think so, boy," came a voice from behind the Kraken, as a lithe figure jumped over the Squidlord's tentacles, a boy struggling in her arms. Her skin was as black as night, shining purple and blue where Moonbrand's light caught it. Her right arm was locked around Casper's throat, her clawed left hand open, ready to strike the child.

"Drew Ferran, the Wolf of Westland," she said, cocking her bald head, looking him up and down. "This floating bonfire was the last place I expected we'd meet."

"Opal," Drew said with a snarl of recognition. The Panther was the second female felinthrope he'd met, and she bore a striking similarity to the first. The Weretiger Taboo had been battle hardened in the gladiatorial arena on the volcanic isle of Scoria, years spent fighting for survival breaking down her trust in everyone. In time, Drew had managed to repair that, to the point that Taboo had considered him her friend. Every move Opal made was poised and deliberate, as if she might strike out at any moment. Taboo had been just the same, her wary nature easily misconstrued as constant, simmering aggression. Opal seemed every bit as deadly. A handful of Krakenguard stood behind her, silver shortswords raised before them.

"You're feeling foolish now, Wolf, aren't you?" said the woman as Casper squirmed in her grasp. "Drop your sword and turn yourself in. You're coming with me to Highcliff, you *and* the Shark. King Lucas wants to speak with you."

"And the boy?"

Vega grunted where he was pinned high to the wall, his

heels kicking out at the Kraken's tentacle, but Ghul simply pushed harder, forcing the fight from him.

"This one?" asked Opal, turning to look at Casper. She kissed his forehead tenderly. "He's precious to you, too? I understand he's the count's boy from the *Maelstrom.* I promise you nothing, Wolf. The longer you delay dropping the sword, the more chance I may just kill him."

Drew wavered, the weightless Moonbrand suddenly heavy in his grip. He felt the wolf retreating, withdrawing beneath his skin, his heart growing cold. It was bad enough that Ghul had Vega, but he couldn't risk Casper's life as well.

"Hold that sword, my lord," came a voice from behind. "Don't be thinking about dropping it."

Drew turned to find Florimo had joined him, the severed chain from his manacles taut in his gnarled hands. At his back, more figures began to appear through the balcony, a steady stream of freed prisoners from the fortress walls. Chains and lengths of wood were the weapons of the humans, while those therians among them who had shaken off their shackles began to shift. Another Shark, a Wereray, a Lobsterlord: all manner of marvelous Werelords of the Sea materialized. Drew's heart raced. Suddenly the advantage was theirs.

"About those demands," said Drew, snarling as he let the wolf back in. "I think we need to renegotiate."

"I still have the boy, remember?" said Opal, twisting Casper roughly in her arms. "And the Kraken has the Shark!"

Drew ignored her, pacing forward, the Panther's comrades looking doubtfully at one another. More allies continued to clamber and crawl into the war room, adding weight to the Wolf's cause. The tower lurched again, another mighty groan sounding from its base.

"You hand them to me, you leave with your life, Opal. You harm a hair on their heads, you die, here, tonight. I give you my word."

"Over my dead body it is, then!" said the Beauty of Bast, her voice lacking confidence.

The Werewolf turned his attention to the Krakenguard. "That goes for you, too, gentlemen: drop your weapons. Leave now, and we spare you. I make this offer only once. Refuse, and we all die together in an inferno!"

That was enough for most of them. Weapons clattered to the floor as those who'd served the Kraken called an end to that association. While some dashed for the exit, a handful turned their blades toward Ghul and Opal, taking an even greater step away from their former masters. Only a single Krakenguard remained loyal, standing beside Opal.

The mob backed away from the Kraken as it flung its tentacles out indiscriminately, striking anyone it could reach.

"Let Vega go, Ghul!" roared Drew, refusing to stand down. As the tentacles struck out at him, the young Wolf ducked, jumped, sidestepped, and parried the blows.

Opal had seen enough, now retreating toward the exit.

Florimo lashed out with his chain, catching her guard in the head. The links snared around his helm; with a tug, the soldier was thrown into the mob of freed prisoners, falling beneath their blows.

Drew spied Opal making her getaway. He was forced to choose between Vega and Casper. The decision was easy.

The Werewolf bounded away from the Kraken, low to the ground, Moonbrand trailing behind him. One more leap and he'd be across to the arched portal that led to the staircase; she'd be trapped. The Werepanther hissed, her back arching as the lycanthrope tried to cut her off. Lifting Casper over her head, she threw him toward Ghul, the boy snatched from the air by one of the Kraken's lashing tentacles. With that, she turned and ran through the war room's grand entrance.

The punch that Opal took to her face was delivered with righteous fury. The attack came out of the darkness at the top of the spiral staircase, the heavy ursine fist catching her face dead center, the felinthrope landing in a broken heap.

A familiar-looking gang dashed in through the archway, a partially transformed Werebear leading them, the woodland green cloak instantly marking her out as Whitley. At her side came Figgis, first mate from the *Maelstrom*, dagger in one hand, shortsword in another. The wooden frame buckled as a huge figure squeezed through the arched entrance, filling the portal.

"Release them, Ghul!" roared the Whale of Moga, his feet threatening to splinter the floor beneath him.

Baron Bosa was unmistakable. At sixteen feet tall, his vast body was hatchmarked with old war wounds, the white skin stretched taut over brawn and blubber. Head and torso had merged into one, a mountain of muscle and menace. His mouth was a chasm, lined by rows of hard, stubby teeth that could crush rocks. In one giant hand he held a trident that glistened black by the torchlight.

"You fat fool, Bosa!" screeched the Kraken. "You come to my fortress and think you can command me?"

"Let them go," said Bosa, striding toward the Weresquid as Drew slunk through the smoke, his eyes never leaving the boy who was suspended in Ghul's grasp.

Prisoners rushed past now, dashing for the stairs, keen to be out of the structure before it finally collapsed. Dust fell from the ceiling in clouds, dispersed through the smoke as the Kraken struck out at the Whale, Bosa batting a tentacle away with a clublike fist.

"The scum that adorned my walls were a warning to you all!" screamed the Kraken. "A warning for you to stay away, lest you face the same punishment!"

"A warning?" the Whale said scoffingly, smacking another tentacle aside. "You idiot Squid. It was a surefire way of attracting my attention. Well," he said, his laughter vanishing. He raised his trident. "You have it now, Ghul."

"All of you!" cried the Kraken, raising Casper in the air and shaking him. "Stand down or Sosha help me you get your boy back in pieces!" The monster held Casper by his arms, a tentacle wrapped around each of them. The lad let out a cry of pain as the Squidlord's limbs went tight, threatening to tear him apart.

The mob hesitated, wary of what the enraged Kraken might do next. Moonbrand came down with a flash as Drew bounded at the monster, the blade slicing through a tentacle. The strain in Ghul's hold went instantly as the severed limb released Casper, the stump of its chopped tentacle spitting inky black blood into the air. Casper sailed over the flailing mob, out and over the open balcony, swallowed swiftly by the billowing black smoke.

Drew could see Vega suddenly coming to life. He raised his hands, which had now become clawed gray talons, shifting as he took hold of the tentacle that pinned him to the ceiling. Blood flowed from his wrists where the manacles were fixed, but Vega paid the wounds no heed. His fingers disappeared into the Kraken's flesh alongside his mouth, his jaws transforming enough to allow the Shark's teeth to come to his aid. The Kraken's violet limb parted, torn in two by the count's sudden, determined, and potentially suicidal attack.

Vega landed, rolling into a tumble, snatching the silver saber from where it stood buried in the floorboards. The Kraken turned its attention toward Count Vega now, away from the Wolf, but only in time to see the count's blade flash down diagonally across its body, from the uppermost side of its mantle on one side to the lowermost edge on the other. The wound opened instantly, threatening to separate the Kraken's wobbling body, but Vega wasn't done.

Drew staggered clear as the saber sang, ribbons of Squid flesh fluttering through the air, bloody black ink erupting from the beast. The Kraken was no longer fighting, a mess of blubbery flesh and twitching, suckered arms that trembled in their death throes.

"Vega!" cried Drew, trying to pull the Sharklord out of his vengeful reverie. Slowly the count turned to look at the young Wolf, and Drew stared into the depths of the man's sorrow, his black eyes emotionless and wet with tears. The saber clattered to the ground as the count wavered where he stood.

Drew jumped forward, catching Vega before he fell.

"We need to get out of here, my lad," boomed Bosa as another thunderous explosion shook the tower. The Whalelord raised a giant hand to the ceiling above, bracing the timbers should the roof collapse, the smoke now beginning to overwhelm them.

"I know," replied Drew, as Whitley placed a trembling hand on his shoulder and they looked down upon the distraught Vega.

"My boy," whispered the master of the *Maelstrom*. "My poor Casper."

"Captain!" shouted Florimo, the old sailor hopping deliriously from one foot to another as he pointed toward the balcony. All in the war room followed his excited finger out into the black sky beyond as the smoke swirled and eddied, a shape rising from its depths. Casper hovered in the air unsteadily, his body held aloft by two beautiful hawk wings that rose and fell from his slender back.

"Casper!" repeated Vega, his voice joyful now as he rose, the deathly black shade of the shark vanishing in a blink from his eyes.

6

Crossing the Redwine

STANDING ON THE enormous balcony of Redmire Hall, Gretchen looked down upon the flotilla that crossed the Redwine. The grounds of the Boarlord mansion were alive with activity, civilians crowding the gardens, yards, and wharf below. In happier times, Gretchen had summered here with her cousins Hector and Vincent. The Werelords of the Dalelands had always been especially close, and Huth had looked out for the young Foxlady as one of his own. These gardens had once been hers. Presently they belonged to the people of Redmire.

The crowds had gathered with all their worldly goods—chests, sacks, and trunks piled around them—waiting for transport across the surging river. The constant din of livestock accompanied the anxious chatter of the people as, family by family, they waited in turn. A steady stream of vessels traversed the Redwine, ferrying the townsfolk from shore to shore. The famed river barges, so often loaded with the fresh produce of the Garden of Lyssia, were now weighed down with the people they'd once served. Already a gaggle of Romari tents had appeared on the opposite bank, a temporary halfway house for the horde of Dalelanders who had chosen the Dyrewood as the safest destination in these troubled times. The nomads worked alongside Greencloaks, helping the people of Redmire alight on the other side. Gretchen gripped the banister. She couldn't help but wish she were with them, crossing the river, disappearing back into the haunted forest and heading for Brackenholme.

She glanced around the balcony, letting her mind wander back to her first encounter with Drew. He'd arrived here half naked and nearly starved after escaping the Lionguard with Hector. She'd taken an immediate dislike to him, as had he to her, the two of them worlds apart in ideology and outlook. This was the balcony where he'd taken her hostage, his claws at her throat. So had begun their grand adventure, with Hector in tow, as they'd traveled the rivers, woods, and terrible seas of Lyssia, ultimately to Highcliff where he'd faced down the Lion to claim his crown. Only that bauble had never found its way onto Drew's head. Before any coronation had taken place, those worlds—once so different but now so close—had been turned on their heads as Wolf and Fox were torn apart. What might have happened if they'd remained together?

An awkward cough clumsily alerted her to the fact that she was no longer alone. Turning, she found Trent standing at the doors that led out of the mansion. His newly acquired gray cloak hung to below his knees, the hood down across his broad shoulders revealing the thick mop of blond hair. One gloved hand rested on the pommel of his Wolfshead blade, sitting proud in its scabbard, while the other was folded neatly behind his back. He bowed. Inexplicably, Gretchen blushed, immediately looking back to the river.

"Since when did you cough to attract my attention, Trent?" she asked, Drew's face still fresh in her troubled mind. "And why the need to bow, all of a sudden?"

"You have visitors, my lady," said the Ferran boy, standing to one side as a man and woman joined him on the balcony.

"My lady," they said in unison, each bowing low as Gretchen turned and smiled, composing herself.

"Captain Gerard," she said to the first, stepping up to embrace him. "It's so splendid to see you fully recovered after your ordeal."

"I've never felt better," replied the old soldier with a smile. "All thanks to your brave Harriers. I never expected a reprieve before the executioner's block."

"And Captain Quist," said Gretchen, hugging the tall

green-cloaked ranger. "I can't express how good it is to see your face again. That it should be you who reaches out to us from the Dyrewood truly gladdens my heart, for I feared I'd never see anyone from Brackenholme again."

The woman smiled. "Nor we you, my lady. When you disappeared from Brackenholme during Vala's attack, many assumed you were killed. We have dear Stirga to thank for passing news to us that you had survived, Brenn bless his soul."

"Stirga, dead?" Gretchen gasped. She glanced at Trent, whose face instantly darkened.

"The last we saw of him was when we fled the city from the Wyldermen attack," said the young Graycloak.

"He died preceding the battle for Brackenholme, alas," replied Quist. "Though not in vain, I might add. It was the sword-swallower, on his deathbed, who urged Drew Ferran to come to the city's aid. Stirga was the bravest fellow and played a large part in ensuring that the Romari now patrol the roads of the Dyrewood alongside the Woodland Watch. The ancient forest isn't a place the Lion will dare enter in a hurry."

Gretchen kept her eyes on Quist, aware that Trent was intently watching her.

"And what of Drew? How is the Wolflord? That he lives comes as joyous news to all of us."

"Lord Drew remained with us in Brackenholme briefly, overseeing the initial rebuilding of the city, but he departed many weeks ago, searching for help in the struggle against the Catlords."

"Searching for help?" asked Trent. "Where did he go looking?"

Quist squinted at Trent momentarily. "You'd be the Wolf's brother—Trent Ferran, isn't it? I've heard much about you. You must be very proud of Drew."

Trent managed an awkward smile as Quist continued. "He headed to the White Sea. Seemed the only place where anyone was giving the Lion a run for his money was on the water. Drew went looking for Baron Bosa, the Whale of Moga. He reckoned the baron's force could help turn the tide of war."

"Have you heard anything of his success?" asked Gretchen. She couldn't hide the note of hopefulness in her voice. "Did he find the Whale?"

"I've no idea, my lady. Word's been trickling in to the Dyrewood that Bosa's strength wanes, that the Kraken's found some way of defeating the Whale. One can only pray that Drew is all right—and Lady Whitley, for that matter."

"Whitley went with him?" exclaimed Gretchen. "Surely she should have remained in Brackenholme. She would've been safer there, and her people need her! Who let her accompany Drew on his journey?"

"Let her?" said Quist, shaking her head. "Believe me, Lord Drew tried to prevent her, but she wouldn't have it."

"She'll get herself killed," said Gretchen angrily. Where the anger had come from, she couldn't tell, but for some reason the fact that Whitley and Drew were out there, together, irked her.

"My lady, I've worked alongside Whitley in the Woodland Watch. She's every bit as capable as any scout who's ever taken the Green. She's left the city in the hands of her uncle, Baron Redfearn, while Duchess Rainier convalesces. General Harker's there also. Brackenholme's in safe hands."

"Let us indeed pray they're both safe," Gretchen concluded. "While you're here with your people, overseeing the evacuation, please treat Redmire as your home, Captain."

Quist nodded as Gretchen turned back to Gerard.

"Any sign of the Lionguard?"

"None," said the captain. "Seems they turned tail and ran once Vorhaas was killed. Quite an unexpected victory for the people of Redmire."

"It's just a shame that victory comes at such cost," said Gretchen, the others muttering their agreement.

Thrilling though it had been for the people to chase the Redcloaks out of the Boarlord town, they knew the Catlords surely wouldn't stand by and let an uprising go unpunished. King Lucas was bound to send troops once news of Vorhaas's defeat reached his ears. In light of this, the decision to abandon Redmire had been quickly, and reluctantly, made.

"We've no choice but to leave the town, my lady," said Gerard. "It's with a heavy heart I leave—I was born here—but to stay would be suicide. This is the first place Lucas will come looking for revenge."

"Will you not come with me to Brackenholme, my lady?" asked Quist. "Surely the safest place for you to be is with your friends in the forest."

"Believe me, Captain, don't think I haven't considered it."

The Greencloaks had appeared at first light, news clearly having reached them of the uprising in Redmire. Two branches of the Woodland Watch had crossed the river by boat, quickly informing the Dalelanders of the sanctuary that awaited them within the Dyrewood and promising them safe passage along the Dymling Road.

"Where will you go, then?" asked Quist, following Gretchen as the Werefox headed back to the rail, looking out over the busy river.

"As enticing as it would be to run to the Dyrewood, I cannot leave the people of my realm to the Catlords. Lucas will strike out for what we've done to his army in Redmire. When he does, the Harriers and I need to be in the Dalelands, waiting for him. If he thinks we're scared of his Redcloaks, he's got another think coming."

"Aye," agreed Gerard, the old captain's chest swelling with pride.

"The city of Bray lies upriver of here," said Trent, "on the other side of Badgerwood. Perhaps Count Fripp's sympathetic to our cause. If the Harriers can cover the terrain swiftly, silently, leaving no tracks, that might be the perfect place for us to seek shelter ahead of the coming fight."

"Indeed," said Gerard. "Fripp's an old friend of the late Baron Huth. He sided with the Wolf when the Lion was overthrown in Highcliff. He may have bent the knee to Lucas in recent months, but I have my suspicions about where his loyalty truly lies."

"The Badgerlord knew my father also," added Gretchen. "He's a good fellow who loves the Dalelands. He won't turn us away."

"Very well, my lady," said Quist. "If you'll pardon me, I'll get back to the river and rally the townsfolk."

"Rally them?"

"Indeed," replied Quist. "Understandably, they're nervous about what awaits them in the Dyrewood."

"And they're saddened by what they're leaving behind," said Gerard.

Gretchen didn't even have to think. She turned back to the balcony's edge and called out over the Redwine.

"Do not fear the path that lies ahead!" she called, causing all on the river and those who crowded the banks to turn and face the balcony.

"You travel with friends into the Dyrewood. The Greencloaks

of the Woodland Watch know the land like no other, and you'll never find nobler guides than the Romari. Only enemies of the Woodland Realm consider the great forest haunted—it should hold no fear for you!"

She cleared her throat, aware that this last line rang hollow in her heart. The Dyrewood held plenty to fear, from the beasts lurking in the dark to the Wyldermen who still inhabited the forest. She and Trent had faced down monsters that had hunted them on two legs and four, even some that had slithered or scuttled through the trees. But the Dalelanders were fortunate that they traveled in huge numbers, with Greencloaks and Romari to escort them. *Just get to Brackenholme,* she silently prayed, *and then you'll be safe.*

"This is not the end of Redmire," Gretchen continued. "The Dalelands will breathe again, will rise from whatever ruin Lucas wreaks upon them. Shed no tears for the lives and land you leave behind. Look back at her and be confident that you shall return. This will be your home again one day. I give you my word!"

At this, the assembled folk of Redmire cheered, waving hands, scarves, and hats in the air as their spirits soared. Smiles appeared on faces. Gretchen smiled back, though inside her stomach was bound in knots.

"Brenn protect them," she whispered.

"That's my job, my lady," said Quist. The captain bowed once more before shaking hands with Trent and Gerard. With that she left, the aged captain following her, leaving Trent and Gretchen alone.

"You can go with them, you know," she said, without looking back at Trent. "You'll be safe in Brackenholme. You saw how well defended it was. The Wyldermen got in once—nobody ever shall again."

"No."

"If you travel with the Harriers to Bray, there's no guarantee what awaits us. Lucas may already have one of his cohorts in position there, just as Vorhaas was here and Krupha held Hedgemoor."

The fear gripped her heart, rising now, threatening to overwhelm her. It was true: who knew what awaited them in Bray?

"We could be marching toward a fate far more terrible than what awaits us here. I could be walking to my death," she said, her voice reed thin, catching in her throat.

"You won't walk alone," said Trent, leaning forward on the tips of his toes until he could whisper in her ear. She felt his fingers twine between hers as he gave her hand a firm, comforting squeeze. His breath blew her red ringlets against her pale cheek.

"I'll be right by your side."

7
The Lion Rides Out

MAGISTER SHURIKO'S HANDS, usually so sure and steady, shook with tiny tremors as he drew the thread through the torn flesh. He came from a long and troubled line of healers, each having served as court physician to the Panthers of Braga. The life span of many of Shuriko's forefathers had varied, the wisest living to a ripe old age while the clumsier, less elegant surgeons found their stay in the waking world curtailed. The Panthers had never suffered fools gladly, their tempers often famously getting the better of them. This was occasionally awful news for those magisters who were in service at the time. Shuriko was painfully conscious of the strange death of his own father, Magister Shappora, who had drowned in a shallow bowl of wine. This had been only a few years ago, with the young healer hastily propelled into his father's vacant position, thrown wide-eyed into the court of Braga. The fact that Shuriko's father had always abstained from alcohol had left a damning finger pointing at the Werelord he'd been serving when he'd met with his "accident," the same Shuriko now served: Onyx. The wound Shuriko was presently tending ran across the Beast of Bast's belly.

Onyx stood with his arms out to either side, as if he were being measured by a tailor rather than stitched back together. The injuries he'd received in combat with Duke Henrik had left a trail of bloody marks across his body, the most grievous of which ran from his right shoulder diagonally down to his left hip. Onyx should have died from that cut, at the hands of the White Bear, but instead their fates had been reversed by Lucas.

A misplaced jab of the needle provoked a flinch of discomfort from Onyx, his enormous black jaguars growling in response where they lay. Shuriko paused for a moment, gripped by fear.

"Don't be afraid of Kibwana and Kibibi, Shuriko," said Onyx. "They're only kittens. Wait until they're fully grown. Please, continue."

"I'll say one thing," said General Gorgo as he swilled his drink in his cup. "The battle's certainly swung our way. The Sturmish are on the run. Another big push and we'll have driven them out of the mountains."

"With the White Bear gone that leaves us free to march on Icegarden," added Count Costa as he watched Shuriko at work. "Then we can have our reckoning with Blackhand and the Crows. See what the Boar and his friends make of the king's Wolfmen."

This last comment brought a nervous laugh from the Hippo. The two Werelords sat by the fire in the center of Onyx's tent, relaxing after a fraught and frantic day in the field. The tent was modestly outfitted, his previous accommodation commandeered by the Lion upon his arrival. Gorgo and Costa looked weary, their armor soiled and pitted, but the men shared a look of relief that they were finally crossing swords with the enemy.

"Don't be so pleased to see our new 'allies' put to work, Costa," said Onyx as the magister pushed the needle through the pinched skin of his stomach. "This war might have suddenly tipped dramatically in our favor, but at what cost?"

"You have to admit," said Gorgo, "they've broken the deadlock."

"Indeed," said the Vulturelord. "Our men were growing fat and lazy, waiting for the thaw so the fight could begin. Lucas's Wyld Wolves have put fear into Sturmish hearts like nothing we could've done."

"Their unpredictable, savage nature terrifies our enemies," concurred the Hippo. "Demons like these don't live by our laws or fight by our rules."

"Something they hold in common with the king, then," said Onyx. "You speak about these Wolfmen as if they're heroes, Gorgo. They're abominations, bastardized therianthropes with no understanding of the power they hold. Cannibalizing their enemies? They strike fear into their allies' hearts as well!"

"Love 'em or loathe 'em, they've put us on the front foot," said the general. "Another week with them running riot ahead of us and we can start thinking about home. Nobody will stand in our way after victory in the Whitepeaks. These mountains were the Wolf's last hope."

"They disgust me," said Onyx, "and that won't change anytime soon. Ours will go down in history as a hollow victory, one that we couldn't achieve without the help of another."

"They're already saying that," muttered Costa. "After all, are we not here fighting Lucas's war for him?"

"I've said it before," growled Onyx. "An attack on one of the Catlords is an attack on Bast. Our war is just. As instructed by the Forum of Elders, we'll help this boy king achieve the victory his father was so incapable of. And then we'll remind the young Lion of what loyalty means."

"I don't follow," said Gorgo, sitting forward in his chair suddenly.

"I'd mind what you say, my lord," said Costa to Onyx, nodding at the healer who was hard at work stitching.

"Don't worry about Magister Shuriko," said Onyx. "He's been in my family longer than the young Lion has been alive.

He and his predecessors all understood loyalty. Isn't that right, Shuriko?"

The magister nodded quickly but didn't speak, his eyes locked on his work.

"Lucas needs . . . a gentle reminder of what it means to be a Bastian Catlord," continued Onyx. "A few lessons in loyalty, which I'm happy to administer."

"What if a gentle reminder doesn't work?" whispered Gorgo.

Onyx smiled. Before he could answer, the growls of his jaguars alerted the Werelords that someone approached his tent. The enormous cats suddenly rose, causing both Gorgo and Costa to flinch in their seats. Their massive heads faced the entrance flaps, which opened suddenly as Sheriff Muller stepped in. There was no waiting for admittance, no request for audience. The male cat, Kibwana, hissed at the human, but Muller ignored it as he spoke directly to Onyx.

"You need to come at once!"

Magister Shuriko rushed along, his case still open, the contents rattling as he struggled to keep pace. Onyx strode ahead of him, Muller at his side, pointing the way forward. The thread and needle still dangled from the Panther's torso, the magister's work unfinished, the wound still hanging open. A throng of Redcloaks and Bastians had gathered on the southern edge of the camp. As Onyx strode forward, the press of soldiers parted, allowing the Werelords through.

The other members of the war council were already present, General Skean at their center, the rest assembled around him. Beyond the councilors, a great deal of shouting and whinnying rose in the darkness as a heated exchange took place inside the stables. A man's body lay in the dirt at Skean's feet, one of the Lionguard's field surgeons tending him. Steam rose from the sweating mount that stood over him, the horse clearly ridden half to death.

"Major Krupha?" said Onyx to the injured man. "An odd time for you to pay a visit, isn't it?"

Though his greeting was sarcastic, it was clear by his voice that Onyx was concerned. Krupha was a good man, from the Panther's home city of Braga, and a most able commander in the field. That the major should turn up alone in the Badlands late at night was an alarming development.

"My lord," said Krupha, punching his chest by way of salute. The man's face glistened with a sickly hue. "I'd have sent a rider ahead to announce I was coming but couldn't find one faster than I."

The Lionguard surgeon carefully rolled Krupha, trying to make him comfortable. The pile of bloody rags beside them told their own tale, in addition to the arrow that had been removed from the hapless officer. The major was clearly in a lot of pain, struggling to remain conscious.

"Shuriko," said Onyx. "Lend a hand."

"But your stomach, my—"

"Help him now," ordered the Panther. "I want my best magister working on my best officer!"

Krupha's pained smile was suddenly hidden from view as Shuriko crouched over him.

"What happened?" asked Gorgo. "Why's Krupha here? Where's Vorhaas?"

General Skean turned to the Pantherlord, talking over the Hippo. "It would appear these Harriers of Hedgemoor are more determined than we gave them credit for. Redmire's fallen and Vorhaas is dead."

"These rebels killed the Ratlord?" asked Count Costa, incredulously. "How many did they number?"

"Hundreds, so Krupha reports," said Skean, the Cranelord looking down his long nose at the wounded major. "Then again, it wouldn't be the first time the sole survivor of a fallen outpost exaggerated the scale of his enemy."

"Don't be so quick to dismiss the major," said Onyx. "Krupha's a good soldier. Would you rather he'd remained and died with the useless Lionguard he'd been saddled with?"

The Redcloaks in the surrounding crowd grumbled their discontent at Onyx's description, but not a soul challenged him.

"I'd rather he'd have stayed by General Vorhaas's side," said the Cranelord. "We've lost a good general there."

"If he'd stayed by the Ratlord's side, he'd have been the

second to die, as well you know," grunted Gorgo at his rival.

"How has Vanmorten taken the news of his brother's demise?" asked Gorgo.

"How do you think?" replied Muller with a sneer. "With much gnashing of foul teeth and wringing of corrupted flesh. It's one big act with the Rats—they hate one another as much as any enemy."

"Would anyone care to explain exactly what we know?" asked Onyx.

The Pantherlord listened while General Skean recounted what Krupha had told them, from his earliest encounter with the Harriers on the Low Dale Road to their successful attack in Redmire. While the councilors argued over the precise details of what the major had said, Onyx was constantly aware of the noise from the nearby stables, the frequent snarls and hollers a backdrop to the bickering Werelords.

"The girl who led the attacks," said Onyx, now looking toward the stables. "You're sure he said she was a Werefox?"

On this Gorgo and Skean were in agreement.

"Yes." The Cranelord nodded. "She transformed and attacked Vorhaas up on the scaffold as he was about to execute one of the Harriers' leaders. Some blond lad with a Wolfshead blade did the rest."

"And Lucas is aware of these details?" asked the Panther with a grimace.

"Indeed," said Skean. "He went straight for the stables with his Wyldermen to—"

Onyx was running through the camp, bounding ever nearer the stables. As he arrived there he found a handful of frantic farriers, a couple nursing twisted limbs, one a bloody nose. One poor scrawny-looking youth crouched on his knees, nursing a bite on his forearm. Vanmorten stood among them, the Ratlord turning to Onyx as the Panther approached.

"I tried reasoning with him," screeched the Lord Chancellor, "but to no avail! If anything it is *I* who should be riding out, to seek vengeance for my brother's murder!"

The snorting and stamping of twenty horses caused the stable boys to scramble clear, leaving just Onyx and Vanmorten standing in their way. The Ratlord backed up a step as the stampeding horses almost ran them over, but the Werepanther stood his ground, unleashing a roar. The approaching beasts reared up in surprise, threatening to throw their riders from their saddles, but the Wyld Wolves held on. The monstrous riders snarled, snapping their jaws at Onyx as their horses stepped nervously. The Panther could see the mounts were as scared of their riders as they were of him, their eyes rolling wildly in their sockets.

"Stand aside, Uncle," snarled Lucas as he rode out from the midst of the mounted Wolfmen.

"No," the Panther replied simply. His stomach was bleeding again. "You're needed here, Lucas. You and your mob of . . . *Wyld Wolves.*"

"It's King Lucas, remember?" shouted the Lionlord furiously as his gray warhorse trotted forward. "And you may have heard: my future queen's been spotted in the Dalelands. I intend to bring her home."

"We need you here, Your Majesty, with your army. You assumed command from me, remember? You can't abandon that responsibility now. Your actions the other night—as much as I abhorred them—have proved decisive."

"I'll take that as a compliment," said Lucas.

"Don't," replied Onyx. "You've set a precedent for how this war shall be fought now. Any rules that we might have abided by in the past have been flung out the window. There can be no bartering, parlaying, or reasoning with the Sturmlanders now, not after what you did to their lord and what your Wolfmen did to their brothers!"

"You *needed* my intervention, Onyx! If the Wyld Wolves and I hadn't stepped in as we did, who knows how long we'd be fighting this war?"

"Spring is here!" roared the Panther, as a crowd began to gather behind him. "We were about to launch our offensive. Now is the time that suits my Bastian warriors—clement weather as opposed to the nether-withering cold of winter! I would've had the Sturmish out of the Whitepeaks before the week was out."

Gorgo, Costa, and the rest of the war council had joined Vanmorten, a sea of Redcloaks and Bastians at their back.

"You still can, Onyx," snarled Lucas. "My Wyld Wolves have made the job very easy for you. They've paved the way for you to march on Icegarden now, mopping up whatever resistance is left. I'm afraid I'm in need of Darkheart and his brothers, though. They won't be able to help you as they did the other night."

While the rest of the Wyldermen frothed and snapped at one another and their horses, only Darkheart remained in control. The shaman sat upright in the saddle of a black charger beside the king, his lupine eyes fixed upon the Pantherlord.

"That's my horse!" gasped Vanmorten suddenly, only for Darkheart to bare his teeth at the Ratlord.

"You must finish what you started here, Lucas," said Onyx. "My men of Bast shouldn't be held responsible for the atrocities your Wyld Wolves committed. Neither should the Lionguard or Muller's Skirmishers. You've unleashed these abominations upon the Sturmish. You must answer for their actions."

"You can answer in my absence, Uncle," said Lucas, dismissing Onyx with a wave. "My betrothed awaits me in the Dalelands. Who knows what nonsense they've filled her head with, but I'm confident I can rekindle our love."

"She hates you!" Onyx laughed.

"You and the other Catlords have always envied the passion of the Lions, Onyx," snarled Lucas. "Our strength and rage:

it must have been hard for the other felinthropes to stomach, my father's long shadow cast across the Lyssian Straits to Bast. He had his faults, but he conquered these Seven Realms, as shall I again. . . ."

He leaned forward in his saddle. "Once I have my bride."

Lucas kicked his warhorse hard, and the gray mount was off, the Wyldermen following after. Onyx stood where he was, his feet rooted to the ground, as the troop of horses parted like the sea around him. He turned slowly as they galloped away, heading south.

"He's right about one thing," said Count Costa, coming to stand beside Onyx, who glowered after the fading dust cloud. "Those Lions certainly are passionate."

8
The Reckoning

HECTOR STOOD IN the shadows of the Strakenberg Gate, ranks of Ugri warriors lining the road on either side, the swirling snow swallowing them from sight. Spring might have been on Sturmland's doorstep, but high in the Whitepeaks the weather remained cruel. Behind him, to the south, the distant sound of battle echoed as the Lion's army at last mounted its offensive on Duke Henrik's force. The Boarlord had stood on the walls of Icegarden alongside the Crowlords the previous night, staring out over a sea of fog, listening to the snarls and screams on the wind. Lord Flint and his brothers had traded thoughts on what therianthropes—or creatures—Onyx had unleashed upon the Sturmish. Nobody was sure, but all were in agreement that a line had been crossed, the Catlords playing a brutal, never-before-seen card, forever changing how this war would be fought.

For Hector to be beyond the walls was rare. The recent months had seen him locked away indoors, either questioning prisoners in the dungeons or scouring the mines for fabled relics. He'd come up short on both fronts. Duchess Freya and her Daughters of Icegarden remained tight-lipped as to the whereabouts of the Wyrmstaff, while the mines themselves were a warren of interconnecting caverns and smithies. On his forays, Hector had insisted on not only being accompanied by Ringlin and Ibal but also having a smith or two in tow. The mines were a dangerous enough place for a stranger to get lost in, but that peril was heightened by the magma and steam that flowed and flared deep within the Strakenberg.

The running of Icegarden had for the most part been left to Lord Flint, since Hector's search had kept him away from the throne room. This concerned those closest to him, Ringlin especially uneasy with the Crows taking a greater hold on the city. Flint had even begun to order the Ugri about, and what was more, they'd obeyed. The Crows were as untrustworthy as the Rats. Letting Flint make decisions in the Boarlord's name was the thin end of the wedge. As Ringlin saw it, Hector needed to be in the throne room, his eyes on those he called his allies. Yet instead, he stood outside the gates of Icegarden—*his city*—awaiting the arrival of prisoners who'd been captured in the Sturmish port of Shannon.

News of these three particular prisoners had piqued Hector's interest: an old man, a white-haired woman, and a girl, so the messenger reported. They'd been traveling east from the port town of Roof, far to the north. This wasn't any old man, either. He was a Werelord, having transformed and slain a number of the Ugri, before they'd overpowered him, with the great horns on his head that tore their fellow warriors in twain. *Could it be?* Hector wondered. *Could they* really *have walked straight into my grasp?*

Hector's flesh prickled with anticipation as he looked down at his hands. His right remained gloved, wrapped in black leather, protected against the elements. His left was bare, the withered, dead flesh creaking over his knuckles as he flexed his fists.

What will you do, brother? How will you greet them? hissed the Vincent-vile excitedly, wrapping itself around his shoulders like a spectral scarf.

"How do you think?" Hector said in a sickly whisper.

Ringlin glanced over from where he stood to the right, having caught his master's words, while Ibal hopped from one foot to the other. Two Axes stood to Hector's left, his commander within the Ugri force of Icegarden. Since Hector had taken the city, more Ugri warriors had traveled from their homeland of Tuskun to join the Boarlord in the Sturmish capital.

A crowd of Ugri emerged through the snowstorm, the honor guard rattling weapons against shields as they passed between their ranks. They were led by the Creep, the eagle-eyed scout who had first joined Hector alongside Two Axes. Three distinct, shadowy figures could be seen in the warriors' midst, the prisoners' heads bowed as they trudged ever nearer the Strakenberg Gate. Hector felt a wave of emotions rush through him: joy and sadness, fear and rage. These were his betrayers, brought back for the reckoning he'd promised himself.

Duke Manfred walked in front of the two ladies, his hands bound with thick ropes, Queen Amelie to his left and her lady-in-waiting, Lady Bethwyn, to his right. Bethwyn, the young Wildcat of Robben, kept her eyes fixed to the floor, while Manfred lifted his head as he approached. He squinted through the snow as it lashed his face, the whiskers of his straggly gray beard coated with ice. His narrow eyes widened when he realized whom he faced.

"Dear Brenn, no," he said, his voice heavy with dismay.

Hector stepped forward, struggling to form a response. The Boarlord's hand went to his hip, whipping the jeweled dagger from his belt, thrusting it forward, and jabbing it in the air toward the Staglord Manfred. Whatever hopes Hector had harbored of a witty, sophisticated speech had dissipated, washed away by a wind of fury. The duke took a faltering backward step as the magister came at him.

"You *left* me for dead in Friggia!" Hector raged.

Manfred stood his ground now, staring Hector down.

"You're a murderer, Hector. We know full well what you did to Vega. How *could* you?"

"He was a killer! Don't shed a tear for that monster—he couldn't be trusted!"

"He'd sworn an oath, to the Wolf, just as you and I had. When did it happen?"

"When did *what* happen?" Hector spat out, his Boarguard moving around him, the tension beyond Icegarden's gate threatening to melt the city's frozen walls.

"When was it that an oath no longer meant a jot to you?"

Hector clenched the dagger, sorely tempted to run the old fool through the belly.

Pompous old deer! Who does he think he is, Hector? Kill him, now! Let the snow taste his innards!

Hector ignored the vile, fighting the rage with every fiber of his being. He wanted to show them what kind of man he was, what kind of Werelord he'd become. He couldn't throw it all away with the flash of a blade. These turncoats were worth more to him alive than dead, especially the queen. She might buy him Lucas's forgiveness for his betrayal, and Hector needed that if he wanted the new king to accept that another power existed in the Seven Realms, one he could work alongside rather than against. The cards were falling into place. The Boarlord's time was at hand.

"The Wolf's Council was sundered once Drew disappeared, Manfred. Those oaths now mean nothing."

"Not true, Hector, as well you know," said the duke with disdain. "Word reached Shannon before your Ugri thugs seized us: Drew's alive, isn't he?"

Hector struggled to hide his annoyance with Manfred.

"Indeed, Drew lives. But what of it? He provided us with hope when the council was formed, but that didn't last long. Lyssia's a different world to the one that Drew's light briefly flickered in. If he has returned and is prepared to join me, for the good of all the Seven Realms, then this is great news for all."

"And if he isn't?" asked Manfred. "If he sees you for what you are? A traitor?"

Hector sneered at the Staglord. "If Drew cannot work with me . . . then he is against me. If it came to this, none would be more saddened than I. I loved Drew. But what allies—or hope—does Drew still truly have? His bridges have crumbled; his friends are all but dead. He needs me a fine sight more than I need him, Manfred. Look around you: where is your savior of the Seven Realms when his people need him?"

Hector's head twitched to one side as Amelie's legs buckled at the comment, his words striking her like a physical blow. Ringlin stepped forward and caught her before she fell, Ibal stepping in to assist him.

"I'm sorry, Your Majesty," said Hector. "Truly I am. Drew was the dearest friend I've ever known. But times have changed, as have the stakes."

"You're a monster," Amelie, held up by the Boarguard, cried out with a sob.

"I'm a servant of Lyssia."

"You serve yourself," Manfred shot back.

Hector ignored the duke. "With the last of the Gray Wolves gone, Lyssia needs someone to step into the vacuum. There are thrones that need filling, *throughout* the Seven Realms."

His eyes settled on Manfred, a knowing smile spreading across Hector's pale, sunken face.

"What news from Stormdale?" whispered Manfred, his fierce look replaced with one of hope in an instant.

Hector walked up to him, coming face-to-face with the cantankerous old duke. The Boarlord knew of the fate of the Staglord's home, Stormdale—that the city had survived the relentless attack of the Lion's army and driven the invading forces out of the Barebones. But the duke didn't know.

"Your precious city fell, Manfred, as did those within its walls. Last I heard, the Crows and the Rats were tearing it apart brick by brick, plucking ripe eyeballs from the dead. Your time's over, Staglord."

Manfred's head went down, his chin landing on his chest. Hector turned to Ringlin and Ibal, who nodded approvingly, the queen hanging between them by her arms. As he turned back to the duke, Manfred's head was already rising, the antlers erupting from his brow and catching the Boarlord in his chest, lifting him off the ground. Hector felt a puncturing sensation in his chest, the air escaping his torso as the spiked tine found a lung.

Ringlin and Ibal dropped the queen into the snow and, joining the Ugri, circled the Staglord as he held the maimed magister on the antlers over his head. Hector writhed, the pain absolute and immeasurable. He couldn't breathe, his body weight forcing the antlers deeper with every passing moment, the tine sliding between his ribs.

The Creep's fist struck Manfred's kidneys, sending the exhausted Staglord to his knees. That was all it took; his head fell forward and Hector slid off the antlers. The Boarlord fell into the snow, withered hand clutching the chest wound, his lips running red.

"Kill him!" he ordered, gurgling, the blood catching in his throat as he glared at the Staglord. Two Axes stepped forward, raising his weapons.

"No!" cried Bethwyn, the young lady of Robben throwing herself in the way of the Ugri's axes. Two Axes faltered, unsure of what to do, glancing back at his liege for direction.

Hector's black hand flew out, the vile seizing its moment. Quick as a snake, it coiled around Bethwyn's throat, the Ugri recoiling as the girl's hands went to her neck, clawing at the invisible phantom.

Hector shook his head, his vision blurring. What was happening? Why was he in pain? Where was he? He lurched up, his left side seeming to crumple, sending him back onto one knee in the snow. The metallic taste of blood was thick in his mouth, coating his gullet. He staggered to his feet between the Ugri, jeweled dagger in hand.

Bethwyn spun on her toes, doing a grisly dance in the snow, Vincent's phantom attacking her indiscriminately, her audience the warriors of Tuskun. Manfred reached up, trying to help her, but two mace blows sent him down to the ice. Hector could see the vile, working its wicked magic, a thin black noose of smoke constricting the throat of the girl he'd once fancied. He raised his hand to call it back, trying to concentrate, but his mind was still fogged with pain, leaving him unable to master the demon.

A movement and a cry to his right caught his eye, a shape coming forward into his field of vision. Instinct told him to lash out, knock the intruder away, and his right hand connected with the figure's chest and sent it backward. The jeweled dagger was suddenly out of his hand—there one moment, gone the next. He turned to see whom he'd struck.

Queen Amelie staggered back along the road, her back turned to him. The fury and anger that had consumed Hector vanished, his mind refocusing in an instant and causing the vile to cease its attack.

What are you doing, *Hector?* hissed his brother, enraged to have its moment of indulgence snatched away.

"Silence!" cried the Boarlord with wheezing breath, taking a faltering step of his own after the queen. "Your Majesty . . ." he said, both hands raised before him, taking her by the shoulders and turning her to face him.

Amelie's skin was paler than ever, her blue lips trembling as the tears froze in her fading gray eyes. Her hands trembled around the dagger hilt, where it protruded from her chest, buried into her heart. She fell into the magister's arms, her lips brushing his earlobe as she tried to speak.

"I . . . I forgive you. . . ."

A horror like he'd never known engulfed Hector. Amelie's head lolled back, her eyes shifting from gray to yellow as they stared into the heavens. White lupine fur raced from her flesh, her teeth sharpening as her mouth opened for one final cry to the heavens. The lingering howl that emerged was the most mournful wail Hector had ever heard, a scream of sorrow that leapt higher than the Strakenberg and echoed across the Whitepeaks. The Ugri ran clear, covering their ears, looking away, terrified by the noise. Hector held her, his body reverberating, alone with her in his arms. The white fur receded, the canines disappeared, and as the howl's last note escaped Queen Amelie's lips, her life went with it.

PART V

TURNING THE TIDE

I
The *Nemesis*

BEING A SHEPHERD boy who'd grown up on the Cold Coast, Drew had limited nautical knowledge, but even his novice eye recognized the *Nemesis* as something spectacular. "Dreadnought" was the word Count Vega had used to describe such a vessel, a towering, four-masted man-of-war that dwarfed the ships of the White Sea. While the galleons of Westland's navy were impressive affairs, fifty to sixty yards in length, the dreadnoughts were in excess of seventy strides from aft to figurehead. Most striking of all was the *Nemesis* battery, three artillery decks as well as cannons mounted on the quarterdeck and forecastle.

Standing at the prow presently, Drew found himself staring at one such cannon, a long, bronze monster that squinted toward the horizon. A chest was positioned beside it, nailed to the deck, its iron shot loaded within. Somewhere belowdecks was no doubt the blasting powder used to fire these projectiles. He prayed it was safely under lock and key. Vega had been at pains to point out that although many warships of the White Sea had cannons, the Lyssians hadn't yet mastered control of the deadly blasting powder. Accidents still happened all too often. The Sharklord was right to be concerned. That the Bastians had harnessed the power of the black powder, loading their battleships with three decks of the cursed cannons, was an alarming development.

"Your sight may have returned, but your hearing's not what it was."

Drew jumped at the voice, turning to find a smiling Whitley standing close behind, the Lady of Brackenholme clearly having taken great delight in sneaking up on him. He embraced her without thinking twice, so happy to be reunited.

"You also smell a lot better now," she said, laughing as they parted.

"Crawling through a sewer can wreak havoc upon a boy's bouquet," he replied. "If there'd been another way of getting into that sea fortress, believe me, I'd have taken it."

"You've quite the following, Drew," she said, glancing to either side of the *Nemesis*. A fleet of ships kept formation with them, a dozen on either side. Many of them were Bastian, the remainder pirate ships, all of them seized from the Squidlord

Ghul. The Kraken's sea fortress had been destroyed, the White Sea finally claiming it as its flaming remains crashed and sank beneath the waves. The hundreds of pirates who'd been imprisoned by Ghul now manned the armada, loyal to Drew. The *Maelstrom* kept pace at the *Nemesis*'s starboard bow, with Bosa's ship, the *Beluga*, flanking port side.

"*We* have a following," he corrected her. "These people aren't just fighting for the Wolf, Whitley. They fight for Lyssia's freedom."

"They're calling for you," she said.

"Best not keep them waiting then, eh?" he replied as the two set off aftward.

Drew found it almost impossible to resist saluting the smiling sailors who passed them by. The Bastians from the *Nemesis* had been put ashore on the uninhabited island between Hook and Cutter's Cove, along with the other survivors from Ghul's force. Until the war was over, they'd remain marooned on that desolate lump of rock known as Blackspire. Those of value to them—captains, therians, and the like—had been kept aboard the *Nemesis*, locked up in the brig. A relieved Casper was back aboard his beloved *Maelstrom* with the count. Drew had yet to talk with Vega about the boy's revelation. The wings that sprouted from his back seemed to have taken all but the Sharklord by surprise.

"I don't know why you've let her live," said the Lady of Brackenholme as they walked.

He didn't need to ask whom she was referring to; there was only one other woman aboard and Whitley had made no secret of how much she despised Opal. The Pantherlady presently languished in the brig with her fellow Bastians.

"She's a prisoner of war. There are codes of conduct we should follow and respect."

"She followed no such code of conduct when she ordered Lucas to kill my brother."

Drew winced at her honest words.

"I'm sorry for that, Whitley. But she might hold the key to unlocking the Bastian stranglehold on Lyssia. We have an asset there—a hostage—who's of immense value, to both ourselves and the Catlords. Can't you see that?"

"All I see is the woman who had my brother murdered, and a friend who's gone back on his word."

Drew stopped and took Whitley by the shoulder, turning her to face him.

"Are you accusing me of betraying you?" he asked incredulously.

"You promised me justice aboard the *Lucky Shot*," she said coldly. "If the Hammerhead hadn't murdered Captain Violca, she'd be my witness to what you said."

"You'll get your justice, Whitley, in whatever form."

"You know exactly what kind of justice I seek, Drew," she replied calmly. "Opal's a monster who needs putting to the sword. She took Broghan from me. The way I see it, this shouldn't even be up for debate." She tugged herself free and continued toward the rear of the ship.

"An eye for an eye," she called back as she went.

Drew trudged up the stairs to the aft deck, not for the first time feeling the weight of responsibility heavy upon his shoulders.

The three commanders of the armada stood examining the vast sea chart laid out before them. A fourth figure kneeled before them, his bony figure sprawled across the giant scroll. Four sabers pinned the enormous map to the deck. Count Vega, Baron Bosa, and Captain Ransome all looked up as first Whitley and then Drew joined them.

"Couldn't you find a bigger chart?" Drew joked.

"Remarkable, isn't it?" said the eccentric old navigator, Florimo, from where he crouched. Clean and changed after his incarceration aboard the sea fortress, he was now every inch the dandy. His white vestments were accented by an enormous pink feather that protruded from the bandanna that capped his head.

"It covers the entirety of the Lyssian Straits," he continued, "from Haggard to Port Stallion."

"It's good to have you aboard, Lord Florimo," said Drew to the sailor. "I hadn't met any of your kind before."

"A Ternlord?" said the navigator. "We're a proud, solitary breed. Ocean travelers, star readers, map enthusiasts, and whatnot. Frightfully exciting folk. Was a time there wasn't a ruler in the Seven Realms who didn't entertain a Ternlord in court, so fascinating were the tales of our exploits. We were once considered Lyssia's greatest explorers, you know?"

"Long, long ago, eh?" said Vega with a smile.

"That's quite the decoration you have there, Lord Florimo," said Drew, pointing to the drooping pink feather on his head. "Where does a chap get such a thing aboard a pirate ship?"

"My gratitude's to Bosa for that, my boy," said the Were-tern. "He's got a chestful below! And you can drop that Lord nonsense. I was never one for flowery talk and highfalutin titles."

Drew didn't miss Vega's grin at that.

"These maps also give us a fine insight into the Bastian coastline, as well as all in between," said the flamboyant Baron Bosa, his jeweled fingers rattling as he clapped his hands together. "Quite remarkable, really."

"It's certainly a coup," said Captain Ransome. "Very little's known about Bast, its waters uncharted by Lyssian ships."

Drew knelt beside Florimo and ran his hand over the scroll. It felt smooth and leathery to the touch.

"What's it made from?"

"The flayed skin of some poor beast," replied Bosa. "Or some poor soul, I suspect. Judging by the resilience of the scrolls, I suspect this came from a butchered therianthrope."

Drew recoiled and stood, instinctively wiping his hand on his thigh after contact with the map.

"You say scrolls, plural? There are more of them?"

"Six in all," answered Ransome. The elderly pirate had been rewarded for his service with captaincy of the *Nemesis*. "One charts Lyssia, as fine as any maps in the Seven Realms. The rest seem to cover the jungle continent and other lands, Sosha knows where."

"To think," said Vega, "when we first encountered the Catlords twenty years ago we thought them savages. How wrong we were: terrific tacticians, incredible ship builders, and a fighting force to rival anything in Lyssia. In addition they've mastered the black powder and have traveled to the edges of the known world."

"And found their way back again," added Whitley.

"So what have we discovered?" asked Drew.

Bosa and Ransome both looked to Vega, clearly the expert when it came to acquiring information from prisoners. The Sharklord smiled. Weary and wounded though he was from his ordeal, he was slowly becoming himself once more.

"Some of the brig's residents are more talkative than others, especially this fellow," he said, clicking his fingers as two of Ransome's marines led a manacled sailor across the deck to Drew.

"The name's Hobard," said the prisoner. "Captain of the *Motley Madam*."

"I know your ship," said Drew, casting his mind back to the pleasure vessel from Ghul's harbor. "The two-master?"

"Indeed she was. Poor girl got burned up proper in that fire."

"Our hearts bleed for your loss, Hobard," said Vega, clutching his chest. "Tell Lord Drew what you told me."

"Right you are, Count Vega," said the man nervously. "You only got a bit of the Cat fleet up 'ere, see? Just a small amount of what Sea Marshal Scorpio brought with him. He must have fifty warships still off Calico."

"Scorpio?" exclaimed Whitley.

"Commander of the Bastian fleet, my lord," replied Hobard.

"Fearsome devil," added Bosa. "A Werelord of the Sea, and that's what name he goes by. I don't actually suspect his parents gave him that name. . . ."

"So if fifty warships remain in the southern sea, and there are ten Bastian ships among our number—where are the rest?" asked Drew. "Vega, you said that there were over a hundred in their armada when they first attacked Lyssia."

"I expect many returned home. They'll have been transporting the Bastian army, remember. They've served their purpose in that regard. The remaining force is the sharp end of Onyx's naval might, and they're anchored off Calico's doorstep."

"Could we attack them?" asked Drew hopefully.

"We number but two dozen, more than half of which aren't dreadnoughts," replied Vega. "It would be suicide to draw the Bastians into battle."

Drew looked up the mainmast to the black flag that fluttered atop.

"They're hardly going to attack their own, though, are they?" he replied with a smile.

"You'd propose we surge into the heart of the Bastian navy, sailing their ships and flying their flags?" said Bosa, his jowls wobbling and eyes bulging.

"Indeed."

"Splendid stuff!" exclaimed the Whale of Moga. "I do love a good ruse."

"We'll need the signal codes to get anywhere near Scorpio's fleet," said Vega.

"There's mates o' mine in the brig who can help you there," said Hobard earnestly. "We might be skippers o' boats that served Ghul, but we never signed up with no Catlords. We know what flags to fly in what manner, y'see, so's not to raise suspicion."

Vega nodded.

"Take him below," said Ransome. "Pick out who can help us and have them brought up. Let's see if any of them want to earn their freedom."

Hobard smiled as he was led away, his manacles rattling as he disappeared belowdecks.

"Can we trust him?" asked Drew.

"The man's a fool, but straight enough," said Ransome. "He and I were both in Ghul's service at the same time. While my *Leviathan* was hunting you down, Vega, his *Motley Madam* was busy running contraband under Lucas's nose, skimming the top off the Lion's taxes. Ghul might've worked for Onyx and Opal, but he was still a thief and pirate at heart."

"So Hobard and his friends can give us the code for safe passage," said Bosa, "as well as alert us to whatever tricks the Bastians have up their blouses."

The sudden screams below startled them all. Ransome was the first to start running toward the hatch. Drew followed, feet thumping the steps as they descended through the gun decks. Sailors passed wary looks to one another as they rushed by, following the cries rattling through the warship's innards, leading them straight to the brig. Bursting through the doors into the dark prison chamber, none were prepared for the sight that awaited them. Whitley crashed into Drew's back, gasping in shock as Bosa let loose a cry.

The iron gate was thankfully now closed, with the one surviving marine slumped against the wall, far away from the barred partition. Within the holding cell, his companion had been slaughtered. In addition, the dead and dying bodies of eight prisoners lay, motionless, twitching, or breathing their last. Opal stood over them, the cutlass of one of the marines in her manacled grasp. At her feet lay Captain Hobard, his throat torn from his body. Though she wasn't transformed, the manacles that prevented her from shapeshifting hadn't restricted her horrific assault. Her chin glistened where the skipper of the *Motley Madam*'s blood stained her jaw.

"I'm afraid none of my acquaintances will be able to assist you, Wolflord," she said with a snort.

Drew felt Whitley's hand grip his forearm, her fingers almost transforming into claws and puncture his flesh.

"I warned you, Drew," she whispered quietly, choking on the hate that had risen in her throat. "An eye for an eye. It's the only way."

2
The Chapel of Brenn

BENEATH THE PALACE of the White Bears lay the Chapel of Brenn. The frigid world above sent chill winds through the corridors, while the fires of the Strakenberg vented heat from below. The sacred chamber was the oldest structure within Icegarden, carved out of the caves by the first ursanthropes who founded the city. The ancient Dragonlords might have lived on the fire mountain long ago, but with the passing of the great lizards, Brenn's children had inherited the world as their own. From here the Bearlords had built up and out, over and through the Whitepeaks, reaching skyward with their colossal citadel as the city grew around it. Spiritually, the tiny chapel of the Bearlords was the beating heart of Sturmland, the first pawprint in the snow.

A domed room that reached thirty feet at its highest point, the walls were covered with crumbling mosaics and fading frescoes, featuring scenes from Brenn's saga that shaped the fabric of therian religion. Candles sat in alcoves, casting their gloomy light across the chamber, their wax running to the floor like static waterfalls. The altar in the chapel's heart was purely ceremonial, as sacrifices were a long-abandoned tradition from less civilized times. The granite table was where Brenn's priests conducted their sermons and prayers, and when a lord or lady of Icegarden died, tradition dicatated that the body should lie in state upon the altar for a week.

Queen Amelie lay on the stone slab, draped in a white funeral shroud. A brazier burned at the altar's head, smoking incense filling the air as its glowing coals illuminated the dead queen's body. Hector sat slumped on the floor beside it, staring at the shadows as they danced across the crooked walls. The pain in his chest was constant. Healers had been put to work, draining the blood from his lung and stitching him up, but it would take a magister to repair the damage dealt by Manfred's antler. Hector couldn't understand why the wound was so slow to heal. He would have attempted the magicks himself, but his mind and body were fogged as if gripped by fever. He might have been alone but for the constant whispering in his ear, his brother's spirit always close at hand with words of torment.

She threw herself upon your dagger, dear brother, said Vincent.

Hector could hear the smile in the vile's voice. *Try not to dwell upon it.*

"I lashed out. I didn't know what I was doing. I should never have had the accursed dagger out in the first place!"

Ah, that blade's a tricksy thing, dear brother, as I learned to my own cost in Bevan's Tower. You remember, don't you?

Hector closed his eyes, willing the spirit to be silent, but the image was emblazoned in his mind's eye: he and Vincent, locked in an embrace, the jewel-encrusted weapon buried deep in his brother's heart.

That's two *therianthropes that gaudy knife's claimed the lives of now, Hector, and it isn't even enchanted! They'll be naming it a thing of legend before long, you mark my words.*

"I was confused. I never meant to hurt anyone."

You meant to hurt Bethwyn, brother. You thought she was marriage material once, didn't you? How quickly your mood changes.

His brother's demented spirit giggled. Since the death of Amelie, the vile had been animated as never before, thriving on Hector's discomfort.

"You did this," the magister whispered, glancing up at the corpse on the altar. "Every poisonous word you've whispered led me here."

That's a bold claim, brother, considering it was your hand that plunged the knife into her heart. So quick to shift the blame. Nothing's ever your fault, Hector. You were always the same, even as a child.

"I don't claim to be blameless," said Hector, sniffing back

a sob. He tugged the glove off his left hand and threw it on the floor, turning the gnarled black limb from side to side, regarding it with disgust.

"I'm weak willed. I let you tell me what to do, allowed you to run roughshod over good reason and common sense. If I'd been stronger, I would've silenced you sooner."

Silenced me? the Vincent-vile echoed scoffingly. *You still think you control me? I'm not some djinn you can force into a stoppered bottle. I'm your shadow, Hector, everywhere you go. You'd be lost without me!*

"I don't *need* you, Vincent!" Hector snapped. "It's you who needs me, feeding off me like a parasite. I have friends. What do you have?"

You have nobody, Hector. You're a loveless, lonely loser.

"I have Ringlin and Ibal," Hector whispered.

I'd sooner be unloved, hissed the vile.

"Quiet!" snapped Hector, rising from the floor to shout at the shadows, finally finding his voice. "I see I've made mistakes now, all too clearly! I realize I've been a fool!"

Hector reached out, clutching the altar's edge in both hands as the grief-stricken sobs shook his body.

A bit late in the day for tears, brother. Who are these in aid of?

"These are the first honest emotions I've felt since . . . since I don't know how long!" Hector cried. "And look what it took for me to see the light: the mother of my best friend dying! Killed by my hand!"

Get a hold of yourself! hissed Vincent, the phantom now materializing before his eyes, the shadows taking shape through the clouds of smoking incense. *You're an embarrassment! You* wanted *this! You've earned Icegarden and your enemies' respect—don't throw it all away now in a moment of weakness!*

"It isn't weakness!" shouted Hector, his face contorted with fury, the veins bulging on his neck. Spittle frothed on his lips as his eyes burned red with tears. He cried out as the pain in his chest struck again, his ruined lung dogging every movement. He wagged his blackened hand at the air, pointing at the fiend as the vile circled him.

"This is how I feel!" shouted Hector, his other hand punching his left bosom. "This is how I should always have felt, but you and your hatred stole it away from me. I had love in my heart once, for my friends, for my family, and you ruined it, killed it. You sucked whatever goodness there was from my soul, Vincent, as sure as a leech gorges on blood!"

I made you stronger, you ungrateful wretch! I gave you purpose and drive, I showed you a life where you had none before. I ruined you? It was you who killed me, remember?

"I wish I'd never become a magister." Hector sobbed. "I thought I could help people with my magicks, serve them, heal them, but it's brought me nothing but misery! I should've wasted my youth as you did, a self-serving, malingering gambler. When did you ever do anything for anyone other than yourself, brother?"

You have the gall to ask me that? You took my life and you've used me ever since, Hector: your attack dog, your slave!

"I don't need you," snarled Hector suddenly, a smile appearing across his crazed face. He nodded feverishly, suddenly onto something. "Yes, that's it. You've served me for the last time, Vincent. I release you from your bond. Go, brother. Take the long sleep at last. Or find some other soul to torment, I care not. But I'm done with you."

You don't get *to release me, Hector. You never summoned me, remember? I was born the night I died. I'm part of you. I will always be beside you, behind you, within you. . . .*

"Get out!" Hector screamed, the jeweled dagger in his hand now.

All the power at the tips of your withered fingers, and you'd throw it away. On the threshold of greatness you'd turn away, step back. . . .

"Out!" cried Hector, slashing ineffectually at the swirling vile.

Wasted on you . . .

The vile was laughing now, mocking Hector as he tried to dispel it, reveling in his misery.

He blinked, trying to see through the tears and sweat that blinded him, his dagger hand weary as the vile cackled. Hector looked to his other hand. The black fingers twitched, as if possessed with a life of its own, skeletal digits clawing at the air before him. Seizing the moment, Hector thrust the necrotic limb deep into the burning brazier, the white-hot coals rolling over the dead flesh as the flames licked up its length. The dark skin crackled and broke under the blistering heat, peeling away to reveal the gray, rotten flesh beneath, the pain registering with Hector for the first time in a long while. His scream shook the chapel, Vincent's cry mixing with his own as the phantom suddenly began to dissipate, its form blown away on the breeze.

Wasted . . . the vile hissed for the last time before blinking out of existence.

Hector dragged his smoking hand out of the brazier and fell against the altar, his body wracked by sobs. He wasn't sure how long he knelt there, his brother's cursed words still ringing in his ears, blood thumping through his temples. Though he knew the shadow was gone, his eyes searched the room for any sign of the vile.

"Hector."

His name repeated, again and again, at last drew him from his stupor. He glanced around the chamber, his eyes finally finding Ringlin, who stood at the open door to the chapel. The Boarguard captain stared at him fearfully.

"Are you all right?"

"He's . . . he's gone," gasped the young magister, collapsing to the floor, the jeweled dagger skittering across the flags.

"Vincent's gone?" said Ringlin, approaching and placing a tentative hand on Hector's shoulder. He glanced at the deformed limb in the Boarlord's lap, the burned and blackened flesh still sizzling, the stench unbearable.

"Yes," sniffed Hector. "The darkness . . . it's lifting. I am . . . myself again."

The boy from Redmire slowly began to sit upright, Ringlin helping him rise. Hector stared down at the withered black limb with fresh, horrified eyes. The hole through the center of the palm, the skeletal fingers, the corrupted flesh—he was a monster.

"How did I come to be this?" he whispered, as much to himself as Ringlin. Lightning quick, his mind raced through the events of the recent past, every poor choice, each regrettable action. "So many decisions I've made, so terribly wrong. And you, Ringlin. You and Ibal helped me. Why didn't you stop me?"

Ringlin shrugged. "Wasn't our place. We worked for you, remember? Still do, for that matter. You tell us to do something, we do it. We're yours to command."

"But you must have *known* that some of those deeds were wicked."

The captain shook his head, showing no remorse. "I'm sorry, but you more than anyone knew that Ibal and I were no angels when we entered your employ. You pay and promise a man enough gold, he'll likely do anything."

These men had killed for Hector, murdering people without a second thought. Could they truly be considered his friends still?

"Epiphany or not, my lord, you can still count on us. I didn't much care for your brother when he was alive, even less so when he was dead. You've been good to us, and we can continue to be good to you. What would you have us do?"

Hector looked at Amelie's body forlornly, shaking his head with regret. His cheeks remained wet with tears, his sorrow a sea he could drown in. Some of his earliest memories revolved around the queen. On their visits to Highcliff as infants, Hector and Vincent were invariably left in the care of the royal nursemaids. Leopold's wife, so stern and serious to all who visited the court, would share a smile or a laugh with the young Boars when alone in their company, rare moments of warmth from the woman who would forever mourn the loss of Wergar, the Wolf she had loved.

"I need to begin righting my wrongs," said Hector quietly, realizing the terrible gravity of his predicament. "Has Flint returned from his travels yet?"

"No. The Crowlord and his brethren are still on the wing, engaged with the Cranelords of Bast in the mountains. That said, I've no idea when he'll return. Why?"

"We need to act swiftly and without his knowledge," said Hector, his mind now firing with ideas. "Icegarden is no longer safe for any of us. We must leave."

Hector placed his pale right hand over the shroud that covered Amelie, his palm gently caressing her brow.

"And what of the prisoners?" said Ringlin. "Freya and the Daughters of Icegarden? Carver and Manfred? All the others?"

Hector turned to his man and smiled. "They're coming with us, Ringlin."

3
A Mother's Love

LEANING ON THE rail of the quarterdeck, Drew watched the crew of the *Nemesis* as they sat in huddles, eating and drinking, their voices low. Florimo had led them in a chorus of shanties throughout the day, to take their minds off the horrors that had occured in the brig. The songs had ceased by sunset, a gloomy mood settling over the warship. The farther south they sailed, the closer they were to the Lyssian Straits and the Bastian armada that awaited them. Considering how well drilled the Catlord forces were, many feared they were sailing to their doom.

Drew turned, surprised to see Vega approach from the aft deck. "You're still here? They'll be forgetting you aboard the *Maelstrom* before long."

"Not for a long time," replied the Sharklord. "I had to consult the Bastian sea charts one last time. See if there was some alternative to striking blind in the dead of night."

Drew arched an eyebrow and Vega shook his head.

"And Whitley. Is she speaking with you yet?"

"No," said Drew. "I'm not sure she will again."

"Not until you let her have Opal's head anyway, eh?"

"I wonder if I should let Whitley have her justice. What use is Opal to us now? She'll never talk."

Drew was grateful Vega didn't provide counsel. He knew the Shark wouldn't have shied away from giving Whitley a silver blade and letting her exact her revenge on the Pantherlady. But Vega knew Drew well enough, too, and rightly suspected that the young Wolflord wouldn't sanction such an act.

"You know it's been many days since we escaped Ghul's sea fortress," said Drew.

"And?" said Vega, stiffening instantly, knowing what question was coming.

"Casper: he's a Hawklord. How long have you known?"

Vega's chin dropped as he smiled. "That he was a Werelord? I've known that since he was a babe in arms. That he was an avianthrope? That's news even to me," he said wryly, shaking his head.

"I asked Casper once how he came into your service," said Drew. "He told me his parents had died and you'd taken him in as one of your own, grooming him for a place aboard the

Maelstrom. You didn't tell him what really happened, did you?"

"And what should I have told him?" asked Vega.

"That his mother was Lady Shah of Windfell and his father was Count Vega of the Cluster Isles. And that they both lived."

Vega grabbed and led Drew away from where the crew were gathered. He bundled him into the shadows and held him against the ship's rail, his voice a whisper.

"Where is she?"

"Shah? The last time I saw her she was in Azra, a guest of King Faisal."

"How is it that *you* know my Shah?"

"She was in the forced service of the Goatlord slave merchant Kesslar, until we overthrew him and his Lizardlord friends in Scoria."

Drew quickly recounted his experiences with the crippled Hawklord Baron Griffyn and his beautiful, reserved daughter. He spared no detail, letting Vega understand what he'd endured escaping the volcanic island of Scoria with his friends from Bast, fellow Werelords who'd been forced to fight like gladiators for the Lizardlords' amusement. Though it was dark, Drew could see that Vega's eyes were wet as he described what Shah had been through.

"I'd given up all hope of seeing her again. Casper's all I have, delivered to me many moons ago by a merchant from the east. The fellow was clearly loyal to Griffyn, to have brought the boy to the Cluster Isles. I had no idea as to her whereabouts."

"Where did you and she meet?" asked Drew, enthralled by the unfolding secrets of the Sharklord.

"Ro-Shann, in Omir. I was a guest of Lady Hayfa, the Hyena. In truth, I was wooing her. My fortunes in the Cluster Isles had recently been stolen from me by Ghul and Leopold. I was looking to make a life elsewhere, and Hayfa had swiftly taken to my charms. I was in my prime back then, Drew. . . ."

Vega grinned wistfully. The young Wolf cleared his throat. "And Shah?"

"Shah was in the service of Kesslar then, too—the Goatlord had many dealings with the Werelords of Omir; Shah must have only been in her second decade at the time. A delicate thing with big gray eyes."

He shook his head, the smile still there. "As beautiful as Hayfa was, Shah was breathtaking. The minute I clapped eyes on her I knew I'd never love another. She and I courted behind Hayfa's and Kesslar's backs for weeks. I'll say this, Drew: never try to carry on an affair when you're the guest of a caninthrope. Hayfa's pack of spies quickly got word back to her of my carrying-on, and I had to make my excuses. And Shah was already on her way out of port with Kesslar, heading Sosha knows where. I never saw her again."

"You still love her?"

"I've been 'in love,' time and again—I mean, what lady of Lyssia could truly resist a catch like this?" replied Vega. "The feeling has never remained long, always carried away on a current as my heart leads me elsewhere. But Shah? I don't think I ever stopped loving her."

Drew couldn't quite believe it. He'd thought he understood Vega, but here was the Sharklord's softer, sensitive side. Drew thought better of mentioning the former slaver, Djogo, who had taken Shah to his heart. Whether those feelings had been since returned, he didn't know.

"The boy's always had his mother's looks," said Vega. "Such a rare thing. Trust Shah to steal my therian lineage from under my nose, gifting the Shark a Hawk for a son! I'll be the laughingstock of the White Sea when this gets out."

"The Seahawk," said Drew. "He'll be the first of his kind, no?"

Vega nodded. "And the last you saw of his mother was in Azra, you say?" he asked Drew.

"Yes, but when I left, the city was preparing for a siege by the Dogs and Cats. Why, do you want to take Casper to her?"

"I'll be damned before I let the Bastians take Shah."

"How do you plan to get there, Vega? We're sailing toward death in the Lyssian Straits, aren't we? You'll never get Casper back to his mother's arms."

Vega was silent, his hands on Drew's shoulders as he stared past the young lycanthrope across to the *Maelstrom*. He stood as still as a statue as the boat rocked and rolled, the wind ruffling his long, dark hair.

"What is it?" whispered Drew.

"Something you just said has stirred a memory. Opal let something slip while she tortured me on Ghul's tower, a piece of information that we may use against her. Wait here."

Drew watched as Vega walked quickly away, heading straight for the hatched door that led below to the brig.

"To what do I owe this late-night visit, Vega?" said Opal, rising from the floor of her cell. "Are you trying your hand at charming me again? I found you infinitely more attractive when you were hanging from the walls of Ghul's fortress."

"You've a lot to say, Opal, but all I keep hearing is arrogance," said Vega as he entered the brig, closing the door behind him. "Typical Catlord. Leopold was arrogant, too, and look what happened to him: he was killed by Bergan in Highcliff."

Opal laughed. "Is that what you think? Silly Shark. It was Lucas who killed Leopold!"

"Lucas killed his own father? Why?"

"Why do you think?" asked Opal. "Just as happened with Wergar and Leopold, a new leader came and took over. Wolf or Lion, pack or pride, it makes no difference. It is the victor's way to slay the predecessor."

"Is Lucas really that twisted?"

"He's suggestible and took very little persuading."

"Why tell me this now? The news that the so-called

monarch of Westland committed patricide could devastate the Seven Realms."

Opal scoffed at that. "Whom are you going to tell, Shark? And who'll listen? You're a dwindling force, while those loyal to the Lion grow in number by the day. The Seven Realms belong to my nephew now."

"Fair point."

"May I suggest a course of action for you, Sharklord?" she purred.

"Speak freely," replied Vega with a smile.

"Take me to the nearest port and let me walk free. Then run as far as you can, for my brother and I shall be coming for you, I promise."

"I was never one for running," replied Vega. "Swimming's more my style."

"Then swim. Better still, fall on your cutlass: take your own life before we find you, for your death will not be swift."

Vega stopped walking. "No?"

"It will be lingering, drawn out, an opus of torture like you cannot imagine. Your nails, your teeth, your skin will be removed. You'll be spared the touch of silver or the claw of the Panther. I want your wounds to heal, your flesh to grow back, simply so I may remove it again. You'll die a hundred deaths before I'm finished with you."

"Are you done?"

"I've hardly started, Sharklord. You'll win no war. Your

Jackals and Hawks are entombed within the Bana Gap. The Bears and Stags are falling as we speak. So sail into the Lyssian Straits with your fleet of stolen ships. You will be blasted, burned, and sent to the seabed by Sea Marshal Scorpio."

Vega clapped his hands together as he stepped up to the barred gate, his palms meeting in prayer as he smiled behind them.

"Ranting over? Good—my turn now, so listen carefully, Panther. You're going to tell me the codes of Scorpio's fleet, every ship that sails under your brother's black flag, every order they might expect to receive from the *Nemesis*, and you're going to do it right now."

"We've danced to this tune already, Shark." Opal sighed.

She sat back down, turning about until she found a comfortable spot to lie. Resting her head upon her manacled hands, she closed her eyes as she spoke sleepily.

"You couldn't pull a hair from your chin let alone a fact from a prisoner."

"You'll tell me, Opal, or I'll travel to your ancestral home outside of Braga, find your children, and kill them."

Opal's green eyes flicked instantly open, the pupils wide and swollen as she stared at the Sharklord.

"A bold threat, but nothing more," she said with a sneer.

"You need to know something, Opal. If I put my mind to something, I see it through. You doubt whether I could reach them? Perhaps you have palace guards protecting them. Maybe you think they're safe behind some grand golden walls. Hear me now. I'll tear those walls down brick by brick and paint that palace red with Bastian blood to reach those children, even if it kills me."

"You're bluffing," said Opal, but her voice caught in her throat.

"Can you afford to take that chance?"

Opal jumped up, chained hands gripping the bars. Her face contorted, black fur bristling from her ebony skin as she snarled and bared her teeth.

"My children are but babies!"

Vega calmly stepped up to the grille, inches from Opal, utterly unfazed.

"My friend up there is a good man, an honest man, one wracked by convictions about what it means to do right and wrong. I can assure you, Opal, I've no such compunction. Your children may be mewling kittens, but it's you and your Catlord brethren who wrote the rule book on how this war's fought. I'll not be accompanying the fleet as they attack your armada. The *Maelstrom* shall remain removed from the battle, ready to sail to Bast and find your children should you betray us."

"You'll never make it to Bast," said the Werepanther in a scoffing tone. "The Lyssian Straits are clogged with Scorpio's ships. You'll be spotted and hunted down."

"At which point I'll dive overboard and swim the remaining

distance, woman," said Vega coldly. "You forget, Brenn and Sosha blessed each of us in special ways."

Opal snarled as Vega continued.

"For all the horrors you've dealt out, in both Bast and Lyssia, upon friends of mine and total strangers, you'll find no compassion in my beaten, black heart. You're a prideful, vain-glorious killer, Opal. You speak of your infants as if they're gems among a sea of dirty stones, somehow better than every other little one out there. Yours aren't the only children in the world, and you aren't the only parent. You underestimate what a father might do for his children. Do we have an understanding?"

She nodded slowly, emerald eyes narrowed as she hissed at the sea captain.

"Now," said Vega, clapping his hands merrily, his mood lifting to one of playfulness in a heartbeat. "Make yourself comfortable; I'm off to get a scroll and quill. I suspect it's going to be a long night."

4

A Darkness Lifted

"IF WE'RE TO believe you, Hector—and I'm not saying we do—where did this sudden epiphany come from?" said Duke Manfred, glowering at the young Boarlord suspiciously. "What's changed?"

"I've made terrible mistakes, Your Grace, done unimaginable things to those I thought were my enemies," replied Hector earnestly. "In my defense, I wasn't in my right mind—though I'll admit that's an awful excuse."

"I told you," said Bo Carver from where he sat chained to the wall beside Manfred. "The boy consorts with demons. Sorcery has led him here. If you're in a quagmire, it's of your own making, Blackhand. We should let you drown."

Ringlin and Ibal stepped forward from behind Hector, the two rogues rankled by the words of the Thief Lord. Hector snatched at his men, catching each by a shoulder and hauling them back.

"He's right," said the magister. "I've been gripped by a darkness ever since I first communed, so long ago." He released his grip on the pair as they stepped back.

"We warned you, Hector," said the Staglord wearily. "Back in Highcliff, when news of your necromancy reached the ears of the Wolf's Council. I said no good would come from it, but you wouldn't listen."

"I couldn't listen, didn't want to, Your Grace. I've spent so long seeking counsel in the dark places that I no longer sought help in the light."

Hector's eyes sparkled, a trace of the old madness still there.

"It got its claws into me, took a hold of me. I couldn't just dip my toe into those waters of knowledge. It was never enough. I had to hold the secret to every scrap of arcane knowledge."

He looked up at the two prisoners where they sat chained to the wall.

"I dived in. I immersed myself in the arts of communion, wasting no opportunity to practice my necromancy. I've gorged upon the minds of Lyssia's greatest living magisters—and even one of its dead ones—in order to master that dark magistry.

And what good has it done me? I've driven away all those I once held dear, betraying and killing those I loved. That you don't trust me now . . . I don't blame you at all. I wouldn't trust me, either."

His speech was a whisper, his cheeks wet once more. He didn't think it was possible to cry so much, every waking moment having been spent mourning his actions, reliving the horrors.

"That Amelie should be dead . . ."

Hector's voice trailed away, his mouth unable to form the words. The room was silent as both Carver and Manfred looked up at him, the young Boarlord wavering where he stood as if mesmerized. Ibal stepped by him, approaching the prisoners and dropping to his knee. He shifted the brass ring around on his belt, fishing through the keys with his fat fingers.

"What's this?" blustered Manfred as Ibal jabbed a key into his manacles.

"You're being freed," said Ringlin. "Baron Hector would see you out of Icegarden at the soonest opportunity."

"We're to flee the White Bear's city only for you to loose an arrow into our backs?" asked Carver. "That's your way, isn't it, Ringlin?"

"Believe me, Carver, it'd be a fine sight easier for his lordship, Ibal, and me to leave alone, under cover of darkness. Freeing every prisoner from the cells beneath Icegarden will likely alert the entire Whitepeaks."

"You're freeing everyone?" exclaimed Manfred as his manacles fell apart, Ibal moving on to the Thief Lord.

Hector snapped out of his trance suddenly, turning back to the men. He wiped a sleeve across his face, sniffing back the tears as Manfred rose to his height before him.

"Every poor soul I stupidly imprisoned," said the Boarlord. "Magisters and miners, townsfolk and traders. I won't leave a man, woman, or child behind."

"And what do the Crowlords make of this?" asked Carver.

Ringlin and Ibal both looked at their master warily, as Hector flinched nervously.

"They're unaware of what you're doing?" said Manfred. "My boy, the Crows of Riven are not to be crossed. If you're in league with them, you couldn't have chosen a more reprehensible ally. These are the folk who destroyed Stormdale in Lucas's name!"

Hector shifted awkwardly, raising his good hand to stop the Staglord.

"Your Grace, I may not have told you the truth there. Stormdale still stands. The forces from Riven and Vermire were repelled by the Stags . . . with the help of Drew."

Manfred grimaced and shook his head. "More lies, Hector—"

"From the *old* me, Manfred," the magister interjected, blushing furiously. "I'm coming clean now, albeit admittedly late in the day."

"How is it that the Crows haven't just seized Icegarden for

themselves yet?" asked the duke. "What stands in their way? You and your snow warriors of Tuskun?"

"I don't doubt that they want Sturmland for themselves. I fully expect them to strike me down any day now. Believe me, I didn't willingly enter an alliance with the Crowlords. But it's fear that's stayed their hand thus far."

"Fear?" whispered the Staglord.

"Formidable though the Ugri are, it is not my army that they fear," said Hector sheepishly. "It's me that they're afraid of."

"You?" exclaimed Manfred incredulously. "I saw your little magic trick, throttling poor Bethwyn beyond the Strakenberg Gate. That's what they're afraid of?"

"A little more than that, Your Grace. Lord Flint has witnessed firsthand my command over the dead. He's seen me commune and hold thrall over the risen. He now wonders if the power can be used as a weapon. He spoke of using my necromancy in the field."

"In the field?" said Carver, rising with the help of Ibal, the Thief Lord throwing his waddling jailer a hard stare.

"The dead," chimed in Ringlin nervously. "Flint reckons that the bodies beyond the wall can serve further purpose against any who try to invade Icegarden. Baron Hector's said before now that the Wyrmstaff might help him achieve this aim, such is the power it harnesses."

Manfred looked confused at mention of the ancient staff, but a quick word from Carver soon set him straight.

"It's some relic from yesteryear, this Wyrmstaff. That's if it exists at all. It supposedly magnifies a magister's strength, channeling his power to greater effect." He smiled at Hector as he rubbed his wrists. "See, I *was* paying attention to your addled ramblings, Blackhand."

"I can't remember—nor care to recall—what rants I've made you endure, Carver," said a shamefaced Hector. "I only pray that my future actions show me in a better light and prove to you that there's still a good soul in here."

Hector tapped his breast with the fingers of his withered hand, his eyes lingering upon the black, blistered flesh. The pain in his chest was hard to ignore, where the Staglord's tine had punctured his lung, but he tried to push it from his mind. He'd see to his wounds once he'd set things right.

"The Crows will bide their time before striking when you're at your weakest," warned Carver, ignoring the Boarlord's overtures. "I've watched in the passing months how you've wasted away, Blackhand, shrinking into yourself, obsessed as you are with that accursed staff. They'll have been watching, too, waiting for their opportunity. Looking at you now, before us, that could be any moment."

"How can you be sure the Crows won't strike?" Manfred asked.

"They ain't here at the moment, although their army from Riven mans the walls," said Ringlin. "The Crows have been sparring with the Cranelords from Bast for days on end. But they'll be back any day now. And they'll want *you* when they get here, Duke Manfred," the rogue added with a crooked smile. "Flint's been banging on about capturing you for months now. Sounds like the Crows are none too fond of the Stags."

"Do you trust your Boarguard?" asked Manfred, glaring warily at Ringlin.

"All of them," said Hector. "The Ugri are sworn to me by blood since I killed their old mistress, Queen Slotha."

"So what you're saying," said Carver, "is if someone were to kill the leader of the Ugri, they would instantly inherit an army?"

Carver left it hanging there, the implication obvious to all. Should Flint strike now and slay Hector, he would have the city and the Ugri nation at his back.

"And where is this army now?" asked the Thief Lord.

Hector scratched his jaw. "Mostly beyond the walls. The Ugri are superstitious of the White Bear's city—they're happier camping in the mountains. Some, such as Two Axes and the Creep, remain within the palace, close by should I need them. But the city is patrolled by the soldiers from Riven."

"And the Wyrmstaff?" asked Manfred. "What of it?"

Hector took a breath. "I'm done looking for it, Your Grace. Let it remain hidden as the Daughters of Icegarden always wished. Clearly it's too dangerous to ever leave the Strakenberg."

"So what's your plan?" said Carver. "How do you free your prisoners without raising the suspicion of the soldiers from Riven? They man the walls, do they not? I can't see them standing by while you march your prisoners out of the Strakenberg Gate."

"There's another way out of the city," said Ringlin. "The miners and smiths know it well enough, an old road beneath the mountain that'll lead you into the Whitepeaks beyond. It's not been used in our lifetime, but it should still serve its purpose."

While Ringlin and Carver put aside their differences to discuss the escape route, Manfred stepped forward and placed a firm hand on Hector's shoulder.

"You know, this is a new beginning for you, Hector. You can start over, put the madness and mayhem behind you."

"The magistry as well, Your Grace. I can't go near it. Never again."

"Don't be so quick to dismiss it, my boy. Your powers can still be used as a force for good—"

"Not as a magister," said Hector, shaking his head. "The temptation's too great. I mustn't even toy with the idea. I'll heal with herbs and bandages from now on, but no cantrips and magicks; I daren't even dabble."

Manfred nodded. "Nobody knows better than you the grip it had on you."

"I was seduced, Manfred. Totally. Haunted by my own brother's phantom, I allowed myself to be dragged into darkness. I can see and hear the spirits of the dead—though the good souls move on, the wicked ones linger in the form of viles, malevolant specters that shadow dark magisters. Vincent was one such monster."

"You fear he'll return, that your torment at your brother's hands isn't over?"

"No." Hector smiled wearily. "He's gone. But I can never allow myself to be seduced by the dark arts again."

"Well, you have your friends back, Hector, and with your blessing I'll be keeping an eye on you like a Hawklord henceforth. I see you so much as mutter a word of magick and I'll crack your skull, right?" Manfred's smile hardened, a sincere look of concern etching his gray face. "No harm shall come to you on my watch, Hector, as Brenn is my witness."

The two men hugged, their heartfelt reunion complete. They turned to the rogues in time to see Ringlin handing Carver one of his long knives, Ibal giggling nervously beside them.

"Try not to stick it in my back," said the Boarguard through clenched teeth.

"What? Like you did to me at the South Gate not so long ago? Relax, Ringlin," said Carver, his eyes narrowed. "We're all turning over a new page here."

"We're to leave right away?" asked Manfred.

"I'll need you to help Ringlin and Ibal free the rest of the prisoners," said Hector. "Lady Bethwyn is in with the Daughters of Icegarden close by. Two Axes watches over Duchess Freya. I'll fetch her myself; I owe the duchess a great many apologies. But there's no reason to linger here—as soon as you've got people moving, you should accompany them, my lords. Who knows what awaits them on the road beneath the mountain?"

"And you?" said Manfred. "You'll be coming, too?"

"Indeed," said Hector. "I'll gather my belongings and come through last of all with Ringlin and Ibal. I need to call by the Chapel of Brenn. Pick up the queen's body . . ."

He sighed, the Vincent-vile having been replaced by shame and misery, shadowing his every move. "I won't leave her here, alone. Ringlin and Ibal can help me carry her out and perhaps I can reunite her with Drew one day."

"Perhaps," said Manfred ruefully, stroking the whiskers on his lip.

"Are you truly done with your dark magistry, Blackhand?" asked the Thief Lord, turning the borrowed long knife in his palm. "How do we know this isn't a trick?"

"That part of me's dead, I swear, upon the lives of all those I find dear, and there are yet many. And Carver," he added, staring in revulsion at his twisted limb, "my name's Hector."

5
The Choice

"OH, VEGA, I could kiss you!" cried Baron Bosa, sloshing his goblet in the air before the Sharklord.

"A toast would do just fine, old friend," said the count politely, placing a firm hand upon the Whalelord's shoulder. He grabbed a chalice from the passing tray as the ship's cook circuited the forecastle of the *Nemesis*. The other captains of the fleet joined him, fully twenty of them celebrating the good news.

"A toast to all, in fact, and the good fortune Sosha blesses us with!"

Bosa raised his goblet aloft as the others followed suit.

"To the Wolf!" shouted Captain Ransome, his words echoed by his fellows.

Drew smiled at the cheering sea captains, their spirits now soaring after being low for so long. Whitley stood across from him and managed a smile, raising her cup. He nodded back.

"I still don't see how you finally persuaded Opal to give up her secrets, Vega," said Drew, glancing over the shoulders of a group of captains who were gathered around a collection of scrolls. Each bore the scrawled handwriting of the Sharklord, with lists of vessel names, thumbnailed maps, and a definitive code for flag flying. Here was everything their ships needed to be able to sail into Scorpio's fleet undetected.

"Yes, Vega," said Whitley. "Tell us, how did you do it?"

"I discovered something of value to her, my lady," he said. "Something that would provide us with leverage. The scrolls you see before you: trust me when I tell you their contents are genuine. There's no way on Sosha's blue sea that she's lied to us."

"But how can you be sure?" asked Ransome.

"Take my word for it, she risks too much to have lied to us. We have all we need right there."

"So Opal's outlived her usefulness," said Bosa. "A shame. I was warming to her charming threats."

"She no doubt still has information that will be of use to us," said Vega. "Her knowledge of the Catlord armada's just the tip of the iceberg. There are more secrets to be extracted from the Beauty of Bast's exquisite head yet."

"I don't like the idea of our keeping hold of her," said

Ransome. "The men aboard the *Nemesis* fear her, and rightly so, regardless of her imprisonment."

"Worry not. I've room aboard the *Maelstrom* for the Catlady if it puts your mind at ease. She's the one I have this . . . understanding with, so it's only right she remain in my custody. We'll transfer her across as soon as it's convenient."

Another round of toasts went up from the captains, as goblets and jugs were refilled. Similar noises floated across the water from the other ships as the word spread that they'd broken the Bastian code. Drew stepped up to Vega as the Sharklord swigged from his cup.

"What did you do, Vega, to buy her secrets?"

"My dear Drew, if it's all right with you, I'd rather you didn't know."

"I'd just hate to think she was tricking us, Vega," Drew whispered, keeping his voice out of earshot of their companions. "What if she's playing you, and we're sailing into a trap?"

"She wouldn't dream of lying to me, my boy. Not now that she knows what's at stake."

Drew shivered, trying to imagine what kind of deal the Shark had struck with the Panther.

"Don't worry about it," continued Vega. "If I were you, I'd be more concerned about getting back into dear Whitley's favor."

"She won't listen to me, Vega."

"It's complicated, my boy. She thinks an awful lot of you. Surely you understand how she feels."

Drew stared at Vega gormlessly, as the Sharklord laughed.

"Good grief, I know you grew up on the Cold Coast, but surely you had *some* interaction with the fairer sex in your childhood. It can't all have been sheep and snow on your father's farm!"

Drew's mouth was dry, his heart quickening as Vega chortled. He'd known since he and Whitley had traveled south to the Longridings just what the girl meant to him. They'd endured much together, side by side, only to be torn apart. Time with the Bearlady should have been precious to him, but he felt he'd taken her for granted, preoccupied with the bigger picture. The war, the politics, the people of Lyssia: all had taken precedent over his relationship with Whitley.

"Whatever you feel for her, lad, just tell her," Vega whispered. "Don't bottle it up, or you may never get the chance. Don't have the regrets that I have over a lost love."

Drew nodded. "I'll speak with her right now."

"Good man. And remember: she'll be hurting still, so go easy."

The young Wolflord looked across the crowded deck for his friend, finding no sign of her.

"Where is she?"

"She was here a moment ago," replied Vega, looking past the other to the spot she'd vacated.

Drew was already walking away, in the direction of the hatch that led below. As he closed in on the open doorway, his stride lengthened. By the time he'd reached the staircase, he was running.

Opal stirred. Her sleep, when it had finally come, had been fitful, her mind dogged by the secrets she'd spilled to the Sharklord. The decision hadn't been easy, not by a long distance, but—not for the first time—she'd had to put family first. The consequences would be terrible for Bast, every flag signal and formation now in Vega's hands to distribute among his fleet. Brave men from her homeland would die, no doubt by the hundreds, and their upcoming deaths weighed heavy on her conscience, but she would do it all again if required. There was nothing she wouldn't do for her babies.

She blinked, her eyes quickly adjusting to the darkness, chains clinking as she rose from where she was curled on the floor. Ransome might have washed the decks down, but she could still smell the blood of those she'd slaughtered within the brig, soaked into the thirsty timber. If only it was Vega she'd opened up. The Sharklord was as low a foe as she'd ever encountered. And the worst of it was, he was right. The moment the Panthers, Lions, and Tigers had taken the children of the Werelords of Bast, this day had been fated to her.

"Who's there?" she asked, rising to her knees. She ran a finger around the collar that encircled her throat. She found scabs, the cuts having already healed from where she'd partly transformed earlier, enraged by Vega's words. The door was closed, but she was sure she'd heard it open. A chair had been placed against it, back to the handle, its legs wedged into the boarded deck. She welcomed the felinthrope in, just enough to heighten her senses, as she scanned the dark cabin. Her cat's eyes shifted, instantly drawn to the shape in the corner of the chamber.

"If you've come to interrogate me, you're a little late," Opal said. "I already gave the Shark everything."

"I've not come for your secrets," replied Whitley with a growl.

"Then you've come to mock and taunt me for betraying my people? Nothing you say will make me feel more wretched than I already do, child, so do your worst."

"It's not that, either. There's something else I want, Panther."

"And what's that?" Opal asked, sighing.

"What you've done in Lyssia is quite remarkable," said Whitley. "Your Bastian army has spread across the Seven Realms like a wave, killing any who stand against it."

"That's how lands are conquered, girl. Such is the way of the world."

"And that's how you seized control of Bast? I've heard that at one point in time it was ruled by many different Werelords. Is the entire continent now under the control of the felinthropes?"

"My father and his cousins showed single-minded ruthlessness when they seized Bast from their neighbors, an unwavering vision where the Catlords ruled over all. It's to be admired, really."

"I'm sure those you conquered feel that way."

"Those we conquered do as we say."

"Or else what?" asked Whitley.

"Or else we kill their children."

"I beg your pardon?"

"You people really know nothing about ruling, do you? The firstborn of each Werelord line is sent to Leos, the seat of rule in Bast. There, under the guidance and tutelage of the three high lords in the Forum of Elders, they learn what it means to be a faithful Werelord of Bast. By the time they eventually return home as adults, they completely understand their people's place and are utterly loyal to the Catlords. And should their mothers or fathers see fit to challenge the order of things . . ."

Opal allowed her words to trail away menacingly.

"And now you plan to use the same system to control the Werelords of the Seven Realms?" spat out Whitley.

Opal stared at her, eyes narrowed, before suddenly clicking

her fingers. "You're the sister of the Bearlord. Lord Broghan was his name, correct?"

"I'm glad you remember his name," said Whitley. "You did, after all, murder him."

Opal arched an eyebrow. "I think you'll find it was Lucas who killed your brother, my dear."

"By *your* command!"

"What can I say? He wanted to prove himself."

"Did my brother beg for mercy?"

"I . . . I don't recall," said Opal, glancing toward the door, wondering now what the Bearlady's intentions were as the girl stepped forward from the shadows.

Opal could see the girl from Brackenholme changing. Her torso had thickened into a heavy trunk of ursine muscles that threatened to shred her clothes should she roar. Her limbs lengthened, hands widening into clawed paws. She shook her head from side to side, the muzzle of the bear appearing with each violent motion, flashes of white teeth emerging as she snarled.

Opal looked at the chains and manacles that adorned her limbs, suddenly feeling terribly vulnerable. She backed away from the barred door as the Werebear approached it.

"What are you doing?" gasped the Pantherlady fearfully.

Whitley seized the cell door. Her muscles bulged as she strained, gradually prizing the lock apart. The iron buckled, unable to resist the transformed Bearlady's anger.

"You've told us all we need to know," said the girl as the mechanism finally sheared apart, the door groaning open with a clang. "Now it's my turn to get what I need: a blood payment for my brother's life."

A hammering at the door suddenly caught their attention, Drew's shouted pleas momentarily halting Whitley's advance. The chair shuddered where it was propped, but the door remained closed.

"Whitley!" he cried. "Whatever you're thinking of doing, I beg you don't! You mustn't harm her! That's not our way! She can still help us!"

The Pantherlady seized her moment, making to dart past the Bearlady, her only hindrance the chains and manacles around throat and wrist. Opal was quick, but Whitley was no fool. Her clawed hand flew out, catching the woman by the collar. The Bastian's feet flew from the floor as she was yanked back and slammed into the barred wall.

"She's helped us already!" cried Whitley as her pawed hand shifted around the steel collar, claws raking Opal's neck. "She pays for her crimes now!"

The door to the brig suddenly exploded inward, the chair that had blocked it reduced to shattered kindling. The Werewolf bounded into the brig, skidding to a halt when he surveyed the situation.

"Put her down, Whitley," he growled. "Don't do this. You'll regret it forever!"

"The only thing I'll regret is not avenging my brother's murder! You said you'd help me, but it appears I'm on my own."

"She's paid already, Whitley," Drew said, stepping closer, trying to make eye contact with his friend. "She's betrayed her countrymen by giving us her secrets! And that's only the start. We can *use* her, Whitley, as a weapon in this war."

Vega, Bosa, Ransome, and the others all piled over the threshold, stumbling to a standstill behind the lycanthrope.

"She's lied to Vega," snarled Whitley. "Played Vega like a fool!"

"Every word . . . was true!" spluttered Opal, Whitley's paw crushing her throat. "No lies . . . mercy . . . please!"

The Lady of Brackenholme released her grip on the Pantherlady's throat and stepped aside, moving out through the twisted gate of the cell.

"She's all yours," said Whitley, the bear receding with each step as the girl returned to the fore. "I think we can be sure that she's told us the truth now."

"You mad witch!" spat out Opal. "You're crazy!"

"Better to be safe than sorry," said Whitley to her companions, ignoring the Panther's strangled outrage.

"I'm sorry," said Drew, his hand now human again as he gripped Whitley by the forearm. "I assumed . . . that you wanted to kill her."

"Don't get me wrong, Drew," she replied. "I'd rather she were dead, but if you think she's more valuable alive, then so be it. I don't have to like it, but I'll go along with it." She glanced back and glowered at the weary prisoner who knelt on the floor, nursing her throat. "But don't for a minute think I'll be letting her out of my sight."

Three of Ransome's best marines entered the cell and took hold of the exhausted Pantherlady as Drew turned to the Sharklord.

"Have her taken to the *Maelstrom*. I'll be joining her on your ship, too, Vega. We won't remain with the fleet. We've a different port of call than Calico."

"And where's that?" asked Vega as Drew embraced Whitley.

"Bast, Vega," replied the Wolflord. "That's where the root of the problem lies. That's where we must strike."

6
Gone Fishing

IT WAS SUCH a simple sound, but to Gretchen's ears, extraordinary. The chorus of children's voices, their song so sweet, could be heard over the rooftops, rising above the sleepy town of Bray. She stopped her stroll in Count Fripp's gardens and closed her eyes, pausing to soak in the joyous noise. She'd almost forgotten what it meant to be happy and carefree. Standing on the lawn of the Badgerlord's villa, the sounds of spring all around her, she could have been back home in Hedgemoor. The irregular footfalls of her companion made her open her eyes and turn.

"A school?" asked Gretchen as Count Fripp caught up with her.

"Not quite, my dear," said Count Fripp, the elderly

Werebadger leaning heavily on his cane. "An orphanage, actually. You won't find any urchins or homeless folk in Bray, my lady. Not so long as I'm the lord of the manor."

Gretchen extended an arm, and Fripp took it by the elbow, the two strolling ever nearer the river.

"It's very good of you to accommodate us, my lord," she said. "I can't imagine there are many Werelords in Lyssia who'd harbor fugitives from the Catlords these days."

"The Harriers of Hedgemoor will find a good many friends in the Dalelands, my dear," said Fripp. "But you must show caution. If you're to stay with my family, you and your friends must remain within my compound."

"Fear not, Count Fripp. We won't be going for an amble through Bray anytime soon. We shall not overstay our welcome, either. Some of my men are injured, but as soon as they're fit for the road again, we'll be on our way."

"I would not see you endangered in the wilds again, Lady Gretchen," said the Badger gruffly. "My villa's your home for as long as you like."

"The offer's most gracious, but I fear every day my Harriers remain here is another day our enemies draw closer. I wouldn't want to endanger Bray."

"Your man's down yonder," said Fripp, changing the subject and pointing ahead with his cane. "I don't think he's had any luck yet. Perhaps you can show the Westlander how we catch fish in the Dales, my dear."

Fripp smiled as Gretchen kissed him on the cheek. Then she was off across the lawns, heading for the riverbank.

"No bites?" she called, approaching the rickety jetty that reached out into the sun-dappled Redwine. Trent sat at its end, his britches turned up, one leg over the side, toes dipped into the chilly water. His other leg was raised, chin resting lazily upon his knee, the fishing rod resting in his idle hands. The boy from the Cold Coast raised his head as Gretchen approached, rolling his eyes.

"If you're here to mock me like the Badgerlord, please don't," he shouted back. "The old chap took great delight in pointing out one end of my rod from the other."

Gretchen stalked along the creaking boards of the jetty on tiptoes.

"Here," she whispered. "I'll be deathly quiet so as not to disturb the fish. Looks like you need all the help you can get!"

"There's nothing wrong with my technique," replied the young Graycloak. "If the fish aren't biting, it's because of this shoddy rod. Just look at the thing: there isn't even a reel on it!"

Trent waggled it in the air as if to emphasize the point, the line caught around his fingers in great, wispy loops.

"A bad workman—"

"—always blames his tools, yes, yes," he said, finishing the proverb for her with a laugh. "Go on then, sit yourself down. Don't be throwing anything into the water, though. I'm determined to catch something in this rotten river before the day's through."

"There's some big beasties in there, I warn you now," she said, remembering the creature she'd mistaken for a rock a few weeks previously. "I'd be careful, Ferran. One might just catch you!"

Gretchen sidled up beside him, dangling her own legs over the edge. She watched as Trent threw the line back into the river, the thread running through his mutilated left hand. The boy was missing the two smallest fingers from his fight with the Wyldermen in the Dyrewood.

"Does it hurt at all?" she asked.

"What?"

"Your fingers," she replied. "Or rather, the lack of them."

"I get a dull ache occasionally, especially when it's cold, but beyond that I can't say it bothers me. Actually, scratch that: I used to be a great fisherman until I lost them. There, that's my excuse and I'm sticking to it."

The two laughed. Their combined strength of spirit had carried them out of the Dyrewood, and in the bubble of Bray, the pair had drawn closer still.

"You know why I was angry at you, don't you?" she asked as their laughter subsided. "The fussing and worrying that you were doing over me. Can you see that now?"

"I can," Trent replied as the line slowly went taut in the

water, the baited hook at its length. "And I'd do it again. I'd do it because you're more important than any living therian in the Seven Realms. You're the hope that the free people can still cling to."

"More important than Drew?" she asked.

Trent shrugged. "We don't know if Drew even lives."

"You *will* see him again, Trent," she said, reaching out and closing her fingers around his maimed hand.

"I hope so," he said. "I want to tell him I'm sorry. Sorry for ever believing he could do anything to hurt Ma. Sorry for taking the Red and fighting for our enemies. I pray to Brenn that day might come."

"It will," she said, resting a head on his shoulder. "Have faith."

Trent was silent for a moment before finding his voice again.

"He's a fool, if you ask me, chasing after some army that might not even be out there. If he had any sense, he'd have come after you."

"There are more important things for Drew to consider than me, Trent. He's the rightful king of Westland. He has the people of his realm to think about. He'd be a fool to have come looking for me."

"Then that makes me a fool," said Trent. "I know what I'd have done if the roles were reversed."

"You know how to flatter a girl, Graycloak," she said, trying to sound scoffing, all too aware of the sudden heat in her cheeks.

"Graycloak? I like it! A definite step up from Redcloak. It's true, though. I wouldn't have let you out of my sight. My brother's a lucky young man to have your affections."

She gripped his hand.

"Drew's very dear to me, Trent. He's a good friend, and the reason we're fighting this war. But he isn't the only soul who's precious to me."

As he turned to her she leaned in, her lips catching his tenderly. A sudden tug on the line caused Trent to lurch forward, the elusive first bite of the day catching him unawares. Gretchen pulled away as Trent fell forward, still gripping the rod as it hauled him from the jetty. He landed with a great splash that brought howls of laughter from the Lady of Hedgemoor.

Surfacing from the river, Trent spat a mouthful of water up at Gretchen, his hair draped over his face, obscuring his eyes.

"You look like a water hound, Ferran." She laughed. "Don't be shaking your coat all over me when you get out!"

He reached up and grabbed her by the ankles, yanking her forward. She followed him into the river with a shriek, disappearing beneath the water before rising in his arms. He grinned as she spluttered in his grasp. Their laughter subsided gradually as she raised a hand to his face and drew his hair to one side. There were the bright blue eyes that she couldn't shake from her dreams.

"You see, my lady," said the boy from the Cold Coast, his teeth chattering. "I told you I'd catch something."

7
The Tale of the Tiger

"BY MY RECKONING we're fifty leagues from the isle of Claw," said Florimo, tracing his scrawny finger over the sea chart.

"Fifty leagues through Bastian water?" said Vega. "Easy as a sunny day on Lake Robben."

Drew and Whitley smiled at the count's grim humor. While the rest of the Wolf's ragtag fleet had stayed in Lyssian waters, heading for Calico Bay under the command of Baron Bosa, the *Maelstrom* had raced ahead of them, sailing on to Bast. All the codes of the Catlord's navy wouldn't help Vega's ship approach the jungle continent. The *Maelstrom* was known to seafarers throughout the oceans. Any sailor worth his salt would recognize her as loyal to the Wolf, with or without Onyx's flag flying. The route they were taking was painfully precarious, and their fortune hung on the wits of the ancient navigator.

"I'm grateful you joined us on the *Maelstrom*, Florimo," said Drew. "Without your eyes and wings I fear the Bastians would've found us by now."

"I'm grateful the count invited me along," replied the man. "I feared he'd heard enough of my shanties by now."

"Perish the thought, old chap." Vega smiled. "I could listen to your dulcet tones all the livelong day, although I fear your rousing songs might attract the attention of the Catlords as far off as Felos."

"Just how good is your eyesight?" asked Whitley, fascinated by Florimo's airborne perception.

"Put it this way, my lady," whispered the Ternlord, tapping his beaked nose, "I could tell you what the Lion had for breakfast in Highcliff."

"And the navigation?" said Drew. "I've seen you use the maps, but there's something more to it, isn't there?"

"Vega can keep his fancy sextants and astrolabes," said Florimo with a dismissive wave. "The stars make up a Ternlord's map and compass. It's all about the moon, young Wolf, as you should well know being what you are, all tooth, fang, and frightful legend. She's up there in the day, too, mind; one just has to look that bit harder for her light. You've heard of the black sun, my lord?"

Drew nodded as Florimo continued.

"We navigators call that an eclipse. That's the moon's work, casting her shadow over the world. And what power lies within it—a Wolf could get drunk on the black sun's shadow. When one understands the cycles of the moon one truly understands her hold over land, sea, and the lycanthropes. A good navigator can predict the weather, the season, and the tides by the sky. Stare long enough and one can see the future writ there."

"Florimo, could you chart the weather that was coming for us?" asked Whitley. "You can forecast such events before they've happened?"

"Most certainly, young Bear."

He winked before bowing low, his drooping pink feather lolling forward. "If you'll excuse me, my lords, my lady, I'd best get back to it. Who knows what awaits us, and the sooner I spy it the better."

Florimo squinted at the sky, licked a finger, and held it up to the wind. Checking his bearings he walked toward the starboard rail and unhitched his shirt, tossing it to Casper, who stood grinning nearby.

"Watch and learn, young Seahawk," said Florimo with a wink. "Watch and learn."

Slender white wings emerged from the navigator's bony back, his bare feet thinning before splaying, the flesh turning red as webbing spanned the joints. His nose grew sharper, longer, jaw joining the protrusion as they shifted into a daggerlike black beak. The wings flapped, feathers rustling as the avianthrope lifted a foot onto the rail. As the sails clapped overhead, a gust of wind caught beneath Florimo's wings, lifting the Were-tern from the deck and elegantly over the sea. Within moments he was rising high toward the sun, disappearing from view in a matter of heartbeats.

"Come," said Whitley, patting Casper on the head. "Let's get back to your ropework. I'll show you how we woodlanders tie *proper* knots as opposed to the raggedy efforts you pirates work with."

As Bearlady and cabin boy headed toward the main deck Drew and Vega made their way aft.

"Casper seems very fond of her," said Drew with a smile.

"He's not used to a woman's company," replied the Sharklord. "This is new to him."

Figgis stood at the helm, hands on the wheel, watching the horizon. Opal stood behind him, her wrists manacled, ankles chained to the deck for good measure, out of reach of the first mate. Occasionally, Figgis glanced over his shoulder, checking that the Werepanther remained where she was.

"Speaking of a woman's influence, have you told Casper yet?" asked Drew.

"We've had a chat," replied Vega as they walked past the first mate. "The lad's now aware I'm his father. We're building up to the conversation about his mother. In the meantime Florimo will act as a surrogate avianthrope for him. Sosha knows how one controls shifting into a hawk!"

"You really think that old seagull can get you to Bast undetected?" shouted Opal as the two approached.

"Did he tell you how he bargained for information, little Wolf?" said Opal to Drew. "How he threatened to kill my children?"

Drew glared at her, chained up on the deck, a sick smile upon her face. She thought she had him.

"He told me that very thing, Opal."

Opal's smile slipped as Vega's appeared. If she'd been hoping to shock him it hadn't worked. Drew had pressed Vega on how he'd achieved his results, and the count had reluctantly revealed his tactic.

"An old Hawk told me not so long ago that one has to be prepared to do ugly things to win a war," said Drew. "I'm coming to terms with his words now. I wouldn't tolerate anyone in my ranks harming a child in my presence, even the Sharklord. Still, I'm not the count's keeper. One thing I do know about my sea marshal is he's not to be trifled with."

"You should have left the Bearlady to do her worst the other night," said Opal. "I'm as good as dead now." She drew her clawed fingernails along the decking, leaving furrows through the timber. "Banishment would be a blessing, but it's my head the elders will take for aiding you."

"Then it sounds like you now need us as much as we need you," said Drew. "Don't wish your life away so swiftly, Opal. We may still be able to provide one for you. And your children."

"I fear for them," she confessed.

"Try not to," said Vega. "If you've told us the truth, you shouldn't be afraid."

"It's not you I fear anymore," spat out Opal. "Once the high lords of Bast receive word of my complicity, they'll go after my children. The Catlords have never been shy of punishing their own for transgressions."

"Like Taboo?" asked Drew, remembering his friend's predicament that left her enslaved to the Lizardlords. "What crime did she commit that got her imprisoned on Scoria, fighting in the Furnace? How is it that a Catlady of Bast ends up fighting in a pit for the amusement of others?"

Opal's face, so hard and fierce, softened at mention of the fiery young Weretiger who'd fought alongside Drew in the arena. One of the Lizardlord's Eight Wonders, she was as tough a therian as Drew had ever encountered, and he was proud to consider her a friend.

"Therein lies a tale, cub." Opal sighed ruefully.

"I'm not going anywhere," he replied, encouraging her to speak. "Besides, anything you tell us regarding the Catlords could be of use. Taboo is a friend of mine; if I can convince your high lords that Lyssians and Bastians can work together, perhaps there's a way we can stop this war for good."

"First I want a guarantee," she said, looking up. Vega stepped closer, coming to a halt behind Drew, hands on his hips.

"Go on," said the Sharklord.

"I need a promise that you'll help rescue my children from Braga."

"We can do that," replied the count. "I'll do everything in my power to get them safely into your arms."

"How strange, Sharklord, that days ago you promised you'd kill my babies if I didn't do as you demanded, yet now you vow to save them."

"You helped us, Pantherlady," replied Vega with a smile. "Now let me return the favor. So tell us, what do you know of this Taboo?"

"You already know," she began, "about the three great houses of the Catlords, three dynasties which together have governed Bast for sixty years."

"The Lions, the Panthers, and the Tigers," said Drew.

"Good lad, you've been paying attention," joked Vega, patting Drew on the head like a lapdog. A glare from Opal silenced him.

"We've worked together, pooling our strength, supporting one another as we turned Bast from a myriad of tiny, warring states into a force to be reckoned with throughout the known world. You've been experiencing our might presently, of course."

Both Drew and Vega nodded ruefully.

"The seat of power in Bast is Leos, the Lionlord capital. Then there's Braga, my home, and Felos, land of the Tigerlords. The Forum of Elders gather in Leos, the senior high lords from the three houses and all the smaller felinthrope lines—Jaguars, Cheetahs, and the like—making up its number."

"What of all the other noble houses, those whose children you took as ransom?" asked Drew.

"Some have risen through the ranks to positions of power, like the Hippo general Gorgo and Count Costa the Vulturelord. But most remain where the Catlords want them, beneath our paws."

She said the last words with a hint of triumph.

"Taboo was but a girl when she joined her grandfather, High Lord Tigara, in Leos. She instantly caught the attention of all in the court, her passion and temper being quite remarkable, even for a felinthrope. You'll have heard of the rage of the Lions—Taboo had her own kind of fury, screaming the steeples down whenever she didn't get her way.

"While a few found Taboo difficult and unmanageable, many warmed to the girl's wild demeanor and unpredictable nature, and found her antics a breath of fresh air within the stuffy council chambers in the capital. Indeed, one young felinthrope took a particular shine to her: Chang, son of Lord Chollo, the Cheetahlord of the Teeth. The attraction was mutual and the two were soon courting. Their tempers were well matched—when they weren't holding one another's hands, they were gripping one another's throats. But we're Catlords. We're nothing if not passionate."

Opal took a deep breath before speaking, the Beauty of Bast's tough exterior melting before their eyes.

"There was another who loved Taboo, a young Catlord who was on the rise. Quiet spoken, he was a man of action, unlike the smooth suitor that was young Chang. Well . . . this shy felinthrope, though he had little in common with the young Tigerlady, approached Taboo one evening, declaring his undying love for her. The girl, still little more than a child herself, laughed at the Catlord who'd proposed to her, throwing his love back in his foolish face."

Opal's eyes were wet with tears as she stared into space, recalling the terrible incident.

"He seized her, distressed by her rebuttal. She struck him, clawing his chest. He hit her back and she fell hard, just as Lord Chang returned to her chambers. The boy leapt to the girl's defense, but he was no match for his rival, who was freshly returned from a military campaign, battle hardened. A few punches from the warrior were enough to crush the Cheetah's slender body. Taboo, enraged, leapt onto the Catlord's back, raking his torso, clawing at his face, biting and tearing at him with all her fury. He grabbed her, he beat her, he throttled her until she was unconscious. Then he fetched his sister."

Drew knew what was coming next. He shivered to think about how complicit Opal had been in Taboo's fate.

"I helped Onyx set the scene. According to our version, he

was with me when we heard screaming. While I rushed for the palace guard, Onyx went to investigate. He found the lovers fighting one another. Onyx leapt forward, valiantly trying to wrestle the Tiger from the Cheetah, but the boy was already breathing out his last, the girl turning her hateful blows on my brother. When I arrived with the guard, and other members of the court, we told our story and she was carried away to a cell.

"High Lord Oba, my father, pushed for execution of the girl—she was sick in the mind, a danger to all as well as herself. She pleaded for clemency, claiming to not recall the events of the night. That was very probably the case—I don't doubt that Taboo suffered a grave trauma at my brother's hands, both emotionally and mentally. She denied she could have ever harmed Chang, swore she loved him, but who were the elders going to believe? A crazed young girl with a history of foul temper and fights, or a many-times-decorated young war hero? High Lord Tigara begged for leniency, for his granddaughter's life to be spared.

"It was left to the Lion, High Lord Leon, to pass judgment. Leon is the father of Leopold, and as old as any of the Werelords of Bast. Even back then he was very fond of my brother. Upon the advice of Onyx and my father, Leon agreed that Taboo should be stripped of all title and position and gifted to the Lizardlords of Scoria, forced to fight out her days in the Furnace. She was banished, and all the felinthrope races turned their backs upon her. The shame upon the house of Tigers was immense, the stain immovable."

Opal rocked forward on her haunches, looking from Vega down to Drew. She lifted her wrists and held the chains out before her. The Pantherlady closed her teary eyes.

"That is Taboo's sorry tale."

8
A Wasted Talent

"IT'S TIME, MY LORD."

Hector looked up from the tome. Ringlin stood at the library's entrance, edgier than he'd ever been. The Boarlord winced as he lifted the heavy book cover, a cloud of dust billowing as it slammed shut. The pain in his chest was a constant reminder of the wrongs he'd committed and how far he'd wandered off the right path. He could have administered his own remedies and magicks, but he'd ceased all forms of magistry. Perhaps Duchess Freya could forgive him once he freed her, and she might help him then.

"Have they all gone?" he asked, rising and hobbling to the door.

"I left Ibal escorting the remaining prisoners from their

cells," said the Boarguard captain. "Once they realized they were being freed, the miners and smiths were more than forthcoming about the road beneath the mountain. They were happy to point it out. Carver and Manfred led the way, with your Lady Bethwyn in their company."

Over his shoulder he carried his backpack, and the cloak he wore was a thick, woolen affair. He was dressed for the outdoors. "If you're going to do this, it has to be now."

"Good man, Ringlin," said Hector, seizing him by the forearm with a gloved left hand. "I had you down for a cold-blooded killer when we first met."

"Oh, I'm still that, my lord. Only there's a time and a place, see?"

"You know this is the right thing to do, don't you?" whispered Hector, pausing at the door.

"That's your decision to make, Hector," said Ringlin, dropping the formalities for a moment. "I'm a Boarguard; I'll follow you whatever you do."

"You're loyal so long as I pay you," said the Boar with a sigh.

"Not necessarily. Your brother paid us, and I could hardly say I was loyal to *that* drunken fool. I like you, Hector. Ain't ever been able to say that about a boss. And this new leaf you're turning over, when all the world is turning to sewage around you: it may be the making of you."

"You flatter me, Ringlin," said Hector, moving into the corridor. "You must be after a wage raise."

"You really think I do this just for the money?" said the other, snorting, as they set off, deep beneath the palace. "Show me someplace I can spend my gold and you might be onto something."

"I've one more piece of business before we leave, Ringlin," said Hector as they walked. "I must free the Ugri from their bond, allow them to return to their homeland. Two Axes watches over the Duchess Freya. I'll give him that news once we collect the queen's body, and then we may follow the others out of here."

"You never know," said Ringlin, taking Hector by the elbow as he stumbled down the sloping corridor. "Two Axes may want to take Icegarden for himself."

"No," replied Hector. "He and his people may kill as many of the Crow's men on their way out of here as they wish, but this city belongs in the paws of the White Bears. I aim to make it theirs again."

Deeper they went into the belly of the palace, following twisting corridors and staircases down into the earth. Hector stopped suddenly, throwing his palm against his forehead.

"What is it, my lord?" asked Ringlin.

"What a fool," he muttered, shaking his head. "I was in such a hurry that I've left a trinket behind."

"What's that?"

"Something my father gave me long ago." Hector sighed. "It's a brooch, a clasp for my cloak: a charging boar fashioned out of bronze. It's the only thing of his I still owned. Damn."

"Let me go back and fetch it," said the man.

"We haven't the time!"

"I'll be quick. Let me do this for you."

"It's on my bedside table, Ringlin. Hurry, and I'll meet you in the chapel."

With that, the Boarguard was off and running, back the way they'd come. Hector watched him disappear, continually impressed by the reformed rogue and the road to salvation the two were now embarking upon. Turning, he continued on his way.

As Hector neared the chapel, he felt cold sweat soaking his robes again, nausea rising in the pit of his stomach. Instantly his hand went to his chest, nursing the wound he'd sustained upon the end of Manfred's antler. He could still feel the ribs grating within, his ragged lung rasping and rattling uselessly. A wave of dizziness came over him, growing with each faltering step, the world turning, the corridor spiraling like a corkscrew. He blinked, trying to fight the vertigo.

"Come on, Hector," he whispered, trying to bolster his fragile confidence. "Get a hold of yourself."

Since his revelation in the company of Manfred and Carver, Hector had felt spiritually reborn, his mind almost returned to normality. He knew that there was a world of recompense due, that his crimes were great and many, but his heart was set upon reparation. His greatest joy came from the fact that he'd dispelled Vincent. There'd been no sign of the vile since his confrontation, and Hector's relief was immense.

Clutching the wall he continued onward, the corridor taking a gradual bend. Around the corner he saw the doorway, a torch spluttering in a bracket beside it. While one hand clutched his magister's case, the other reached out to the wall of the corridor as he composed himself, the dizziness gradually lifting.

Hector took a further moment to compose himself before opening the door, taking the torch and entering the Chapel of Brenn.

Walking up to the altar, he placed his medicine bag at the foot end before stepping up to the table's head. Gingerly taking the sheet in his hands, he gently pulled it back, revealing Amelie's peaceful face. He'd seen to her care in the aftermath of her death, ensuring she received all the funereal attention a deceased monarch deserved. The wound in her breast had been stitched up—by his own hand—and herbs and tinctures had been applied that would preserve the body and prolong its decay.

"I'm so sorry, Your Majesty." Hector sniffed, a trembling hand stroking her frigid cheek. "I promise, I'll return you to Drew, or I'll die trying."

Another wave of dizziness washed over him. He wobbled where he stood, reaching out and taking hold of the altar's edge. Hector shook his head, trying to chase away the vertigo before the attack could escalate. His balance suddenly disappeared along the left side of his body and he staggered down the stone table's length, clattering into his magister's case. The bag tumbled from the table, its contents smashing and spilling across the floor of the chapel.

Hector dropped the torch to the floor and put a hand to his head, forcing his palm to his eye socket to quell the rising nausea. It felt like his skull was being torn apart.

"Make it stop!" he shouted as the pain suddenly intensified. The attack came on hard, far greater than before, an assault upon Hector's every sense. Knives were driven into his ears, his eyes run through by burning pokers, his nose overcome by the foul stench of brimstone. He tried to cry out but his scream was stifled, as if a great beast were forcing itself down his throat, choking the air and despair from his twisted lungs. He tasted blood and bile, salt and sulfur. Hector was no longer aware of his surroundings. All he knew was the pain, overwhelming and agonizing.

Banish me, would you, brother? I'll go when I'm good and ready. All that knowledge in your pathetic little head . . .

Hector's knees went from under him as he went over, his head cracking off the altar's edge on his way to the floor. As the blackout approached, the last thing he heard was Vincent's voice.

Wasted on you . . .

"My lord?"

Ringlin stepped carefully down the darkened corridor toward the Chapel of Brenn. By now the freed prisoners were traversing the road beneath the mountain, firmly on their way out of Icegarden and into the Whitepeaks. Ibal was with them, of course, no doubt keen for him to catch up. His giggling friend wouldn't usually go anywhere without him; this was already the longest the two had been apart in years. Ringlin had his doubts about Hector's plan, but he'd accepted there was no other course of action. Events in Sturmland had taken a distinct turn for the worse. Better to get out of the mountains now in one piece, and perhaps find his way back to the Dalelands.

"Lord Hector?"

He'd hurried after his master as quickly as he could, knowing only too well how impulsive Hector could be. He looked at the bronze brooch in his hand, the heraldic symbol still of great value to the Boarlord. Clenching it in his fist, he called out again as he approached the chapel's open door.

"Hector?" he called and pushed it open.

The room was a mess. Ringlin stepped gingerly through

the debris, his foot sending a glass vial spinning across the floor, rattling as it went. The torch lay on the floor, its fading light illuminating the altar beside it. All around, the contents of Hector's medicine case lay crushed and broken underfoot. Crouching, Ringlin reached out and took hold of the torch. As he righted it in his grasp he could now better see the floor. He caught his breath.

The unmistakable markings of Hector's handiwork were there to behold, a crude brimstone circle etched around the altar. The black candle, the device his master used when communing with the dead, lay on its side, its melted wax pooling around its still-smoldering wick. Ringlin rose, lifting the torch and holding it out before him, dreading what awaited him.

The queen wasn't so different from the beauty they'd laid to rest in the chapel some nights ago. Her long white hair remained braided and piled atop her head, her ivory skin glowing with the torchlight's caress. Her ruby red lips parted ever so slightly as she seemed to exhale. Madness, Ringlin knew all too well: she was dead. Her eyes flickered open, twin flames of the brightest blue roaring into life at the sight of the rogue.

Ringlin stared at her in disgust, his mouth flapping, words failing him. A noise behind made him turn, a figure stepping forward from the shadows. It was Hector. As the Boarlord stepped up he put a hand on Ringlin's shoulder and pulled him toward him. The jewel-encrusted dagger hit home, straight and deep into the soldier's guts. Hector gave it a twist as he gripped the man's thick winter cloak by the scruff, dragging him closer so he could speak in his ear.

"Drunken fool, was I?" he whispered venomously, giving the knife another savage turn. "Who's the fool now, Ringlin?"

"Why, Hector?" spluttered Ringlin, his eyes wide with horror.

Snatching the boar brooch from his grasp, the magister shoved him backward, into the embrace of the waiting ghoul. Pale slender arms came down and around the reformed rogue, Queen Amelie's undead form burying its teeth into Ringlin's shoulder.

"I'm afraid Hector's gone, old friend," said the Boarlord, snapping the bronze clasp onto his cloak and pulling the leather glove from his left hand. He tossed the glove away, tensing the black fist, his sickly face bright with wonder and fascination. He turned back to the undead monarch as Ringlin's screams reached a bloodcurdling pitch. "You're speaking to Vincent now."

PART VI

WAVES OF WAR

I
THE EMERALD FOREST

OF THE TEN pirates from the *Maelstrom* who had volunteered for the landing party, none had ever set foot on Bastian soil before. The oppressive heat, the vast expanse of tropical jungle, and the shrieks and calls of strange, wild animals were a constant reminder that they'd entered an alien world. The fact that they wore the unmistakable armor of Opal's honor guard—constricting golden breastplates and stifling helms—only compounded their misery. For all that, they looked every inch a squad of fearsome warriors, shields strapped to their backs and shortswords swinging from their hips.

Three more travelers completed the group as they trudged, single file, through the humid emerald forest. In among the pirates strode Whitley, while Drew walked ahead of Vega's men, the pair sporting the same armor and distinctive gold helms as their companions. The count remained with his ship, having sailed on to Braga, home of the Pantherlords, to rescue the children of Opal. Florimo, the Ternlord, was scouting their route. The old bird had done an incredible job of getting Vega's ship to Bast without being spotted, but the task of reaching Braga unnoticed was far trickier, with busier waters to navigate.

Drew's expedition was heading directly toward Leos, the Bastian capital. As he strode ahead of the others, listening to their banter as they tried to keep spirits high, Drew couldn't help but be transported back to his time as a slave aboard the *Banshee*, destined for the isle of Scoria. He'd tried to escape his captors in a jungle just like this—Brenn knew where on the map that had been—encountering a crocodile and nearly getting killed in the process. This time he would tread carefully in the footprints their guide left for him to follow.

There she was, stalking ahead of them, the Werepanther leading the group deeper into the jungle. While the pirates struggled with the path at times, tripping or stumbling over vines, roots, or rocks, Opal was the epitome of grace and balance, frequently stopping as her companions caught up. Presently she stood at the top of a fern-covered slope, glaring at the Lyssians. Everyone had noticed how Opal had transformed of late. Since her sharing of information, her aggressive demeanor had been replaced with one of calm. Furthermore, upon landing on the beach, she had a distinct spring in her stride. The Catlady seemed almost happy, which caused Drew concern. When he closed his eyes, he could still see the pile of torn bodies in the belly of the *Nemesis* and the Pantherlady's bloody smile.

"How much longer until we camp?" called Whitley from her place in the group at his back. "Night's drawing in. We don't want to be yomping through the bush in the dark, do we? Brenn knows what manner of beast lives in this strange place!"

"Come along, my lady," Drew replied. "A fine scout of the Woodland Watch, spooked by a bit of jungle? Anyone would think you were as green as the trees!"

He looked back and was relieved to see her smiling as the pirates joined in and laughed. Since Whitley and he had come to terms with the Opal situation, there had been a thawing in their relationship. Whitley's frostiness had been replaced by a familiar warmth that Drew had feared he'd never see again. True to her word, she had accompanied them on their mission to Leos, despite Drew's protestations. Whitley wasn't about to leave Drew in the hands of the Panther. The Lady of Brackenholme didn't trust Opal, and it was hard to blame her after what the woman had put her through. Drew turned back to the trail ahead and stopped. He'd lost sight of Opal.

"Keep it down," said Drew, briefly turning back to them. "Remember where we are."

By the Catlady's reckoning they were around three leagues from Leos. Ordinarily, Drew might have suggested they press on, the distance coverable in a matter of hours, but that would have been back in Lyssia. Here, surrounded by dense undergrowth, picking their way through an inhospitable tropical forest, it would have been madness. The shadows were drawing in, plunging great swaths of the jungle into darkness.

"Opal!" he hissed, running on ahead, following her trail up the rise to see where she'd got to. He pushed the ferns aside, using his hand for extra purchase in the damp earth as he scrambled ever higher. Upon reaching the top he expected to find her halfway down the hill on the other side. Instead, he found more forest and no sign of the woman.

"Curse you, Opal," he snarled, ripping his helmet off. His dark hair was plastered to his face, streams of sweat trickling down his torso within the golden breastplate. He couldn't quite believe she would do this to them. She needed them, just as they needed her. Vega was en route to finding her children. If anything were to happen to Drew and the men from the *Maelstrom*, it would destroy any chance Opal had of ever seeing them again. She was an outlaw in Bast now, though the news wouldn't have reached her homeland yet. How could she turn her back on Drew—and her children—now? Whitley had been right all along. With dread, he turned about, ready to pass on the awful news to his companions.

The jungle was silent.

The only sound came from those oblivious crew members

from the *Maelstrom* who were making a little too much noise as they traipsed through the foliage. From his lofty vantage point he could see the expanse of shoulder-high ferns below, spreading out and covering the forest floor. Drew took a step, about to descend the slope, when he caught sight of a dark shape moving through the ferns, twenty yards away from the group. He waved his hand, miming the need for quiet, but none of them noticed. Brave and loyal they might be, but stiff and regimental they certainly weren't.

Drew leapt onto a tree stump for a better view. There she was, slinking through the undergrowth, stalking her prey. She was enormous, as large when transformed as the mightiest warhorse. She remained on all fours, staying low to the ground, now only ten yards from the men.

"Ho!" Drew shouted. "The Panther's in the ferns! Defend yourselves, now!"

Instantly the pirates were fumbling for their weapons, some going straight for their shields. The sudden animation spurred the beast to attack, the jungle exploding as the predator pounced. Drew started running.

Close to twenty feet long, the giant black cat was larger than any Drew had ever seen. The ebony fur shimmered as its paws and jaws lashed out. The crowd from the *Maelstrom* were bowled over, instantly dispersed as the monster tore into them. A helmet flew into the air, the head within narrowly avoiding accompanying it. The deafening growls and hisses of the panther only raised further panic among the pirates.

Drew was shifting as he ran, his clawed fingers struggling to loosen the clasps on the golden breastplate as his torso swelled within. He'd entrusted their lives to Opal in the foolish belief she'd see them safely through the jungle, at least until they reached Leos. Instead, she'd double-crossed them at the first opportunity, waiting until they were in the deepest, darkest corner of hell before turning on them. Drew snatched Moonbrand in a clawed hand and leapt the remaining twenty feet. Launching himself from the higher ground, the Werewolf was able to fly straight for the monster's long black back.

As the lycanthrope came down, blade shining above his head, the Werepanther suddenly rolled onto its back, ignoring the crew members as they scrambled clear. Four huge paws were raised over the panther's belly defensively as the legs lashed out at Drew. A giant limb connected with him, kicking him away through the air once more. Hitting a tree, he fell to the ground in a stunned heap, gasping for breath. He clawed at the armor, finding the chest of the breastplate crumpled from the impact with the panther's paw. His claws ripped at the leather buckles, tearing the plate free, the young Wolf wheezing and wobbling.

He looked around for Moonbrand, seeing no sign of the enchanted blade. Heaving himself to his feet, he began stumbling back through the ferns toward the melee, where the crew members were valiantly trying to combat the beast. Drew couldn't believe how big she was, fully transformed, and just how much control she had over her therianthropy. She had shifted entirely into the creature, humanity abandoned. The only other two Werelords Drew had seen with this power were Vala and the Kraken, and the Catlady seemed every inch their equal in battle.

"Fight me, Opal!" Drew roared as he staggered back toward the battle. Drew's hand was open, claws tensed and ready to trade blows. He snarled, trying to draw the Werepanther's attention away from the shocked and scattered sailors. Slowly the monster's head swung around toward the Wolf, a rumbling growl emanating in its chest.

Drew's heart stopped. Whitley lay on the jungle floor, twitching, the beast's huge forepaws placed on her chest. The breastplate and helm she wore, disguising her so well as a Bastian should they be discovered, effectively prevented her from shifting into the bear: she was trapped. The armor began to buckle as the panther let its weight descend.

Before Drew could leap to the girl's defense, a blurred shape shot from the foliage nearby, springing onto the creature's back and grappling it around the head and throat. Instantly, the giant panther was toppling, knocked clear of Whitley. More screeches and yowls erupted from the beast, in addition to those from the attacker. Drew now saw the creature for what it was: a giant black jungle cat. Opal, the Beauty of Bast, Werepanther of Braga, was wrapped around the panther's neck, throttling the life from it. Opal's legs hooked about its throat, while her clawed hands were locked beneath its jawline, her thin dress swirling like smoke around her.

The beast threw its head back, a desperate bite at nothing, as the felinthrope roared and yanked back hard. The sharp *crack* told Drew and the dazed crew of the *Maelstrom* all they needed to know. As the giant cat collapsed to the ground, Opal bounded away, springing back to her feet. Drew watched on in awe as the Werepanther rose to her full height, almost eight feet tall, not an inch wasted upon her lithe, muscular frame. Her enormous green cat's eyes narrowed as she glared defiantly at the Werewolf.

She bounded toward Drew, the young Wolflord raising his claws defensively. Instead, Opal moved past him, plunging her hand into the ferns. When the dark-furred limb returned from the undergrowth, it held Moonbrand. She turned the blade one way and then the other, inspecting the workmanship.

"You still want to fight me?" asked the Werepanther, tossing the white sword back to the Werewolf, who caught and returned it to its scabbard.

"Not anytime soon," replied Drew, slowly shifting back.

Opal stepped over the slain beast and crouched beside the body. She placed her broad forehead against the cat's and whispered a prayer. Drew stood beside her, his hand folded over his stump, head bowed respectfully. The ceremony was over with as the Lady of Braga rose once more. She was shifting back to human form, the hairs receding across her body.

"Are you all right, Whitley?" Drew asked as he crouched beside Whitley, helping his winded friend to rise, the concern evident in his strained voice.

Whitley ignored Drew, speaking directly to Opal, her cheeks shot with color. "Thank you."

"I did what I had to," she grunted. "If you expect me to walk into the Forum of Elders without raising suspicion, the least we should do is ensure I've a full complement of bodyguards."

Drew nodded, watching the men as they set about retrieving their dropped shields, helms, and weapons. "I'm sorry," he said, scratching the back of his head. "It was the cat: I just assumed—"

"—that she was me. I know. You've just faced a giant black jaguar, one of the many wild beasts that roam the jungles of Bast. My brother keeps two of these creatures as pets. Fear not—I won't betray you. Until the Shark brings my children safely back to me, you and I are allies, little Wolf."

"She's quite a beast," said Drew, staring at the slain giant cat. "Do you feel sorrow for her?"

"Let me ask you that question, Drew Ferran," she called back, "the day you're forced to slay a wolf."

2

Bad Blood

ONYX STARED ACROSS the battlefield, searching for signs of life. The waning gibbous moon rose behind the Strakenberg to the east as midnight approached. Up on the ridge, the remaining forces of the White Bear were camped, guarding the mouth of the Icegarden pass. At their backs was their fabled city, its doors barred to them. Once the Sturmish had been disposed of, Onyx's army could march upon the frozen city. He'd already sent word to his sister in Highcliff. He wanted cannons, and plenty of them. Bastian blasting powder would help open up the walls of Icegarden. There was too much at stake to leave the Strakenberg in Blackhand's perverted grasp. The wealth of Lyssia was within that mountain, and it would be in the Panther's hands soon enough.

The Sturmish numbers had dwindled in the past week since the death of Henrik and the advent of the Wyld Wolves. Onyx expected Duke Bergan had assumed leadership of the remaining Sturmish army. *Another Bearlord I'll have to fight, perhaps,* he mused, squinting at the moonlit horizon.

Taking his leave of the eerie grounds littered with the frozen bodies of fallen Sturmlanders, Onyx strode back to camp, his enormous black jaguars flanking him. As he approached, Sheriff Muller hurried to his side.

"My lord, a word?" said Muller, wringing his hands. The jaguars hissed at the Lord of the Badlands.

"I can give you two," growled the Catlord as he stormed in the direction of his tent.

"It's to do with the Wyldermen!"

Onyx stopped in his tracks, turning his head enough that he could hear Muller speak.

"You'd best come and see, my lord," he finished, unable to say more.

Onyx and Muller were quickly moving through the camp, the big cats following, heading toward the long tents that made up the military infirmary. Shouts could be heard from within the cluster of canvas huts. The Lionguard's guild of healers, a team of medics who had trained under the watchful eyes of magisters back in Highcliff, took care of the wounded. They relied solely on traditional, natural remedies, plus the blessings of a priest of Brenn. As the fighting had intensified in the past week, they were busier than ever.

"It's my lad from the stables, the one the Wyld Wolf attacked last week," said Muller.

"Stay," said Onyx to his black jaguars, the two creatures instantly dropping onto their bellies outside the tent. One of the soldiers pulled a door flap to one side as the Pantherlord stooped and entered, Muller hurrying behind.

The first thing that struck Onyx was the absence of other beds, just the one in the center of the infirmary. Whoever else had previously shared the chamber with the unfortunate stable boy had been removed. The wailing, snarling patient was presently obscured from Onyx's vision by a crowd of onlookers, the gurney he lay upon rattling and creaking as he thrashed about.

Onyx pushed through the crowd. A sorrowful-looking healer fingered his beard nervously, while a priestess of Brenn whispered anxious prayers at his shoulder. All of the members of the war council were present, too, their faces drawn and haggard.

"Such a collection of noblemen and notaries," growled Onyx as he drew closer to the convulsive patient. "If I didn't know you better, I'd suspect a coup was under way."

"Don't speak too soon," warned Skean, the Cranelord standing aside to reveal the stable boy.

The thrashing figure that lay strapped to the bed bore little resemblance to the fresh-faced lad who'd been bitten at the beginning of the week. His twisted limbs strained against the bonds, the leather sawing into the flesh. The youth's torso was twice as big as it should have been, his chest distended to monstrous proportions. A layer of dark, bristling fur blanketed every inch of his malformed body, thickening around the throat.

"I see now why she prays," said Onyx, glancing back at the mumbling priestess.

The boy's head looked as if it had been crushed and rebuilt in mockery of the Wolf. The jaws were enlarged, harboring a set of monstrous canines that were still too large for the space within. They were locked together, the stable boy snarling, foam frothing at his rabid lips. His nose was sharper but upturned, the skin at its tip darkened. The boy's eyes rolled in their sockets, yellow and bloodshot.

"How long has he been like this?"

"The wound itself, incredibly, healed over within a day, while his fever worsened," said the healer. "My colleagues and I suspected he had blood poisoning, such was the speed with which his body was shutting down. He was given his last rites this afternoon," he added, nodding in the direction of the whispering holy woman.

"And the change?" asked Onyx, reaching his hand out toward the transforming boy.

"It commenced at dusk, my lord," said the medicine man. "I wouldn't do that if I were you!"

The stable boy's awful head strained up suddenly, his spittle-covered jaws snapping at the Pantherlord's hand. Onyx kept his open palm there, a hair's breadth from the poor lad's rabid face.

"Have any of you ever heard of anything like this before?" asked the Beast of Bast, looking deep into the insane eyes of the former stable hand.

"Well, there was the Wyldermen—" began General Gorgo.

"Not the Wyldermen, you idiot Hippo," snapped Onyx. "It was Darkheart's Wyrm Magicks that transformed the savages into Wolfmen. They willingly entered into that arrangement, with the help of the Wolf's paw. I'm talking about *this* . . ." he said, casting his hand over the deformed boy.

"The passing on of therianthropy by bite is just a myth." The Hippolord snorted, clearly affronted.

Onyx glowered at him for a moment, hooking a thumb over his shoulder to indicate the thrashing stable hand.

"*Was* a myth, you mean. I think it's fair to say that this lad isn't simply changing from a boy into a man. He is suffering . . . with lycanthropy."

"Suffering's a fair description," agreed General Skean, the Cranelord walking around the table and drawing the wolf-boy's attention. "He's out of his mind, utterly wild. The moon could be the trigger. Feel his skin: he's burning alive."

"Bitten less than a week ago and now he's a living, breathing parody of a Werelord," growled Onyx. "All thanks to the witchcraft of that shaman Lucas adopted. Ever since the king began listening to Darkheart's whisperings, we've been on the path to this," he said, gesturing to the creature on the bed. "This . . . abomination goes against all that's holy and precious."

"Precious? A surprising show of empathy for this mockery of the Wolf," said Count Costa.

"Enemy though the Wolf is, as a fellow Werelord the lycanthrope deserves our respect, Costa. The gift of therianthropy is what separates us from mortal man. Besides, this starts with Lucas and his Wyld Wolves, but where does it end? With each injury dealt out by Lucas's monsters, so this disease will spread. It needs purging, or Drew Ferran won't be the only Wolf we must worry about."

"How would you propose we do that?" asked Gorgo.

"Check the prisoners we've got locked up, Muller, survivors who were wounded by the Wyld Wolves. If we're lucky, they won't have begun turning yet. Have them removed from their cells and dispose of them accordingly."

The sheriff snapped his heels and nodded.

"Generals Gorgo and Skean: you've work to do. The wild men attacked indiscriminately on the first night. Have your officers discreetly investigate their own troops. Anyone else who has been injured by the Wolfmen on the battlefield, have them rounded up."

"And then what?" asked the Hippolord, drawing a groan from Skean at his side.

"Does everything need spelling out, Gorgo?" said the Crane slyly. "Consider it done, my lord."

"And Count Costa," said Onyx, returning his attention to the doomed youth. "You need to find the whereabouts of Lucas and his Wyld Wolves. I fear the Lion needs reining in."

"I'm happy to find the king, my lord," replied the Vulture-lord. "But what if he won't be reined in?"

"Then there are other ways of rectifying a problem," said Onyx. "If I get a splinter in my paw, I pluck it out."

Some of the members of the war council gasped as they realized what Onyx was saying. He ignored their concerned mutterings, instead snatching a dagger from Gorgo's weapon belt. In a moment, it was buried in the chest of the hideous Wolfman, his torment over at last.

"It sounds like you talk of removing the king from the throne, my lord," said Muller.

"Don't be such an alarmist, dear sheriff!"

The group turned to find the black-robed Vanmorten appearing from the shadows. The hooded Ratlord walked through their midst, coming to stand beside Onyx like a loyal soldier. The Werepanther looked into Vanmorten's cowl, turning his nose up at the rotten stench that rolled off the Lord Chancellor. He couldn't be sure, but he thought he glimpsed a smile on the Wererat's disfigured lips.

"Let us all pray to Brenn," said Vanmorten, "that the king's in the mood to listen."

3
The Burning of Bray

AS SETTLEMENTS IN the Dalelands went, there were few so sleepy as Bray. Few Werelords throughout the Seven Realms enjoyed the love of their people as much as the fair-handed and kindhearted Count Fripp. The neighboring towns and villages held him in esteem, and Bray had remained untouched by conflict and invasion. The tumbledown perimeter walls, overgrown with ivy and covered in birds' nests, were evidence of how little importance the Badgerlord placed on defense.

As Bray basked under the waning moon's beams, King Lucas rode through the gatehouse and onto the main thoroughfare. Ahead, the town was silent, while at his back the hungry snarls of the Wyld Wolves could be heard as they dispatched the guards at the gate. At times, the trail from Redmire had gone cold, but the tracking instincts of the Wyld Wolves had soon set them back on the right path. The road appeared to lead straight through the town, no doubt to Fripp's estate on the banks of the Redwine. Smaller streets branched off from the main avenue, each one lined with trees showing the first signs of spring. Picturesque houses buttressed up beside one another, no two buildings the same, each one rich with charm and character. This had to be the quaintest place the Werelion had ever laid eyes upon.

Lucas turned as Darkheart appeared beside him on Vanmorten's black stallion. The shaman was the only Wolfman to still have a horse, the rest having slaughtered and eaten their mounts since departing Onyx's war camp in the north. A waste of fine beasts, Lucas had commented, but his Wyld Wolves were insatiable creatures. Under the light of the moon, their transformations had intensified, making them more hideous than ever before. His own gray warhorse, Envy, threw her head and snorted.

The Lion leaned over in his saddle to speak directly to the shaman.

"Find her."

Gretchen pushed through the corridor, fighting against the crowd who came the other way. Count Fripp's estate had been thrown open to the townsfolk the minute he'd caught word of Bray being under attack. Parents dashed by with screaming children in their arms, old folk knocked over as the panicked mob surged through the villa. Where they were heading, Gretchen had no idea. The gardens were at the rear of the estate, and beyond that, the river. Perhaps there were boats that could be used to escape the town by water. With a sickening dread she realized she hadn't seen any.

"Turn back, my lady," said an old man being carried past in the opposite direction. "The monsters come!"

Gretchen ignored him, ducking through an archway and into a side chamber. Tall windows overlooked the graveled courtyard, the booted feet of men-at-arms crunching and kicking up the ground as they charged by. Ripping back the latch, Gretchen raised the sash, slipping out of the villa and into the night. She quickly fell in, following the flow of steel and shield as they ran toward the gated entrance to the estate. She searched for a recognizable face, one of the Harriers, but she was lost in a sea of strangers.

The iron gates of Count Fripp's ancestral home were closed, polearms and staves pinning them in place. The ornate metalwork was for show, the gates serving little practical use against a concerted foe. While some of the soldiers put their shoulders against the iron, others jabbed between the bars with spear and sword, stabbing desperately at the enemy. Terrible shapes moved in the darkness beyond the gate, the occasional creature trying to scale the groaning iron defenses before a well-placed weapon sent it tumbling back. They grew in number all the time, the wails of townsfolk fading eerily as the luckless lay dying behind them.

"Trent!" she shouted, hoping he might hear over the din of battle. All she wanted was to be reunited with him, then find the rest of the Harriers, and perhaps they could coordinate a response against their enemy. The beasts beyond the threshold began attacking the gates in unison, hammering them together, howling as they tried to force them open. The household guard were struggling, staves splintering beneath the relentless pounding, polearms threatening to shatter.

"To me!" roared Count Fripp, the Badgerlord suddenly appearing among the throng. The elderly therianthrope was shifting, his robes torn free to reveal the black and white pelt beneath. His broad head lengthened, a snout full of gray whiskers revealing ancient but powerful teeth. Holding his longsword over his head, he pushed through to the front, thrusting the blade through the wrought iron and finding one of the monsters.

"Gretchen!"

She heard Trent's cry and immediately turned, trying to place it, the voice already swallowed by the tumult and chaos. Soldiers bent their backs, putting shoulders to the iron, seizing bars between hands as they tried to hold back the enemy. Claws and teeth sliced between the rails, ripping apart collarbones and shredding flesh from forearms. With an almighty crash the wobbling gates finally tore free from their brackets. Down came the iron doors, landing upon those defenders who'd kept them shut. Limbs snapped as bodies were crushed, the horde of black-furred devils clambering over the twisted metal.

Gretchen caught a good look at the monstrous caricatures of Werewolves. Everything about them was a hideous pastiche of the lycanthrope, powerful limbs overloaded with twisted muscles. The striking lupine head, so often the feature of Drew's transformations, had been replaced by a disfigured mess of yellow eyes and jagged teeth, demonic ears sprouting from their manes of dark hair. There was nothing graceful or grand about them. They jumped onto the backs of their enemies, burying fangs into necks, rending meat from bone. Some ran like humans, others like dogs, covering the ground on all fours as they chased down Fripp's men.

Count Fripp struggled to rise from beneath the gate, lashing out with his sword as the grotesque creatures ran by, pouncing upon his guards. A gray warhorse reared up and stamped down on the gate, forcing the heavy metal down onto the wounded Badgerlord. The sword tumbled from Fripp's clawed hand as the hooves smashed down repeatedly. When the old therian had no more fight, the rider's greatsword fell upon the count.

Gretchen's scream was out of her mouth, the combined

horror of Fripp's death and the fellow who'd dealt it striking her like a lightning bolt. Lucas looked about as his horse turned, stepping over the broken gates and fallen soldiers. His wild eyes found Gretchen, and the girl from Hedgemoor ran.

The Wolfmen dashed past her as she sped through the courtyard, bringing down guards all around. None had targeted her, the monsters instead singling out armored soldiers as foes. She noticed feathers, leather thongs, and bone necklaces adorning the bestial invaders, some of them carrying flint daggers from belts around their waists: Wyldermen. How they had come to shape-shift she couldn't imagine.

With some of the attackers now bursting into the villa, she had to find another way to the river. An eight-foot wall separated the private gardens from the courtyard, and some of the guards were dashing along its edge, searching to find a way over it. Shields had been dropped, breastplates stripped, as they tried to unencumber themselves. Gretchen changed as she ran, allowing the fox to come to her rescue. Her gait lengthened as her speed picked up, claws emerging from her russet-furred hands and feet. She leapt as she neared the wall, landing atop it and scrambling onto its edge. She glanced back.

Lucas was following, spurring his horse through the crowd of fighting soldiers and Wolfmen. Even from this distance she could see him screaming to the hideous Wyldermen, pointing his sword her way.

Gretchen threw her arms down, hauling some of the

fleeing guards up the wall's edge as the enemy dashed closer. She was about to tumble down the other side of the wall herself when she felt a wicked pain in her calf. Glancing down, she spied one of the Wolfmen, his claws buried in her lower leg, his other hand about to strike her. Her own fingers flashed down, tearing four deep furrows across the beast's face. With a howl it released its grasp, leaving Gretchen to tumble over the wall.

Landing in the bushes on the other side, the Werefox was up again, limping as she crossed the lawns. The cut in her leg was deep, a steady flow of dark liquid pumping over her fur from the torn flesh. The villa was burning now, and it wasn't alone. Lucas's killers had brought fire as well as fangs to Bray, unleashing all manner of hell upon the sleepy settlement.

"Find me the Fox!" roared Lucas from beyond the wall.

Many of the townsfolk had spilled out of the rear of the manor house, falling over one another in their desire to reach the river. The awful cries of the young and old reached deafening proportions as they hit the water. A few boats awaited them, tied up to the private launches, but they were soon overladen with panicked people and tipping or taking on water. A handful were managing to pull away, desperate swimmers trying to board them as they departed.

A steady stream of more sensible souls had headed north along the riverbank, seeking a way out of the gardens that might deposit them beyond the walls. From here they could follow the Redwine, putting distance between themselves and the monsters. Gretchen found herself among these people. One woman shrieked, backing away as she discovered a transformed therianthrope among them.

"Quiet, please!" Gretchen warned, reaching out with clawed hands. Her fingers were covered in blood, her own as well as the maimed Wolfman's. This only further antagonized the woman, whose shriek became a terrified wail.

That was all it took. The first Wolfmen that had hurdled the wall were running toward the Werefox and the fleeing townsfolk as they raced through the gardens, the woman's cries directing them Gretchen's way. Cursing, the girl pulled away from the escaping humans, waving her arms while snarling and shouting. Quickly one of the Wolfmen changed its angle of attack, heading straight for the vulpinthrope. Gretchen found herself limping up to the river's edge and arriving at the fishing jetty. She slipped and stumbled, falling onto her knees as she traversed the rickety pier. She looked back, hearing the beast's growl.

Before it could reach the jetty, the dark-furred monster was sent off its feet by a figure bowling into it. The two went down, the Wolfman bringing its jaws around to snap at its assailant. Instead of tasting flesh, it found a steel Wolfshead blade smashed into the roof of its mouth, the pommel punching its head back. The Wolfman lashed out with its claws, but Trent wouldn't be caught, rolling clear. The two rose, Trent a touch quicker. His father's sword flew, slicing the mutant Wylderman across the belly. The beast didn't stop, ignoring the opening wound as it jumped for the boy, jaws open wide. Trent was spinning on the spot, the next blow already flying around. The top half of the Wolfman's head was cleaved off, sending the semi-decapitated monster to the earth.

He looked toward Gretchen, who crouched at the pier's end. Waving a three-fingered hand, Trent set off toward her, the burning villa at his back. Only that wasn't all, Gretchen noticed. She screamed his name as the dark shapes fast appeared behind him.

The Graycloak turned in time to see the Wolfman coming down upon him in midair, two more close behind. The Wolfshead blade wasn't up in time, the beast landing over his shoulder, legs and arms embracing him. The jaws came down, disappearing into Trent's collar. Finally the sword connected, punching through the creature's stomach and out its back, but Trent was already falling. The slain Wylderman tumbled into the water as Trent's hand went to his throat, trying to stanch the flow of blood. His sword went up as the next Wolfman hit him and he was lost beneath its merciless blows.

Gretchen tried to scream once more but nothing came out. She teetered on her knees, leaning over the jetty's edge, the moon reflected upon the surface of the rushing Redwine. This was where Trent had held her. Never again. Her own blood continued pumping from her leg. Her eyes were lidding over as another Wolfman landed on the pier, stalking closer. He carried a long, serrated flint dagger in each clawed hand, a headdress of capercaille feathers rising from his shaggy, deformed head.

"You might remember me as Rolff," snarled the monster, terrible teeth catching against one another. He held out a filthy clawed hand. "But I am Darkheart, and your king will see you now."

Gretchen closed her eyes and let her body topple into the Redwine. The sudden cold of the fast-flowing water was surprisingly invigorating, her pain instantly ceasing, to be replaced by a numbing calm. Any further thoughts were quickly vanquished as the river took her into its frigid embrace.

4

The Forum of Elders

DREW TRIED TO keep his head down as he marched across the giant bridge that led to the Tower of Elders. It wasn't easy. Upon arriving outside the walls of Leos, he and his companions from the *Maelstrom* had encountered one breathtaking wonder after another. Windows and ballista decks pockmarked the enormous walls, housing the garrison throughout their length. Within these battlements, Leos overflowed with opulence. From the towering marble residences with their own hanging gardens to the elaborate fountains that appeared on every avenue corner, everything made it clear the people of the Lion city were well accustomed to luxury. Two enormous rivers charged down out of the jungle-covered mountains overhead, finding their way through the walls over a series of falls. Increasingly beautiful bridges spanned each of these waterfalls, the tributaries finding their way around the Tower of Elders before meeting beyond it on their way to the sea.

Drew looked up, the tower top blotting out the sun and providing a brief respite from the heat. The citadel was crowned by an enormous golden dome that appeared to glow like a beacon. As the sun crept around it, light erupted from the dome, reflected beams finding the jungle beyond the walls.

Opal strode between Drew and Whitley, the Pantherlady having drawn a crowd since they'd arrived at the gates. With the rest of the lads from the *Maelstrom* walking in formation around them, clad in the golden armor of the Bastian elite, they looked every inch Opal's personal guard. Behind them, a procession of well-wishers followed, shouting out blessings of thanks for the safe return of the Beauty of Bast. The aloof Opal gave the people no reaction as she stalked through the city.

"Where do you keep your poor?" asked Drew beneath his helmet. "I see only wealth throughout Leos."

"We have no poor in our cities, little Wolf," she replied proudly. "The citizens of the Catlords all benefit from our good fortune. A lesson you Lyssians would do well to learn."

"Really?" whispered Whitley incredulously, impressed by the equality. "So the cities of the Rhinos and Buffaloes and Crocodiles—they all thrive?"

"*Our* cities, I said. The cities of the felinthropes. It's the tithes and tributes of your lesser races that keep us in such comfort."

Once inside the towering citadel, Opal led them up a series of sweeping staircases that switched back on one another, cutting through council chambers and rising over grand hallways. She was moving fast now, Drew noted, almost threatening to leave them behind. Was she keen to get them to her father? Did she yet mean to betray them? The crowds continued to build, cheers and applause greeting them at every turn. The higher they climbed, drawing ever closer to the tower's golden summit, the more fearful Drew became. They were walking into the beating heart of their enemy's camp, hopelessly outnumbered and trusting the Pantherlady to stand by them. He glanced across to Whitley, catching her looking back. Her big brown eyes were just visible through the slit of her full, golden helmet, the distinctive black horsehair fluttering from its peak. She batted her lashes slowly, just for him. The meaning wasn't lost on Drew.

As the party entered the Forum of Elders, Drew felt his heart skip a beat. The enormous domed ceiling was open in two places opposite one another, shafts of warm sunlight arcing into the circular chamber, a pleasant breeze following them through. Drew had to estimate there were maybe sixty or seventy white-robed Werelords present in chattering cliques.

At the arrival of Opal into the forum, the noise dropped suddenly.

"Your Graces, lords, and ladies," came the announcement, the herald lost somewhere in the throng. "I give you the Beauty of Bast, Daughter of Braga, and High Commander of the Bastian Army, Opal."

The councilors applauded as they stepped back, leaving Drew and his companions in the center of the forum, Opal to the fore. Three enormous marble thrones sat equidistant from one another around the room, a figure upon each. The standing elders seemed to separate into groups, gravitating to these distinct areas of the forum.

With the white-robed therian lords dispersed, Drew now spied guards within the chamber, bearing different uniforms. He immediately noticed more Goldhelms wearing uniforms just like his own; one of these warriors nodded his way, the dark horsehair crest fluttering in the breeze. Drew hastily returned the acknowledgment. A troop of men wearing banded leather cuirasses stood beside another throne, twin sword scabbards on their hips. The greatest number of soldiers wore the red cloaks that Drew knew only too well from back in Lyssia: the Lionguard.

"I'm right here, remember," whispered Drew.

"How reassuring, little Wolf," said Opal as she stepped toward one of the thrones.

"High Lord Oba, I am returned to you," she said, dropping to one knee and bowing.

"Arise, daughter, and let me see you better," replied the ebony-skinned Werelord on the throne.

Opal stood tall before her father, her jaw set, her steely eyes fixed on the old Panther. There seemed no affection between the two, but Drew had to remain alert. This was the Catlord capital, the seat of Bastian government. So much hinged upon how Opal addressed the elders. With one misplaced word their mission—and lives—would be over.

"Back so soon, daughter, and with a war not yet won," said High Lord Oba. "Is there any reason you return to Bast unannounced, while your brother remains on the cold continent?"

"Ask her why she returns to Bast while my grandson fights a war," repeated High Lord Leon, the truly ancient Lionlord having apparently missed the conversation. He seemed agitated by the turn of events.

"I'd be especially keen to hear where you've moored the *Nemesis*," added Oba. "That's my ship you have, child. She'd better be in one piece."

Drew glanced toward the others from the *Maelstrom*, a couple of them shifting anxiously. *Keep your cool, lads.*

"My brother remains in command of the armies that sailed north, obviously under the direction of King Lucas." Opal made sure that she said the last loud enough for the elderly Leon to hear, the venerable Lion sitting up straight in his chair as if suddenly awakened.

"King, you say? He's a good boy. I only hope he can follow in his father's pawprints."

"Indeed," agreed Opal, glancing toward High Lord Oba. "May our forefathers bless the memory of Leopold."

Drew caught the flicker of tension there. *Was Oba complicit in Leopold's death? Did he* know *what they were planning when they sailed to Lyssia?*

"We're fortunate that a Lion remains on the throne," continued Leon, his voice now passionate as he spoke to all in the forum. "Those Westlanders are an unruly bunch of primitives. No wonder they made Leopold's reign so arduous. It's thanks to the intervention of you, my Bastian brethren, that we were able to wrest back control of the Seven Realms from this usurper and his allies. A Wolf will never rule Lyssia, not so long as there's breath in my lungs!"

A roar might have better emphasized his point, but Leon was struck by a bout of wheezing coughs, settling back into his throne. *An ailing Lion,* reasoned Drew, watching the three leaders in turn. Oba seemed in fine condition, every bit as athletic as his offspring, but the Tigerlord Tigara had yet to speak.

"Why are you here, daughter?" Oba asked again, his voice impatient.

"To ask the Forum of Elders to reconsider our campaign in Lyssia. Call back our troops and be done with this war."

High Lord Leon's wheezes transformed into bouts of harsh laughter, those around his throne joining in with him. The laughter quickly spread around the room, first a ripple and then a wave. High Lord Oba remained unmoved, his unblinking eyes fixed upon his daughter. High Lord Tigara of Felos leaned forward in his seat.

"You ask us to withdraw the Bastian army and navy, Opal?" asked the Tigerlord, his voice lacking the mirth of those around him. He was a pale, barrel-chested man, his enormous red sideburns almost comical where they covered his cheeks and jawline. "For what possible reason would we call back our forces now, so close to victory? The Cranelord Skerrett has brought frequent news home to Bast, informing us of your string of triumphs. Westland's under your control, is it not? Our army in the east has the measure of the Omiri, and Lord Onyx is close to crushing the Sturmish. We'd be mad to pull back now."

"Your Grace," she said directly to Tigara, her voice calm and measured, almost lost beneath the hubbub of laughter. "I ask the elders to reconsider our action in light of information I have. Information that's directly relevant to how we proceed, not just as a united army of Catlords, but as individual felinthrope nations."

High Lord Leon had found his voice now.

"What fresh news from Lyssia could you possibly have that would sway us from our course? My grandson *needs* our might to best these northern mongrels. This isn't even up for debate, Opal!"

"You've deserted your post, daughter," added the glaring Oba.

Drew couldn't decide whether the man was always this way; if so, it would certainly explain how Opal had grown to be the way she was. However, the more Drew watched the Lord of Braga, the more he suspected that the Werepanther didn't trust his daughter. For her to arrive back in Bast had been most unorthodox. He was clearly aware that his child brought something monumental to the Forum of Elders.

"No child of mine has ever run from a fight before," continued Oba, his voice barely hiding the menace within. "That you would do so now brings shame upon our family. I would counsel you to hold your tongue for fear of further embarrassment, daughter."

Opal's head dropped, her father's hold over her immense. *This wasn't supposed to happen.* Drew could feel the sweat pouring down his face within the full golden helm. *Speak up, Opal, tell the Tigerlord what he needs to know!* The men from the *Maelstrom* remained agitated, their movements unsteady, unsure, while the other soldiers around the domed council chamber stood to stiff attention. Some of the white-robed elders behind Oba's throne had noticed the uneasiness of Opal's guard, one fellow even pointing it out to his companions. Drew's throat was parched, his heart gripped by fear.

"You said '*fresh* news,' High Lord Leon," said Opal finally, bringing her chin up again. "It's not fresh news I bring. It's old news, not from Lyssia, but from Bast."

"Step down, daughter," said Oba as the Lionlord looked confused, the laughter beginning to die away. "The Forum of Elders isn't the place for clearing one's conscience. If you've a grievance, bring it to me, your father."

"The forum's the perfect place for what I want to say," she said with a growl. "I've kept silent long enough."

Oba's eyes flew wide now, the realization suddenly hitting him. He knew *exactly* what his daughter was talking about. He stood and took a step forward.

"Silence, Opal!"

"What's she talking about?" asked Tigara as the noise in the room suddenly heightened, the white-robed elders raising their concern or shouting each other down.

"Your Grace," said Oba, turning to the Tigerlord, "the fact that my daughter's here at all when she's needed in Lyssia is reason enough for us to doubt her state of mind."

"This is about Onyx—"

Opal never got the remainder of her sentence out. High Lord Oba was up to her, his enormous hand around her throat. He held her at arm's length as she clawed at his skin frantically.

"Still jealous of your big brother, daughter?" snarled the Pantherlord, the room suddenly deathly silent. "So keen to besmirch his good character. You speak of a war hero, child.

A champion of Bast! His reputation's beyond scrutiny, yet you think to fling mud? Lyssia's brought out the worst in you!"

"You're wrong, Oba," said Drew, the tip of Moonbrand suddenly up against the nape of the high lord's neck. "Lyssia has brought out the *best* in her. Now let her go."

The chorus of gasps went up around the Forum of Elders at the sight of the soldier with his sword to the Pantherlord's flesh. Oba kept his hand clamped around Opal's throat, but his grip instantly slackened. Many of the soldiers in the chamber started forward, only for the crew of the *Maelstrom* to draw rank around the Werelord trio, weapons at the ready. Whitley tore off her helmet and snatched at the clasps of her breastplate, tearing it loose so it clattered to the polished floor. Her claws began to emerge, limbs thickening, hair shooting across her changing flesh. She wasn't alone. Around the forum, the therian lords began to shift, all manner of beast materializing from beneath flowing white robes.

"All of you, stay back!" shouted Drew, punching his own helm off with a blow from his stumped left arm. The shining headgear clattered to the polished floor, catching the golden rays as it spun to a halt. Drew's face was already shifting, his yellow eyes gleaming like twin suns from the darkening face of the lycanthrope.

The audience roared as they realized the soldier's identity, but they held back, away from Opal's bodyguard. The majority present were Catlords, dark furred or pale, spotted or banded.

But there were other Werelords from across the Bastian continent—Birdlords, Reptiles, Apes, and Rhinos, to name but a few.

"Let her go, Pantherlord," snarled Drew, the breath of the Werewolf hot in Oba's ear.

Oba's hand opened and Opal fell to the floor, curled up and choking. Whitley went to her instantly, standing over the Pantherlady and growling at anyone who dared approach. Drew's forearm encircled the High Lord of Braga's throat, Moonbrand now lowered to the base of his broad back.

"One thrust is all it would take, Your Grace, so if I were you, I'd let the lady speak."

Drew looked back to Opal, who was now on all fours, coughing blood onto the marble floor at Whitley's feet. High Lord Tigara had descended the steps from his own throne and stood before them. He glared at the Wolf, the Bear, and the men from the *Maelstrom* who held their swords toward him.

"You'd better pray to your Lyssian god they're silver blessed," said the Weretiger as he shifted. The black stripes flashed across his flesh, flaming orange slashes of fur materializing as he loomed over the faltering pirates.

"Keep your ground, lads," said Drew. "He won't do anything. Not yet."

"You're correct, Wolflord," said Tigara. "Your deaths can wait until Opal speaks. I'm intrigued to know what kind of madness would compel a soul to travel countless leagues across an ocean with her mortal enemy merely to die. We've fought your friends for a year now, trying to find what rock you were hiding under. And you come here, to Leos, offering your throat to us."

Tigara looked at the snarling Oba. "Are you well, Your Grace? I promise you, the Wolf is yours when this is over with."

"Don't listen to her," said the Pantherlord.

Drew dug Moonbrand into Oba's back, the Lord of Braga squirming in his grasp.

"You seem more concerned about what your daughter might say than your immediate safety," the Wolf snarled at Oba before looking at the Tigerlord. "Does that strike you as odd, High Lord Tigara?"

"Silence, son of Wergar," growled Tigara as he watched Whitley help Opal to her unsteady feet.

The Pantherlady looked up, rubbing her injured throat.

"I would hear what the Beauty of Bast has to say."

5
Locked In

HECTOR HAD NEVER felt so helpless. He saw the body, dumped on the flags before the stone throne of Icegarden. There was the circle of yellow powder, hastily sprinkled around the corpse, warding symbols fingered throughout it. He watched in horror as his own wax-covered fist rose high into the air. The words of magick tumbled quickly and uncontrollably from his lips as his fist slammed into the ground.

Death in Brenn's Chapel would have been more appealing than the hell Hector now endured. His consciousness had slowly returned, ethereal at first, like a waking dream. A gradual familiarity had initially washed over him as he recognized the symptoms: he was sleepwalking. He watched as in previous nightmares, seeing his body move through the palace of Icegarden of its own volition. The sensation was of being trapped within one's own body, unable to communicate with the physical being. He had assumed he'd wake up at some point, but the moment never came. It was only when he witnessed himself ordering Two Axes and other members of the Boarguard around that he realized he couldn't wake up from this nightmare. His body was no longer his to command.

All those times, he hadn't been sleepwalking; Vincent had merely been practicing, waiting for his moment to take over. Now Vincent was in possession of Hector's physical form, with no intention of surrendering it. The magister was locked behind his own eyes as his brother proceeded along his trail of atrocities. Amelie and the slain Boarguard Ringlin had been the first poor souls Vincent had toyed with. Having witnessed the ritual on a number of occasions while in vile form, he'd known exactly what to do. The only blessing was the fact that the prisoners—Carver, Manfred, and the hundreds of other innocents—had escaped by the road beneath the mountain. Only one poor soul had been left behind, and she was now in Vincent's terrible grasp.

In the past, Hector had taken what he'd needed from the dead and then let them go, freeing them from the torment of being trapped inside a cold, rotting body. But Vincent had no such quandaries when it came to the risen dead. Ringlin was utterly subjugated, snared by a binding spell and beaten into submission. Vincent had squealed with triumph as the utterly obedient corpses shambled after him, obeying his commands. Though Amelie and Ringlin had been his first experiments, they certainly weren't the last. Hector's brother had been busy.

Stop, Vincent, said Hector, his words destined solely for his brother's ears. *I beg you.*

"Rise, creature, and answer to your master's bidding!"

The body rose stiffly from where it was slumped, the head gradually turning the Boarlord's way. The familiar blue flames burned in the creature's eyes as the corpse that had once been Duchess Freya, Bearlady of Icegarden, shambled to her feet. The dead noblewoman cast her gaze around the chamber, taking in the mighty vaulted ceilings and pillars of her former throne room.

"Am I . . . home?" she whispered.

"In a way, Your Grace," said Vincent, rising unsteadily from where he was kneeling. The Boarlord paused, clutching his left breast where Manfred's antler had struck.

Good, thought Hector. *You still haven't repaired my broken body. I pray an infection finds its way into that wretched rib cage.*

"You would wish this body dead, brother?" said Vincent, finally addressing Hector. "Does this mean you surrender ownership at last?"

You hear me? gasped Hector.

"Of course, but I choose to ignore you. Brenn knows, you're a whiny little child. Was I this annoying when I haunted you?"

Stop this madness now, Vincent, before it's too late!

Vincent tapped his jaw in mock consideration. "You know, that sounds like a familiar plea to my ears. I'm sure I've heard it before. Perhaps every poor sap who crossed your path uttered that very thing, no?"

And eventually I saw the folly of my ways, gasped Hector. *Please, for the love of all that's good in the world, cease this insanity.*

"You don't get to tell me what to do. You're not my conscience. You're certainly no moral compass, either, judging by the awful deeds you yourself carried out when this body was yours. Only it isn't yours anymore, is it? And it never shall be again."

The vile had only been in possession of Hector's body for a matter of hours and it was already at home under the skin. Clearly, it was delighted to have freedom of movement again.

"And don't think you'll be able to escape your little prison, either, Hector," said Vincent, turning back to the reanimated Bearlady who still swayed before him. He tapped his temple with a skeletal black finger. "This is your home from now on."

"Why am I here?" whispered the slain duchess. "What happened?"

"You're dead, Your Grace," said Vincent matter-of-factly. "I killed you. You've spent the last few months showing my brother that pompous, haughty, greater-than-thou demeanor of the Bearlords. But you see, my brother refused to acknowledge that one has to be more direct when seeking a straight answer. So now I *command* you."

The ghoul stood slack jawed, Freya's terrible death mask fixed in permanent horror. Vincent clapped his hands.

"The Wyrmstaff, my lady," snarled Vincent. "Where is it?"

"Communing . . . is not alien to the Daughters," said the corpse. "You are not alone in the practice, magister. I have communed once in my life, with my departed grandmother at her bedside. I remember the sensation even now, like holding death's hand. . . ."

Hector listened to Freya's frail voice, instantly empathizing with her. Vincent reached across the circle of brimstone and struck the ghoul across her sagging face.

"I don't have time for this nonsense. Flint will be with us shortly. The Wyrmstaff, Your Grace—I command you to tell me where it is!"

The blue fires roared in the dead duchess's eyes as she spoke, her voice strong now.

"Others have sought it. Even Daughters of Icegarden have searched for the relic, curiosity or greed occasionally getting the better of a misguided soul. We have one of my ancestors to thank for its eventual safekeeping, a lady whose bloodline I was directly descended from. The truth of the Wyrmstaff's whereabouts was passed down from matriarch to daughter, from the deceased mother of the order to the incumbent one. The secret was mine to pass on to Lady Greta, but that day shall never come."

"So it isn't a myth? The staff exists?"

"You must climb to the top of the Bone Tower. At its summit, you shall find a blackened lightning rod bolted to the brickwork. That, magister, is the staff of the Dragonlords."

"You hear that, Hector?" Vincent whooped, dancing a clumsy jig. "It was under your nose all along!"

Hector knew the lightning rod in question, a twisted bit of burned metal, utterly unremarkable. He'd stood beside it enough times when he'd taken to the Bone Tower to clear his head. He understood only too well the need to keep the staff away from anyone. In plain view atop the Bone Tower? Where better to hide an innocuous-looking staff of such profound power?

"What in Brenn's name's going on in here?"

It was Lord Flint, the Crowlord's feet clipping the stone as he hurriedly approached.

"Blackhand!" shouted Flint, slowing as he approached the swaying risen Bearlady. "What have you done? For Queen Amelie to be killed, I can believe that was an accident. When you brought her back, you seemed to have good intentions . . . but this?"

The Crowlord stalked around the brimstone circle, staring at the Child of the Blue Flame who only days ago had been the living, breathing Lady of Icegarden. Vincent paid him no heed, instead muttering excitedly to himself about what his next steps should be. Flint's eyes flitted around the dark throne room as a chorus of moans rose from the shadows.

"How many of these cursed wretches hide in the darkness? You and I struck a bargain, Blackhand, yet you commit dread deeds without consultation. I thought your magistry could be a weapon for us, a force with which we could bend the Seven Realms into a world of our design, but it's clear to me now that you're out of your mind! Using your necromancy in the field is one thing, but *killing* Duchess Freya and then bringing her *back*?"

"I had questions," said Vincent, batting his withered hand at Flint with irritation. "She's finally answered them."

"You're sick! This is a perversion! What if I have knowledge that you seek? What if I'm unforthcoming when you ask your questions? What then, Blackhand?"

Hector could feel his hope rising now. Might the Crowlord be their savior after all? The one soul who could stop Vincent? Flint moved quickly, ripping a scimitar from his weapon belt, oily black wings emerging from his back. Hector's hopes soared with the knowledge that death and its final relief might be on its way.

But Hector's feeling of elation had not gone unnoticed by Vincent. As the scimitar was raised, the Boarlord was already turning, tusks jutting from his lower jaw as he charged the Werecrow. His head thundered into Flint's dark belly, launching the avianthrope backward. As the Crow tumbled into one of the throne room's mighty pillars, his wings beat hard as he made to take flight. As he rose he didn't catch sight of a figure stepping out of the shadows from behind the marble column. He was only aware of the fellow when hands grabbed his ankle, hauling him back to earth, teeth buried into his calf.

Flint slashed down with his scimitar, the blade parting the flesh of the man's shoulder, but still the man chewed on his leg. Blazing azure eyes looked up at the Crow, who recognized the dead man as Ringlin. More Children of the Blue Flame stumbled and crawled out of the darkness, descending upon the horrified Lord of Riven. The risen duchess shambled across to join them, now released from her brimstone bonds. She grabbed at the Crow's other leg as the mob dragged him back to earth, his scimitar ineffectual as they tore into his feathered flesh.

Sweet Brenn, what are you doing, Vincent? Where will this madness stop?

"Hush, dear brother," said Vincent. "You always were a worrier. My work's only just beginning. I'm going to show you how to wield true power."

Hector's spirit sobbed as the full ramifications of the horror hit him. The Catlords and Lucas were the least of Lyssia's problems. It was one of their own that the Seven Realms had to fear most of all. In Vincent, Hector had created a monster.

"Now," the new Lord of Icegarden said, rubbing black hand over white, "time for a bracing climb."

6

The Broken Triangle

ALL EYES WERE on Tigara. The High Lord of Felos's own gaze was fixed upon the elegant Pantherlady who stood before him. Her tale told, Opal had straightened, prepared for whatever might come. Her pride was restored, and with it her confidence. She searched Tigara's face for a clue as to his mood. The temper of the Weretigers was legendary, never more infamous than in the case of Taboo, whose sorry story had been finally laid bare. The atmosphere in the Forum of Elders crackled with tension.

"This cannot be true," said Tigara, his voice a husky whisker.

"You know it to be," said Opal. "I don't lie, Your Grace. I'm only sorry it's taken the Wolf to provoke such honesty."

"Don't listen to her," shouted High Lord Oba. "She's allied herself with the Lyssians, brought the Wolflord, our enemy, into our highest council chamber."

"You made me your enemy, Oba," snarled Drew. "When your brethren invaded Lyssia in Wergar's time, stealing Westland from my father, you drew the battle lines."

"Listen, Tigara," growled Oba, ignoring the Wolf in his ear and the blade at his back. "You and I have known one another for many years, old friend. Have we ever had a cross word? Has there ever been a moment of contention between us?"

"I sent my own grandchild away, Oba," said Tigara in disbelief, looking across at the hostaged Panther. "I allowed her to be banished, handed over to the Lizards of Scoria. All for a crime she didn't commit?"

"She was *guilty*, Tigara!" shouted High Lord Leon, stepping forward from his own throne, his loyal vassals and Redcloaks around him. "You witnessed her temper firsthand like the rest of us. She put a Lion's rage to shame!"

"Being wild didn't make her a monster!" said Drew, turning toward the approaching Lionlord, the Panther still at sword point before him. "I met Taboo on Scoria. It's true, she has a fury like no other, but she's a loyal, honest soul. I'd trust her with my life."

"She yet lives?"

"She does indeed," replied Drew, "and I'm proud to call her a friend."

"You make my point for me, Wolf." Leon snorted, pointing a gnarled finger at the lycanthrope. "Regardless of whether Taboo lives or not, this beast from Lyssia would trust her—a *known enemy* to the Catlords of Bast—just as he trusts this traitorous Panther, Opal."

"He was my son."

The words were quiet, but somehow cut through the din and raised voices. The high lords, Drew, Whitley, and Opal all looked across, every head in the forum turning to watch the Catlord as he stepped forward.

"Chang was a good soul with his whole life before him," said Lord Chollo, Cheetahlord of the Teeth. While the other felinthropes had been shifting, he had remained in human form, his olive skin smooth and flawless. He looked fragile to Drew.

"And he was taken from us by Taboo," said Oba, Leon nodding his agreement.

"No!" shouted Opal. "The Tiger was innocent. Onyx killed your son, Lord Chollo, just as he conspired to have Taboo sent to Scoria. And, may the forefathers forgive me, I helped him cover up his crimes. I was complicit, as were they."

Opal pointed at her father and then toward the Werelion. High Lord Leon actually staggered back, as if the Beauty of Bast's damning finger might physically harm him.

"She lies!" shouted the old Lion as Oba's eyes blazed with fury.

"I wouldn't be so quick to defend the Panthers if I were you, Leon," shouted Opal, "after what happened in Highcliff!"

"What do you mean, girl?" gasped the elder, his chest now rippling as the mane bloomed around his throat.

"Want to know how Leopold really died? Then ask my father. Onyx commanded Lucas to kill him. There you have it: your own grandchild murdered your son."

Strong as he was in Werewolf form, Drew felt his arm might tear from its socket as the Pantherlord suddenly exploded. His torso expanded, Oba hunching his back so that his rapidly shifting spine cracked Drew across the muzzle. Oba leapt at his daughter, but Opal was already moving, tumbling and coming up transformed, the two enormous Werepanthers facing each other.

Drew looked up, face-to-face with an advancing mob of Bastian Werelords, red-cloaked and golden-breasted soldiers among them. He lashed out with Moonbrand, a warning that caused them to recoil as he sprang back onto his heels. The men from the *Maelstrom* moved alongside him, some whipping the restrictive helmets from their heads. Whitley was at Drew's side, her ursine teeth bared as she stared at the enemy, focused.

"I always thought I'd die in Brackenholme at a ripe old age. Find my way into Brenn's arms from the comfort of the Great Oak."

"There's time yet, Whitley," growled Drew before roaring to the pirates. "Stay with me, lads!"

The enemy came on in two directions, the Lion's Redcloaks from one side, the Panther's Goldhelms from the other. Among them Drew caught side of tusk, horn, claw, and hoof as he and his allies were caught between two waves. Two of his pirates were snatched from the group instantly, a great fat Wereape catching one in each mighty hand. They were thrown over its broad shoulders, screaming as they landed in the throng at its back. Whitley stamped forward, lashing out with her paws, punching a Rhino across the jaw and sending him crashing into a crowd of Redcloaks. Pirates and Bastians traded blows, steel and silver ringing as enemies held nothing back.

Opal lashed out at her father, her foot catching him in the stomach, but the giant Pantherlord ignored the blow. He snatched the ankle and twisted it. A crunch sounded as Opal screamed. Oba raised his other clawed hand, ready to strike her, when he let loose a roar of his own.

High Lord Leon had leapt upon him, transformed, his teeth buried in the Panther's forearm. Instantly Oba released his daughter, bringing his fist around to punch the great Lion in the face, but the beast wouldn't relinquish his grip. The teeth ground down, bones splintering as Leon worried his enormous head from side to side, his giant mane quivering. Oba's jaws came down now, teeth clamping over the Lion's face and taking hold. The two rolled, huge limbs thrashing and tearing as they struggled to reach one another's throats.

Seeing the two high lords fighting raised the chaos within the forum another notch. Those loyal to the Panthers and Lions now turned on one another, making three factions warring within the room. Whitley found herself separated from her group, the spears and shortswords of Goldhelms blocking her path back. The horn from a Buffalo, loyal to Oba, suddenly caught her in the hip, lifting her up into the air. Before she came back to the ground, the fat Apelords at the heart of the melee had snapped the Buffalo's neck and caught her by the leg. The breath was gone from her chest, her head fogging as she was hauled over the sea of blades and claws toward the Ape's yawning maw. Her progress toward his mouth was cut short as Moonbrand flashed down, cleaving the Wereape's arm at the shoulder and allowing the Werebear to tumble to the floor. Drew was among them, the Werewolf kicking out, sword slashing, jaws snapping, clearing the foes from around his friend.

A roar mightier than the Panther's and Lion's put together suddenly split the air in the forum, causing all to cease battling. The High Lord of Felos's jaws were open wide, spittle flying as he unleashed his lungs at the dueling Catlords. Drew pulled Whitley up from the floor, embracing the Werebear as he backed up, Moonbrand before him, edging back to the men from the *Maelstrom*. Only a handful still stood, the forum's polished floor now slick with the gore of slain humans and therians.

"Fight no more, not here, not in the Forum of Elders, not this day!" Tigara shouted. "Any therian or human who spills another drop of blood in Leos this day will face my wrath. I say this with a heart full of vengeance, and a craving for the blood of Panthers and Lions. You shall each pay for your duplicity, but not today."

"What? You'd command us to leave?" said Oba, his face already disfigured by Leon's attack.

The Lion was likewise maimed, his skull visible where the Panther's teeth had shredded the skin. "This is my city!" Leon cried out, gurgling, his throat full of blood. "You don't order me!"

"This is the Forum of Elders, Your Grace," said Lord Chollo, showing incredible restraint at the enraged Tiger's side. "As such, we vote upon this. You'll let the Panthers depart, and you shall let High Lord Tigara leave Felos. This armistice will last until sunrise tomorrow. All in favor say 'Aye' . . ."

A chorus of anxious approval went up around the forum, the Werelords of Bast agreeing to the uneasy dissolution.

"And what of the Bastian army that fights in Lyssia?" snarled Oba, glowering at his daughter, who slowly rose beside the Tigerlords. Chollo put his arm out and Opal took it.

Tigara shook his head. "All that we worked toward, to achieve together, for the glory of Bast: it was built upon your lies, Oba."

"You have the Panthers to thank for the glory of Bast,"

snarled Oba, staggering upright, his fellow Werelords rushing to his aid. He beat them back, standing by his own strength as he continued.

"It was my vision that brought us together, my vision that allowed us to conquer this continent." He spat a bloody glob onto the floor in front of Tigara. "Our army in Lyssia is *my* doing. It's there because I will it." He glowered at Leon. "They fight for my son, the Beast of Bast, not some child who plays at being king."

"We shall recall this army," snarled Tigara.

"They will remain, and fight for my grandson, King Lucas," spluttered the Werelion.

"The boy who killed his father, you mean?" Oba sneered.

"They will secure a Lion on the throne," growled Leon. "Lyssia belongs to the Lions!"

Oba tore off his bloodied white robe and tossed it onto the floor between the other high lords.

"The union of the Catlords is dissolved. Every felinthrope for himself. I'll see you again soon enough, Tigara, Leon."

He bowed once before turning and walking toward the exit, stepping over the bodies of the wounded, dead, and dying. Many of the Werelords who had earlier been by his side now stood apart, remaining in the council chamber: a Rhino, a Weremammoth, an Ibex, two Cranelords, all manner of therianthropes from the jungle continent. Oba hissed at those who'd turned against him as he stalked past. He paused only once before the young Werewolf who stood surrounded by his surviving men.

"Bravo, Wolf, for your victory here today. But this was just one fight. The war is yet to be won. Take your Bearlady and humans, go to my daughter, seek comfort with your new friends the Tigers. But don't tarry. Lyssia's going to need you."

With that final threat, the High Lord of Braga prowled away, his entourage of Panthers and Goldhelms following him. Drew shivered as he watched him go. Gradually he allowed the wolf to recede, his human self returning as the men from the *Maelstrom* hugged and clapped one another with relief. Across the chamber, Leon was already gathering his loyal servants. Lions and Redcloaks swarmed to him, magisters already tending to his wounds. Just as with Oba, the wounded high lord still had many powerful allies. He kept glancing past them as he watched Drew and his men walk across the abandoned forum toward Tigara's seat.

"High Lord Tigara," said Drew, nodding briefly as he interrupted the Tiger's conversation with Chollo and Opal.

"Most folk—human *and* therian—bow when they address me, Wolflord," he snarled. "And it's 'Your Grace.'"

"All things considered," said Drew, scratching his grizzled jaw, "if you're so bothered by etiquette, perhaps you can call me 'Your Majesty.'"

Tigara snorted. "The Wolf is amusing."

"He's many things," said Opal, her narrow eyes glaring at him.

"You need to free those young therianthropes you took as wards, Tigara," said Drew, the passion returned to his voice. "Halt your tyranny and grant the Werelords of Bast their freedom once more. The kidnapping of therian children is what's brought you to this." He cast his hand over the gore-slick floor of the forum.

"You don't understand, Wolf," said Chollo. "The wards are all that keep the therian races of Bast under control."

"Why do they need controlling?" said Whitley, keen to add her voice to Drew's. "Break the shackles now. Better to have someone fight by your side out of choice than out of fear."

"And if they choose not to fight with us, Bearlady?" asked Tigara, looking the wounded Whitley up and down.

"Then that's their decision," answered Drew. "But those who *do* take up arms by your side will fight with ten times the passion and pride they've shown before."

Drew looked at the therian lords who remained in the chamber, those who weren't Catlords and had chosen not to side with Oba or Leon. There were maybe twenty of them present, of all shapes and sizes. He stepped up to the Rhino.

"There's one of your kin called Krieg, is there not?"

"My cousin, feared dead," said the therianthrope.

"He's alive and well, fighting in Omir for the good of the Lyssian people. And you," he said, patting the shoulder of the Mammoth. "The Behemoth battles by Krieg's side. I made a vow to my friends who escaped Scoria that I would help them to free their people from bondage in Bast. I'm here to make good on that promise."

He turned to Tigara and Chollo. "Your own granddaughter fights for the free people of the Seven Realms, Tigara. She battles Onyx's army and the Doglords of the desert, alongside Krieg and the Behemoth."

"She truly lives? This isn't some Lyssian trick to turn Panther and Lion against one another?"

"If so, it appears to have worked," added Lord Chollo.

"She's the Wolf's ally," said Opal.

Drew smiled and held his hand out to the Tigerlord. "More importantly, she's my friend."

Tigara took Drew's wrist, each clasping the other's forearm. "They're free, as the forefathers are my witness," whispered the High Lord of Felos.

Opal and Chollo reached forward, placing their palms over the Wolf and Tiger's grip. Whitley's hand, still clawed and torn, closed over theirs. Next came the Rhino's hand, followed by the Mammoth and the Ibex. Gradually they were joined by other therians, sidling alongside one another, keen to make good their oath to this new alliance.

"You say she's fighting in the desert?" said Tigara, his voice suddenly grave.

"Indeed, in Omir," replied Drew. "Taboo went to the aid of King Faisal the Jackal-lord, alongside the Hawklords. They're currently trapped in the Bana Gap by the combined forces of the Cats and Dogs."

A grave look passed between Tigara and Opal.

"The army that fights for Lucas in Omir, the one that has Taboo and your friends trapped in the Gap," said Opal, "it's led by our most fearsome commander. He might not be as brutal as my brother in battle, but he's twice as cunning. If he's laid siege to your allies, they're doomed. He won't stop until they're all dead, be it by steel, silver, or starvation."

"Who is he?"

"Field Marshal Tiaz," Opal replied. "The Tigerlord."

"He's my son," added Tigara, his face now pale. "Taboo is his daughter."

7
The Long Sleep Can Wait

HE WASN'T ENTIRELY sure what brought him back. It might have been the freezing water of the Redwine, lapping around his legs and waist, threatening to dislodge him from the bank where he lay. It could have been the sun on his face, its life-affirming warmth coaxing him back from the long sleep. Perhaps it was the smell of the still-smoldering buildings, the smoke sparking his world-weary senses. The crow on his chest, pecking away at him, certainly played its part, hopping clear as he stirred.

But Trent Ferran suspected the real reason he'd returned from death's dark door was love.

He lifted his head from the mud and looked down his body. He was submerged in the water from below the waist, his legs lifeless and unresponsive. How long he'd been there he dreaded to think. He turned his head to look up from the bank, trying to find his bearings. Fiery hot pains shot from his left shoulder as he moved, causing him to cry out. It felt as if a blacksmith's poker had been plunged into his collarbone and twisted about. Gritting his teeth, he rolled over. Raising his hands, one after the other, he dug them into the bank and began to climb. The ascent was arduous, the youth from the Cold Coast frequently sliding back down to the river. His legs remained paralyzed, a dead weight.

Eventually reaching the top of the incline, Trent hauled himself onto the grassy bank and lay there for a moment, catching his breath. Reaching down, he began poking his thighs with his fingertips, punching and tugging the muscles until sensation slowly returned. The anesthetized flesh slowly prickled to life, thawing under the sun's bright rays.

When sufficient movement had returned, he pushed himself upright and looked about. The smoke drifted across Count Fripp's gardens, much of it billowing from the still-burning villa. The once beautiful structure was now a blackened shell of charcoaled timber and collapsed walls, orange flames occasionally flickering within its scorched remains. Trent's mind drifted back to the night's terrible events.

Had they truly been Werewolves? He struggled to imagine that the bloodthirsty monsters that had spread chaos were the same creatures as his brother. He'd seen Werelords shift on a number of occasions—they had control, retaining the human nature that separated man from beast. The monsters that had slaughtered innocents and put Bray to the torch had shown nothing but frenzied bloodlust. There wasn't an ounce of humanity within their grotesque forms.

The image that returned to him, time and again, was of the regal figure on the great gray charger, trampling soldiers underfoot. It had been Lucas who had led the storming of the gates, cutting down Count Fripp as his Werewolves bounded past. Trent had been in no doubt at all: the Werelion had come for Gretchen, the bride who'd slipped from his grasp. The Fox of Hedgemoor would sooner have died than wed Lucas. *Where is she?* Trent's memory was hazy as he recalled the night in fits and starts. *What's happened to her?*

He distinctly recalled the jetty—*their* jetty—as the last place he'd seen Gretchen. Rising onto wobbling legs, he staggered across the lawn through the pall of smoke, following the riverbank back toward the villa. He saw shapes through the mist, lying on the grass, torn open, dismembered, and left for the crows. He recognized two figures immediately, a man and a boy, side by side, the fellow's savaged arm flung protectively over the lad's body. The slain man was Captain Gerard, friend to Drew and the soldiers, whose rescue from the executioner's block in Redmire had signaled the fightback in the Dalelands. Tom, the blond stable boy who'd been with the Harriers from the beginning, lay facedown in the mud beside him. Trent shooed the birds away from their corpses before whispering a prayer to Brenn. He rose and walked on, spying more bodies he recognized, old friends he and Gretchen had fought alongside in the name of his brother. All the while the crows accompanied him, their constant squawking the new sound of Bray, replacing childrens' hymns and birdsong.

"Gretchen?" he called as the jetty's vague outline appeared through the fog, disappearing into the Redwine. Stepping onto the planks, he saw a great dried pool of blood where he'd fallen beneath the attack of one of the creatures. Flies buzzed over the burgundy stain, disturbed by his footsteps as he approached. It was coming back to him. The beast had taken his Wolfshead blade through the guts, just before Trent had lost consciousness. His sword, still painted dark with gore, lay beside the bloody puddle. He winced as he bent to grab the sword, the wound at his shoulder aflame once more.

Trent was stumbling along the planked jetty, following a spattered red trail. He remembered now. Gretchen was injured; he'd seen her limp onto the pier. His pace quickened. If she was wounded as gravely as he had been, who knew if she was even alive?

"Gretchen!" he cried as the jetty's end materialized.

There was nobody there. Another large bloodstain adorned the wooden boards, but the girl from Hedgemoor was nowhere to be seen. Trent collapsed, choking back tears. If she'd fallen in, she was dead. Therian or not, there was no way she could survive the cold, especially with the amount of blood she'd lost. Her body might have been carried all the way to Redmire by now. Trent shook his head. He refused to believe that had been her fate. No, Lucas and his Werewolves must have captured her. That had to be it: the Lion had his bride. Gritting his teeth, Trent hauled himself upright again.

The pain in his shoulder seared once more, making him cry out as he stepped uneasily back down the jetty. The snorting of horses and the grating of armor caused him to halt. He was no longer alone. Low voices were carried along the wind from the blackened villa. Numerous footsteps approached the jetty across the lawn, their heavy, metallic sound informing Trent that these men were fully suited for battle. Gripping the Wolfshead blade in his shivering hand, he squinted through the smoke.

One by one the plate-mailed soldiers emerged like phantoms, converging upon the wooden walkway. There were three of them, the one in the middle shorter than his companions by a good foot. He advanced, his heavy feet clanking as they alighted on the jetty. The knights wore soot-gray cloaks that hung to the ground, and in their hands they carried longswords and shields.

"Drop your weapon," said the short soldier, slowly approaching Trent. His voice was light, almost feminine.

"In whose name?" asked Trent, ready at any moment to

leap into the river. Better to take his chance in the Redwine's cold embrace than face the Lion's justice.

"In the name of the Knights of Stormdale," said the warrior proudly. Trent could see the heraldic device upon the man's breastplate now, a leaping buck: the symbol of the Staglords.

"Back up, Milo," came another voice from behind the knights, this from a figure on horseback. The smaller soldier instantly retreated, allowing the rider onto the jetty's edge. He wore no helm, his long face set in a frown as he looked down upon the boy from the Cold Coast. The gray cloak he wore was trimmed with white fur around his shoulders, and it was clear by his manner he was the leader of the knights. His horse stepped nervously, snorting, perhaps disturbed by the rushing water.

"My lord," said Trent, half nodding into a clumsy bow.

"Am I?" replied the rider, eyeing him suspiciously. "We find Bray destroyed, its people dead and gone. All but you. What's your name, boy, and whom do you serve?"

"I'm Trent Ferran, brother to the rightful king of Westland. I fight with the Harriers of Hedgemoor for Lady Gretchen."

The rider slowly smiled. "Then that makes us friends, Trent Ferran. My name's Reinhardt, and I'm the Lord of Stormdale in my father's absence. Come, lad, let Magister Wilhelm take a look at your wounds."

"I was bitten," muttered Trent, pulling the shirt back at his shoulder to finally inspect the wound. A large scab came away with the material, revealing a fresh pink scar underneath. The skin tingled to the touch, the muscle aching beneath. *The wound is already healing: how can that be?*

"What's that, lad?" said Reinhardt.

"Nothing," said Trent, nervously pulling his bloodstained shirt back over the injury. "How many do you number? I can hear horses."

"Five hundred Knights of Stormdale," he replied. "We might even have a spare mount for you, Wolf brother, if you'd join us on our ride?"

"Your ride?" asked Trent, hobbling closer to the Staglord. The horse snorted again, seemingly unnerved by the young Graycloak.

"Indeed," said Reinhardt, as many more knights began to materialize through the smoke at his back. "We ride to war."

Read an excerpt from the sixth book,
Wereworld: War of the Werelords

I

The Bull Pen

THE YOUNG WOMAN stopped in her tracks, taking a moment to look back over the harbor while the steady stream of men-at-arms strode past. Calico Bay was a fractured reef of blackened masts and half-sunk ships, their twisted timbers reaching out of the waves like the fingers of drowning men. The occasional trawler bobbed between the wrecks, hopeful fishermen slowly taking back their sea from the fallen invaders as they made for the deeper waters beyond. One small vessel bobbed past the *Nemesis,* the man o'war blotting the sun from the sky above. The fishermen saluted the men aboard, a mongrel crew from Bast and Lyssia who had sailed with her in the name of the Wolf. Her men waved and cheered back, hollering encouragement as the plucky boat headed for open water. The young woman admired the trawlermen's optimism, the never-say-die attitude of a people who'd been prisoners within their own city for so long, reclaiming their livelihoods. A feeling that took some getting used to—hope didn't come easy to the girl from Brackenholme.

"Are you ready, my lady?"

Whitley turned to Captain Ransome, the elderly pirate captain straightening his gray whiskers as he waited for the Bearlady on the crowded drawbridge. More of their ships remained anchored further out to sea, their human cargo having alighted in the harbor. Whitley had witnessed the Goldhelms and Redcloaks march across Lyssian soil, but here was a different kind of Bastian: the Furies, twin-sword wielding warriors of the Tigerlords. They numbered fewer than their cousins, but their reputation was equally frightful. They crossed the giant timber walkway into the walled city, the men of Calico looking down warily from above as the leather armored Furies crossed the threshold.

"You think they're happy to see more Bastians come ashore, Ransome?" she asked, falling in alongside him as they vanished into the shadows of the mighty gatehouse, the sandstone walls towering overhead.

"Well Calico's open for business," said the old sea captain. "I doubt Duke Brand welcomed Scorpio with such open arms."

"I was expecting a king, and they send me a girl?"

Whitley marched through the hall, known to all in Calico as the Bull Pen, as the assembled great and good parted excitedly to let her by. Captain Ransome remained at her shoulder, back straight and jaw jutting out sharp as a cliff, pushing back the years as they approached the duke's table. Though old enough to be her grandfather, the former pirate had proved his worth time and again to the girl from Brackenholme, having first saved her pelt from the jaws of the terrible Sharklord, Deadeye. There was only one other soul she'd prefer by her side, and he was now far away.

"Girl I may be, but I speak on behalf of the Wolf and my father, the Lord of Brackenholme."

Her voice rose over the noise in the Bull Pen as all eyes turned back to the giant fellow who stood behind the long table. He lifted his bald head and snorted at the young lady as she came to a halt before him. His neck was lost amongst a knot of enormous muscles that were piled across his shoulders. A long black cloak was held in place by a straining gold chain about his throat, its ermine-lined edge trailing onto the ground at his feet. It was clear by the way in which his court looked to him that he commanded their utter obedience. Whether this was born out of respect or fear, Whitley had yet to decide.

"Bergan's child?" said Duke Brand.

"Lady Whitley, your Grace," replied the girl with a respectful bow. "Thank you for opening the gates of Calico to our men. Your hospitality is most welcome."

"Good job you sent word ahead," replied Brand gruffly. "Chances are, had you turned up unannounced, we'd have blown you out of the bay with that Bastian blasting powder."

"Then I'm pleased we weren't mistaken for an invading force. The warriors you no doubt saw in my company are allied to the Wolf, sworn into his service in the name of High Lord Tigara, the Weretiger of Felos."

"Strange that those you once considered enemies are now called friends, Lady Whitley," said the duke.

"Alliances shift like the grasses of your Longridings, the winds of war often unpredictable, occasionally fortuitous."

Whitley wasn't about to be intimidated by the old Werebull. She'd done a lot of growing up in recent years, the once wide-eyed apprentice scout a dim and distant memory. Her confidence was born out of a host of events that would have broken a lesser spirit. She saw nothing to fear in Brand.

"Baron Bosa has moved on already, I hear?"

"Indeed," replied the duke. "He said there were bigger fish to fry along the Cold Coast. Talk of even more of these Bastians making for our shores. I'm grateful to the Werewhale and his fleet for their timely incursion in Calico Bay. Had they not come to our assistance when they did, Brenn knows what fate would have awaited my people."

"You mention Bosa's fleet, your Grace, but those were actually the Wolf's ships. The Baron was one of Drew's men, having sworn fealty to the rightful king of Westland."

"And why does this Wolf King not show his face to us? Do I not warrant an appearance from the fabled son of Wergar, the lycanthrope at the heart of this sorry war?"

"Lord Drew is otherwise engaged," replied Whitley, her own annoyance just about in check. She hadn't wanted to leave his side, but circumstances had dictated that their paths had to part. "He has sailed on to the desert realm of Omir, while I headed straight for Calico and the newly liberated lords of the Longridings. My path takes me north, your Grace. I mean to carve a path directly through Lyssia, taking me north to Sturmland where our enemies await us."

"Your enemies are your own business, my lady," said the Bull. "I've stomached enough of this war already. You may go north with my blessing."

Whitley stood agape, staring at the assembled court of the Lord of Calico. She turned to each of them, hoping for a response, but found every man and woman looked toward Brand, the duke speaking on behalf of all of them.

"I didn't come here to seek your blessing, your Grace," she snapped. "I came here seeking soldiers."

"You've brought soldiers of your own I see. No need for you to take any of mine."

"There is *every* need for men and women of the Longridings to join us on the march north. It may have escaped you, but those are Bastian warriors who fight on our side, brothers in arms against our common enemy."

"More Bastians coming to fight in Lyssia?" scoffed Brand. "Well, isn't that just what the Seven Realms needs? I hardly see these Tiger warriors as being an answer to our worries."

"They're but a small fraction of the solution to our problems," said Whitley, fists curled earnestly as she took another step forward to lean against the table. "I'm gathering an army, your Grace. The Longridings can have a large say in how powerful that force might be."

Brand waved a mighty hand dismissively, tired of talking. "March north alone, my lady, with your swarthy southern friends by your side. The Longridings never asked to be part of the Wolf's war, but somehow managed to get dragged into it."

"War was always coming, regardless of Drew's emergence in Westland. King Leopold was only ever the thin end of the wedge. Did you really think the Cats of Bast would be content with just a small portion of our continent? They want the lot, Brand. They want everything."

"Mind your manners, child," rumbled the duke. "I doubt your father raised you to speak to your betters in such a charmless, graceless fashion."

"Presently, *your Grace*," she said, scouring the Bull Pen, "I've yet to spy any betters."

Brand punched the table, enraged.

"Insolent little wretch," he snorted. "Come to my hall and

disrespect me, would you?" His brow split, horns sliding out of his temples like two monstrous spears. The audience of assembled nobles gasped, stepping away, even Ransome staggering clear as the Werebull shifted before them. Only Whitley remained motionless, feet locked firmly in place, her eyes fixed fierce upon the duke, while inside her heart quaked. *So perhaps there* is *something to fear after all?*

Brand grabbed the table and pulled it to one side, his temper exploding in the face of the contemptuous girl from Brackenholme. His powerful legs had transformed, great cloven hooves striking the flagged floor like steel against stone.

"You seem to forget, your Grace," she shouted over his fury, "you have Drew Ferran to thank for your freedom. It was Baron Bosa's fleet, sailing in the Wolf's name, that came to your aide, scuttling Scorpio's fleet. Tell me, how close to starvation were the people of Calico before Bosa sailed into the bay and liberated you? Before the Wolf was victorious on your behalf?"

Whitley moved now as the Werebull went to snatch at her, ducking under his grasp and moving around him. She kept him turning, light on her feet, making mockery of his petulance before his cowed and trembling courtiers. Some of the noblemen and ladies cried out, panicked by the sudden, violent turn of events. Whitley was vaguely aware of shouting and a fresh commotion at the entrance to the Bull Pen, but her attention was focused solely on the duke and his terrible horns.

"Is that how you win a war, Duke Brand?" she called out.

"Cowering behind your giant walls while other men—better men—give their lives so you may live? What of the other lords of the Longridings? The Bull of Calico grants you shelter, a savior during these troubled times, and you have to leave your backbones at the door? Will none of you come to our aid?"

"Shut up, you wretched child," roared the Werebull, stamping the floor as he lowered his head, blinded by rage. "Silence or so help me . . ."

"What?" she growled back, skin darkening as rust-brown fur emerged. "You'll attack me? You probably think you can take me, Brand, what with me just being a girl. Perhaps I'm worthy opposition for the once powerful Lord of the Longridings? Well I promise you this," she said, claws and teeth emerging as she prepared for his charge. "I'll leave you with something to remember me by."

Before the Werebull could lunge at her, another figure burst from the ring of onlookers, snatching at his monstrous head. The two crashed across the chamber, leaving a breathless Whitley, half-transformed, watching on in wonder. Her would-be-savior had Brand in a headlock, twisting and turning the duke as he tried to wrestle free. His own cloven feet struck the ground, the clatter of hooves rattling off the Bull Pen's walls as the two struggled for dominion over one another. Spittle flew from the Horselord's gnashing teeth as his mane shook with the strain. Finally tearing himself loose, the Bull collapsed at his back. "But not mine. You remember my son, girl?"

Whitley shook her head, trying to recall if she'd ever met him. Her mind was blank, adrenaline coursing through her body, having been so close to being gored by the duke. "I cannot say I do."

"He was a ward to Baron Ewan, the Ramlord of Haggard. Just a lad, my dear, sweet Dorn. And then he met your friend the Wolf. Death followed swiftly, Bearlady. He took up arms alongside Drew Ferran, and died for his troubles. I can never forgive the Wolf for what happened to my son."

Whitley cast her mind back now, the memories returning, cloudy and distorted. The grim events of Lord Dorn's death had been lost to her, shrouded by the hundreds of others she'd witnessed in the intervening time. But the truth was there. The young Bull had sided with Drew as they had escaped the horrors of Haggard, prisoners of the Goatlord Kesslar. Dorn was murdered for his troubles, little more than a boy, the same age as Drew.

"Go with her if you must, Horselord," muttered Brand miserably, remaining in the alcove's shadows. "Take your brother Stallions with you. But count me out. I owe the Wolf nothing."

through a darkened alcove, crashing into the wall, plasterwork crumbling with the impact.

"Have you taken leave of your senses, Duke Brand?" shouted Whitley's champion. "I return to court to find you trying to kill our guest?"

"She's no guest of mine," snorted Brand, glaring at the Werestallion as he positioned himself between the duke and the girl. "Stand aside, Conrad."

"Why?" asked the blond-maned Horselord. "So you may harm her?"

"So I may turn her out of my city!" shouted the Bull.

"Then you turn my brethren and me out too," replied Conrad, gradually shifting back to human form as his temper sub sided. "Whitley is a friend to the people of the Longridings. Sh is an ally of ours."

"Of yours, young Horselord."

"Of ours," repeated Conrad, pointing at the girl as h fur receded. "The Bears of Brackenholme have suffered m than anyone in this war, yet still they fight on. I witnes her brother slain at the hands of Lucas and many of her pe butchered on the street in Cape Gala. We owe them our f dom, your Grace. Don't treat her this way, I beg you. The is our ally."

"Yours perhaps," said the Bull, shifting slowly ba human form as more plaster crumbled free from the b

through a darkened alcove, crashing into the wall, plasterwork crumbling with the impact.

"Have you taken leave of your senses, Duke Brand?" shouted Whitley's champion. "I return to court to find you trying to kill our guest?"

"She's no guest of mine," snorted Brand, glaring at the Werestallion as he positioned himself between the duke and the girl. "Stand aside, Conrad."

"Why?" asked the blond-maned Horselord. "So you may harm her?"

"So I may turn her out of my city!" shouted the Bull.

"Then you turn my brethren and me out too," replied Conrad, gradually shifting back to human form as his temper subsided. "Whitley is a friend to the people of the Longridings. She is an ally of ours."

"Of yours, young Horselord."

"Of ours," repeated Conrad, pointing at the girl as her fur receded. "The Bears of Brackenholme have suffered more than anyone in this war, yet still they fight on. I witnessed her brother slain at the hands of Lucas and many of her people butchered on the street in Cape Gala. We owe them our freedom, your Grace. Don't treat her this way, I beg you. The Wolf is our ally."

"Yours perhaps," said the Bull, shifting slowly back to human form as more plaster crumbled free from the bricks at his back. "But not mine. You remember my son, girl?"

Whitley shook her head, trying to recall if she'd ever met him. Her mind was blank, adrenaline coursing through her body, having been so close to being gored by the duke. "I cannot say I do."

"He was a ward to Baron Ewan, the Ramlord of Haggard. Just a lad, my dear, sweet Dorn. And then he met your friend the Wolf. Death followed swiftly, Bearlady. He took up arms alongside Drew Ferran, and died for his troubles. I can never forgive the Wolf for what happened to my son."

Whitley cast her mind back now, the memories returning, cloudy and distorted. The grim events of Lord Dorn's death had been lost to her, shrouded by the hundreds of others she'd witnessed in the intervening time. But the truth was there. The young Bull had sided with Drew as they had escaped the horrors of Haggard, prisoners of the Goatlord Kesslar. Dorn was murdered for his troubles, little more than a boy, the same age as Drew.

"Go with her if you must, Horselord," muttered Brand miserably, remaining in the alcove's shadows. "Take your brother Stallions with you. But count me out. I owe the Wolf nothing."